PIECES

WITHDRAWN

OF

ME

Natalie Hart

Legend Press Ltd, 107-111 Fleet Street, London, EC4A 2AB
info@legend-paperbooks.co.uk | www.legendpress.co.uk

Print ISBN 978-1-78719803-6
Ebook ISBN 978-1-78719802-9
Set in Times. Printing managed by Jellyfish Solutions Ltd
Cover design by Anna Green | www.siulendesign.com

Natalie Hart is a writer, researcher and communications adviser, specialising in conflict and post-conflict environments. She has worked extensively across the Middle East and North Africa, including three years in Iraq where *Pieces of Me* is set. Natalie has a BA in Combined Middle Eastern Studies (Arabic and Spanish) from the University of Cambridge and an MA in Creative Writing from Lancaster University.

Follow Natalie on Twitter
@NatalieGHart

For Richard Hardy-Smith

TABLE OF CONTENTS

PART ONE
PRE-DEPLOYMENT

1

I did not cry when he told me he was leaving.

We both knew that the war would draw him back eventually. We both knew that it was a question of when, not if. That sooner or later equipment would be organised and bags would be packed and months of separation would follow. But still, it has happened sooner than I imagined.

I did not cry when he told me he was leaving, although his words slammed into my chest and forced the air out of my lungs. Five months ago I was there myself, but I exchanged the beige of Baghdad for the vast skies and rolling peaks of Colorado. After three years of filing asylum applications for Iraqis, I found myself entering the details of my British passport into the US spousal visa form. And now, I am here. And now, he is going back.

When he told me he was leaving, I recognised the breathless excitement and the shine behind his eyes that said his mind was already there, training troops in the heat and the dust. I have watched the television footage of American soldiers going off to war, leaving behind women with mascara-smeared faces and children waving small plastic flags. What they don't show is the excitement and the tingling limbs and the twist of anticipation in the gut. What they don't show is that although the soldiers don't want to leave, they often want to go.

Adam wants to go.

He wants to go and do the job he was trained for. The war needs him, or he needs the war, I am not sure which. He has lived out the battle from stateside for too long this time. He has read the reports and watched the footage. He waited while friends were deployed. He waited while I stayed out there myself. Now it is his turn.

When he told me he was leaving, I spilled over with questions.

"What's the mission?" I asked. "Where will you be?"

"You know I can't tell you details, Em."

"But it's me," I said. "I was there. It's different."

He shook his head.

"No, Emma, it's not. I can't."

Before we married I used to think how lucky we were to have met in a war zone, to understand deployments. Poor wives, I thought, who knew nothing about Iraq. Poor wives who had not seen the golden glow of the reeds on the river at sunset or woken to the dawn call of the muezzin. Poor wives who knew Iraq only from the television and the internet and the radio; who knew the land only as a place where husbands go to die. I thought that knowing and understanding would make it better, but now I am not so sure.

I did not cry when he told me he was leaving, but now we are in bed and I lie with my body curled into his and a pillow wet with tears. I cry for him and I cry for the me I left out there. I was the linguist, the migration specialist, the adventurer. But now I am an army wife, living in Colorado. I am a woman who followed a soldier. I am the woman who followed Adam.

I know what it is to leave. I do not know how to be the person who is left behind.

2

I must have fallen asleep eventually, because Adam's side of the bed is empty when I wake. The indentation of his head is barely visible on the pillow and the sheets are cold. This is what it will be like every morning when he is gone.

In the kitchen, I make coffee. It has been five months now since I moved to Colorado Springs and tried to make a home in this place where I don't quite fit.

"It will be easy," my friends said. "After Iraq, America will be a breeze." But in Iraq I knew who I was. What I was doing. I haven't worked that out here yet.

I take my coffee and stand on the front porch, watching the steam rise up and disappear into the cool morning air. The street is a peaceful place, with large houses that are faded lilac and duck egg blue and the colour of tea with too much milk. Our neighbours are a mix of retired couples and families. They wash their cars on Saturday and mow the grass on Sunday and wave hello as I pass.

Most mornings this week I have sat on the step with my laptop, applying for local jobs, something to give me a purpose here. The search has been a struggle, but I have taken comfort in watching the easy morning routines of my neighbours. Not today though. Today, I am restless.

From where I stand, I can see the mountains. Amid the peaks is the Incline, Colorado Springs' notorious hiking trail. The route climbs 2,000 feet in less than a mile. My eyes track the sandy brown path that cuts through the dark green woodland, a seam in the middle of the mountainside.

I tried to climb the Incline a week after I moved to Colorado. It seemed like an initiation rite, a way to prove that I could fit in amongst the outdoor aficionados and extreme landscapes of my new home. But the Incline was too much for me, too soon.

I wasn't even five minutes into the hike when my chest started to ache from sucking in the thin air. Families, children and old people all passed me, but I could go on no further. After stopping for a while, I picked my way carefully back down, feeling defeated and wondering what I thought I was doing there.

Today, I feel the fresh call of the challenge. Adam has offered to go up with me before, but I am determined to succeed on my own. This morning I crave the cool empty air to quiet my racing mind. The months to come will be full of their own mountains and I want to prove to myself that I can take them on too.

I throw the dregs of my coffee decisively onto the lawn, then pull on my trainers and get in my Jeep. The closer I drive to the Incline, the more imposing it seems. Shadows from passing clouds darken the top of the path. The route looks vertical and I feel the low buzz of adrenaline that I got every time I flew back into Baghdad. It's a feeling I've missed.

In the car park at the base of the Incline, I check my backpack: water, energy bar, phone, tourniquet (a habit I still have from Iraq). I lock the car and put on my sunglasses. They say that Colorado has 360 days of sunshine a year. It is nothing like England and a different kind of light to Baghdad. The daylight here is more blue and the sunrises are more yellow. The colours have sharper edges than in Iraq, where soft beiges and peaches blur and run into each other.

As I walk along the path to where the Incline trail starts, I can already feel my chest rising higher. Although I have acclimated to the altitude, it will never feel entirely normal to me. But today I can push through. This deployment will happen whether I am ready or not.

At first the gradient isn't too steep. The steps are wide, so I do a half step between them, which enables me to alternate the leading leg. It isn't long before I feel the burn in my muscles, but I fix my gaze on my feet, trying to ignore the seemingly insurmountable task ahead. As I move up one step, then the next, I remember the advice that my history teacher Mrs Edwards gave me while I was preparing for my A Level exams.

"Rome wasn't built in a day, dear. Take it one brick at a time." Mrs Edwards loved a classics-related proverb, even when it didn't quite fit. Her enthusiasm was contagious. In class we talked about culture and war and romance and went on school trips to see the remains of intricate mosaics in Roman villas that told stories about all three. Maybe for me that was where everything started. I wonder how Mrs Edwards would feel if I told her that now.

I take another step. One brick, one step, one day at a time.

I pass the place that I sat last time, frustrated and breathless, before turning back. The trail gets steeper, but I continue. My legs give the occasional wobble but I am okay. I am strong.

A few minutes later, I hear pounding feet and heavy breathing behind me. While I haven't looked up at the ascent, I haven't looked down either. Now I stand to the side and glance back, realising just how far I have come.

A group pass me, easily recognisable as military by their army T-shirts and matching black shorts. In the International Zone in Baghdad there was a monthly 5K run, which was usually a mix of soldiers and contractors. I see these men and women on the Incline and I am taken back to the pad of running shoes on gravel. Clouds of dust rising from feet. Light grey shirts turning dark with expanding patches of sweat. It feels strange not to be part of this group, but I am not one of them now.

I continue walking steadily as the group moves away from me, their shape stretching out up the mountain the further they get. The fibres in my legs are burning now, but I push on. I focus on the satisfying sound of stones crunching together with each successful step.

I look up. I must be nearly there. But what I see, just a few steps ahead of me, is not the summit that I had been aiming for but more mountain face. More steps.

I stand, catching my breath, overwhelmed – the combination of the hike and a long sleepless night. I notice another woman nearby, also pausing. She is middle-aged and stocky, with light hair that is pulled back by a nineties-looking scrunchie. She looks at me and grins.

"Did no one warn you about the false summit, honey?" she asks.

I shake my head.

"Happened my first time too. My trail partner thought it was better not to tell me. I couldn't decide whether I wanted to throw her off the edge or myself!"

I let out a breathless laugh, pushing back the wisps of blonde hair sticking to the sweat on my face.

"Do you want to do this last part together?" she asks.

"Oh, yes please!" I say, glad for the company. I see her notice my accent. I noticed it too. It is more pronounced here.

"Penny," she says, holding out a hand.

"Emma," I say, wiping sweat onto my trousers before taking her hand in my own. Her grip is strong but her palms are soft. I notice that her hands are flecked with colour.

We set off, maintaining a slow but steady pace for the remainder of the hike.

"When we get up there, I'ma ask you where you're from," the lady says between breaths. "I just can't be sparing the oxygen right now."

I smile, relieved that she is feeling it too.

The last part of the hike feels easier. Perhaps it is the company, or perhaps it is the reassurance that the end in sight is definitely the summit this time.

As I take the final step, I make a noise that is somewhere

between a whoop of joy and a relieved expulsion of air. The woman wraps her arm around me and I feel the heat radiating from her. I notice again the flecks of colour on her hands and it tugs at something in me.

"You did great, honey," she says, "you should be really proud. First time up the Incline is a big deal. Here, let me take your picture."

She takes a photo with my phone that confirms I look as red and exhausted as I feel, but there is something else there too. The dark shadows that were a permanent feature under my eyes during those final months in Baghdad are gone now. My face looks more relaxed. My smile more easy.

In the picture, the trail drops away behind me. A patchwork of green and brown landscape melts into the grey of a distant town. My dad would have loved this place. When I was young, we would go on family walking holidays in places with peaks and valleys, my father carrying my sister while she was still tiny. When we were all tired and aching, he would stop and take in a long deep breath, as if he was inhaling the very landscape into his being. Savouring the struggle, savouring the beauty. Then he would open his eyes, smile and say, "Yes, there it is, we can keep going now."

"So where are you from, sweetie?" Penny asks me. "And what brings you to these parts?" She has been taking photos of the landscape herself and now zips her phone back into her pouch.

"England," I say. "And my husband."

"Ah, you came here for love, of course," she replies, pulling out her scrunchie to retie her hair. "He military by any chance?"

I nod. I hope that she doesn't ask what I do here. I used to wait keenly for people to ask me my job, but I have nothing to tell people in Colorado. Not yet.

"What about you?" I ask her.

"You know the little art shop in Old Town? That's my baby. I've had her for nearly twenty years."

The flecks of colour on her hands make sense now. An art shop. An artist.

"Oh, how lovely," I say and Penny chuckles at the expression. "My mother loves to paint," I say. Or at least she used to. After my father died, the painting stopped. The paint palette and the easel were moved out to the shed, covered with a sheet, left unmentioned. And now? Now I do not know.

"Do you paint too?" Penny asks.

"No," I say and pause. "But I've been meaning to take up something now I'm here. Perhaps not painting, but something creative… I just don't know exactly what yet."

"Well you should drop by the shop, sweetie," she says. "Have a coffee with me and see if anything sparks inspiration."

"I'll do that," I say.

Penny gives my shoulder a squeeze.

"I need to start heading back down. The shop won't open itself!"

"Thanks for the support on the way up, Penny."

"It was all you, honey. All you."

She gives me a final sweaty hug and leaves. I lean against a rock to rest my legs and take in the view. The burning in my lungs has lessened and my legs feel like solid objects again. I feel good. Colorado stretches out before me. Clouds cast giant shadows that move quickly over the ground. Manitou Springs is directly below and my eyes follow Route 24 as it meanders out of the town towards Colorado Springs. After that the land keeps going until somewhere it transitions into a bright blue sky.

Baghdad was all boundaries and barriers, compounds and checkpoints. The blast walls that flanked the sides of the roads were supposed to keep explosion impacts out, but it felt more like they just kept us in. Baghdad meant claustrophobia. But here the world is vast. Open. Glorious.

I look down for a moment and notice a smooth square piece of rock by my foot. It is a deep yellow colour, the colour of the mountain between the trees. I pick it up and run my finger around the edges, testing the corners against the flesh of my fingers, then I slip it into my pocket. I raise my eyes once more. This place, this space, is what I needed. I close my eyes and take a deep breath in.

Yes. There it is. I can keep going now.

3

I did not go to war looking for love. I did not go to war at all really, although I was locked deep in its heart, in a compound where the cogs of war ground steadily against each other. The razor edges of the International Zone separated me from Baghdad, but I was still close enough to feel the tremors from downtown explosions and taste burning metal in the air.

I do not remember why he was in the International Zone that day. At the time, he was just another man in uniform, and there were plenty of those around. The International Zone was a melting pot of military personnel, international politicos, security contractors, journalists, aid workers, construction workers, translators and kitchen staff. It had the same mix of nationalities as an international airport and the same sense of transience too. Not many people stayed for long, although some of us stayed longer than others.

I know it was a Friday when I met him because I was at the pool. While the vortex of conflict raged around us, we lived and worked in a surreal calm at its centre. Sometimes we wondered if the storm would ever pass.

Many of us in the compound worked six or seven days a week. Friday afternoon was our time to relax, so the sun loungers were inevitably full. We would laze around with cheap beer, listening to the latest American country music or thumbing through dog-eared novels, generally pretending we were somewhere else.

When I first arrived in Baghdad, I didn't go near the pool. I couldn't reconcile the idea of sunbathing and swimming with being in a conflict zone. How could people discuss casualty figures in one breath and backflip techniques in the next?

My job in Iraq was to listen to the stories of what happened outside the walls of our compound. Each day, I interviewed Iraqis seeking special immigration visas to the US. They talked to me about the relatives they had lost, the threats made on their families, the fear they felt each time they left their homes. I recorded each story in minute detail, preparing the case for the next stage in the application process. I hadn't come to a war zone to sit by the pool. I had come to Iraq to help people find safety; to help people leave.

I learnt early in life that in the pursuit of purpose, sometimes sacrifices had to be made. As a doctor, my father often worked long hours and would be called into the hospital at odd times of the night. It wasn't unusual to wake up for school and find his place at the breakfast table empty. He never complained. My father was not a religious man, but the faith he did possess was an unwavering belief in the importance of doing the right thing.

"Some people, like your dad, are put here to help," my mother told me on my eighth birthday when I refused to blow out my candles because my dad was late home from work. When I was finally cajoled into puffing over the cake, I made the wish that I would become someone "who helps" one day. I wanted to make him proud.

After he was gone, I clung to that wish. I studied hard at university. When other people were in the bar, I was in the library. I went home less and less, even during the holidays. My mother and sister would call me, concerned, and the more they called, the less I would phone them back. I stayed on to do extra reading, extra assignments. And all the while, I was planning my escape.

When the job in Baghdad came up, I jumped at the chance. I dived right in, ready to sacrifice myself for my work, but it was not long before the long hours and the strangeness of compound life began to take their toll. Eventually my manager took me to one side.

"I know this place is tough, Emma, but you need to find an outlet, some way to relax here," he said. "Otherwise you're going to burn out fast and we need you too much to let that happen."

I did not so much hear his words as feel them. If I burnt out, I became useless to them. I would have failed. I needed this job as much as they needed me. Perhaps more.

The first Friday I went to the pool I didn't even own a swimsuit. I had to fashion swimwear out of my gym shorts and a sports bra that I bought from the PX, the military store on the compound. The Turkish shop sold swimsuits too, but the cheap Lycra was notoriously bad at surviving the combination of Iraqi sun and over-chlorinated water.

Around the edge of the pool were sun loungers, which I navigated awkwardly with my towel wrapped tightly around me that first day. I walked past the private security guys who were busy flexing and slathering themselves in tanning oil and past the women from the State Department who drank wine and watched from behind their expensive sunglasses.

I found where my colleagues were sitting and joined them, accepting the beer that was handed in my direction. Everyone seemed completely at ease with being partially clothed in front of their colleagues. I settled on a sun lounger, took a sip of the beer and hid behind my book. It wasn't long before I started to sweat.

The heat became too much and I moved to sit tentatively at the edge of the pool. I dipped my feet in and gasped as the cold water rushed between my toes. I pulled my feet out and glanced around guiltily. I imagined the faces of the Iraqi family I had interviewed that morning, shaking their heads in disappointment. But the moment of repose felt like a drug and I kept going back for more, until eventually I was there every Friday. Just like everyone else.

By the time I met Adam I had swapped my shorts and sports bra for a normal bikini I bought on R and R. It was Anna who introduced him to me. She was the only other Brit in the office, a couple of years younger than me, and had embraced the social side of compound life far more easily than I had. Within a few weeks of arriving, she had become a regular fixture in Baghdaddy's, the US Embassy bar, but our friendship was slower to form.

The first real conversation I had with her was a few months after she arrived. A group from the office were in Baghdaddy's one evening, sitting around a small table and discussing the latest episode of *Sons of Anarchy*. Whenever a new season of any major programme came out, it was the talk of the compound. Outside of war, there was little else going on.

Anna went up to the bar to order for the group. While she waited for the drinks, she spoke to the man next to her, who had headed over from the pool table at the other end of the bar. He had a shaven head and a thick neck and was probably ex-military, but none of us paid much attention. It was only when Anna slammed down the drinks and marched out of the bar that we took notice.

"Damn liberals," we heard the guy mutter as he returned to the pool table with his beer. I wondered for a moment if anyone was going to follow Anna and quickly realised that all eyes were on me, the other British female. I scraped my chair back and followed.

I found Anna leant against the wall just outside the bar, palms covering her face. When she peeled away her hands, I noticed for the first time how exhausted she looked. Her tears had left streaks in her foundation, revealing the raised bumps of a breakout on her skin. I was shocked at not having recognised her fatigue sooner. I had been there myself.

"God, I'm sorry," she said, trying to regain her composure. "It's just… God, he was just being such a dick."

I didn't need to ask what he'd said. Comments from men

like that tended to be sexist or racist or just generally ignorant and weren't worth repeating.

"These people can't live in the States with such violent inclinations. It doesn't fit with our culture," one man in the Green Beans café had told me after finding out my job. I didn't bother reminding him about the levels of gun crime in the US, nor that these people were the ones fleeing the violence not spreading it.

I searched my handbag for a tissue to give Anna, but found only a squashed cereal bar and a broken ID badge holder. Anna wiped a hand under her eye and dragged mascara across her face.

"Uh, do you want to come up to my room?" I asked awkwardly. "I can make you a cup of tea or something."

I wasn't expecting her to say yes, but she nodded silently and so we started walking towards our accommodation block, East End.

East End was about mid-rung in terms of the compound's accommodation hierarchy, which dictated not only the relative comfort of your living quarters but their safety level too. Diplomatic staff had their own kitchenettes and shatterproof windows. The CHUs (containerised housing units) were close to the edge of the compound and offered zero protection in an attack. These were for third country nationals who had lost the passport lottery and were shipped in for the logistics of running a war. East End was somewhere in the middle. We didn't have windows but we did have privacy.

Inside my room, Anna sat down on the flowery bedspread I bought on my first R and R, after I realised the only ones available on the compound were green and scratchy. I also brought back a magnolia-coloured table lamp and some brightly patterned cushions so the bed could double as a sofa, as it was doing now. They were small additions, but they made it feel more like a bedroom and less like a hospital room or prison cell.

24

I filled my travel kettle with a bottle of plastic water and rinsed out the spare mug I'd been using as a pen-holder.

"PG Tips? Wow, I would've cried in front of you sooner if I'd known," said Anna as I pulled out the teabags. I laughed.

After I made the tea I sat down on the bed next to her, my head resting back against the photos taped to the wall. One was a printed-out photo of my dad, holding a very young version of me upright in a paddling pool. Another was of my friends at our graduation, our faces shiny from achievement and a Prosecco breakfast. The third was a photo of a painting, with a blue sky and a small pond and splashes of red and pink flowers.

Anna and I were quiet at first, both adjusting to the unexpected intimacy of being in a location that was neither the office nor the bar. Eventually I spoke.

"Some days here just suck."

She sighed.

"Usually I can deal with it, but, I dunno, it just hit me today…"

She trailed off, unsure of where the boundaries of our fledgling friendship lay. I nodded, assuring us both that she should go on.

"I… I haven't slept much this week," she said, and took a sip of tea.

It had been a tough week for everyone in the office. Two of our Iraqi staff had left and we were struggling to get through the number of interviews needed to stem the ever-growing backlog of applications. However hard you worked, there was always the worry that the speed of the process was failing the people who needed it. I should have realised that Anna was suffering too.

"You can always hang out with me in here if you need a break," I said. "We can drink tea and talk about the royals and do all the other stuff people assume us Brits must bond over."

Anna smiled. In the awkward confines of my windowless room, our desert friendship was formed.

When Anna came over to me at the pool a couple of months later, I knew it wasn't to talk about work. We didn't talk work by the pool. Anna and I had grown increasingly close over the past months, our friendship extending beyond tea into gym sessions, lunches, coffee breaks and even an R and R vacation to Thailand. We interviewed visa applicants during the day, drank gin and tonics together in the evening and lay side by side under our desks amid dusty computer cables whenever the mortars fell a bit too close.

Relationships in the compound intensified in a way that would be deemed unusual in the outside world. Sometimes now, this friendship from Baghdad is the only one that feels real. Anna knows parts of me that friends and family from back home will never know. Adam knows Baghdad Emma too. Even when I am not out there, he keeps that part of me alive.

Anna sat on the end of my sunbed and I lowered my magazine.

"Hey, Em," she said. "How's it going over here?"

There was a forced casualness to her question that made me suspicious.

"Fine..."

"Good. Cool. Hey, Em, I have a bit of a favour to ask. There's someone I want you to meet."

I rolled my eyes at her and lifted the magazine back up to my face. Although our friendship had developed, Anna's interest in socialising still extended far beyond mine. She hadn't been dissuaded by the many stories going round about secret wives and awkward office dynamics and the occasional chlamydia outbreak. The only difference was that now Anna tried to rope me into her compound escapades too. She pulled my magazine back down.

"I know you're not interested, but Ryan is here and he brought a friend. Help me out this one time, please?"

Ryan was Anna's current infatuation. I wasn't sure exactly

what his job was, but he turned up at the International Zone every couple of weeks to do something at the embassy.

"It's hardly just one time, Anna. I'm practically your designated wing woman at the moment," I said, then raised my head slightly out of curiosity. "Where are they anyway?"

Anna pointed towards the entrance of the pool. Two men stood uncomfortably next to the glistening water. Ryan had taken his sunglasses off and was wiping them vigorously. The other guy was staring at his feet.

"God, I've never seen soldiers look so out of place in a war zone," I said. The military bases where most soldiers lived were different from the International Zone. I suspected that the only women Ryan and his friend saw on a daily basis were wearing military uniforms or cargo trousers and loose shirts. No wonder they didn't know where to look at the embassy pool, where girls in bikinis sipped beer from their sun loungers in all directions.

"They need to get the Rhino back up to VBC in an hour," Anna said. "So they wanted to go to the chow hall first and grab some food."

We slipped easily into the odd vernacular of the International Zone by that point. The Rhino was the Baghdad bus service, in the form of a giant armoured vehicle. It delivered military personnel and contractors between VBC, the military's Victory Base Complex, and the IZ, the International Zone.

I wasn't pleased to abandon pool time, but women tended to move around in pairs in Iraq. Personal safety was something drummed into us. It became normalised. There was even a "personal safety awareness" cake in the chow hall one day, although they didn't need much excuse for a themed cake out there. We referred to it from then on as the rape-cake day, although technically I suppose don't-rape-cake would have been more accurate. The joke doesn't seem so funny now.

I pulled on my clothes and followed Anna over to where Ryan and his friend were standing. The friend was wearing dark Oakley shades and stood with arms folded across his chest and feet apart in an unmistakeably military stance.

Ryan gave an awkward close-range wave as we approached.

"Hi Emma," he said. "How's it going? This is my buddy, Adam."

The friend lifted his sunglasses to reveal impressively green eyes and extended a hand.

"Hi."

He was polite but detached and I mirrored his disinterest. To me, he was just another soldier. To him, I was probably just another compound chick, lazing around the pool while other people got on with the business of war.

"Hi," I replied.

Adam and I walked side by side to the canteen. Anna and Ryan were ahead of us, their arms brushing occasionally against each other. Neither of us spoke, but I sensed Adam taking in the compound bar, the people walking back from the pool, the relaxed Friday atmosphere. I assumed that there was disapproval on his face, I had felt it myself after all, but I didn't bother commenting.

Inside the canteen, Anna and Ryan continued their flirtation as we queued up at the food station. There was something distinctly school-like about the whole situation. Anna's giggling, the chicken nuggets being spooned into our partitioned trays, me being left with the sullen friend. I couldn't believe I was in Baghdad and still dealing with this kind of thing.

I took my food and sat down at a free table. Adam sat opposite me. I waited for Anna to come and save us with her dimples and laughter, but when I looked for her, I saw that she and Ryan had gone to sit somewhere else, alone. Adam followed my gaze but returned to his food, saying nothing. I silently swore that I would never help her out again.

"So, uh, it was Alan right?"

The fork that was being raised towards his mouth froze mid-air.

"Adam. My name is Adam."

"Oh right. Sorry, Adam."

He shrugged.

"You live on Camp Victory then?"

"RPC."

I racked my brains for the words behind the acronym but came up short. He sensed my hesitation.

"Radwaniyah Palace Complex."

"Oh, I thought that Anna said you guys were waiting for the Rhino back to Camp Victory."

"We are," he said, not giving anything away.

"But you live on RPC?"

"Yes."

"So, um, that would be…?"

"Connected to Camp Victory. The other side of Liberty and Slayer."

"Ah, right okay."

I pushed lukewarm chicken nuggets awkwardly around my plate.

"What do you do here? Other than hang out at the pool of course?" he asked.

"I put together special visa applications for Iraqis," I replied. "People who have somehow or other been involved with Americans and now need to leave. What is it that you do? Apart from generating work for me of course."

When I looked up, I caught him examining my face with a strange look that could almost have been a smile. I looked down again quickly. He took his time to respond to my question. He was a man who was comfortable with silence.

"I do a bunch of different stuff," he said. "But at the moment I mostly train Iraqis."

There was an unexpected softness to his voice when he said more than a few words.

"What do you train them in?" I asked. I knew that sometimes US and Iraqi soldiers worked together, but I didn't understand enough about the inner workings of the military to know what kind of unit that would be. From Adam's broad shoulders and muscular arms, I assumed he was the kicking-down-doors type, but training local forces was something different; something interesting and more considered. It pointed towards creating a sustainable solution to the insecurity and the almost inconceivable dream of a smooth handover and withdrawal.

"Y'know, military stuff," he replied.

I tried again.

"Which Iraqi forces do you train?"

"It's not something I can really talk about." It's a phrase he must have used a thousand times before. He gave me an apologetic shrug and that half-smile again. I noticed for the first time the small fleck of a scar above his left eyebrow.

"Right," I said, smiling back despite myself. I'd been in these dead-end work conversations before. I knew there was no point pushing further.

We sat quietly for a couple of minutes. He ate carefully – cutting his food into small precise mouthfuls. It was oddly delicate and I found it endearing. I was used to brash men here; big men with big personalities who grabbed the chance to regale a female audience with their war stories (although the ones that bragged the most usually had the least to brag about). There was something different about Adam.

He finished his food and raised his eyes again, catching my gaze. I pretended I was trying to catch Anna's attention from where she was sat a couple of tables behind him.

Outside, I could see the compound being bathed in the pinkish glow of late afternoon, the most beautiful time of day in Baghdad. It was my one chance in the week to enjoy it and, even though I was more intrigued by this man than I cared to admit, I wasn't going to miss it. I pushed back my chair decisively.

"Well, enjoy your Rhino trip back, Adam," I said. "I'm going to catch the last bit of sun by the pool."

"Have fun, Emma," he said. "It was good to meet you."

He looked up and for a moment I almost considered staying.

"You too, Adam," I said, picking up my tray and feeling his eyes still on me as I walked away.

4

As I exhale, the low grumbling of my stomach draws my attention away from the view at the top of the Incline. The sweat that saturates my T-shirt now feels cold against my skin. It is time to go down. I cannot wait to tell Adam about my success.

I start off confidently, but the steps seem steeper in this direction. I angle myself sideways but with each step I can feel my muscles fighting to stabilise my knees. There is no way to avoid looking down the path and the sight makes me dizzy. I rest every couple of steps. I thought the hard part was over.

People pass me on the way up the trail. Most of the time my eyes are fixed carefully on my feet, but the couple of times I look up I get sympathetic smiles. I think I hear one man say 'brave move' but by the time the comment registers in my tired brain he has already passed. At least no one seems to be passing me going in the same direction. I can't be doing that badly.

About two thirds of the way down, I stumble. My ankle rolls and my body just keeps going. I realise I am falling but I can't stop the momentum. After three steps, maybe four, the protruding ledge of a railway sleeper prevents me pitching forwards even further.

I am still for a moment, dazed. I tentatively flex my arms

and legs to check that everything is working, but when I try to stand, pain darts through my ankle. I quickly sit back down on a step.

On the trail below, I see that two teenage boys have broken into a jog. They are barely out of breath when they reach me. I pick gravel out of my trembling hands.

"Are you okay, ma'am?" the first boy asks. "You really ate dirt there." They both look about fifteen.

"I lost my footing," I say, by way of explanation.

"We saw. But are you okay?"

"I think so." My mouth is dry and I look for my water bottle, seeing that it fell a few metres further than I did.

"Here, take this," says the second boy, handing me a bottle of water. He has a mop of blond hair that he pushes repeatedly off his face.

"Thank you."

They wait awkwardly while I drink.

"Was it your first time up?" the first, dark-haired boy asks.

I lower the bottle and nod.

"Is it that obvious?"

"Well, you came down the front, so you're either a total rookie or a pro."

"What do you mean, came down the front?" I ask.

"Most people take the Barr Trail down the side." He pushes his hair back again. "It's a bit longer, three or four miles I think, but it has a bunch of switchbacks. Nowhere near as brutal."

"Are you kidding me? So I went down here for nothing?" No wonder someone muttered "brave move". I turn and look up the trail behind me. Now he's said it, it seems obvious. Everyone is moving towards the top.

The boy shrugs.

"You don't sound like you're from around here, ma'am. It's an easy mistake to make."

I couldn't feel more out of place. I try to stand and wince at the pain.

"How's your foot?" asks the blond boy. "Do you want us to go back down with you?"

"Yeah, I think we should help you out," the other says.

I want to protest and say I'm fine, but I realise that my stubbornness is not useful here.

"If you don't mind, I'd appreciate it," I say.

The boys stand either side of me and I loop an arm across their shoulders. They are considerably taller than my five foot four inches, so with each hop I am suspended in mid-air before they lower me down.

Our progress is made even slower by the concerned questions of other hikers, asking what happened and if we need anything. My cheeks light up anew every time the boys explain that I'm "not from round here" and "didn't know about the Barr Trail". Everyone responds with knowing nods.

"So are you on vacation here or something?" asks the dark-haired boy.

"I live here," I reply. The words still feel strange in my mouth. It has been a long time since I've really lived anywhere. No one said they lived in Iraq, even though we did. It was somewhere you worked rather than lived. "My husband's in the army," I add. Husband. How long has it been now? Eight months? Nine? Still new enough for the word to be strange.

"Is he American?"

"Yeah. We met in Iraq though," I add, more for my benefit than theirs. "I used to work there."

"Are you military too?" he asks, looking more interested.

"Civilian."

"My dad's army. He's off to Iraq in a few weeks."

"Oh cool, my husband too," I say. Then I wonder if "cool" is an appropriate response. Not everyone loves it as much as I did.

By the time we reach the car park at the base of the Incline I am probably as red as I was when I reached the top. My good leg is shaking with fatigue and my ankle has become a throbbing ball of pain. I remove my arms from the shoulders of the boys and lean against the jeep with relief.

"Are you sure you don't want us to wait?" asks the blond one, while the other wipes droplets of sweat from his face with his T-shirt.

"I'm sure," I reply. "Thank you so much for your help though."

"Not at all ma'am. It's good to mix it up a bit. Happy to help."

The boys say goodbye and head back towards the base of the Incline at a light jog. As soon as they round the corner of the path that takes them to the ascent, I try to get up into the Jeep.

I hoist myself up onto the driver's seat and gasp at the pain that jolts up my leg. I raise my foot onto the dashboard to examine my ankle properly. It has begun to swell already and I loosen the laces to give the expanding flesh some room. I know that Adam keeps ice packs in the freezer, I just need to get back home.

When I was in Baghdad, I once sprained my ankle tripping down the stairs of our accommodation block. Anna was with me at the time and joined me in a heap on the floor, laughing hard. I was just about to go on R and R and I wasn't impressed by the prospect of seeing everyone in the UK with a Tubigrip around my ankle.

"Just make up a good war story," said Anna. "Say you were diving into a bomb shelter or something like that."

"No chance. That would mean admitting to my family that we do actually get attacks here."

I spent my entire visit home hobbling around with clenched teeth and hoping no one would notice.

I turn on the engine and test my foot on the accelerator. Another jolt of pain causes spots to dance at the edge of my vision. There is no way I am able to drive.

Adam is at work. Even if I can get hold of him, it will be a thirty-minute drive for him to cross town and collect me.

But who else can I call? Five months here and I still don't have any proper friends. Our neighbours are nice enough, but I don't have any of their numbers. There are the other army wives, the spouses of Adam's colleagues, but they all treat me with caution. Theoretically I am one of them, but I am also part of the world their husbands inhabit.

"You chose to go there? You weren't deployed?" one of them asked me the first time we met.

Another woman looked shocked. "I thought there weren't any women when he went away," she said and I shifted awkwardly, unsure how to react. "Perhaps it was better not to know," she added quietly.

The worst incident was bumping into Ryan and his girlfriend in the supermarket on post. At first I struggled to place the familiar face and bright red hair picking out tomatoes. I realised too late that it was the woman Anna and I had spent a wine-fuelled evening Facebook-stalking in Baghdad, after it transpired that Ryan wasn't as unattached as he had claimed. I turned to escape but in doing so bumped straight into him.

I saw a look of horror flash across his face. His girlfriend did too. She eyed me with suspicion as Ryan introduced us.

"So, wait, did you guys work together out there?" the redhead, Kelsey, asked.

"Uh, no. Not exactly," Ryan stumbled.

I sat in the car park afterwards and emailed Anna about the run-in.

Oh my god! It was as if she suspected ME of having something with him. She clearly doesn't trust the guy at all.

Anna shot back an email quickly that mainly contained expletives in capital letters. I was relieved when Adam told me a couple of months later that Ryan had moved to North Carolina.

In the Jeep I continue to scroll through my phone looking for a name to jump out, but there is no one. A feeling of isolation hits me. I will have to call Adam. What would I do if he was deployed already? What will I do if something happens while he is gone?

I press dial and the phone goes straight to voicemail.

"Hey, hubby. I hope your day's going okay. Sorry to have to call, but I rolled my ankle on the Incline and now I can't get home. Could you come and give me a lift? I'm in the car park at the bottom. Love you. Bye."

I hang up, wondering how long it will be before he gets the message. I shiver in my damp clothes. I reach for the hoodie that Adam has left on the back seat. It swamps me like a dress, but I immediately feel more comfortable. What I really want is a giant mug of tea, preferably the way my mum used to make it, with extra sugar. We drank a lot of tea the year dad died.

I decide to take off my trainer entirely and the surge of blood makes my ankle throb even more. I recline the seat as far as it will go and elevate my foot on the dashboard again – I know that's what Adam would tell me to do. My father too. I remember lying on the sofa aged 10 as he balanced my foot on a cushion after a netball accident. Sometimes these memories come unannounced, closing their grip around me for a second and then drifting away as quickly as they came.

I lean back and close my eyes, willing Adam to arrive soon.

A hard knocking on the window jolts me awake. I sit up, disoriented, but the sharp pain in my ankle throws me back into my seat. I see Adam's worried face inches from the window.

"Emma! Em! Unlock the door."

I gather my thoughts and remember where I am, what has happened. I unlock the door and Adam swings it open. He leans in and wraps me in a hug. My nose is buried in his shoulder and I breathe in his comforting smell.

"Hey," I say sheepishly when he draws back.

"God, you had me worried, Em," he says.

"I'm fine," I say. "Really. I just rolled my ankle."

"I know, but I could tell that you were putting on a brave face in the voicemail. And then you didn't answer any of my calls. The traffic was a nightmare getting over here. I didn't know what was going on."

I look at my phone. I've been asleep for nearly an hour. There were eleven missed calls from Adam.

"Shit. Sorry," I say.

"It doesn't matter," he says. "As long as you're okay. Now, let's have a look at that ankle."

I take my foot off the dashboard and lower it into Adam's large, cold hands. He gently rolls down my sock and carefully turns my ankle from side to side. He places his palm against the sole of my foot and tells me to push. I grimace.

"There's a bunch of inflammation already, babe."

I nod.

"It must be sore. Have you taken anything yet?"

"No, I didn't have anything with me."

"Okay, we'll sort that out. Good job with elevating it."

I smile.

"Thanks. I met this hot medic in Iraq once, taught me everything I know."

He leans in and kisses me.

"Okay, let me get a cold-pack and some Advil," he says. He disappears for a moment and returns with the kind of ice pack that freezes when you crack it.

"Prepared for everything," I say.

"I wouldn't be much of a medic if I didn't carry an ice pack with me," he replies. "Actually, let's move you into my truck first."

Adam slides a hand behind my back and I loop my arms around his neck. I turn sideways and, with his other arm, he scoops me up, manoeuvring me carefully out of the jeep. He lifts me easily, supporting me with one hand when he opens the passenger door of the truck. Once I am inside, he hands me painkiller tablets and a bottle of water. I lean in and kiss his head while he adjusts the ice pack on my ankle. There is a familiar smell of sweat and shampoo. However hard this transition to Colorado has been, I do not question for a moment the man I have done it for.

"So, how far did you get?" he asks, gesturing back towards the Incline with his chin as he climbs into the driver's seat.

"To the top," I tell him.

"Wait, what? You carried on with your ankle like that? Or did you fall on the Barr trail?"

"Um, neither," I say. "I fell on the way down, but at the front."

"But why were you... Oh, wait, Emma... you went down the front?"

"I didn't know there was another way!" I protest.

"Didn't you see that no one else was going down?"

"Obviously not! I wasn't trying to do the more difficult thing on purpose."

He smirks. "Wouldn't be the first time if you were."

I try to give him a light thump on the arm but he dodges.

"Easy, tiger. But seriously, Em, that's pretty impressive. No wonder your ankle gave way – going down those steps would be brutal."

He starts up the engine.

"I've gotta say though, I'm really glad you're getting out and making the most of Colorado. All that time writing those damn job applications... You need to take it easy sometimes too."

I nod, even though I know that until I have some kind of purpose here I will never truly relax.

"Are we going to leave the Jeep here?" I ask.

"I'll ask Dave to give me a ride back later," Adam says.

"The new guy at work? The one you knew from before?"

He nods. Adam has been talking about Dave and his wife a lot recently. Dave is the new team sergeant, or the "team daddy" as Adam refers to him. Adam worked with Dave after he'd just come out of the Special Forces Qualifying Course and it sounded like he'd been a real mentor figure. Adam expressed a mix of relief and excitement when he told me Dave was joining the team. Now I know how close they are to deployment, I understand why.

"Actually, you'll get to meet him this week – there's a pre-deployment briefing for spouses Wednesday morning," Adam says.

I lean forwards to adjust the ice pack, distracted.

"A what?"

"A pre-deployment briefing. Usually it's just the wives. They come in for a talk about what to expect, how to prepare, that sort of thing. But I think they're having us guys there too this time, so you won't have to suffer through it alone."

"But I can miss the briefing, right? I mean, I know what it's like in Iraq."

Adam takes a hand off the steering wheel and rubs it round the back of his neck.

"Sorry, babe. It's kinda compulsory."

"Compulsory? But I'm not in the army. They can't make anything compulsory for me."

Adam looks at me and realises he isn't helping his case. He changes tack.

"They talk about some important stuff that you should know. What happens if I get injured or something."

I try to ignore the "something" that he is referring to, although it has hovered at the edge of my mind ever since I found out he was going back.

"I'd really appreciate it if you come and it'll give you the chance to meet more of the wives."

"Okay," I say. "Okay, I'll come." I stare out of the window and now we sit in silence. I am learning to shift my identity here, but it feels wrong. I need more. I know he senses it too.

5

Iraq has invaded our home.

It is the images that flash into our living room, with close-ups of stomping military boots. It is the burning metal wreckages that used to be cars. It is the grieving women who beat faces streaked with tears.

Iraq has invaded our kitchen. It is the fridge full of the foods he will miss when he leaves. It is the faded cover of an old *Time* magazine on the counter with the face of General Petraeus and the question *How much longer?* It is a photo in a newspaper of a coffin draped in a flag.

Iraq has invaded our bathroom. It is the long hot showers he takes while he still has privacy. It is the almost empty tube of toothpaste that he is eking out until he leaves. It is the hair from the fresh buzz cut that didn't quite wash down the sink.

Iraq has invaded our bedroom. It is the dust-coloured boots and desert camo uniform in the wardrobe. It is the heavy box of gear that is waiting to be shipped. It is the piles of unidentifiable equipment that I trip over on the bedroom floor.

Iraq has invaded our bed. It is the cool space next to me when he leaves early for work. It is the way I explore his body, mapping it into my mind for when he is gone. It is the unexpected desire to conceive.

Iraq has invaded our conversations. It is the casual queries that cannot be answered. It is the plans we cannot make. It is the envy I do not put into words.

Iraq has invaded. The space between us has been occupied.

6

After I met Adam in Baghdad, the war rolled on. It rumbled forwards with the steady determination of an armoured vehicle, crushing the country beneath its heavy tracks. Nothing could divert it from its course.

Life in the International Zone continued. Days and weeks and months melted into one. We lived Groundhog Day over and over. The same routine, the same work, the same interviews with Iraqis. The faces behind the stories changed, but everyone wanted the same thing – to get out.

We found ways to mark the passing of time in the compound. Anna sometimes joked that we should scratch a tally of days into the wall, but I reminded her that was what prisoners did. Unlike most people in the country – Iraqis and international military alike – Anna and I could leave at any time. We chose to be there.

There were better ways to mark the time, anyway. Mondays were when Mexican food was served in the chow hall. On Tuesday there was a step aerobics class. On Wednesday our manager would bring cookies into the office to celebrate getting through half the week. On Thursday evenings we set up a projector in the office to watch some grainy pirated movie. And Fridays, of course, were for the pool.

As the war rolled on, I tried not to think of Adam.

Ryan continued to visit the International Zone, although

since Anna had found out about the pretty redhead on Facebook, he just gave an awkward wave from a distance that neither of us returned. Anna had spent a heartbroken week drinking cheap wine in my room, but things improved when she met a blond-haired Air Force sergeant in the queue for the salad bar one lunchtime.

Anna and I had a routine of working out in the morning, then driving into work with a large coffee and box of semi-frozen melon we'd picked up from the chow hall.

Inside our office, a converted warehouse structure, Anna and I shared a desk in the open-plan area used for doing paperwork and inputting biometric data into the organ-isation's extensive and temperamental database. There was also a series of small interview rooms with bare walls and a mishmash of furniture left over from other parts of the compound. If the visa applicants arrived at the office expecting their first insight of the American dream, they left disappointed.

The morning Anna mentioned Adam, I was sat at my desk stirring milk into my coffee. By the time I left Baghdad, my taste buds had been Americanised and I was adding a sickly-sweet vanilla creamer that seemed to be the norm in the chow hall.

As I stirred, I went through a mental checklist of the work that needed completing that day. I had two sets of interviews. The first was with a single man who had been a US interpreter, and the second was someone who had worked on a USAID project and had submitted an application that included his wife, children and elderly parents too.

I took a sip of coffee. Anna cleaned dust from between her computer keys with a can of compressed air that had a long thin tube at its nozzle.

"Ryan emailed me last night," she said, between squirts.

"What? Why?" I replied. I thought communication between them had stopped completely after the Facebook incident. "You didn't reply, did you?"

"It was weird. He wanted your email address actually."

"My email address?" I stopped stirring.

She gave the keyboard one long final blast of air and then placed the can down, satisfied.

"Yeah, not for him though. For his friend Adam."

"What, you mean the guy you left me with in the chow hall?" I said, as if searching my memory for him.

"That's the one."

"Why does he want my email address?"

"Apparently it's work-related," Anna shrugged.

"Work?"

"Yeah. I wondered whether you'd been secretly recruited by the Yanks and hadn't bothered to tell me."

I laughed.

"Not yet. Did you give it to him?"

"Of course not. I wanted to ask you first."

"I don't see how it can be a work thing when I don't even understand what they do," I said to Anna.

"What do you mean?"

"Well, like, who are they?"

Anna considered me for a moment.

"Did your conversation really not even get that far?"

"I tried," I said defensively, "but he wasn't exactly forthcoming."

"They're Special Forces."

"Oh," I said and was quiet. I still wasn't that much clearer and made a mental note to google it later.

Anna sensed my confusion.

"They work a lot with the local forces," she said, trying to help me out. "They train them, doing missions, that kind of thing. Apparently they were some of the first troops to enter Iraq – did a lot of work with the Kurdish Peshmerga in the north, even before the invasion"

"Did Ryan tell you all that?" I asked, surprised by her knowledge.

She laughed.

"No, not all. He just mentioned his unit and the internet told me the rest. I like to know who I'm getting into bed with," she said with a wink.

"Shame you didn't research his personal life so thoroughly," I replied.

Anna threw a sugar packet in my direction.

"Shall I give him your email address or not?" she asked.

I took a sip of my coffee, thinking. I was torn. I distrusted the motivations of anyone who had chosen combat as a career path. I also distrusted the motivations of most males in a place where females were in short supply. Men here went to great lengths to spend time with the civilian girls in the compound. The Italian Carabinieri even printed off flyers advertising "pizza parties", promising better quality wine than we could get in the compound bar. I knew more than one girl who had been enticed by the promise of a good Pinot Grigio. But something about Adam seemed different.

"I'm not entirely convinced…" I said to Anna. "But yeah, give him my email address. Just make sure he doesn't go circulating it around all the other sex-deprived guys on PRC or RPC or whatever their weird part of the base is called."

Anna picked up her phone.

"Done," she said with a grin. "You know, Emma, perhaps I'm starting to rub off on you."

The first email arrived that evening.

Usually when I remember Baghdad, the weeks and months are barely distinguishable. I see much of it as if through the haze of heat. The edges are softened and everything has the gentle blur of another lifetime, different to the one I inhabit now. But some things cut through the haze and split time with a sharp edge. The emails from Adam were one of those things. They changed everything.

I was lying on my bed when the first email arrived. It had been a long day in the office and a low-level headache had gathered around my temples at lunchtime and hadn't shifted despite taking multiple Advil from the industrial-sized tubs they sold in the PX.

I knew I should be asleep already, but I was on my third episode of *Grey's Anatomy*. I found something comforting about hospital dramas, even though the American doctors with their bright white teeth and complicated personal lives were nothing like my father.

I was debating watching a fourth episode when the email from Adam came through. I probably should have ignored the bleep of my BlackBerry, but most of us in the office were guilty of not having a firm distinction between office hours and personal time. Part of the problem was never actually leaving the place that you worked. The other part was the importance of being contactable at all times for accountability in case of an attack. Phones couldn't be switched off.

I opened the email without registering the email address and squinted into the bright light of the screen.

Ms. Cooper,
This is Staff Sergeant Adam McLaughlin. We met in the International Zone, through my colleague, Sergeant First Class Ryan Nova. I hope you will forgive my obtaining your contact details, however I would like to ask your advice on the procurement of US visas for local nationals. I understand, from our brief conversation, that this is your area of expertise. Please let me know if this is something you may be able to assist with.
V/r,
Adam
SSgt Adam McLaughlin
+964 750 7464928

It certainly wasn't the communication I expected to get from him. I knew Anna had said it was work-related, but I had still expected mention of a get-together, or hanging out, or something else with social connotations.

It was also an unusual request to come from military personnel. Plenty of Iraqis who worked with the US Army applied for asylum in the States, but usually the military didn't get involved until they had to produce references or confirm employment dates. Who was it that he wanted to help anyway?

I replied quickly, my fingers speeding through phrases that were second nature to me.

Dear Adam,

Thank you for your correspondence. Yes, I do recall meeting you. I was at the pool at the time, if I remember correctly. I am indeed able to advise on visa applications. To clarify, my role is to prepare case applications for Iraqis seeking passage to the United States under the Special Immigrant Visa programme. However, the final interview is conducted by the US government and, as such, I have no influence on the ultimate decision made on the individual(s) in question. Furthermore, in order to be eligible for this particular visa, you should note that the applicant must be deemed to have provided services for an entity representing the interest of the United States of America. This includes, but is not limited to: armed forces interpreters, employees of American companies, Iraqi subcontractors, employees of any charity, organisation or media entity that has received funding from a US body. I hope this helps.

Regards,

Emma

I put my BlackBerry down, knowing I wouldn't sleep straight away, and decided instead that I would watch one more episode of *Grey's Anatomy*. I got off my bed to change the disc in the DVD player when the bleep of an incoming email sounded again.

Dear Emma,

Affirmative about meeting at the pool – apologies for any inconvenience caused. Yes, noted about requirements for visa eligibility. Individual in question previously provided services at a US funded medical facility. Also, understood that you have no influence over the final decision on entry to the USA. You are, after all, British.

Would it be possible to meet in person to discuss further? I can come to the IZ if so.

V/r,

Adam

I was intrigued. Who was it that this US Special Forces soldier wanted to help? How had he come into contact with someone working at a medical facility? Could it be a woman he'd had some kind of interaction with? Stranger things had happened. I'd heard stories about soldiers meeting local women in Kurdistan and trying to take them back to the States. I felt a surprising jolt of envy at the thought of this imaginary woman, which I quickly pushed away. From the little I knew of Adam's personality, it didn't seem to fit anyway. He seemed too straight. Someone who played by the rules.

I answered. It must have been the tiredness. Maybe it was just the intrigue.

Hi Adam,

Yes, meeting is fine. Let me know the date and time. Preferably not Friday afternoon.

Best,

Emma

7

Adam was already in Green Beans on the embassy compound when I arrived, although I didn't see him straight away. I knew he planned to take the morning Rhino down from Camp Victory, but the schedule was unpredictable. He'd already cancelled on me twice at the last minute, citing operational issues. I arrived late at the café that morning, wondering if he'd turn up at all. It was the last chance I was giving him.

I did a brief sweep when I walked in, checking the place for colleagues. The café was full, but there was no one I knew, I noted with relief. I didn't want to be the subject of compound gossip, even if I was meeting Adam for official purposes.

Sampath, a young Sri Lankan man who worked in the café, greeted me. He was wearing the same uniform he wore every day – a pale yellow T-shirt with a dark blue apron bearing the chain's slogan "Honor First, Coffee Second". Sampath came to Baghdad from his tiny coastal village to serve lattes to a mix of diplomats, contractors and soldiers who thought it was completely normal to have a gun slung over their shoulder while they ordered their morning muffin.

"Why does your name badge say Sam, not Sampath?" I asked him once.

"They said my name is too difficult for the Americans," he replied with a good-natured shrug.

Sampath sent all of his earnings home to his family each

month and spoke to them once a fortnight via an old Nokia phone that was passed around the other KBR workers.

"How are you today Miss Emma? Americano with half and half, yes? You are looking smart today – big meeting?" he said with a smile. There was a comfort in being known on the compound, even if only slightly, even if among strangers.

"Something like that," I said, smoothing my clothes down self-consciously. I had exchanged my normal dark linen trousers for a pair of grey office trousers that I usually saved for important events. I was also wearing my only blouse that had survived the compound's extreme-boiling laundry system. Adam had met me in a bikini and summer dress, and I was keen to reassert my professionalism.

It was at that point that I noticed Adam sat among the other uniformed bodies in the coffee shop. His head had been bent over a *Stars and Stripes* newspaper, but he must have looked up at the sound of my name.

"Wow, I guess you're a regular in here," he said, standing up and walking towards me. I held my hand out to shake his and noticed he was taller than I had remembered. I wondered just how much of Sampath's comments he had heard and willed my cheeks not to burn.

"Hi Adam, glad that you could make it this time," I said, sounding more assured than I felt. It was his turn to look uncomfortable now.

"Yeah, uh, I'm really sorry about that. Stuff came up last minute."

"It's fine, I get it," I said. "The fight for freedom doesn't wait for anyone."

"Yeah, freedom, something like that. Can I get your coffee? Americano with half and half was it?"

"It's fine, I've got it."

"No, please, I asked for your help. At least let me get the coffee."

I noticed Sampath watching the whole exchange with interest and I shifted awkwardly.

"Well, okay, thanks. I'll get the next one."

"Oh, we're having another coffee?" he teased, unexpectedly.

"Actually, it was just the polite British thing to say," I replied.

I went and sat down at the table where Adam had been reading the newspaper, facing myself towards the counter. I caught Sampath grinning at Adam as he handed over the coffees, then as Adam turned, Sampath shot an approving wink in my direction. I gave him a warning glare. Adam joined me at the table with an Americano and a towering latte that smelled of caramel and vanilla.

"I know, it's like two days of calories, but it was an early start," he said, almost apologetically. "Lots of waiting around for the Rhino."

"No judgement here," I said, holding my hands up in front of me. I didn't tell him I was actually noting that he waited for my arrival to get a coffee, despite the red of his eyes betraying how desperate for caffeine he must have been.

"So," I said, taking a sip of my coffee, "now that we're both here, tell me what's going on."

Adam started talking. Based on the chow hall experience, I had expected our conversation to be stilted, awkward. But today was different.

"So, there's this woman... Ameena," he said. I felt strangely deflated for a moment, but then he continued. "She's the cousin of my 'terp, Ali. He's a solid guy. I said I'd try and help him out."

Adam wanted advice about the special visa programme for the cousin of his interpreter, or "'terp" as the US soldiers tended to call them. He said he didn't know much about Ameena personally, but Ali was worried about her. And a distracted interpreter in a conflict zone wasn't good for anyone.

Adam said Ali had been a Special Forces interpreter for the past three years. He came from Basra, a city in the south where he had been training to become a doctor. Adam spoke about Ali with a mix of professional respect and genuine affection.

"You know, when Ali was studying, they didn't even get to learn on real bodies. Some kind of religious regulation apparently. Can you believe that? Dead bodies all over the damn place and med students are all just examining one single body that was preserved in the seventies."

I raised my eyebrows slightly and Adam went on. There was something undeniably attractive about his passion.

"I don't know how they learnt anything at all. Y'know, back in the day, this place was way ahead of the rest of the region in terms of medicine... Sorry for ranting about it, it just makes me really mad," he said. "I'm a medic too, so I guess that's why Ali and I kinda bonded, talking about training and treatment and stuff. He's a smart guy."

"Wait, you're a medic?" I said. He had surprised me again.

"Uh, yeah..."

"I thought you trained Iraqis."

"Well, I do that too. We do a bunch of stuff."

"Oh," I said, trying to wrap my head around the information. "So, does it take a lot of training to be a medic?"

"I guess. I mean, it adds an extra year to your training, but I knew most of what we learnt already."

"Why? Were you the kind of kid that operated on cats or something?" I joked and immediately regretted it. I had a tendency to make inappropriate jokes when I was nervous.

"Actually, I studied medicine at college," he said. "But you know, us SF medics train on cats sometimes too."

I laughed.

"No, really. At least, we used to. Wait, you're not a cat lover are you?"

"I'm more of a dog person."

"Good. Me too. Luckily we didn't have to practise on them."

I smiled and he looked down and stirred his coffee. I found myself doing the same, as if embarrassed by the lightness of the exchange between us. I was intrigued.

"So, you studied medicine at college?" I asked, encouraging him to continue.

"Yeah. I was going to be a doctor, but then, well, SF happened. Or 9/11 to be exact. Both my brothers were military and I knew I couldn't stay in the States while they were deployed. Especially when I had skills that could be useful."

I had the sudden desire to tell him that my father was a doctor. That I had grown up around medical terms. That I shared my father not only with my sister but with thousands of patients I never met. But I held back this surge of personal information. I barely knew the man, why was I so keen to tell him so much?

"So, anyway," he said, turning his cup between his hands, "Ali didn't get to finish his studies like I did. His brothers were killed, so it was down to him to support the family. Can you imagine? He left his studies and got a job as an SF 'terp through some contact of his. But he says he'll go back to school when—"

I shifted in my seat and stretched out a leg, which came to rest against Adam's. Realising this, I withdrew it quickly. Adam paused, as if he'd forgotten what he was saying.

"—When, um…"

"When this is over?"

"Yeah. Right. When this is over."

Adam cleared his throat and I felt the red begin to creep up the base of my neck. With pale skin there was no hiding my blushing. There was a moment's silence, which was interrupted by the buzz of my BlackBerry on the table between us. It was a reminder that I had a meeting in half an hour. We'd already been talking for thirty minutes and I still wasn't much clearer about the woman he wanted to help.

"Sorry," I said. "So, um, Ali sounds like a really great guy, but you said the visa was for his cousin, not him?"

"Oh, yeah," said Adam. "Ameena – she's the cousin. Second or third cousin, I think. She worked in a medical centre that received US funding, but she stopped because she started getting threats. Ali said it could be because of the job, but someone killed her husband a year or so ago, so it could be linked to that too."

"Can she prove it? The threats, I mean," I asked. It was a question I hated, but it was part of the job.

"I don't know. Does she have to? What's she supposed to do – ask them to wait while she gets out a voice recorder?" Adam looked annoyed.

"No. No, of course not. It just strengthens the case if she can. Could speed things up a bit. Does she have children?"

"Er, I think so. A young one. Ali said she lives with the kid and her mum."

I nodded, thinking about the application form. Single mother. No direct male relatives. I hoped for her sake it was a case I could put through quickly.

"So what now?" Adam asked. "Shall I find out more information about the family?"

"First she needs to go onto the website and fill in the online registration form," I said. "Then she'll be invited in for the first interview, in my office. After that there will be background checks, which can be slow, then another interview with the US Citizenship and Immigration Services. It's a long process and there are no guarantees."

I rummaged in my bag for a business card.

"Tell Ali to give her this. If she calls me when she's registered I'll try to interview her myself."

Adam took the card and turned it over in his hand.

"Do you think she has a chance?" he asked. I saw a worry in his face that I hadn't noticed before. He rubbed a hand around the back of his neck. His other hand was on the table in front of me and I almost reached to touch it with my own. "I really want to help Ali. I... I owe him one," he said.

I felt more words rise up in Adam and then get pushed back down, not yet ready to be released into the air between us.

"I'll do what I can, Adam," I said, placing my hand on the table so close to his that our fingertips were almost touching. "I promise."

8

This is not what I expected.

The man at the front of the briefing room who is giving the presentation keeps using the word "we". It punctuates his sentences, this reminder of an army family of which I do not feel part. I did not expect to find it this hard.

"It is four weeks until your husbands leave for Iraq," he says, but the name of the country that leaves his mouth sounds foreign to my ears. "Eye-rak". The "eye" is harsh and the "rak" is emphasised and the country is mutated into a place that I do not recognise.

The k catches at the back of his throat. I see other women flinch at the sound. It is the click of the gate closing behind the men as they leave the base. It is a bullet sliding into a chamber. It is the moment before detonation.

I must not let myself believe in this American version of Iraq. I must not let it transform into a different place now I am not there. I shut out the man's voice. In my head I say Iraq in my voice, over and over. I say Iraq the way I say it when I talk about my work, my life, about how I met the man I love. I say it like a mantra. I make it softer. I make it true.

Is this how Iraqis in America feel when they hear the name of their country from someone else's mouth?

This week Adam came home from work with a "deployment readiness pack", like a child sent home with letters from school. This pack was supposed to prepare us for everything that is war – the paperwork, the logistics, the emotions. I know what it is to be in a conflict zone, yet these pamphlets made the experience into something alien. Something to be feared.

I searched military spouse blogs, to read the experiences of women who have been there, done that, come out the other side.

Deployment survival guide! said one title. *How to survive your first deployment!* said another. And I paused because I thought he was the one who was supposed to be surviving. Not me.

The articles told me *how to say goodbye to your soldier* and *how to communicate when your soldier is away* and *how to prepare for you soldier's return.*

I read it all but I could not find us anywhere in the words. I did not recognise me and I did not recognise him. He is not *my* soldier. He is my husband, my friend, my lover. He is the army's soldier. Not mine.

"Em. Em? Are you okay?" There is a quick squeeze of my leg. "Hey, babe, anyone home?"

The PowerPoint presentation has ended now and there is a slide in front of us that says *ARMY STRONG* in giant letters. Underneath is the black, yellow and white five-pointed star of the army logo.

"Oh, yeah. Sorry. I zoned out for a bit there." I turn towards him and force a smile. I want to reach out and hold his hands in mine, but there is a rule against public displays of affection when soldiers are in uniform.

"No worries," he says. "That last part went on for ages."

I don't even know which part he is referring to. I stopped focusing about halfway through. The presentation had driven home the reality that Adam was leaving and I was going to be left in Colorado with no purpose. Nothing.

"Look, there's coffee over there. Do you want one?" he asks.

I want to leave but I say okay and he puts a single finger on the small of my back, guiding me between the groups of people until we reach the table with coffee.

We stand quietly, holding our polystyrene cups. I look around the room at the other wives and notice that many seem to be standing much closer to their husbands than usual. When I look down, I see that my arm is pressed against Adam's too. I feel my pulse thud in the place where our skin meets.

He is leaving. I feel my pulse quicken. Thud. Thud. Thud. He is leaving and I am staying here.

"Hey, there's Dave and Kate," Adam says, moving the arm that was touching mine to point out a couple. "Let's go say hi. I really want you to meet them."

"Just give me a second," I say. I hand him my coffee and slip away before he can answer. I find the bathroom and shut myself in a cubicle, trying to gather my thoughts. Thud. Thud. Thud. I put the toilet lid down and sit with my feet up, staring at the grey of the door, taking long slow breaths. What is going on with me? It is just Iraq. It is just for a little while. Everything will be okay.

It's just Iraq, I say again, but images, tastes, sounds begin to flash through my mind. The office. The alarm. The dust on my tongue. The tremors of the ground. The relief. Then Sampath. The blast wall. The arm on my neck. The blood in my mouth. And now I have nothing.

STOP, I tell myself.

Please. Stop.

Two women enter the bathroom. I am grateful for them disturbing my thoughts. They are discussing some new teacher at the local elementary school who came from a military family herself.

"She's really helped Joe," one of the women says. "He acted out a ton during the last deployment, but I think with her he'll be different." I flush the toilet. One of the women smiles at me as I leave the cubicle. I wash my hands and reapply lip balm. My lower lip is red. I must have been chewing it during the presentation, a nervous habit I developed at university. I am fine.

When I come out, Adam is already talking to Dave and his wife. Dave is a tall man with dark hair and the same broad shoulders that seem to be standard in Adam's line of work. He is almost matched in stature by his wife, an athletic-looking woman wearing ripped jeans and an oversized sweater with long brown boots. Her hair is pulled into a messy knot at the back of her head. She looks different to the other wives I've met and I like her already.

"Ah, here she is," says Adam as I approach. "Emma, this is my old friend Dave and his wife Kate."

"Hey, easy on the 'old' part there, Adam. You're catching up fast!" jokes Dave as he shakes my hand. "Glad to finally meet you Emma. I've heard a lot about you!"

"Uh-oh. All good I hope?" I say, trying to smile.

"Well, apparently there's a new British girl in town who likes to throw herself down the front of the Incline," says Kate, extending her hand.

"Oh God, you heard about that?" I ask her, shooting Adam an exaggerated disapproving look.

"Word got round fast," Adam says. "Dave heard the Sergeant Major saying his son had just helped a British lady down the front of the Incline before I even got back to the office. You sure chose your rescue party."

I groan. This is not the first thing I want people to hear about me.

"Well, I thought it was impressive to go down the front," said Dave.

"Me too. I like a woman with a bit of grit," says Kate. "And the British accent just makes it even cooler." She pauses. "Hey, can I ask you to say something for me, Emma?"

Dave rolls his eyes and shakes his head.

"Already, Kate? Seriously? You've only just met the poor woman."

I laugh. Requests to hear my accent are normal for me these days. It's a constant reminder of how I don't quite fit in.

"Of course," I tell her. "What do you want me to say?"

"Predator," she says, clasping her hands together.

This is a new one.

"You want me to say predator?" I ask.

She grabs Dave's shoulder and lets out a loud laugh that makes some of the other women turn around. Perhaps they don't consider laughing appropriate at pre-deployment briefings.

"Brilliant," she says, in a voice that I could almost swear is purposefully louder.

"That was it?" I say. "Predator? As in, *Predator* like the movie?"

Dave runs a hand down his face, trying to stretch out the creases of a smile.

"That's a really good one, Kate," says Adam, openly smirking.

Kate, meanwhile, is trying to copy my pronunciation herself.

"Preh-duh-tuh. Preh-duh-tuh."

I look to Adam.

"You say it," I tell him.

"Predator," he says with a shrug. The t has become a second d and the r rolls long at the end of the word. *Preh-deh-dorrr.*

"Yeah, okay, that's pretty good," I concede.

"I've been waiting to hear you say it since I found out Adam married an Englishwoman," she tells me.

Dave checks his watch and looks at Adam, then me.

"Emma, do you mind if I borrow your husband for a quick work chat?" he asks.

"Of course not. But no promises about what your wife might be saying by the time you get back."

Kate claps her hands together in excitement.

"Love you, babe," Adam whispers in my ear, then follows Dave out of the room. With the men gone, the mood between Kate and I shifts slightly.

"So… How did you find the briefing?" she says.

"Um, it was interesting," I reply. "A lot to take in. I

haven't had to think about the other side of it before. What about you? You must be a pro at these by now."

Adam had mentioned that Kate and Dave have been married fifteen years. They had been to the same high school apparently. She doesn't look old enough to have been married more than a decade, but I remind myself that Americans (especially the military kind) tend to marry early.

"Yeah, I could pretty much recite the whole thing by heart," she jokes. "But I never enjoy them. They tend to freak the crap out of the new wives and remind us older ones about all the admin bullshit we have to deal with when the men are gone."

I take a sip of my near-cold coffee.

"I was kind of interested about how you'd react to it though," she continues. "Having been out there too, y'know, on the civilian side of things... How are you settling into Colorado?"

"It's lovely," I say. "The scenery is amazing and everyone seems friendly..."

"I feel like there's a 'but'," she says.

I laugh. She is perceptive.

"To be honest I'm just a bit, well, bored."

"I'm not surprised. It always takes Dave ages to adjust after a deployment and he has a job to come back to."

I try not to wince. Adam must have told them I'm not working. That's part of who I am now. She notices my expression.

"But hey, we've heard impressive things about you. I'm sure you'll find something soon."

"Thanks," I say awkwardly. I hope she's right. I am about to ask her about the son Adam mentioned when a woman with a pastel pink jumper and a perfect blow-dry walks towards us.

"Ah. It's Olivia," Kate says. "Have you met her yet? She likes Europeans. I saw her at a meeting once explaining to one of the German wives what pancakes are."

I have met Olivia only once before. She has something

to do with the unit's Family Readiness Group, or FRG, which seems to mean she's a ringleader among the wives. Our single exchange had been strained. She kept using acronyms I didn't know and then asking me to repeat things because she didn't understand my accent.

"Hello, Kate, Emma. Good to see you both. Would you like a muffin?" she asks, holding out a tray of small cakes with intricate frosting on top.

"They look delicious, Olivia," I say. We both take a muffin and one of the pink napkins, which match Olivia's outfit but are at odds with the many shades of green and beige in the room.

"It's a family recipe, with extra chocolate. I'd never indulge in one myself, of course, but the men seem to love them," Olivia says as Kate is midway through her first mouthful.

I try not to laugh at Kate's face and take a bite myself.

"I can see why they are popular," I say.

Kate nods in agreement through another mouthful. The compliment softens Olivia's face into a more natural-looking smile.

"Thanks. So, will I be seeing you at any of the FRG meetings soon?"

"Um, yeah… I'll try…" I say awkwardly.

Kate is far more upfront.

"Oh come on, Olivia, you know me. There's no point me making a promise I can't keep. It's a busy time of year for sports injuries."

"Sports injuries?" I say.

"Yup, I'm a physiotherapist," she says, turning to me. "I used to work in a practice downtown but then I went private, so now people just come to the house."

I hate myself for having assumed that she doesn't work. I didn't even ask her.

Olivia sighs a little at Kate's response and I almost feel sorry for her, but I know it can't be this difficult to get other spouses along to FRG meetings. Some of the women in the front row of the briefing raised their hands so often in the Q and A section that I thought it would never end.

"It's fine," she says. "I just think it's important that we stick together during this deployment, that's all. Especially after what happened to that poor man from Fifth Group last week."

"What happened to the man from Fifth Group?" I ask. Fifth Group is who Adam's team will be replacing.

Kate shoots a warning look at Olivia, but she is already swelling with the importance of having information about Iraq that I do not.

"You know, maybe you should ask Adam about it," says Kate quickly, cutting in before Olivia has a chance to speak. "There was an accident, but the guy is okay. He's at the hospital in Landstuhl at the moment. I'm sure Adam will want to explain it to you himself."

"It was the medic that got injured," says Olivia. I try to control my expression on hearing Adam's specialisation. I don't want Olivia to see how unsettled I am. "He was shot in the shoulder."

"Where was he?" I ask.

Olivia looks confused. "Um… Iraq."

"Yeah I know, but where exactly?" I ask her, sounding harsher than I intended.

Olivia is flustered by the question. She is on the back foot now. Iraq is my territory.

"Oh, well, I don't know. Somewhere central I think. Or was it southern?"

Kate senses the tension and interjects.

"Hey, Emma, I think it's about time we find those husbands of ours, don't you? I need to go and rescue my neighbour from my grumpy toddler."

Olivia gives us her best cheerful goodbye, but her voice is too high-pitched. I let Kate lead me away, then when we're at a safe distance she turns and squeezes my arm.

"Hey Emma, I'm sorry about that. I don't know you that

well, but I do know Adam. I'm sure he was just figuring out a good time to mention it."

I nod, but there is no time to reply because Adam and Dave are walking over to join us. Adam catches my eye and smiles.

"Hey, Kate, are you about ready to release my Brit?" he asks, returning to my side.

"Ugh, if I must," says Kate, "but make sure she gets my number. We have a bunch more hanging out to do."

As we leave Fort Carson, I stare out of the window of the truck in silence. We pass by the checkpoints where soldiers examine the IDs of people entering the base. It is still strange to me to see checkpoints outside a conflict zone.

"You and Kate seemed to hit it off," Adam says to me.

I continue to stare, my head resting against the gently vibrating window of the truck. We pass row upon row of military accommodation, cookie-cutter houses separated from the rest of Colorado Springs by a high wire fence that reminds me of the CHUs in Baghdad.

"Em?" says Adam.

"What? Oh, yeah, she seems cool," I reply. I do not want to talk right now.

"Did she tell you she's a physio?" he asks. "I meant to mention it last week after your fall, but then your ankle seemed to be healing well and I forgot."

"Yeah, I heard," I say. Adam shoots me a sideways glance.

"Are you okay, Em? Did the briefing upset you?" he asks.

It did, because I had not expected it to be this hard.

It did, because it made me think about scenarios I did not want to consider.

It did, because it reminded me that he was leaving and I had nothing.

But that is not the problem.

"Adam, why didn't you tell me that the Fifth Group medic got shot?"

"Shit."

Adam hits the steering wheel and I flinch. I have never seen Adam hit anything before. I know only the level-headed, reassuring Adam who I imagine must be a comforting sight if you are bleeding on the battlefield.

"Who told you?" he asks. "Was it Kate?"

"It doesn't matter who told me," I say. "What matters is that it wasn't you."

Adam runs a hand around the back of his neck and takes a deep breath, shaking his head.

"Honestly, I'm not sure," he says. "I knew I should, I was going to, but the time never seemed right. What with you looking for a job and dealing with the deployment news already, I didn't want to worry you more."

"Worry me?" I ask. "Adam, I *know* people get injured in Iraq. I know people who *have* been injured out there. Since when have you had to shelter me from that kind of thing?"

"I just thought that with the deployment coming up..."

"What? That you'd start treating me like a clueless army wife? In fact, even they all knew. So it's worse. You just shut me out completely."

"No, Em, it wasn't... I..." He falls quiet. He doesn't look angry anymore. His hands wring around the steering wheel and a crease forms on his forehead.

Iraq has invaded. An invisible wall is rising between us and I scrabble to break it down. I claw at the bricks with broken nails and bloody fingers. This isn't the way it works. This isn't who we are.

I take a breath.

"Did you know him?" I ask.

He nods. "Yeah, we went through selection together."

He didn't just know him, he knew him well.

"So what happened?" I ask.

"Unexpected contact while they were out," he says.

"Where?"

"It got him in the shoulder."

"No, I mean where did it happen?"

"Sadr City," he says. The Shia district used to be a hotspot for clashes. The military were tied up there a lot, especially back in 2008. But we're in 2011 now. It's supposed to be safer.

"So that's where you're going?" I ask.

"I'll be on RPC again. You know that's all I can tell you, babe. Now can we please talk about something else?"

9

Music pumped inside the gymnasium as Anna and I thrust our hand-weights into the air and tried to move in unison, left then right, up onto the step and then back down. The song playing was by some female singer who was popular in the States at the time. I don't know her name, but sometimes when I am in Colorado I hear the song in the car or in a store and my muscles twitch with the memory of movements from the class.

The aerobics instructor was a tiny woman called Jessica, who was the admin and logistics assistant at the US Embassy. Her dark hair was pulled into a neat bun and she wore bright patterned leggings and a black tank top, with the neon pink straps of her sports bra peeking out from underneath. She was in flagrant disregard of the rule about not displaying shoulders, but if anyone called her up on it the class would be over. Perhaps the prominence of shoulders was one of the reasons for the high popularity of aerobics on the compound.

Anna and I were positioned at the side of the hall, next to a large fan. Military personnel tended to gather at the front and back (near the exit routes) or in the centre (away from the windows). Anna and I had weighed up the risk mitigation options carefully and decided body temperature regulation took priority over safety in a rocket attack. Survival of the latter would mostly be down to chance anyway.

On the other side of the hall were a few private security

contractors. These were the men more commonly found in the weights section of the gym comparing protein shakes and creatine powder, but they sometimes joined us to lift tiny pink dumb-bells in the hope of getting Jessica's number. I remember they were all looking particularly orange that day. Rumour in the compound bar was that they'd taken too many carotene tanning pills.

My favourite person in the aerobics class melting pot, however, was Sampath, the Sri Lankan guy from Green Beans. He always positioned himself at the front of the class and never missed a beat. You could tell when he liked a song because he added in extra steps and flourishes with his hands. Once I saw him add a whole double spin into a Rihanna song. It came as no surprise when he finally admitted he'd been a traditional dancer back home. Apparently the security guys even asked him for a couple of private lessons, trying to up their game to impress Jessica.

At the end of the class, I picked up my empty water bottle and sweat-soaked towel. Anna and I gave a wave of thanks to Jessica, then headed towards the exit so we could fit in a quick shower before going to the office. Sampath caught up with us on the way out.

"Good morning, Miss Emma, Miss Anna. How are y'all today?"

His accent was a funny mix of Sri Lankan and American, having worked on military bases for so long.

"Good thanks, Sampath. How about you?" I replied.

"Good thanks, ma'am. And how is your other friend?"

"Other friend?"

"You know. The soldier man who bought you coffee when you had your smart clothes on."

Anna raised an eyebrow at me.

"Oh. He's not a friend. That was a meeting."

"Ah, okay," said Sampath, with an exaggerated wink. "Nice meeting. I must go for work now, but y'all have a good day."

He jogged off, energised by the morning's dancing.

"So you put your smart clothes on for Adam, did you?" Anna teased. I felt the red burn of embarrassment creeping into my cheeks as I tried to think of an excuse for my outfit.

"No, I... It wasn't for him," I stumbled. "We had something else that day. You know, that briefing in the afternoon."

"You weren't wearing smart clothes in the briefing though," she pointed out. "In fact, none of us ever wear smart clothes for that briefing."

She was right. I knew that my smart trousers would have caused questions in the office, so I went back to my room and changed straight after seeing Adam.

"Sometimes we do," I argued feebly. I was digging myself into a hole. "Also I spilled some coffee on my blouse."

"Sure," said Anna, clearly enjoying seeing me squirm. "So why didn't you just change your blouse then?"

"Er, I don't think I had one that matched the—"

"Oh, come on, Em!" Anna stopped walking and raised her hands up at her sides. "This is me! Seriously, just admit you made an effort. He's a handsome guy. I would have done the same."

I had been hesitant to tell Anna about my meeting with Adam at first. Although she claimed to be over the Ryan episode, I knew the betrayal still stung. But when I finally gathered the courage to tell her about meeting Adam and explained about Ali and Ameena, she was supportive.

"I'm glad Adam wants to help them," she said. "God knows we could do with a few more soldiers treating Iraqis like humans, even if he is only doing it to get in your pants."

We got to our accommodation block and trudged up the stairs with tired legs.

"So have you heard from him since the Green Beans meeting?" she asked.

"No. Not really, it was only last week. He got in touch with a couple more questions, but just application stuff."

"Really?" she asked, with an eyebrow raised in a sceptical arch. "Application stuff? Is the woman even on our system yet?"

"Well, no, not yet," I stumbled, "but he had some queries."

"Sure. I bet he did."

It wasn't completely untrue. Adam had been in touch with a question about the references that needed to go on the application form. I didn't need to tell Anna that the conversation had then drifted a bit, that we had discussed where I should go if I ever visited the States, how much he would like to go to London one day, what a coincidence it was that we both liked reading Tim O'Brien and how bored we were of chow hall food. But it was just chat, that was all. As I reminded myself, soldiers weren't my type.

Incoming. Incoming. Incoming.

We were sat in the office when the alarm sounded later that morning. Chairs pushed back. Stiff wheels scraped against the floor.

Incoming. Incoming. Incoming.

"Get down," a voice shouted. We knew the drill. Away from the windows. Under the desks. Get flat. But you couldn't get flat under desks, not really. So we got on our knees, curled up into balls, strained our necks as we ducked our heads down instead.

Incoming. Incoming. Incoming.

THUD. A hit. One… Two… Three…

I saw Anna's foot in the tangled mass of extension cables where our computers met. I wondered if the electrics were safe. There was a thick line of dust on the power outlet where the cleaning hadn't reached. Was it a fire hazard? What a thing to be noticing, I thought, as we were…

CRACK.

The C-RAM sent out a round to hit the incoming rockets mid-air.

Incoming. Incoming. Incoming.

"Fuck."

"Anna?"

"Yes?"

"You okay?"

"Yeah. You?"

THUD.

"Shit. That felt close."

"Fuck. Yeah."

Incoming. Incoming. Incoming.

Nothing.

Nothing.

Nothing.

"Stay down!" the voice yelled again. "Keep your heads down!"

I pulled my chin in tightly against my chest and concentrated on breathing in, breathing out. My heart beat, beat, beat in my ears. It had been a while since they'd been this close. It had been a while since they hit.

Listen. Wait. Breathe.

The waiting seemed endless. People began to shuffle, move around. My left leg cramped, so I shifted position and pummelled my fist into the side of my thigh.

Listen. Wait. Breathe. Then the speaker system.

This is the Command Post. All clear. All clear. I say again. All clear. All clear.

Movement. Footsteps. Cursing.

I reached out my hand to Anna.

"We're fine," I said. "We're fine."

One of us laughed. It might have been me. Then the voice again.

"Is everyone okay? Right, get up. Let's do accountability."

It was the same voice that had yelled at us to stay down. I crawled out from under my desk and our office manager Nigel began the accountability check, working his way quickly through a list of names. I waited, ready to answer. It was like being at school and waiting for the teacher to say your name in the register, except during accountability you prayed that everyone was present.

"Anna."

"Here."

"Emma."

"Here."

"Hana."

Nothing.

"Hana?"

Beat. Beat. Beat. My heart quickened again. Another spike of adrenaline ran hot through my blood. Where was Hana? Beat. Beat. Beat. It felt like an eternity passed.

"Where the fuck is Hana?"

"She's over here," said Mohammed, crouched down by a desk. "Hana, it's okay. You can come out."

Hana emerged slowly. She was covered in dust and had streaks on her face from where she'd been crying. Hana was from Anbar Province, but things got bad there and she didn't have much family left. That's why she didn't like loud noises. Mohammed and Lina tried to comfort her, whispering in low fast Arabic. Hana nodded and adjusted her hijab. Nigel finished the accountability check. In our office everyone was present. Safe. Unharmed, physically at least.

Anna held out a hand in front of her. It was shaking. I held out my hand. It was shaking too.

"I think that's the closest they've come," she said again.

"Yes."

"Tea? Smoke?"

I nodded yes to both.

"I'm going out to check the situation," Nigel said loudly. "No one leave until I'm back."

Anna went to the tiny kitchen at the back of our office that had a kettle, a small fridge and a coffee machine. She offered the rest of the team tea on her way through, but no one accepted. It was the British response to stress. Hana was on her phone trying to cancel the meeting she had in twenty minutes, but the phones lines were down. It's what normally happened after an attack, but I never found out whether the lines were just overloaded by the sheer quantity of calls or whether the military jammed communications intentionally.

I opened the bottom drawer of Anna's desk, the one that didn't fall out, and looked for our emergency packet of cigarettes. I found it wedged under a pile of papers, some desk cleaner and a half-eaten Cliff bar. I opened the crushed cardboard box. Three left.

I didn't smoke before Iraq or after. I didn't smoke in Iraq, not often anyway. Attacks were the exception. I opened the back door of our office building and sat on the step. It was dirty, but I didn't care. I was coated in dust from the floor anyway. Anna joined me with two large mugs of tea. The air around us was quiet, but there was the sound of sirens somewhere else in the IZ, keeping us on edge.

I lit Anna's cigarette and then my own, trying to steady my hands long enough for the end of the cigarette to glow red.

"At least they didn't interrupt pool time this week," I said. The joke hung restless in the air, unable to find somewhere to settle. I drew slowly on the cigarette and held the unfamiliar smoke in my lungs for a second. I felt momentarily light-headed. I exhaled and coughed.

"That one felt close," said Anna for the third time.

"It was," I replied. "Closest one I've felt. I think I heard the zip before the thud."

By the base of the step I spotted a flat sand-coloured stone. I picked it up and turned it again and again in the hand that was not holding the cigarette, digging it into my palm. My nerves were receding but I felt charged with something else. The muscles of my cheeks started to tighten as if to smile. What was it? Elation? Exhilaration? I shoved the stone into my pocket. Anna saw.

"Another one for the jar?" she asked.

A door shut loudly and we both jumped. A man came out of a warehouse building near ours and leant against the wall, lighting up his own cigarette. The post-attack smoking habit was common. He raised his eyes and nodded in greeting. I recognised him from the compound, but I wasn't sure what the people in that building did, even though it was barely metres from our own.

"You guys all okay in there?" he asked, gesturing towards our office with his chin.

"Yeah. You?"

He took a long drag on his cigarette before answering.

"One down on accountability. Hopefully he just went back to his room or something stupid."

We nodded.

"Fingers crossed," I said, then felt foolish for invoking such a trivial symbol for luck. The Iraqis in the office would have known what to say. They would have had more powerful words for a situation that was doubtlessly more familiar to them. But not me. Interlacing my digits for luck was the best I could come up with for the unknown fate of an unknown man.

"Any idea what happened?" Anna asked the man.

He sucked on the cigarette again and lifted a hand to shield his eyes from the sun.

"Rocket attack," he said. "No damage this side, but apparently one hit over by the US Embassy gym."

"Shit," I said. "We were there this morning."

"So were a lot of people. Lucky it wasn't earlier."

The Iraqis wouldn't call it luck, I thought. They would call it the will of God.

"Casualties?" I asked.

"A couple by the sounds of it."

I wondered who it could be. There were a lot of people in the International Zone, but we were all connected in one way or another.

He dropped his cigarette and crushed it into the ground with the toe of his boot.

"You ladies have a good day. Stay safe."

"Thanks," said Anna. "You too."

"Hope your guy shows up," I said.

73

"Appreciate it." The door of the office building shut. Anna lit the third cigarette, which we passed between us.

"Fuck," she said. "The gym. Shit. I need a drink. I wonder whether the bar will be open tonight."

"It'll be full if it is, but there's wine in my room too."

"I hope Brad will be around."

"The Air Force guy?"

"Yeah."

There was always something hedonistic about the International Zone in the aftermath of an attack. People drank more. Danced more. Shared other people's beds. We had existential crises and bathed in the relief of being alive. We wanted to touch, feel, forget.

There was movement inside the office. Nigel was back with an update.

"Only one hit. Quite lucky really. It was outside the gym, so the blast wall took a lot of the impact. Could have been much worse." There was that word again.

"Did you hear anything about the casualties?" asked Anna.

"One fatality and a few injured."

"Do you know who?"

"Too early for them to say officially, but I overheard someone mentioning one of the Sri Lankan KBR workers – maybe one who works at Green Beans."

"Sampath," I breathed.

"Who?" asked Nigel, confused.

"Sampath. He's…" I paused. A friend?

Anna put her hand on my shoulder.

"No, we don't know it's him, Emma. There are tons of other Sri Lankans around."

"Actually, that name does sound familiar," said Nigel. I was silent, but Anna did not want to listen to him.

"No, it can't be. He was going to work when we saw him this morning. He wouldn't have been there. It isn't him."

I tried to tell myself it couldn't be true. Sampath belonged to a different Baghdad, one of aerobics classes and morning lattes. He was not part of the fighting. He could not have been a victim of this.

Nigel's BlackBerry beeped.

"It's my KBR buddy," he said, looking down at the device. His thumb moved quickly as he scrolled through the email, then he looked up. "Sampath, you said? I'm sorry... Not official yet, so don't spread it around."

Back in my room later that day, I sat at my desk. Nigel told us to take some personal time if we needed it, but we all said we were fine. No one got any work done. I spent the next two hours staring blankly at my computer screen. Mohammed knocked over a mug in the kitchen and we all jumped. Someone swore. Eventually Anna left and I followed her.

"I just want to switch my brain off for a while," she said. "Watch some mindless TV or something."

I didn't fully understand how I felt. It was not grief exactly, because Sampath was not a real friend. Not in the normal sense anyway. I did not know his surname, or much about his family. But he was a friend in the way that strangers could be in the IZ. He was part of life on the compound, part of the routine. He was the closest I had come to experiencing loss from the conflict first-hand.

I wanted to talk to someone but I didn't actually want to talk. I wanted someone who would not ask questions or try to understand or fill the silence. I wanted Adam.

I would email him, just to tell him about Sampath. He had met him. He should know. I opened up my laptop slowly, composing the email in my head.

As I logged on I noticed how slow the internet was. There must have been a lot of people in their rooms, Skyping home to remind families they loved them or streaming movies to block off their brains.

When the page finally loaded, there was already an email waiting for me.

Subject: You okay?

Emma. Apologies for getting in touch again, but we got a report in – sounds like you've had a bit of action down in the IZ. Just wanted to check that you and Anna are okay?

Adam

Of course Adam knew about the attack already. His team must get situational updates all the time. I read the email twice, three times. The exhilaration, the disbelief, the numbness of the day were all ebbing away and I was suddenly overwhelmed by the urge to cry. I wiped tears from my face with the back of my sleeve as I typed a reply.

Subject: Re: You okay?

Hi Adam. Anna and I are okay thanks, just a bit shaken. Sampath was killed. He was the man working at Green Beans when we met there. I think he's the only fatality.

Emma

I hit send and moments later my laptop made the distinctive ping noise of Instant Messenger. Adam's name appeared. My stomach tightened with nervous excitement.

[Adam.M 16:04]	Hey Emma
[Adam.M 16:04]	Really sorry to hear about Sampath. He seemed like a good guy.
[Ems82 16:05]	Hi.
[Ems82 16:05]	Thanks. Yeah, he was.
[Adam.M 16:05]	Are you sure you're all right? Must have been pretty rough down there.

[Ems82 16:06]   Yeah. I think I'm okay, but I don't really know what I feel.

[Ems82 16:06]   It's weird.

[Adam.M 16:06]   Understandable.

[Adam.M 16:06]   From a medic's perspective, you're probably still in shock.

[Ems82 16:07]   Maybe. I guess.

[Adam.M 16:10]   I'm glad you're okay.

[Adam.M 16:10]   They said it hit near the gym. Remembered you mentioning you went there in the morning sometimes.

[Adam.M 16:10]   Just wanted to check in.

[Ems82 16:11]   Yeah. We were there this morning. Sampath was in the class too.

[Adam.M 16:12]   Shit. I'm sorry.

[Adam.M 16:12]   Might sound weird, but I'm here if you need to talk about anything. Training and all that. We're probably a bit more prepped than civilians.

[Ems82 16:12]   Thanks. I appreciate it.

[Ems82 16:14]   And thanks for emailing too. I was…

[Ems82 16:14]   I was actually going to email you myself. You know, to tell you about Sampath.

[Adam.M 16:15]   No need to thank me. And I'm glad you were going to tell me.

[Adam.M 16:19]   Emma?

[Ems82 16:20]   Yes?

[Adam.M 16:21]   I'd really like to come down and see you.

I inhaled deeply and quickly. The knot of excitement and nerves wound tighter in the pit of my stomach. I finally let myself acknowledge that this was what I wanted, but I knew that once I replied there was no going back. I realised I had been holding my breath and let it out slowly as I typed.

[Ems82 16:25]   Yes, Adam. I'd like that too.

10

This evening, we go to a Mexican restaurant. It is my favourite place to eat out here. Colourful paper bunting flutters as we come through the door. People talk and laugh over Latin pop music. I breathe in the familiar smell and I smile.

Adam brought me here the first time I visited Colorado Springs, after I told him I loved Mexican food. Adam didn't tell me at the time that he didn't usually eat anything spicy and that he'd called up a friend for the recommendation. He sweated through the first meal with mild salsa and three cold beers. Now we come here every Thursday and he has upgraded to the medium salsa.

A waiter comes over to us.

"Hey. Usual table, guys?" he asks.

"Yes please," says Adam, and we follow him to a table near the window.

Adam sits with his back to the wall, the way they all do. I face him. Our knees rest gently against each other. The waiter puts the menus down on the table and leaves. Adam reaches across and picks up my hand. His thumb massages circles into my palm.

"I'm going to miss this," he says.

"Me too," I reply, although I do not know if he is talking about the restaurant or the feel of his hand against mine or all of the life that we have created here, together.

"I'm sorry about this week, babe."

I look up from watching the way our hands fit together.

"It's fine," I say. "This is different for us. We'll figure it out."

He reaches across the table and pushes a loose bit of hair back behind my ear.

"I love you," he says.

"I love you too."

The waiter comes over and we order. Tacos for me and enchiladas for Adam. The beers arrive first. I take a sip of mine and then press the lime down into the top of the bottle, squeezing it as I do so. Adam removes the lime from his beer, reaches across the table and puts the wedge into my bottle.

"Remember the first time we ate together?" Adam asks.

"In the chow hall?"

"Yeah, after you came over from your sunbed all sulky."

"It was pool time!"

This is a favourite conversation of ours. How we met, how we fell in love. We tell our story over and over to each other. Sometimes the details change. We disagree about whether he was eating chicken nuggets or fishcakes. How long he waited to come over to my car the first day the Rhino dropped him off. Whether I lifted my lips to his or he lowered his mouth to mine. "You knew what you were doing all along," he teases. In the retelling of our story we strengthen our foundations. This is how our love began.

The food arrives.

"I was so glad when Anna and Ryan sat on a different table," he says, as I pinch together the tortilla of my taco and lift it to my mouth.

"You didn't look it," I say, before taking a bite.

"I was terrified."

"You were aloof."

He laughs.

"Do you know how many times I had lunch with a hot British chick on deployment? I had no idea what to say."

"So that's why it was so awkward," I laugh. "You're lucky I gave you a second chance."

"Yeah. Thank goodness for Ali giving me an excuse."

"I mean, I don't think the situation was ideal, but yeah... It worked out."

We continue eating, lost in memories of the story.

"Have you heard from him yet?" I ask.

"Ali?" Adam says.

I nod.

"Not yet, but he was never good with emails. I'll look him up once I get there."

When Adam first left Baghdad, Ali sent him the occasional email, especially while Ameena's application was being processed. The contact trailed off eventually, but that was normal.

"Give him a hug from me," I say.

"Maybe I can get him on Skype for you. He'll ask why you're not back out there with me."

I smile but it is forced. I am trying not to ask the same question myself.

Adam sees it. "What?"

"Nothing."

"Emma. What is it?"

"I'm just... nervous, that's all."

"About me being deployed?"

"Yes, and about being here with you gone. You're off on an adventure and I'm just in Colorado with no real purpose. I'm wondering if I should start looking into the conflict consultancy stuff again."

"I know it's rough, Em. But the conflict stuff... We agreed you'd take some time out of it. Focus on settling in here. Have you not heard from any of those emails you sent off yet?"

"Nothing. Not a single response... What if nothing ever comes up?"

"It will, Em, I'm sure of it. And there's other stuff you

can do here while you figure it out, like enjoy the mountains. Didn't you say you wanted to work on some projects too? Do something with all those bits of stone you collected?"

"Yes." I did, but I have not told him it is more complicated than that. It is not just opening the jar, but opening up everything else that goes with it. The memories. The feelings. The guilt.

"Maybe I'll stop by the art shop to see Penny this week," I say.

"The lady from the Incline? That's a great idea, babe. Maybe she can help you with some ideas."

He is trying to help. He wants me to find something. I know that for him to be okay he needs me to be okay too.

I take his hand and hold his palm against my face.

"You've got this, babe," he tells me. I nod and feel the toughened skin against my cheek.

I am a different person with him. Love has softened me. I have let my edges merge and fuse with someone else's. Our stories and selves have intertwined. When he leaves, it will not be a neat separation, like pieces of a jigsaw puzzle that cling together temporarily then return to their full self. I will be torn from him like a ripped piece of cloth, my fibres still reaching out to his as we are forced to become two.

11

To take:
CAT/SOF-T tourniquet
Combat Gauze
HALO chest seal
Kerlix/Ace Wrap
Israeli dressing
NPA
ET Tube
Epi
OTFC
Morphine auto-injectors
Narcan
Naproxen
Phenergan
Invanz
Alcohol pads
Betadine pads
10cc syringe
18g cath
18g hard stick

The deployment date sits between us like a giant hourglass, our moments slipping through its sweeping glass curves. We navigate our way around it to reach each other. I press my back against the wall, sucking in my breath and taking tiny steps.

We do not count the time aloud in case our words cause the grains to fall through faster. Instead I pretend that I am fine and that I do not dream of abacuses and measuring cups and scales and an alarm.

We go to Garden of the Gods. These huge rock formations are my favourite place to go in the evening. The rocks formations glow a deep red in the lowering sun, jutting into the sky. Layers of sediment lend deep grooves to the rocks that run vertically up the structures, as if the world has been turned on its side. Beyond the rocks, the sky is clear. The only thing to break the vast expanse of blue is the dark silhouette of the mountain range in the distance.

We walk with our fingers interlaced. There is a chill in the air so our sleeves are pulled low over our hands. The thick band of Adam's wedding ring rubs against the inside of my finger.

It is a quiet time of day in the park. The coachloads of visitors have all left and the area has been returned to the people who live there. Dog walkers, runners, climbers and the occasional cyclist, all giving a nod as they pass. But for most of the walk it is just us, wandering between the prehistoric rocks.

In our bedroom we have a huge canvas of the Garden of the Gods on the opposite wall to the bed, so it is the first thing we see in the morning. The photo is a panorama, the same contrast of red rocks and blue sky and green trees we see now. In the bottom right corner of the picture, you can just about make out Adam and I, walking hand in hand, the train of my wedding dress dragging behind me. In my jar is a smooth red stone. It will always be a special place for us.

"I need to talk to you about a deployment thing," Adam says as we walk. "You know, logistics."

I work through a mental checklist of bills, medical records, power of attorney, contacts details and all the other conversations we've had since finding out the date, trying to work out what "logistics" were left. When Adam suggested the walk this evening I thought it was just to spend time relaxing together, but I realise now that there is something else.

"Haven't we covered it all?" I ask.

"Not quite," he replies. "We need to talk about what happens if I get hurt, or if I don't make it back at all."

What comes next isn't a discussion exactly, more a transfer of information. He tries to be practical. Emotionless. I can tell that this is something he has rehearsed. If there is an incident I will only be contacted by the military if Adam is physically unable to contact me himself. He doesn't want me to hear the news from a stranger on the end of the line. If he is mentally unresponsive, he does not want prolonged life support. If he dies or is in a critical condition, I will be informed in person by a member of the military.

"This is all written down," he adds at this point. "But I wanted to tell you myself."

The order of service for his funeral is in his will. His father knows all the details. He doesn't want flowers at the service but he wants a good chunk of money to be left behind the bar at the wake. We should also start my application for citizenship, he says, because a spousal visa won't keep me in the country if he is dead. I can't imagine staying in America without him.

We walk and he talks and I don't interrupt him. The words spill from his mouth as if they are secrets held long inside. Perhaps it is a relief to share the things he's had to think about. I have thought about them too.

The sun has almost disappeared now and the rocks no longer glow but look an ominous dark red, as if soaked in blood.

12

I'd like that too.

That's what I wrote on messenger. And it was true. But now he was coming to the IZ on the Rhino and we both knew that once he arrived there wasn't any way for him to leave until the morning.

I pushed my chair back from my desk. Stood up. Every millimetre of my body tingled. I moved restlessly around my room, avoiding the laundry basket containing my gym kit from this morning. I forced my mind away from thoughts of the aerobics class and Sampath and what would have happened if the attack were hours earlier.

My phone vibrated.

We load up in ten. All good?

My thumbs hesitated briefly over the keypad. I could feel the heat of my blood as it moved through my body and pulsated through my stomach. He was giving me the chance to change my mind, but I was decided.

I sat down on my bed, took in a breath and willed my hands to be steady. I typed slowly.

All good. See you down here.

I pressed send and put the phone down on the bed, then exhaled.

There are some decisions that you make instantly, even though they terrify you. You know that after the decision is made you can process it, work your way through the pros and cons, panic for a while, eventually settle. But you know from the beginning what the answer will be. *I'd really like to come down and see you.* I knew as soon as he said it.

I stood again and went into the bathroom. I stared at my face in the mirror under the harsh white glare of the light. My body felt heavy from grief.

I stared at my skin, pale and blotchy from the earlier tears. *You are fine.* My eyes were wide, tired, red. *You are in Baghdad and there was an attack, but you are fine.* I stand and breathe and stare. *Sampath is dead, but you are okay. You are fine.* I lifted a hand and touched my bottom lip, feeling the dry skin tighten as I drew my finger down. I had not remembered to eat or drink since the cup of tea on the office steps with Anna. *Sampath is dead, but you are okay, and now Adam is coming.* I moved my hand to my cheek and felt the warmth of the flesh beneath my palm. *Adam is coming. You will be fine.*

I drifted around my room more, smoothing out my bedspread and piling up the books that were scattered on my bedside table. I gathered up a couple of pens, a packet of tissues, my phone charger and a Cliff bar and stashed them into the drawer of my desk. But then I looked around and my room seemed too tidy, so I took them all out again and spread them about as they had been before.

What was Adam thinking, sat in the Rhino, rocking back and forth as they rumbled down the potholed road?

I checked the time. It was forty minutes since his message. I grabbed the keys for the SUV. It was time to pick him up.

As I drove to the Rhino drop-off point, the IZ felt subdued. There were few other people outside. Those who wanted company had crowded into Baghdaddy's as soon as office hours were over, some before. Other people stayed in their rooms, calling home or watching TV. No one had gone near the gym.

When I got in the car, there was a CD playing that Anna had made for our drive into work, a test run for a UN party. I thought the music would distract me, but the throb of the bass felt like the thud of mortars. I kept turning the volume down, straining my ears to listen for an attack. Eventually I turned the music off completely and cracked open my window to be sure I would hear the incoming alarm if it sounded.

The vehicle route to the drop-off point was less direct than going by foot. I drove past the rows of concrete blast walls that flanked each road and building. I shifted my hands on the steering wheel. The sweat on my palms caused them to slide against the synthetic material. *I am fine*.

Although the stillness of the IZ was eerie, it was a beautiful golden evening. The buildings of the International Zone looked like they had been drizzled in honey and sand-coloured bricks glowed in the changing light.

Two Blackhawks moved in unison across the sky, patrolling over the city, making the American presence known. They passed across the large face of the sun as it lowered.

I reached the drop-off point and sat in the car. I took long slow breaths but my heart was still pounding. I wiped my hands on my trousers and checked my watch again. *They must be nearly here. They must be fine. The Rhino drives this route all the time.*

I waited. Nearby was a large black SUV, a private security vehicle waiting to transport its human cargo to one embassy or another. The driver wore dark glasses, even though the sun was now almost down. I recognised the man in the passenger seat from the bar. He stared at me, perhaps wondering what I was doing out on my own. Especially today. I looked away and checked the lock on the door. I waited.

I felt the Rhino approach before I saw it. The deep rumble of the engine caused the windows of my vehicle to shake.

When the vehicle had juddered to a stop, a tall skinny man got out of the front. I had heard people talk about him before. He came back each deployment to do the same job – a bus driver on Route Irish, which was one of the most dangerous routes in the world at the start of the invasion. He opened the side door of the vehicle and people started to get out.

Two men in crumpled suits emerged first and were quickly ushered into the SUV that had been waiting nearby. The military personnel moved at a more leisurely pace, passing bags between each other and shaking hands with the Rhino driver before finding their ride.

Adam was last out of the vehicle. He climbed easily down the steps and looked around. If he noticed me waiting, he didn't give any indication. I stayed where I was. There were strict rules about military fraternisation with civilians, or with anyone in fact. Even though everyone knew it went on, I didn't want to draw attention to either of us.

He took off his helmet and ran a hand through hair damp with sweat. As he did so, he looked up. This time he caught my eye. A smile flickered across his lips and then he looked away. My heart was thudding so loudly I felt sure that even from there he could hear it.

Adam stood and talked to the other soldiers who were waiting. I saw him nod towards the embassy and guessed he said that's where he was going. A couple of military vehicles turned up and the remaining soldiers clambered in. One of the men he was talking to gestured towards Adam to join them, but Adam smiled and waved a hand in front of him. The man with dark hair looked at him questioningly and glanced around, clearly looking for another military vehicle. His eyes locked on me and understanding flashed across his face. I looked down and pretended to be searching for something in my bag and didn't raise my eyes until I heard the vehicles drive away.

When I looked up, Adam was walking towards the car. Behind him the sun had almost completed its descent and everything had a deep golden glow. Adam's shadow stretched out before him, impatient for his body to arrive. For a moment it all melted away. The taste of dust as we pressed ourselves into the floor under our desks. The way the ground had trembled with each impact. The curl of smoke from the cigarette of the man leaning on the wall outside the office as he told us there were casualties. And the name that had circled in my head all afternoon.

All of that was replaced with one thing. One person. Adam, who was walking towards me.

I fumbled with the door handle as I got out of the car. I took a few steps and stood in front of the vehicle while he covered the remaining metres between us. He came to a halt in front of me, standing close. I remember looking down at our feet, almost touching, and thinking how little I would have to move forward for my body to be pressed against his.

"Hi," I breathed.

"It's good to see you," he said.

I didn't know what to do with my hands so I shoved them in my pockets.

"You too."

We stood silently for a moment in the fading light, looking at each other. Then, without saying anything else, I turned and climbed back into the vehicle and he did the same.

I turned on the engine and put the vehicle into gear, noticing how close my hand was to his leg. He glanced down too. The air between us was charged.

"So, how was the journey down?" I asked.

"Long," he said. "It took forever." I could feel his eyes on my face as he spoke, but I kept my attention on the road that was taking us back to the East End. Back to my room.

"Was there a lot of traffic?" I asked.

"None at all."

I wondered briefly whether there should be an incoming alarm for this kind of thing. Run, take cover, this can never end well, it should say. But by that point it was already too late.

"So, how are you doing?" he asked.

"Fine," I said, too quickly, checking my mirror as I took a slow right turn. "I mean, I don't really know. But okay... I think."

He nodded. Neither of us spoke for the rest of the journey. It was the kind of silence that filled the space between us like water, seeking out the gaps and expanding to fill them. It was a silence made thick by expectation.

"So, this is home," I said, pulling into the East End parking area. I closed the car door quietly and prayed we wouldn't see anyone from the office on the way to my room. The crunch of gravel under our feet was loud in the stillness of the night. In the distance, I heard the voices of people making their way home from the bar and I halted briefly, but they didn't come in our direction.

I put the key in the lock of the building door and Adam reached over me to take hold of the handle, pulling the door open when I turned the key. The inside of his arm brushed against my shoulder and I felt his body close behind me. I turned my face towards him as he opened the door and his face was so close to mine that I could smell the mint of recently chewed gum.

"Thanks," I smiled.

He followed me up the stairs and along the corridor.

"It's like being back in college dorms," he said.

I pushed open the door to my room. We hesitated awkwardly in the doorway, each insisting that the other go through first.

Once inside I felt strangely exposed. Adam, in his uniform, looked out of place among my few possessions. I became hyperaware of the pink flowery bedspread, the photos of my friends and family, the scented candle that probably wasn't within regulations. All the details that made my room homely came from a different world to the man standing in the middle of my floor.

"You've really, um, personalised the place," he said.

"Yeah… I thought I'd make it a bit more of a home."

"It smells nice. Really, well, womanly."

"Oh." I wasn't sure how to respond.

"Sorry, I didn't mean…" He looked embarrassed and I

noticed again the way he rubbed his hand around the back of his neck. "I've been living with dudes for a while, so I guess I'm just used to everything smelling like ass."

Adam shifted slightly.

"Do you want to sit down?" I asked, wondering whether he would choose the wheelie chair by my desk or my bed. Both options seemed equally awkward. He considered the question for a moment, then made a decision. He took a step towards me and put a hand on the top of each of my arms. I had to tilt my head back to look up at him and he dipped his chin forwards. Our faces were inches apart.

I examined his face. The striking green of the eyes that had first caught my attention. The small crease on his forehead that soon became a familiar mark of concern. The slight sheen of his lips.

"Emma, are you sure you are okay?" he asked. "Do you want to talk about what happened?"

I raised a hand and put it on his chest, feeling the thick material of his uniform under my fingertips.

I shook my head, but I didn't know which question I was answering. Then I raised my lips to his. The hands that held my arms now moved around me, drawing my body up towards him. Finally I was able to forget.

13

Last week at night I woke to him sat at the end of our bed, polishing the buttons of his uniform.

I squinted into the light of the bedroom, rubbing at my eyes. His head was bent over and his lips were pressed together in concentration. The flick of a scar on his eyebrow disappeared the way it does when it is swallowed into a furrowed brow.

"Adam, it's late. What are you doing?" I said.

"Prepping my uniform."

"For what?"

"Got my hero photo tomorrow."

My eyes refused to open properly and his words barely penetrated my haze of sleep. I thought I blinked, but when my eyes reopened it was dark. I stirred and sensed his presence in the bed next to me. I moved towards him and pressed my chest against his back, felt the steadiness of his breathing, draped an arm over his body.

I found the photo this morning, tucked away in the filing cabinet with other deployment documentation. He wears a jacket heavy with decorations. The crease in his green beret lines up with his left eye. In the background are the stripes and stars of his flag.

He looks handsome and serious. I know this is the kind of photo that his mother would love to have on the wall, alongside his brothers. But it is not a photo for our home.

When we moved to this house, we decorated with photos and a map on the wall. The map tells our story. It is a story that spans countries and continents and oceans. A story of love that begins in conflict. I call it our love atlas and he teased me for being sentimental, but now he calls it that too.

We attached pieces of string to the map, which reach out to photos. We marked our homes first, our roots. We laughed when the first drawing pin covered up my country and when the second drawing pin got lost in his. Then we put up photos of the places we have been together. Our road trip to Yosemite. My first trip to Virginia to meet his family. He joked that we should put up photos of Skype calls and emails and lengthy waits in arrivals halls at airports too. By telling the story, we made this place ours. We made it home.

Next, I put up photos of my travels alone, before our story began. He laughs at the younger version of me in the photos. A sunburnt teenager in Greece. A backpacker in Peru with a rucksack that is too big, and feet that are either dirty or tanned.

Then we searched for pictures of his travels too. But in this photo he wears a uniform and in that one he holds a gun and eventually we gave up. That is not who he is in this apartment. That version of him is not for here.

On the wall across from the photos and the atlas is a painting, the only painting in our house. It is a painting of an English garden in the summer, with a small pond and a blue sky and flowers in full bloom. It used to be on the wall of my childhood home, opposite my father's chair. A photo of it was in my bedroom in Baghdad. The garden was ours and the brushstrokes my mother's.

Looking at the painting, you might imagine that the garden was empty when she painted it, but I know better. I know she preferred painting landscapes to people. I was thirteen the summer of that painting, and my sister was ten. I look at the canvas and I can feel the stickiness of the strawberry ice pop that melted down my arm and onto my book that day. I can hear that barking of the neighbour's dog, the distant hum of a lawnmower and the buzz of the wasp that stung Rebecca's arm as she played swingball.

I see my mother stood in front of her easel in cut-off jeans, flip-flops and one of my father's old white consulting jackets, sleeves rolled up and splattered with colours that are testimony to everything she painted that year. The colours are bright, vivid. So is she.

And now I see my father, coming out of the house and passing her a cool drink, kissing her on the cheek as she works. He comes over and ruffles my hair, then picks up a bat to join Rebecca. He looks relaxed, happy. He always did when we were all together.

I don't remember many summers after that. After my father died, my mother stopped painting. She tried to start again a couple of times, but the paintings always looked empty – as if they needed the admiring gaze of my father to bring them to life. I emailed Rebecca last week to tell her about Adam's deployment and in her reply she mentioned that Mum had finally started painting again. She sent me a photo of the most recent piece and in the delicate detail I found an almost forgotten version of my mother. It caused my throat to constrict, but I couldn't quite tell whether it was from happiness or pain in the knowledge that they are moving on. Even after all this time, I'm not sure that I am.

This evening when Adam got home, I mentioned the photo in the filing cabinet and I asked why he didn't show it to me.

"It's my hero photo," he said. That phrase again. And still I didn't understand. He began to explain and he chose his words carefully, but there is no comforting way to say it is the photo they will use if he doesn't come back. It is the photo that will be at the memorial, in the media, on the wall of the Joint Special Operations Medical Training Center. In death he will be a soldier, not my husband.

I look at the photo again and wish I had never found it. I

replace the photo. Close the filing cabinet. But the image of his death is burned into my mind.

I walk into the sitting room and stand staring at the painting on the wall, a memorial in its own way to a different part of my life. Except my mother and sister are not gone, it is me who disappeared. It is part of me that can be recovered. I will go to the art shop tomorrow. It is time to open the jar.

14

Ameena came into the office for her asylum application interview almost a month after the day that Sampath died and the first night that Adam stayed over. I saw her name on the schedule and walked into the waiting room to find a young woman, bouncing a baby up and down on her knee. Next to her was an old woman, whose fingers worked their way anxiously through a string of rose-coloured prayer beads. Ameena looked younger than I expected. She was younger than me.

"*Sabah al-khair*," I said, greeting them. "You must be Ameena. Would you like to follow me?"

I took them through to one of the small sparse rooms where we conducted interviews. Ameena and her mother sat down on the metal fold-out chairs. The baby on her lap gurgled and grabbed at one of Ameena's bangles, which was a deep shade of purple that matched her hijab and her handbag. I wondered what she made of me, with my baggy blouse and faded linen trousers.

Ameena passed the little boy to her mother and spoke. Normally we conducted interviews in Arabic, but she addressed me in careful English with a slight American inflection.

"Thank you for seeing us," she said, smoothing out her long skirt. "It was a relief to be invited in."

"Thank you for coming," I replied. "I am sorry to hear about your situation."

She nodded, holding my gaze. I felt her mother's eyes

watching my mouth as I spoke, with the intense concentration of someone trying to find meaning in unknown sounds.

"Would you like us to switch to Arabic, for your mother?" I asked Ameena.

Her mother heard the word "Arabic" and understood the question. She waved her hands hurriedly.

"No, no. English. Please."

"She likes hearing me speak in English," said Ameena with an embarrassed smile. "She says she's glad I paid attention at school. Not like my brother. He was always skipping classes to play football."

"Your brother?" I asked, flicking through her online application that I had printed out. "Are you including him in your application? You know that you can include all immediate–Oh."

My eyes found the information on the registration form at the same time as she spoke.

"He is dead," she said. "He died, with my father, in the Sadriyah market explosion."

"I'm sorry. *Allah yarhamu*." I said, switching to Arabic briefly because English words were awkward on my tongue when invoking God. I had heard of the attack. At least a hundred people had been killed, maybe more.

"My husband is dead too. Not in an explosion though. He was killed while I was pregnant. Now it is just me and my mother and baby Yusuf," she said, gesturing to the boy on her mother's lap. "At least we have another man in the family now, even if he is so small."

"I'm going to have to ask you a lot of questions about all of this today," I said. "I know that might be difficult for you." Sometimes I wondered whether I had repeated this script so many times that it sounded insincere. Empty.

"We have been through many difficulties. This will not be worse," she said. She pulled a folder of documentation from her handbag and placed it on the table resolutely. "Let us begin."

I started the way I always did.

"First, tell me about your life before the invasion."

The interview took two hours in all. Ameena was articulate and composed. Some interviews could take much longer as there was so much to get through. As part of the application process, I had to record the applicant family's history with all its details: biographical information, family tree, education and work history, military service, Ba'ath party membership. Their story. It was especially difficult with older people, and even more so with those who couldn't read or write. It was also difficult with some of those who had gone through trauma.

Trauma does funny things to a person's brain. Some people block out events completely, but for many the problem is that the memory becomes fragmented. For some it may splinter and for others it divides into delicate stretches of thread that are wound tightly together. They cannot reach one part of the thread without unravelling the part before. When you ask them "Who do you think killed your husband?" they must first tell you about the food that their mother was cooking at the time, or the washing that their neighbour was hanging on the rooftop, or the peculiar red of the dust that day. Sometimes I wondered about the kindness of what I was doing. If the erasure of traumatic memories is a coping mechanism, what happens when the experiences are brought to the surface again? Who helped to organise and fold and pack away the memories once I was done?

I tried to unravel the memories delicately, but it took patience and understanding and I knew that at other stages of the process the approach would not be the same. Most applicants went through two rounds of interviews. First there was an interview with my office, and then, much later (after many background checks and often months or even years), another with a United States Citizenship and Immigration Services official who made the final decision. These officials were not usually trained in the local language or culture. They barked questions and expected answers that were immediate and matched directly with anything we had written down from the first round of interviews. Any variation could be construed as an intentional attempt to mislead them. There was minimal room for error.

I did not need to worry about Ameena's responses. All of her replies were clear and detailed.

After her father and brother died, Ameena and her mother had struggled on their own. When her late husband Hussein, a man from their neighbourhood, asked for her hand in marriage, she knew she had no other choice but to accept. He knew it too. It was unseemly for two women to be without a male family member.

Hussein wasn't the kind of man Ameena thought she would marry. He was a lot older than her, uneducated and with conservative ideas. It was an unhappy marriage and she said she wasn't surprised when her husband was killed.

"He was not a good man," she told me. "I do not know who killed him, but he had many enemies."

When her husband was killed, Ameena was already pregnant.

"He left my mother and I worse off than before," she said. "He spent the little savings we had and when he was gone he left only debts. And me with a baby on the way too."

It was Ali, her second cousin, who had helped her out.

"I thought he was working in a hospital," she said. "I knew he hadn't finished his degree, but someone said he had got a job anyway, *alhamdulillah*. I thought he could help me get a job too. But when I called him I found out he was an interpreter for the Americans. Then I didn't know what to think."

But Ali had come through. He got her a job working part-time at a local medical centre, which received USAID funding, where she did basic nursing and acted as a translator if there were ever donor visits. The hours were long and the conditions were tough, but Ameena said she enjoyed the work and sense of purpose. I recognised the sentiment.

"So what happened then?" I asked.

Ameena told me that the threats began a few months after

she started work at the clinic. At first she thought it was the same people who had killed her husband, because she knew he owed a lot of people money. But then the threats started using words like traitor and infidel and she thought it must be to do with her work and the US involvement.

"It could even be both. Who knows?" she said, sounding tired now. "But my mother said I must stop working at the clinic and now I have no way of earning money. Ali is giving us what he can, but I feel bad – we are not his responsibility."

That was the first time I wondered whether there had ever been anything between the two of them. Ameena was a pretty and intelligent woman. Marriages between cousins weren't unusual here. Adam had told me Ali had never been married.

I looked at the birth date on her form again. Three years younger than me and she'd already been through so much.

At the end of the interview, I scanned Ameena's documentation and told her that the next step was the background checks that would be completed. I was not allowed to tell her how the interview had gone or say anything to raise her hopes, but I wanted to reassure her somehow. I planned on taking her file straight to my manager to request expedition once she left. I wanted to help everyone that came through my office, but I was always extra invested in cases of young women. Perhaps part of me was doing it for Adam too.

"You gave me a lot of useful information today. I know it can't have been easy," I told her. "Thank you."

"Ali helped me prepare," she said, with a shy smile. "He researched the type of information you might need to know. He helped me to remember."

15

Before Adam leaves, we head to the mountains. We go in search of green forests and cool air and space. We go in search of everything that is different to where he is going.

"One final trip," I say and he frowns at me. Our conversations have been saturated with words like "final" and "last". My words weigh us down with expectation. Everything has to be better, the best. The pressure of superlatives is too much.

Last week, he said I was talking as though he wasn't coming back.

"Mountain biking is a first for us, not a last," he says. It is true. We have been intending to go ever since I arrived, but the snow was slow to melt this year and the paths weren't clear enough for a beginner like me. Now the snow has melted.

"This is our last chance to go," I say, despite myself. And so we leave.

The drive there is quiet. Conversation is stilted. We don't want to talk about his departure so we try to talk around it, but Iraq looms over everything. I even keep in my news. Next to Iraq it feels like nothing.

Adam brings his own bike with us on the trip, strapping it onto the back of the truck, but I need to hire one.

"It's cheaper to rent for a season," the man in the shop says. "Do you plan on coming more than once?" The answer is no, but I do not want to explain why.

Adam speaks instead. "I think we'll just see how we go."

The metal frame of the bike feels foreign underneath me as we set off, but Adam corrects me with gentle, specific advice.

"Put your weight back," Adam says. "Don't lean on the handlebars. You're doing great."

At first, I wobble unsteadily over the uneven ground, but with his reassurance I start to settle. The trails are peaceful. Sunlight shines through the trees and sends dappled patterns across our path. My arms vibrate as the wheels roll over rocks and roots. I loosen my grip on the handlebars and relax, watching Adam's shape as he expertly navigates the path ahead of me.

After a corner, he disappears from view. After every twist in the path, I expect to see him again, but he is gone. Surely he will realise I am not with him and wait, or turn around and retrace his way to me. I keep pedalling forwards. He does not reappear. This was supposed to be our trip together. I am cycling on my own.

Up ahead there is a fork in the path. I stop, unsure of which way to go. Both routes head down the mountainside; both paths look uneven. I can see no sign of Adam. Perhaps I should stay here rather than risk the wrong direction, but I am not the kind of woman who sits and waits and so I ride.

I choose a path and pedal hard and fast. Faster than before. The speed is exhilarating. Air hits my face, drying my sweat as it forms. I feel a rush of adrenaline and welcome the familiar feeling. The bike speeds over a bump and for a moment we are weightless. I soften my knees to absorb the impact of landing and hear other tyres on the track behind me.

"Em, wait up!" Adam shouts.

I brake slowly, not wanting a sudden stop to pitch me forwards. He catches up.

"Wow, you were really speeding along," he says.

"I didn't know which way you'd gone," I reply.

His chest heaves as he tries to catch his breath. He must have been some way down the other path before he realised I wasn't with him.

"I'm sorry," he says. "My head was somewhere else."

I know, I want to reply. *You're already half there*.

We continue on together. We find a sign with a map and we pick a line and say let's go that way. The path is steep and twists and turns and we twist and turn with it, dirt flicking up our backs. Sometimes he leads, sometimes I do. We stay together now.

By the time we get back to the truck it is late. We drive to the nearest town and find a motel to stay in. At the reception desk, the woman talks to Adam and not me. I wonder if there will be women who look at him like that where he is going.

We search for somewhere for dinner, but now he is hungry and I am tired and everywhere is shut. Eventually we see the familiar white and red of a Wendy's burger sign.

"I guess it's burgers then," I say.

"I guess it is."

There are two other cars in the parking lot. They are old and dented. I shut the truck door and the sound reverberates into the night. A disturbed bird flies up from a tree.

Inside Wendy's we squint at the harsh strip lighting. There are no other customers, just a bored-looking kid behind the counter who must own one of the beaten-up cars. His eyes are red and his shirt is crumpled.

We order our food and wait in exhausted silence. A large clock on the wall ticks loudly. Adam rolls up his sleeve and examines a small graze on his elbow. I rub at my eyes. I want to tell him not to go. I want to tell him I want to go too. But then the bleary-eyed boy puts our food on the tray and we take it to a table.

We eat quickly. Adam orders another burger and I play with the straw of my soda, causing it to squeak loudly against the lid of the polystyrene cup. I feel better now I've eaten. More relaxed.

"Adam, I have something to tell you," I say.

He looks up quickly from his burger.

"No, don't worry, it's good. Very good actually, I think. I have a job."

"What?" he swallows. "For real? What is it? Not that consultancy gig right...?"

"No, not that. It's just part-time actually. Remember we talked about me going to the art shop? It turns out Penny needs help."

"Babe, that's great!" he says. The look of relief on his face makes me realise just how much he has worried about going away when I have nothing. "Seriously, awesome. When did this happen?"

"Only a couple of days ago," I tell him. "I was just waiting for a good moment to tell you."

That is almost the truth. I was waiting to feel content with it myself.

I went into the art shop early this week, in Old Colorado City, tucked between a small café and a shop that sells Christmas decorations all year round. It looked dark from the outside and I paused for a second before entering, wondering what memories I was about to unravel and whether perhaps leaving them packed away was better.

When I entered the shop, I was hit by the smell of oil paints and charcoal pencils, but I didn't have long to dwell on the nostalgia the smells triggered because at the sound of the bell, Penny emerged from a back room. She looked different out of her hiking clothes. She wore a long top in a drapey fabric that flowed as she walked and a large pair of bronze earrings. Instead of having her hair pulled back into a ponytail, it fell neatly at her shoulders, and the only remnant of the Incline outfit was the burgundy scrunchie that now sat on her wrist.

"Emma!" she said when she saw me. In a place where I am a stranger, it came as a surprise to be recognised. "Sweetie, I was wondering whether you were ever going to drop by! I was telling one of my customers last week that I had met a British woman up the Incline and I was cursing myself for not taking her number."

"I'm sorry it took me so long, Penny," I said. "Just, you know, life stuff got in the way."

"Life stuff?" She gave me a long look that made me realise I would not leave the shop until she had got everything out of me. "Let me pour us both a coffee, honey. Then you can tell me all about it."

I was in the shop for almost two hours. I sat in a cushioned chair near the counter (there were a couple dotted around the shop, which seemed to fit an extraordinary amount in it despite its relatively compact size). When Penny left me to serve a customer, I looked around at the array of oil paints, brushes, crayons, canvases and, by the window, a small mirror that glinted in a beam of morning sunlight. Around the edge of the mirror was an intricate mosaic with tiny pieces of blues and greys and greens. It somehow made the mirror feel like you were looking into the mountains.

"Sorry about that," said Penny, returning. "So, where were we? Your husband is going away. You want a job, or at least a hobby or something. You both agreed that you'd stay away from that awful war-related work…"

"It's not awful," I said. "But yes, we agreed that I would do something different. I just can't imagine being here and not doing anything. I like to be busy. I need purpose."

"And you didn't happen to notice the sign by the counter? Of course you didn't. You've been mesmerised by my spinning mirror this whole time."

Penny gestured towards the counter and I shifted my eyes. There, taped to the dark wood of the counter, was a sheet of paper with the words *Help wanted* written in a curled script.

"You're hiring?" I asked.

"Indeed I am, my dear. While you're working out what you're going to do in Colorado, maybe you could help me out in here. It might give you ideas for your art project too. The customers will love your accent. It'll be like having a royal in the shop."

"I'd love to," I replied. It was one of those decisions you

make quickly and figure out afterwards. I needed to say yes to something.

"That's so great, babe. Really great," says Adam again, after I have told him the story. "When do you start?"

"Next week. I thought I'd jump right in," I tell him. I do not add that I hoped it would divert my attention from his impending departure.

"Great," he says. "And it's not forever, Em. I know you must want something that's a bit more… you. But it's a good place to start. And hey, perhaps your mother's painting won't be the only artwork on the wall when I get back."

"Perhaps not," I say with a smile.

We say thank you and goodnight to the boy who is now leaning on the counter with his chin resting on folded arms. Adam opens the door and puts his hand on the small of my back as we go through.

We drive through the winding roads back to the motel. We are still high up and the sky is clear. The grey glow of the moon lights up the silhouettes of trees on the mountainside and makes the jagged peaks look almost purple. I struggle to stay awake and my head tilts forwards. Then I feel the car slow.

"What is it?" I ask.

"Look," he says.

There is something moving across the road.

Lit up in the headlights is a skunk. It shuffles slowly forwards, sniffing the tarmac, ignoring our waiting vehicle. When I was young, my father bought me a skunk soft toy after he went on a trip to Canada. Adam knows I have wanted to see one since I arrived in the States.

There are no other cars on the road so we sit and watch as it moves across the road, its bushy tail forming an arc behind its body.

When it disappears into the undergrowth on the other side of the road, I realise I have been holding my breath.

"I guess that makes another first," says Adam.

16

The commissary at Fort Carson is full. Full of people. Full of children. Full of shopping carts stacked high with family-sized packs of cereal and soda and other weekly staples. Everything is colour and noise, carts and elbows jostling against each other. I wouldn't have come if I'd remembered it was payday.

The art shop was quiet this morning. After the first few shifts I can already feel myself settling into its calm rhythm. It is a different pace there. People come not just to buy equipment, but to be in the shop itself. To talk to other people, to share community news, to just soak up the infectious creativity that seeps from the dark wood shelves. It is finding its way into me too. I feel it, working between my broken parts and fragmented memories. Fusing me unexpectedly together.

A woman with her cart bumps into me. Crowded places never used to bother me, but they do now. My heartbeat starts to rise. Someone in another aisle drops something and I jump. I look around for someone in uniform to see if they jumped as well. I can't be the only one feeling this way.

I return the jar of peanut butter in my hand to the shelf. I have been standing and staring blankly at the label but I can't remember what I was reading it for. Then I hear a voice I recognise.

"Hey! Emma! British girl! Hey!"

Kate is pushing a shopping cart towards me, waving. In the front of the cart is a toddler with dark hair and large eyes, chewing on the end of a carrot.

"Wow, what planet were you on?" she asks, hugging me as if we've known each other for much longer than the duration of an army briefing.

"Planet pre-deployment I guess," I reply ruefully, glad for the distraction.

"Tell me about it," she says. "Dave is being a frickin' nightmare at the moment. Noah and I just came here to get out of the house. Hey Noah, this is Emma. You wanna say hi?"

"Memma?" he says questioningly, pointing the carrot at me and then looking back towards his mother.

"Hey Noah. Nice to meet you," I say. I am always awkward around children, which I put down to lack of experience. I guess that he must be a bit younger than my niece Sophie, but I could be wrong. My relationship with her consists of intermittent appearances on Skype calls, and each time I see her I am always surprised about how much more she has grown.

"So how's it all going?" Kate asks. "I hope the thing with the medic didn't cause too many issues. Trust Olivia to put her foot in it!"

"I wasn't exactly happy," I say. "But it's fine now. At least I think it is. Adam's not been very talkative the past couple of days."

After we got back from our biking trip there was a shift in him. He became quieter.

"Oh, he's one of those?" Kate says knowingly, wiping away the carroty trail of drool that was escaping down Noah's chin. "Dave used to be like that too. He'd just completely check out weeks before he went away."

"And now?" I ask.

"He got better after this little guy came along. I told him that if he was going to ignore our son then he needn't bother coming home. That seemed to do the trick!"

"Good to know," I laugh, partly at Kate's brazenness and partly with relief that even someone as experienced as Kate found this part difficult too. "Although I'm not sure I'm ready to have a baby to sort things out."

"Oh, we'll see about that," she replies with a wink. "Are you sure you're okay though? You do look a bit, I don't know, distracted."

She's right of course, but I cannot tell her that I had another one of the dreams last night. It was a market attack this time, like the one that killed Ameena's family. I cannot tell Kate that I dreamt of a shopping bag abandoned with its contents spilling onto the road, fleshy tomatoes burst open on the ground, a wall that was plastered with chunks of meat from the butcher's stand. I cannot tell Kate that I am scared of Adam going this time, but I cannot put my finger on why.

"I'm fine, just a bit tired," I tell her. She gives my arm the same reassuring squeeze as after the pre-deployment briefing.

"The build-up is always rough," she says, "But once he's gone you'll settle into it and everything will be much easier. Come and hang out with us sometime, okay?"

"I will do. That sounds great," I say and then Kate is gone, pushing her cart away down the aisle, leaving me among the debris of my dream.

17

Tonight I dream of Penelope bidding farewell to Odysseus. She stands in front of a low grey sky. The wind whips around her. One hand is raised in a wave. The other clutches her thin dress against the pale skin of her chest. Strands of hair come loose and thrash against her face.

Penelope's gaze is fixed, unblinking. She will not lose Odysseus from her sight for a second. There are not enough moments left for one to be wasted. I follow her eyes, expecting to see a hollow ship rising and falling on a black sea, but instead a vast expanse of tarmac stretches before her. There is a vessel, but it belongs to the sky not the ocean. A dark grey C-17 stands in wait. Its metal wings stretch out in welcome as Odysseus and his men file up the ramp at its rear.

The propellers roar and Penelope turns away. I hear a voice that sounds strangely like Mrs Edwards, asking "When does he return?" Penelope cannot answer. She does not know.

18

People are not supposed to enjoy going to war. It is a dirty secret shared by those of us who have been. People understand the difficult parts of war, or rather, they know that the bad bits must be beyond what they could ever imagine. But it is the good bits that confuse them. The reasons that we love it. That we miss it. That we keep going back. It is in the wistful looks of men and women who say "Fuck, those days were awful, but damn they were the best." That is harder to explain. It is this feeling that bonds those of us who have been there and makes us different from those who have not.

I always enjoyed Iraq. The good and the bad. But with Adam I came to love it. I came to love him.

I remember the first time he used the word, like a scene from a movie. In my memory I do not inhabit myself, but rather see us both. Two bodies with an iridescent gleam in the darkness of the water and the night.

It was late. We were in the pool at RPC. I visited regularly by this point. We took it in turns to ride the Rhino between the IZ and VBC for visits. Jessica, the aerobics instructor, booked me onto the vehicle, the same way she did with herself when she visited her boyfriend Mike.

At first, it was Adam who would visit me. He came to the IZ when he could, but it was never enough. Each morning the question *Will I see him today?* buzzed through my head as I drank my coffee. I checked my phone more often than before. I sat at my desk and my mind would wander, to one or two or three nights before. The feeling of his body against mine. The weight of his arm around my waist as I slept. I craved his presence.

I had not realised I was lonely.

If I'm honest, I was happiest when I started to visit Adam. It wasn't just seeing him, it was the adventure that went with it. I would feel a rush of adrenaline as the Rhino door slammed shut each time. I pressed my face as close to the window as my helmet would allow and watched dented old Iraqi cars and ghostly lines of logistics vehicles crawling along the route. It was my tiny glimpse of real Iraq.

Adam wasn't keen on me taking the Rhino. He said it was a war zone not a school outing, but he couldn't dissuade me. The adventure was mine.

Unlike most of the military, Adam's team lived in a building that was once one of Saddam's palace complexes. Adam's bedroom was upstairs, above the team room, and where we spent most of our time. For our weekly movie nights I would roll his bivvy bag out onto the floor as a picnic blanket. He would bring sandwiches from the chow hall and I would bring two kinds of popcorn from the PX. It was the closest we could get to a date night there. There was nowhere to go without being seen.

"God, I can't wait to have a real sandwich after this deployment," he said one night. "There's this great place downtown in Colorado Springs, they do the best subs. Seriously, they have this pulled pork that's just heaven."

"Okay, well put that on the list of places you're taking me," I replied. "But I want to go to a good Mexican first. And that BBQ place you mentioned."

"Perhaps you should just move to the States with me and we can spread the eating out."

These comments had become more frequent between us. Me visiting him in the US was something we joked about, but we both knew it wasn't a joke really. We were testing the idea, to see how it felt on our tongues and in our bellies. It was still too fragile to address directly, to hold between our hands and examine. So instead we nudged it between each other, nurturing and normalising it with our conversations, silently excited as we sensed it grow. The "ifs" that punctuated our sentences transformed quietly into "whens". And with our words we built foundations.

Adam and I only ever went to the pool at night. The pool was barely used compared to the one in the embassy compound, but there was a heavy rock in the bottom that the men would compete at carrying and a couple of chairs where people would sit and drink root beer in the evening. The nights were getting cooler by that point, but sometimes I would convince Adam to sneak out for a dip with me. We would leave his room quietly, past the closed bedroom doors and the sounds of rap music, murmured Skype calls and porn.

The first time he used the word, I had just got back from R and R. It was only a ten-day break, but by that point it seemed like an eternity to be away from each other.

The night I got back, I went straight up to RPC. Later in the evening, we slid from the edge of the pool silently, the water rippling like dark silk around us. Above the pool was one of Saddam's palaces, raised up on a hill covered with palm trees that rustled in the occasional breeze. A bright moon behind the palace lit up its imposing silhouette and gave the dark angles of the structure a white glow. An aerial protruded from the top with a red light as a warning for passing aircraft.

I rested on my back, looking up at a cloudless sky that was awash with stars. My hair spread out around me and the water covered and uncovered my earlobes as I floated, periodically muffling the silence. My exposed skin rose to meet the coolness of the night air. It was a strange and surreal kind of peace. I was glad to be back.

Adam was treading water, watching me. I swam over to

him and he took hold of my hand, drawing my body towards his. I wrapped my legs around his waist. Our bodies felt slippery and weightless in the water.

"Any update on Ameena's background checks?" he asked me. I shook my head.

"There won't be for a while yet. Even with her application expedited it takes such a long time." Adam asked me regularly about the application and I always wished I had more to tell him.

"I'm sorry to keep asking," he said. "I just see what the worry is doing to Ali. It's such a tough wait."

"There's something between them, isn't there?" I said.

"Ali and Ameena?"

"Yeah."

"I think so. I think that's why it's hitting him so hard."

"And you?"

I released my legs from around Adam and trod water, looking hard into his face.

"What do you mean?"

"Why is it hitting you so hard? Tell me why you want to help Ali so much. It's not just that he's a good guy. It's more than that, Adam. You said you owed him. Why?"

Adam took a deep breath before he answered. The only sound in the night air was the water as it moved gently around the pool, disturbed by our bodies.

"I do owe him," he said finally.

"For what?" I asked.

"Everything."

"Everything?"

"Yes. For being here, now."

"What do you mean?"

"He saved my life... He saved my life by risking his."

"Can you tell me about it?" I said, moving my limbs silently to keep myself afloat.

"Not really," he said. "But he found out information and he had a choice, to stay quiet and protect himself or to protect me and put his own life at risk. He chose the latter. And I'll never be able to fully pay him back for that."

I swam towards Adam and gave him a long chlorine-tasting kiss. I knew I would never be able to fully pay Ali back either.

Adam lifted a hand and smoothed back a piece of hair that was stuck against my wet cheek. He was studying my face, that small crease appearing between his eyebrows.

"What? What is it?" I asked him.

"Emma, you know I'm in love with you, right?"

Above us the unmistakeable sound of propellers filled the skies. The palm trees knocked against each other and ripples raced across the pool. The water vibrated as the sound got louder and I looked up to see the dark shadows of two Blackhawk helicopters move over us, coming in to land on the base nearby.

"Em?" he said.

A shiver ran through me and I ran a hand over the goosebumps that had raised up on my arm.

"I'm scared," I told him.

"Of what?"

"Of this. Of us. Of what comes next." I was not scared of loving him, but losing him. I felt like I was on the edge of a diving board, the moment you start leaning forward. Your feet still touch something solid, but by then you have committed to plunging through the air and into whatever the watery depths may hold. I was already falling.

"I love you too, Adam," I said.

19

There is a particular time of morning in the art shop, 9.25am to be exact, when the early sun comes through the window and hits the spinning mirror perfectly. The small pieces of mosaic tile that surround the mirror glimmer in the light. It reminds me of the way the water sparkled during one of our few family holidays abroad, when my dad taught us how to snorkel. Everything glimmered that holiday. The sea, the scales of small silver fish, my mother's blue earrings that she usually saved for special occasions but wore to dinner every evening that week. Looking back, I think they already knew.

"That sure has caught you, hasn't it?" says Penny, coming out to the front of the shop. "I see you staring at that mirror almost every morning."

"It's beautiful," I say, embarrassed that she has found me stood watching it again. Sometimes I forget that the slow pace of the shop is its beauty. I feel like I should be busy, working, filling every minute. "I love mosaics."

"A customer made it, you know."

"Really? Who?"

"Nora. She doesn't come in anymore. Her kids moved her to California to be closer to them when the arthritis started getting bad. Such a shame."

I am disappointed that the lady is no longer around. I would have liked to ask her how she cut the tiles, how she glued them, how she found their form.

"Such a shame," I say, repeating Penny's words.

I enjoy Penny's company when she stays in the shop during my shift. As we check stock and discuss rearranging the shelves (something she talks about but will never do), Penny tells me endless stories about the shop and the people who come in.

It is safer to listen rather than talk with Penny. I do not talk about Iraq with her. I do not talk about the Iraqis I helped move to the States. To her, foreigners are a different species and she does not deal well with things she doesn't understand. Iraq is a part of me that I switch off when I am with her.

As I move around the shop, lining up the paint pots, dusting the shelves, I struggle to ignore the gnawing feeling that this is not enough. It is enough for now, I remind myself, but I do not know how long this will be true.

Later in the morning, Penny goes out to meet a friend. Customers trickle in and out. Browse, chat, occasionally buy, but the day is slow. Around lunchtime, the bell over the door rings again. This time it is a young woman on the phone. She is speaking a language that sounds familiar to me, although I do not understand it. It is like Arabic almost, but with more "ch" and "sh" sounds and I think I hear a "p". It is some kind of Kurdish.

I try not to stare at the young woman as she moves around the shop. She has long dark hair that falls in loose curls, an oversized shirt rolled up to the elbows and a large turquoise necklace. I guess at her age. Younger than me by a few years, I think. Twenty-four or twenty-five perhaps. I am already trying to work out her story. Colorado Springs is not a melting pot like London or the IZ. If you are different, you stand out.

She moves around the shop, picking up coloured paper and ribbons with an ease that indicates she has been here before. Penny's shelves have a mismatched feel to them that tends to confuse new customers. She comes to the till and puts down the armful of items she's picked up, the phone held between her chin and shoulder.

"Okay if I leave these here while I grab the rest?" she asks, switching to flawless American.

"Sure," I say.

A few minutes later she is back with another armful, her phone returned to her bag.

"Sorry. A lot to pick up today," she smiles.

"Are these all for you?" I ask.

"I wish! No, my students. I'm an art teacher at the high school."

"Oh, that makes sense," I say. She smiles again. It is a warm smile.

"I haven't seen you in here before. Are you new?" she asks.

"Yeah, this is my second week," I say. "I moved to the States quite recently…" I wait hopefully for her next question; I want to tell her that I am different too.

"Where from?" she asks.

"Iraq. I'm British. But I was living in Iraq." The words fall out quickly, betraying my eagerness to form a connection.

She looks at me surprised.

"Iraq? Seriously?"

"Yeah, I spent a few years working there. What about you? I overheard you speaking – was that some kind of Kurdish?"

She smiles.

"Yes, I am Kurdish. My family is from Duhok. Usually I just say Iraqi though…"

"Oh?"

"No one knows about the Kurds here. The war sort of made me Iraqi overnight. Suddenly everyone in America knew Iraq, or thought they did. Kurds spent so long fighting Saddam's Arabisation, but when the US invaded it's like they Arabised all the Kurds here without even realising…"

"That's an interesting way of looking at it," I say.

"It's the only way I have," she says with a shrug. "So did you enjoy being there?"

"Yes and no," I say. "It was different. Challenging." There

is a flicker at the back of my mind. Thud. Sampath. The arm on my throat. The blood in my mouth. Thud. Thud Thud. I push it all away. "But I loved it."

"I am desperate to go back," she tells me. "I was young when we left and I haven't been back there since."

"I hope that you get the chance to one day."

"*Inshallah*," she replies and I automatically repeat the phrase back to her.

"*Inshallah*." God willing. The words taste familiar and inside I feel a different version of myself stir. The version of myself that I was in Iraq. That has been pushed down since I came here. My stomach flutters for a moment, my body greeting itself like an old friend.

"So, how are you finding Colorado?" she asks.

"Also different. Also challenging," I say, and she laughs.

"I bet. Listen, I have to get back to the school, but I'll leave you my cell. Let me know if you ever want to grab a coffee. I'd love to hear more of what you made of it over there."

She grabs a pen from her bag and scribbles down her number.

"That would be great… What was your name?" I ask her.

"Noor."

"That would be great, Noor. I'm Emma."

"Well, hopefully see you again soon, Emma," she says and scoops up her bags to leave. I hope that I do see her again soon. I am excited to have found a link with Iraq. Someone who "gets it" a little bit more.

For the rest of the day I let my brain wander back to Iraq; to the long days and the pink evenings and the green lights of minarets at night. I let myself miss it.

When I get home, Adam is back from work already. He has moved the coffee table to one side of the room and he is sat on the bivvy bag that I haven't seen since Baghdad.

"Hey, babe, I've been waiting for you!" he says enthusiastically as I come in.

"Hey, you, what're you doing down there?" I ask him. He taps the floor by his side, beckoning me to sit down next to him. On the floor are two polystyrene clamshell boxes that look like the takeaway sandwich containers we used to get from the chow hall.

"I thought it was about time we had a Baghdad-style date-night picnic," he says. He reaches behind his back and pulls out a bottle and a corkscrew. "Except this time with wine."

I leave my bag and shoes by the door and kneel down next to him, taking his face between my hands and giving him a long deep kiss, silently repeating the internal mantra that accompanies all of our contact now. *Remember how he tastes. Remember how he smells. Remember how he feels. Remember.*

"You sure know how to woo a girl," I say, drawing my face away just slightly so our noses touch as I speak.

"Well, it worked for me in Iraq," he says.

I sit cross-legged among the array of cushions Adam has pulled from the sofa onto the floor. He opens the polystyrene boxes with a flourish, to reveal two large sandwiches from our favourite place downtown.

I laugh. He is home, this man. The blueprints and foundations of our conversations in Iraq have become walls and a roof. We have decorated the rooms with our love. The olive tree has grown roots and we shelter under its protective boughs.

"So how was your day?" he asks.

"It was good thanks... Yeah, good," I say. I arrived home bursting with news of Noor and our fledgling friendship, but now the words lodge in my throat. This is the time to focus on us.

Adam adjusts his laptop. It is balanced on a sturdy black box that is three quarters full with the equipment he will take to Iraq.

"You know we have a TV now, right?" I say.

"That's not the point, babe. It wouldn't be the same."

He presses play on his laptop and a film begins. I think I recognise it.

"Have we seen this before?" I ask.

"I watched it in Iraq. You fell asleep about five minutes in."

We watch the film and eat our sandwiches. I lean my head against him and feel my jawbone moving against his shoulder as I chew.

"Pause it a minute," I say.

"Why?"

"Just pause it."

I push myself to my feet and go to the kitchen, opening one of the cupboards and reaching into the back. I pull out two bags of popcorn, one salted and one caramel, that I bought in the commissary the day I bumped into Kate. I come back holding them triumphantly.

"Emma McLaughlin, you are the best," he says, grabbing the belt loop of my jeans and pulling me down towards him. I drop the popcorn and sit across his lap, my arms around his neck, his mouth now on mine, the film forgotten. *Feel. Smell. Taste. Remember.*

Let the flames of desire lick at our bodies, leaving their scars. Let his shape be burnt onto the back of my eyes so even in darkness he is visible. Let my hands know his contours so that in his absence they can follow his shape. Let his kisses sear their outline onto my flesh. Let his love be tattooed across me, for after he is gone.

20

The day he told me he was leaving, we were on top of Radwaniyah Palace. Unlike many of Saddam's other palaces, Radwaniyah hadn't been converted into a warren of offices after the invasion. There were no makeshift plywood screens at odds with the marble surroundings or paper door-signs telling you who was occupying a certain room that week.

Instead, you could wander around the cool echoey halls of the palace, everything coated in a thick layer of dust and sand. Even in its derelict state, it was impressive, in the over-the-top way of many of Saddam's buildings. I wondered what would happen after all the troops left and hoped that the complex would be opened up for regular Iraqis to see, not just visiting foreigners with ID badges swinging from lanyards.

Some of the furniture – what had not been looted for offices elsewhere on base – remained. In one room was a large chair with high armrests and peeling gold guild. The centre of the chair was dark, the dust kept at bay by people sitting and posing for photos. In another room was a deep indoor pool, now empty, with a rusty diving board and broken tiles. The entire palace was a maze of marble staircases, giant chandeliers and faded opulence. It made me giddy with excitement and nauseous with disgust.

My favourite part of the palace was where we were that day – on the roof. There wasn't much up there, other than a giant aerial and various other bits of communications equipment, but I loved the views. This area of base jutted out into farmland and from the roof I could get a glimpse into normal Iraq. Outside the perimeter wall were fields, where a few farmers worked the land from morning to evening. An unidentifiable crop grew in low green rows. A man drove a rusting tractor between the crops. A woman's figure folded over as she gathered herbs in the evening light.

The wall around the edge of the roof was low enough to sit on, so I leant back onto my palms and lifted myself up onto it, then swung my leg over and sat sideways. This made Adam nervous.

"I don't see how you can jump out of planes but be scared of heights," I said to him.

"When I jump out of a plane I have a parachute," he replied. "Plus, it's my safety at stake, not yours."

Adam stood next to me and rested his hand on my knee. I could tell he was working himself up to say something. He had been uncharacteristically quiet all evening. I knew what was coming. I knew it must be time.

"Em, I've got some news," he said, running his other hand around the back of his neck.

"When do you go?" I asked. Surprise flicked across his face.

"The replacement team arrives in a couple of days. We'll do the handover, then head out. So next Tuesday maybe, or Wednesday."

I nodded, feeling calm. I'd run this scene through my head so many times that now it was happening it didn't feel real. Adam once told me that this is how soldiers prepare before an operation. They run through each detail in their head again and again and again. Each possible scenario, down to the smallest detail, so nothing can surprise them.

"Are you okay?" he asked, unsettled by my silence.

"Yes," I said. "We knew this would happen."

He took one of my hands, then the other. He pulled me gently off the wall. As he did so, a small piece of blue tile caught my eye. I released a hand and dipped quickly to the ground, slipping it into my pocket.

"Emma." I gave back the hand I had freed and we stood face-to-face, hands clasped between us.

"Emma, I want you to come with me," he said.

"What?"

"Hand in your resignation. Leave Iraq. Come with me. Come to the States, like we talked about."

"Don't ask me that, you know I can't," I replied. "We never talked about it really. I have a job here, a life."

"It's Iraq, Emma. This isn't living."

"Maybe not for you. But we don't all just swoop in and out on deployments. Some of us stick it out a bit longer than that. Some of us care." I heard the harshness in my words but was unable to stop them.

"Don't get angry, that's not what I meant," he said. "I know your job is important to you, but…"

"But what?"

"I love you."

"I love you too. But I'm not leaving. You know that's not who I am. You wouldn't love me if it were."

I looked up. The sun was setting fast, throwing the palace into a brilliant orange. In the distance, mosque minarets flickered green as they lit up. Bats darted around us in the night air.

I looked back at Adam. I loved him, but I wasn't ready to leave this place.

"Okay, let me ask this a different way," he said. Adam lowered himself onto one knee. "Emma Cooper, I understand that right now you do not want to leave Iraq. But one day, when you're done, I'd like you to come and live with me. And until then, would you do me the honour of becoming my wife?"

21

When I wake up, Adam is gone.

He left our home when it was still night. He kissed my forehead and adjusted the covers around me. I tried to fight through sleep to tell him that I loved him, but I don't know whether the words got as far as leaving my lips.

When I went to bed last night, he was adding the final touches to his packing. Loading movies onto his laptop for the journey. Checking he had enough Ambien. I knew he had done this all already, but he was filling time. Killing time. I told him to come to bed, but he was restless. He must have come in at some point, but I do not know if he slept.

I try to stay in bed longer, dozing, avoiding the reality of what is to come, but eventually I get up. I pad to the kitchen wearing one of Adam's T-shirts. The floor feels cold under my bare feet.

Adam's mug is in the sink, the dregs of his coffee at the bottom. Next to the sink is a note.

Have a good day, babe. See you when I get home. I love you!

No one would think that he had left for months.

The house is different now. In just hours it has changed and become the way it will be until he gets back. It is full of his absence.

The clutter that has filled the living room for weeks is gone. There is nothing waiting to be packed or shipped. No medical kits or uniform or unidentifiable bits of sturdy black equipment. No notebooks filled with scrawled lists. Nothing. Just me and the fading signs of his presence. But I have imagined this already. I am prepared.

I make coffee in a daze, his face grinning out from photos as I open the fridge for milk. I sit out on the porch and stare at the Incline, tucking my legs under me and hugging my mug. I do not want to talk to anyone or listen to the radio or turn on the television. I want the last voice to have touched my ears to be his. I sit and I stare but I do not cry. I am numb.

I decide to shower. In the bathroom there is a towel on the floor. It is still damp from drying water droplets off his body. I hang it on the towel rail to dry, then remember he will not be here to use it again. I throw it in the laundry basket instead.

I go to brush my teeth and I notice there is only one toothbrush in the metal holder now. This I had not imagined. This I am not prepared for. This is the moment when I break.

PART TWO
DEPLOYMENT

22

My ringtone wakes me and for a moment I am back there. It is not the regular bleep of my morning alarm, but the sound of someone calling – it's an Arabic pop song I downloaded after Hana played it on repeat in the office for about a month. It reminds me of polystyrene coffee cups and dusty laptops and the early days of being in love.

After leaving Iraq I couldn't bring myself to change the song, despite the looks people give me if my phone rings when I am grocery shopping on post. Adam once joked that my choice of ringtone probably set off PTSD episodes in at least a few of the soldiers. I replied that it was nowhere near as bad as the idiot who downloaded the sound of the incoming alarm for his.

The song continues. But I am not in Iraq now. I am in Colorado and it is too early for my phone to be ringing.

My alarm clock says 5.30am. Since Adam left, I have become used to sleeping in a little later, not being woken by the sound of him getting up to shower or his heavy footsteps as he goes out the door. I am not usually awake at 5.30am.

A phone call at 5.30am. My brain starts to fight through the haze of sleep. No one calls this early. I am not still there. Something must be wrong. I am suddenly filled with the tingling anxiety that the incoming alarm used to bring. Except now it is not fear of an incoming rocket that terrifies me, but incoming news.

I fumble for my phone. Press answer without looking at the name. Try not to let my thoughts race ahead of me.

"Emma," the voice says. It is Kate. "Emma, there's been an attack. US soldiers… Casualties… I can't get through to Dave."

"Shit. What? Where? How do you know?" It's like I'm curled up on the floor under my desk as the rockets fall. Helpless. Just praying this one won't be mine.

"I read it…" she says, "the news…" Her voice sounds strangled.

I push back the covers, frustrated at how they try to hold me back in the bed. Then I am in the living room. I turn on the television. I search for the twenty-four hour news channel. I half expect to see Dave and Adam's faces staring out of my television screen with the rolling ticker tape headline telling me that my husband is dead. Except that it is 2011. Dead soldiers don't make headlines anymore.

When I find the news, it is showing the highlights from a baseball game that was on last night. There are no dead husbands. Mine or otherwise.

"What did you read? Where was it?" I ask Kate. "What did it say?"

I hear her take a breath, then begin forcing words into sentences.

"It was something about an Iraqi policeman. He opened fire. Killed two soldiers."

My laptop is open on the kitchen counter from where I emailed Adam last night. I type *Iraq*, *shooting*, *US soldiers* into the news search engine. Several news stories come up, one with today's date. The word *policeman* catches my eye.

"Got it," I say. My eyes scan across the article, looking for clues.

Iraqi policeman. Checkpoint. Shooting. Mosul. Everything comes into focus.

"It's Mosul."

"I know," she says. "Have you heard from Adam? Could it be them?"

"No, Kate, listen to me. It's Mosul. That's not where they are."

"But it's Iraq. What if they went there? What if–?"

"No, stop. It's okay. I promise. It's not them, Kate. It's too far north. It's not them."

When Kate speaks again, there is a crack to her voice that I have not heard before.

"Oh. Oh, I'm sorry, Emma. I panicked. I… "

I slump down on the sofa, relieved.

"Hey, it's okay. Don't worry," I tell her, waiting for my heart rate to return to normal.

I am concerned about Kate. She has looked tired recently. Last week she cried when Harvey escaped his lead in the park and wouldn't come back when she called him. We laughed about it afterwards and she said it was just the frayed nerves of deployment, but I wasn't convinced. I look at my watch, 5.34am. My shift at the art shop doesn't start until 9.00am. Noor is going to stop by for coffee at 10.30am today, which has become a regular Friday morning routine for us. There is still plenty of time.

"How about I bring over breakfast?" I say to Kate.

"That would be great."

I pull on denim shorts and a sweater, and leave the house without looking in the mirror. The names of the dead soldiers weren't in the news article, which means that next of kin haven't yet been informed. I imagine a woman waking somewhere to a black sedan pulling up outside her house. She opens the door and they start to talk. White noise fills her ears. She braces herself with one hand against the wall. Her legs give way.

The report from Mosul worries me. Not just that soldiers died, but how. Iraqi police was supposed to be better now. Reformed. Cleared of "bad apples". I guess not completely. I suppose the Iraqi Army isn't either.

I stop at Dunkin' Donuts on my way over. Kate claims it serves the best coffee in America. I overheard the same comment in Iraq once, from a contractor in a baseball cap whose belly hung over the top of his cargo trousers.

"Not Dunkin' Donuts, is it? But it'll do," the man said as he ordered a large vanilla latte in Green Beans. Sampath picked up a black marker pen, crossed out the Green Beans logo on the cup and wrote *Dunkin' Donuts* instead.

"There you go, sir," he said, as he handed it over with a smile.

Inside Dunkin' Donuts there is a bored-looking girl examining her nails at the counter. I order two large coffees and the most sugary doughnuts I can see. She smiles at me and asks if it was a late night. I wonder whether I should have checked the mirror after all.

When I get to Kate's house, Harvey comes bounding out of the front door and down the garden path to meet me. Noah follows behind as fast as he can with bare feet, wearing his favourite red pyjamas with pirate ships on.

"Memma!" he shouts. In the fourteen weeks since Adam and Dave left, I have spent a lot of time with Kate and Noah. I haven't spent so much time around a child since I was one myself. It makes me realise how much of my niece's development I have missed. Not just the big markers like taking steps and speaking, but the subtle changes in behaviour and personality that you only pick up on by seeing a child regularly. I realise that I do not really know my niece at all.

Fourteen weeks. We might even be past halfway.

Kate stands in the doorway and takes the coffees from me, ushering her son and dog back inside. Her voice is cheery but the smile doesn't reach her eyes.

"You're a star," she says between sips. "I'm so tired, I couldn't even work the coffee machine right now."

"Well, next time you want a breakfast delivery, just tell me. You don't have to pretend our husbands are dead," I say. The dark humour slips out. It seemed completely normal in Iraq but doesn't sit comfortably in the "real" world. I scan Kate's face for a reaction.

"I have all the tricks, Em. This ain't my first rodeo," she says. Perhaps military spouses have their own dark sense of humour too.

In the kitchen, Kate slices up a banana and lays it beside the doughnut on Noah's plate.

"I can at least pretend I'm being a responsible parent," she says.

Noah eats half of his doughnuts and runs out into the back garden to play. We finish all of ours and Kate starts to clear away the plates

"So, are you going to tell me what's up?" I ask her as she loads the dishwasher. "You can't pretend a freak-out like that is normal."

"No, you're right," she says, standing with the dishwasher door half open.

"Is it stress?" I ask.

"Not exactly." She closes the dishwasher door firmly. "Actually, not at all. I'm pregnant."

"Kate! Oh my god. Congratulations!" My voice comes out weirdly high-pitched and Harvey bounds in through the door, excited by the noise.

"Harvey, get out! Go play with Noah!" Kate shouts.

I stand up and hug her.

"How far along are you?"

"Four months."

"Wait, so *just* before they went?"

"Yeah, I didn't find out until after he left."

I thought about how I'd felt before Adam went away. The desire to keep a part of him with me, an insurance against the what-ifs. I feel a twinge of envy. But it would have been too soon for Adam and I. For most of our relationship one of us has been somewhere else. But still, I feel it.

"Why didn't you tell me?" I ask her. I have spent so much time with Kate in Colorado, it unsettles me that there has been such a large secret between us.

"I was nervous, I guess," she says. "I miscarried after

Noah. It made me cautious. But I would have told you soon. I won't be able to hide it much longer."

She runs a hand over her belly. I think I see a slight rise, as though she has eaten a big meal.

"So, are you feeling okay? Is there anything I can help with?" I ask. I have no idea what pregnant people need. I watched my sister's pregnancy develop via Facebook status updates. I left for Baghdad when she still had six months of her pregnancy left. I didn't think she'd ever forgive me.

"I mean, bringing doughnuts is good, whether I'm pregnant or not. But I do have a scan next month, if you'd be free to come to that?"

"Sure," I say, in my new American way. "Of course."

23

I did not tell anyone what Adam asked me on top of the palace before he left Iraq. Not at first anyway. I did not tell them the question he asked and I did not tell them that I said yes.

I visited Adam in Colorado as soon as I could after his deployment ended, on an R and R that was scheduled for one month later. For those few weeks I sleepwalked through my life in Baghdad. Even though Adam had only been gone a few weeks, our time in Iraq already felt like a strange dream. I thought again about Jessica's tearful words after the first and only time she went to visit Mike. "He was just a different person in his real life."

The journey from Baghdad to Colorado took a day and a half. I flew from Baghdad to Kuwait, Kuwait to Washington DC, DC to Denver.

During the long flight from Kuwait to DC, I stared mindlessly at films. When the lights were dimmed and the other passengers slept, I sat, my face lit up by the small screen in front of me. My mind ran in anxious circles. I arrived in DC exhausted.

A bored-looking immigration officer with thick bushy eyebrows flicked through my passport.

"Where are you arriving from?" he asked.

"Kuwait," I said. "Well, Iraq. Via Kuwait."

The eyebrows moved towards each other and his eyes rose to meet mine.

"Iraq?"

"Yes. I work out there."

"Are you military, ma'am?"

"No. Civilian."

"What do you do in Iraq?"

"I work with Iraqis seeking special visas for the US."

The caterpillars rose this time.

"Hm," he said. I thought about all of the Iraqis that I helped to move here and wondered what kind of reception they received at immigration. Out of the corner of my eye I noticed people in the queue shifting impatiently. The immigration officer was typing rapidly, not giving anything away.

"I work on the US embassy compound," I added hopefully.

"So what brings you to the States?" he asked.

"I'm visiting someone."

"Who?"

"A US soldier."

"That you met in Iraq?"

"Yes sir." I don't know why I called him sir. I don't call anyone sir. The immigration officer typed a bit more and then handed back my passport.

"Enjoy your stay, ma'am," he said.

I emailed Adam to tell him I was in DC. He replied quickly.

This day is taking forever. I can't wait for you to arrive. I'll camp out at the airport if I have to.

I don't remember much of the flight from DC to Denver, other than being sat next to a friendly plump lady who thought my nerves were flying-related and repeatedly patted my hand.

When I got off the plane, I went straight to the bathroom to try and pull myself together. I stood in front of the mirror, taking in my image. My eyes were red and itchy from dehydration and the in-flight AC. My hair was knotted into clumps at the back of my head from three flights' worth of friction against the headrest. My mouth was stale from travel.

I pulled a toothbrush from my bag and brushed my teeth, then splashed water on my face and rubbed in moisturiser. I began to feel better, even though my reflection looked the same. A woman next to me leant in towards the mirror to re-apply her lipstick. I looked at myself again. Maybe it was me who would seem different in the real world, not him.

I checked my phone and saw two messages. The first was an excited email from Anna.

OMG, ARE YOU THERE YET? HOW IS IT???!!!! XXX

The second was from Adam.

The board says your flight arrived. Where are you, babe??

I couldn't hide in the bathrooms any longer. I shoved my toiletries into my wash bag and walked back out into the airport.

I saw Adam as soon as I entered the arrivals hall. He was stood back a bit from the crowd, with his arms crossed and feet apart in the same stance he'd been in that first day by the pool. He wore a blue checked shirt and I realised I'd never seen him in a collared shirt before. He looked different, not quite real. I'd become used to the 2D Skype version of him already. Perhaps this was what it was like for people who saw celebrities in the street, out of context or out of place.

His eyes locked with mine and a smile broke across his face and now he was moving quickly through the waiting crowd, dodging children and roller suitcases. I felt sick and awkward and remembered I hadn't reapplied deodorant.

Then he reached me. He wrapped his arms around my body and my head was buried into his chest. I closed my eyes and breathed in his familiar smell. I was back in Iraq, with the whir of helicopters and the rumble of military vehicles and the warmth of the night. I was back with Adam, my Adam.

I leant back and looked up at him.

"Hey," I said, smiling. He lowered his head to kiss me and his lips felt familiar on mine.

"Hey," he said. "I was beginning to think you'd changed your mind."

"The journey home might take a while," said Adam as we got into his car. It was a large truck-type thing, not so different to the one he drove in Iraq. "It's usually about ninety minutes, but we're gonna hit peak traffic."

"That's fine," I said. "Honestly, I'm just glad to not be on a plane."

As we drove away from the airport, I looked in the rear-view mirror and saw the white tent-like peaks of Denver International. Everything felt wide and spacious, so unlike the claustrophobia of Baghdad. I finally relaxed.

For the first part of the drive we talked about my journey over – the films I had stared at, the merits of British Airways versus United, the concerned lady on the final leg. Adam asked me a bit about Anna, work, but there wasn't much new to talk about.

When Adam was in the States and I was still in Baghdad, we talked on Skype almost every day, right up until I finally left, six months after he did. Sometimes the conversations would be a snatched "How are you? I miss you. I love you." Other times they would last for hours.

Sometimes we spoke about how we met, the same way we still do now. Other times we spoke about the future. Sentences began with "One day" and "When" and we imagined our love in a future far beyond Skype calls and emails and short, intense periods together. But always we talked. We lived half-lives. Our own and each other's. Our relationship filled the space between us.

In Adam's truck we fell into an easy silence. I sat, one hand resting on his leg, marvelling at how the landscape seemed to roll on forever, transitioning from plains to hills and eventually the mountain range. Occasionally Adam would reach over and run a hand over the back of my head or wrap his arm around my neck and pull me towards him to kiss the side of my face. Other times he just looked over and smiled.

Gradually darkness fell and the deep grey mountains melted into a purple sky. Headlights lit up the wide roads. We passed stores and restaurants with flickering signs that advertised liquor and fast food. Then we took the back roads and when I looked out of the window there was the type of deep reassuring darkness you could never find on the compound. I rested my head against the low vibrations of the window and closed my eyes.

When I opened them again, we were stopped at traffic lights on a busy street. Groups of people walked along the pavement, enjoying their Friday night out. They wore jeans and jackets and even cowboy boots; real leather boots, not the fake type that had been popular in England one summer while I was at university. Some women wore skirts and I stared at their bare legs. I wondered how many men coming back from deployment must have done the same. Even with the windows of the car shut I could hear a medley of country and pop music blaring out of bars, the kind I had only ever come across in Baghdaddy's at the weekend.

Adam looked over.

"Nearly there, babe," he said.

I nodded and rubbed at my eyes, looking out at the made-up women and feeling the staleness of travel anew.

The traffic lights changed and we carried along the strip a bit further. I noticed a couple of men in military uniform stood outside one of the bars.

"What are those soldiers doing?" I asked Adam.

"Military Police," he replied. "They keep an eye on things in town. Make sure the guys don't roll out drunk and start causing trouble."

The MPs I had been used to seeing were mostly on Camp Victory, lurking around corners with their speed guns to stop you if you rolled through a stop sign or broke the 10mph limit. There was the other time I spoke to them too, but my trip was before that happened. Things hadn't changed.

"Doesn't it bother you?" I asked Adam. "I mean, isn't it

up to you what you do when you're not at work? It's not as if you're deployed."

He shook his head.

"A soldier's a soldier, Em, off-duty or not."

I hadn't realised that the military permeated everything, even so far from the battlefield. Seeing men in uniform out on the streets was something I associated with Iraq, not normal life.

"It's not a big deal," he continued, glancing at me. "They only get involved if you're being an idiot. Plus, it keeps relationships with the community on track."

I noticed the way he said "community", as if he saw himself and the army as separate from everyone else living in Colorado Springs. I started to realise that Adam was defined by his identity as a soldier at home just as much as he was in Iraq.

"Here we are," said Adam, turning off the main strip of bars and restaurants and into a small parking lot outside an apartment building. It wasn't what I'd been expecting and he must have read my face. "Like I said, a lot of single guys live in condos downtown. The married guys have bigger houses further out."

"Makes sense," I said. "I guess you're close to the bars."

"Yeah," he hesitated. "But it's just temporary. We can find somewhere better, that suits both of us, if, when... Well, y'know."

"I know," I said, with a nervous smile. "But I'm sure it's fine. We're not even inside the place yet."

The apartment was on the sixth floor of the building, second from the top. He wheeled my suitcase through the door of the apartment block and across a shiny floor that smelled of cleaning products. Inside the lift I rested my head on his shoulder, turning away from my tired reflection in the mirror. When we arrived at his floor, the lights flicked on in the hallway. We walked to the furthest of the four doors and he fumbled with his keys as he tried to let us in, reminding me of the nerves I had felt the first time he came to my room in Baghdad. He reached into the apartment to turn on the light, then stood back and motioned me in.

I walked inside and looked around. I had seen the place countless times on Skype. A glimpse of part of the wall or the television or the kitchen behind his head. Once, he'd tried to give me a tour, but the angle of the camera wasn't quite right so I had little sense of space or how the different rooms fit together. It was strange to see it in real life, the same way I found when booking accommodation for R and R that the hotel rooms were simultaneously the same and totally different from the photos that advertised them online.

The decoration in the apartment was basic. Functional. No wonder my soft lighting and throw pillows in Iraq had surprised him. The walls were white and most of the furniture was a combination of blacks and greys. There was a brown leather sofa that didn't quite fit with the rest of the decoration, a large television with a neat stack of DVDs to one side of it and a small glass dining table that looked like it had never been used.

"I don't remember seeing the table before," I said to him.

"Yeah… I, uh, got it for your visit," he said, his hand running around the back of his neck.

The open-plan kitchen didn't look like it had been used much either. On the counter was a bunch of gerberas in a pint glass of water. The bright pinks and yellows looked almost embarrassed at their vibrancy amongst the controlled hues of the other decoration.

"Sorry. I didn't have a vase," said Adam coming in behind me. "And I didn't know what kind of flowers you liked. Or if you even liked flowers."

"They're lovely," I said, standing with my rucksack still hung over my shoulder.

"You can put your bag down," he said.

I put it on the stool by the counter. I had become used to his room in Baghdad, but in this space I felt foreign.

"Sorry it's not very… homely."

"It's fine," I said. "It's nice to… Well, to see your real life, I guess."

He wrapped his arms around me and lowered his head for a kiss. It was still Adam, still us, just somewhere else.

"Would you like a glass of wine?" he asked.

"I'd love one," I said.

He opened the door of his almost empty fridge and pulled out a bottle with a familiar label.

"You remembered," I said.

"Of course I did."

Adam had seen me drinking the Sauvignon Blanc in Baghdad with Anna on my birthday. The three of us were sat on the floor in my room with a bottle of wine and a squashed birthday cake that Anna had brought back from the UK. Adam had reached for his pocket knife to open the wine, but Anna beat him to it and opened the bottle by pressing the lid of her nail varnish into the cork.

"We've learnt important life skills out here," I told him.

Now, in Colorado, he opened the bottle the way people do in the real world and poured me a glass, then got himself a beer. He lifted his bottle and I raised my wine to meet it. The glass touched gently together.

"Welcome home, babe," he said. "I'm so glad you're finally here."

24

It is 8am in Colorado and seventeen hundred hours in Baghdad. The Skype connection is good today. I can see the flick of the scar on his eyebrow, the slight angle of his left front tooth, the pinpricks of stubble on his face.

"Hang on," he says. "I have a photo for you."

I watch as the loading bar fills from white to blue and click open. It is a picture of Radwaniyah Palace. It must have been taken late afternoon, because there is an orange tint to the colour of the stone. The photo is blurred slightly, as if it has been taken in a rush before the phone was shoved back into a pocket. There are a couple of military vehicles in the foreground and a man in uniform is walking out of shot, casting a glance back to the camera.

Everything about the photo is familiar. The antennae on the palace roof. The thick trunks and long, pointed leaves of palm trees. The dark yellow dirt under the vehicles.

"Bring back memories?" he smiles.

It does. Adam and night-time and water like silk. Thick warm air that swims around my limbs. The taste of dust and dirt and burning metal. The arm on my neck. The taste of blood.

"Sure does," I say.

"It's a shame we didn't manage to get engagement photos up there," he jokes.

"Maybe one of the blimps got aerial footage. You should ask."

He laughs.

"So what have you been up to?" he says.

Adam's face pixellates. I worry that our good luck with the connection has run out, but then the details of his face return.

"I went over to Kate's for breakfast yesterday," I say. "Did you know she's pregnant again?"

"Yeah, Dave's stoked," he says. "He's wanted another one for ages."

"Oh. How long have you known for?"

"A while," he says with an apologetic shrug. "There's not exactly a lot to talk about out here. Did she tell you about Dave too?" he asks.

"About Dave?"

"Yeah. About him getting out."

"Out? What, of the army?" I ask, surprised.

"Yup. He's been considering it for a while. I guess the baby has just kinda sealed it for him."

"So this is his last deployment?"

"Yeah. He'll start transitioning once he gets home. It takes a while, but at least he'll still be in Colorado. Actually, I think they're planning on sticking around even after."

"I really hope so," I say. "I'd miss Kate if she wasn't around."

Adam nods but says nothing. We both know the nature of this lifestyle is transient. There's no guarantee of anyone staying anywhere.

"So what have you been up to?" I ask him.

"The usual," he says. "Lots of training the Iraqi guys. Lots of sweet FA."

Work was probably a bad thing to ask about. Adam's boredom is a constant theme in our conversations at the moment. This deployment is different to his last; 2011 in Iraq is different. US troops are only supposed to be there in

146

an advisory role now, not leading the way in, kicking down doors or picking up targets. There are still a lot of doors that need to be kicked down, but there are far more restrictions and bureaucratic loopholes for the chain of command to jump through to make it happen. It doesn't feel like mission accomplished, but everything takes longer and time is running out. I change the subject.

"Any news on Ali yet?" I ask.

"Still nothing." We're both getting worried. Ali wasn't working on RPC when Adam got back to Iraq, and no one there recognised the name. We told ourselves that he'd show up when word got to him that Adam was back, but it hasn't happened.

"I'm due a Skype with Anna soon. I'll ask if she can find anything on the system. Maybe he finally went to find Ameena."

"Let's hope so," Adam replied.

Ameena's visa application was approved a few weeks before I moved to the States. Ali was ecstatic. We all were. It wasn't fast, but still quicker than expected. Ali came to the IZ to thank me with a huge tray of baklava, which Adam had told him was my favourite Middle Eastern treat.

I took him to Green Beans that day and we sat drinking coffee and eating, laughing as the sugar syrup and walnuts stuck to our fingers. It was one of my favourite moments in Baghdad. It was a small victory in the scale of things, but in one family's life it was huge. It made it all worth it.

"Do you think you'll ever go to the States?" I asked him then.

"One day I will visit them, *inshallah*. It is difficult to imagine Ameena being so far away, but right now my duty is here – to my parents and to my country."

I put another piece of baklava into my mouth and nodded. I wondered whether he would say more about Ameena if I stayed quiet, but he started asking about my plans for the States instead. I began telling him and immediately felt guilty that it was so easy for me to come and go as I pleased.

As we left the café, Ali noticed the picture of Sampath on the counter.

"Did he die?" he asked.

"Yes."

"I'm sorry," he said. "He must have been so far from home."

"How's the new 'terp doing?" I ask Adam. "What did you say his name was?"

"Kareem... I dunno." Today's conversation is not going well. His hand moves round the back of his neck. "I mean, he's okay. Just not Ali. I don't like moving through them so quickly."

There has been a lack of consistent interpreters since the start of Adam's deployment. With the military withdrawal looming, many were finding ways to get out.

"Ali's a hard act for anyone to follow," I say, but I am worried. A team's relationship with their 'terp is important. "How do the rest of the guys find him?"

"Fine, as far as I can tell," Adam says. He pauses and I think he is going to say something else, but he changes the subject. "Anyway, tell me more about what's going on with you."

This is the pattern of conversations between us at the moment. Each wants to be in the other's reality more than their own. We bat the conversation back and forth between us, thirstily soaking up the details of each other's lives.

"I saw Noor again yesterday," I say.

"Cool, the Kurdish lady? How's she doing?" Adam asks. I introduced Noor into our conversations slowly. Adam joked that only I would manage to find an Iraqi friend in Colorado Springs. Kurdish, I reminded him.

"She's good," I say. "Actually, I'm going to her art group next week."

"Art group? Cool. Is that part of her high school gig?"

"No, actually, it's really interesting. It's an art group for immigrants and refugees. I'm going to do some volunteering with them."

Adam is quiet.

"Volunteering?"

"Yeah. You know, just help out if it's needed. Or even join in. I'm not quite sure yet."

I am excited about the group. The first time Noor mentioned it I knew I wanted to get involved. It is exactly the kind of thing I've been looking for. I had hoped Adam would be enthusiastic too. Instead he is silent.

"What's up?" I ask.

"It's just... Well, didn't we decide that you were going to stay away from that kind of thing for a bit...? Just while you settle into Colorado."

I am immediately defensive.

"It's an art group, Adam, I'm not jumping on a plane back to Iraq. And this *is* settling in. It gives me something to do. A way of meeting more people."

"But, well... refugees?"

"What?"

"It's not really settling into normal Colorado, is it?"

"Do you only want me to be friends with white people or something?" I can't keep the annoyance from my voice.

"No, of course not, it's just that we agreed... You know what, never mind, Emma. Do what you want."

"I will."

Silence stretches out the distance between us.

"Okay, so I'm going to the chow hall to grab some food. I'll catch you later, babe," he says.

"Love you."

"Love you too." Whatever the conversation, it must always end with this.

Adam disappears from the screen and leaves me sat in our kitchen in silence. Outside, I see my neighbour's kids climbing into the car to go to school. A woman jogs past with headphones and a small dog on a lead. The mailman cycles by. I am annoyed with Adam and yet now I am alone I ache for his presence.

*

I walk numbly to our bedroom and open the wardrobe door. I put my face between his clothes. His blue checked shirt brushes against my cheek. I take the sleeve and put my nose into the cuff. Close my eyes. Inhale. It smells of laundry detergent and deodorant and aftershave and him.

I press myself further among the clothes. Coat hangers slide across the half-empty rail. There is the T-shirt he wore on our bike trip. The ski jacket from the time we went sledging. The shirt that makes his eyes look extra green.

I inhale again. With each breath, I am closer to him. With each breath, I miss him more. Yearning twists in my stomach. I press further into the closet.

His clothes, his smell, his presence surround me. I slide to the floor, knees raised to my chest. I curl into the corner, sit among his shoes. The hanging clothes caress my shoulders. My wet mascara leaves a dark smudge on a sleeve.

When I am in our house, I am closer to him. Even when he is not here. This place is full of him. It is full of us.

I close my eyes and wrap myself in the memory of him. This is why I stay even when he is gone.

25

I give you my life
With all that I am
And all that I have
I honour you

There is a day, three months after that first visit to Colorado. The day it begins. There is family from two sides of an ocean. Everything is wrapped in love.

Pink and yellow petals blush as Sophie scatters them before me down the aisle. I walk with steady even steps, trying not to focus on the absence beside me. The silver toes of my shoes peek out from beneath my dress. My body hums.

At the front, Adam waits. Then he turns and our eyes meet and I do not know how my soul can feel so much. Our love glimmers in the July sun.

At dusk I hold his hand. We walk between the rocks at Garden of the Gods under a vast open sky. The train of my dress soaks up the red dust. I look up at the first stars and this is perfect.

Later there is music. Laughter. Dancing. Sophie's dress umbrellas outwards as she twirls. Adam's older brother teaches my mum how to two-step to country music. Rebecca's husband cheers. I love them for coming so far for me. The night is cool but warmth radiates from our bodies and our hearts.

Now they are gone but Adam and I remain. We sit and gaze at the dark silhouette of the mountains. His coat is around my shoulders and his hand plays with the folds of white fabric of my skirt.

The night sighs around us and there is the faintest caress from the breeze and there is the feeling that this is it. This is safe. This is the start.

26

"As most of you already know, my name is Noor. I'm the art teacher at this school."

We are sat around a large table in one of the high school's art classrooms. Noor doesn't have official permission to use the room for the group because the principal isn't particularly open-minded. Noor once joked to the women that they should claim to be cleaners if he ever came across them in the hallways. It was funny until one had to use the excuse and it worked.

Noor says we should introduce ourselves and say something about our art. As much or as little as we want. Whatever we feel is important.

"I'm 27. I moved to the US in my early teens," she continues, "from Duhok, a city in Iraqi Kurdistan. My family were fleeing Saddam." Around the table there are murmurs, nods. Most of them have heard this story before.

"I work in collage and oil paints. I started this group two years ago as a way to bring people together – people who come from other places, have different stories. It is a place for us to explore our experiences through art. It is a safe space to talk and discuss our work and anything else that is on our mind." More nodding.

"Today we have two new members of the group. I'd like you to welcome Emma, who is from the UK but has been living in Iraq, and Marie-Luz, who is Guatemalan, and a friend of Paz and Laura."

I smile at the group and Marie-Luz gives a little wave.

"Okay," says Noor. "Who's next?"

There are eight of us in the group today, although Noor tells me the number fluctuates week by week. Myself, Noor, Marie-Luz, Paz and Laura (both Mexican), Hope from Somalia, Afsoon from Afghanistan, and Zainab, who is from Iraq.

We go round the group and everyone shares their story. The women are familiar with each other. They add in details to each other's lives if someone forgets to mention something. They correct each other's stories.

"You've been here seventeen years now, stop saying fifteen," Paz teases Laura.

"Hush, woman, you're making me feel old," says Laura with a laugh.

The level of English in the group varies. Hope speaks haltingly. She moved from Somalia three years ago but she is painfully shy. She manages to tell the group her name and that she likes making clothes. In front of her, I see a tunic that I think Penny would like and a colourful patchwork skirt. Afsoon, the Afghan girl who must be a similar age to Hope, gives her hand an encouraging squeeze. I notice that the girls sit close together, offering physical comfort even when language fails them.

Afsoon makes jewellery out of silver wire, which she twists and melds to hold the semi-precious stones that I have seen for sale in souvenir shops around Manitou Springs. Paz does coloured sketches and Laura embroiders anything she can get her hands on – purses, tablecloths, shirts – in bright Mexican patterns. Marie-Luz says she wants to make the Guatemalan worry dolls that she watched her grandmother make as a child. They are tiny figures that are kept in a bag and then placed under the owner's pillow at night-time, to absorb any anxieties. Marie-Luz says, somewhat shyly, that she had spent a long time trying to think of something to make because Paz and Laura talked about the group so much she was jealous. She says that she feels like a bit of a fake because she hasn't done anything artistic before, but Noor reminds her that they meet for fun and support – they are not professionals.

As each person introduces themselves, it occurs to me that although Noor invited me here to volunteer, I have no idea how I can actually help. I am happy to be among this mismatched medley of people, but I am not an artist or an organiser. I am just another stranger. My palms begin to feel clammy as my turn approaches. I still struggle to introduce the Colorado version of myself.

While Laura and Paz's conversation goes off on a tangent about the Mexican traditions they brought with them, I notice the easel that is stood behind Noor. Although she mentioned she works in oil and collage, she did not introduce her piece specifically.

At first glance what I see is a burning tyre. It is the central part of the piece and painted with vivid colours that make the licking flames seem to move off the page. Either side of the tyre are young men, standing, looking ready to leap into action. They wear traditional Kurdish outfits: red and white scarves and billowing trousers that are bound tightly at the waist. In that first glance it seems like a scene of destruction, but then I look closer. The background of the picture is a mixture of newspaper collage and oil painting. The torn newspaper pieces are photos of bombed-out buildings. Crying children. Chaos. But the painting that fills the gaps between the clippings is of deep green landscapes and plunging valleys, picnicking families. Then I understand. The burning tyre is not part of an attack or protest, but the Kurdish festival of Nawruz to celebrate spring. A new year. Jumping over fires is a part of the festival. Even I, who have lived in Iraq and knows its people, assumed the worst.

I shift my focus to the introductions again when I hear my name.

"Emma, would you like to tell us a bit about yourself?"

"Oh, yes. Hi, I'm Emma McLaughlin," I begin. "As Noor

said, I'm from England but I spent the last couple of years in Iraq. I work in the art shop now and I want to begin my own project. It's an idea I've been playing with for a while... I want to make mosaics."

Everyone is smiling at me. Perhaps it is the intimacy, the feeling of being at home among outsiders, that prompts me to continue.

"It is an old hobby," I tell them. "When I was a child, we used to collect pieces of stone and tile and washed-up glass whenever we went somewhere special. It was my father's idea. He said that each piece was a place to store our memories. We kept them all in a jar and when we had enough we would make them into some kind of mosaic. Sometimes we set them into concrete on the patio, sometimes we made a picture, this one time we stuck them to the side of a huge flowerpot. Then my father would always say the same thing: 'Look how much beauty can come from broken pieces.'"

I look to Noor and she nods encouragingly.

"My dad died a long time ago now and I haven't made anything since, but I still collect pieces. I have all these fragments, but I haven't done anything with them. So that's what I want to do here. With you. Find a way to make them into something beautiful."

With these words I feel like I've been broken open. I have recognised part of myself, allowed myself to be known. I look around, surprised at myself, and everyone is smiling still.

"Like Hope's clothes," says Afsoon. "Making scraps into a whole." She's right. Maybe we are all trying to do the same thing.

The conversation moves on and the beating in my chest slows. I can relax now I have spoken. Now it is the Iraqi woman's turn.

"Hello. I'm Zainab," she says quietly. She speaks in short sentences, pausing between each as if rehearsing the words in her head before releasing them into the world. "I have been in America for five months. I have been in this group for one month. I come from Iraq and I like to paint." She gestures to the material in front of her and sinks back in her chair slightly to show that the introduction is complete. She looks relieved and I wonder whether she was more nervous than me.

In front of her is a tiny palette of paint, a canvas that is the size of a tea coaster and a paintbrush so fine that the tip must be like the end of a needle. There is a partially complete scene on the canvas, painted in intricate detail. It looks like part of a garden or courtyard. I can make out the edge of a white plastic table, the gentle curve of a teacup catching the morning light and in the background a tree heavy with figs bathed in dew. It moves something in me, a different version of home. I lean forward to look closer.

"It's beautiful," I whisper. She puts her hand to her chest and dips her head in thanks.

For the next two hours the group works on their projects. Paz pulls out a flask of coffee and a tub of tamales for everyone to share. Afsoon bends over a tiny pair of pliers as she bends wire for her jewellery, her face almost touching the table. Hope adds stitching to the skirt that is so small and precise it is barely visible.

I am not entirely sure what to do. I brought the jar of pieces with me but I am too embarrassed to empty them onto the table, so I move the jar from side to side so I can examine its contents. Then I borrow some paper from Noor and start sketching ideas of what the mosaic might look like. I start by drafting a frame around a mirror, like the one in the art shop, but I have too many pieces, so the frame would be huge. I sketch the plant pot from my childhood, but that is not right either.

I see Zainab looking over at my sketch and I give her a shrug.

"It's not right," I tell her in Arabic which is far more halting than her English. Her eyebrows raise in surprise but she replies with a smile.

"Patience," she says. "One day it will be."

"Is your piece a painting of Iraq?" I ask her, gesturing to her work.

"Yes. It is my garden."

"It's lovely."

At the end of the group, after everyone has left, I help Noor pack away the equipment and wipe down the tables.

"They like you," says Noor. "We haven't had anyone from England before. It's a nice addition to the mix."

"I like them too," I tell her. "But I don't really see how I'm helping at all, Noor. I'm just participating."

"I know," she says. "To be honest, I actually had something else in mind."

Noor tells me that when Zainab moved here with her two children and husband five months ago they were assigned a volunteer "mentor" to help them settle in. The mentor is an older woman from the church, who is well-intentioned but "not too worldly", Noor says. She just isn't the best fit.

"My friend runs the mentor programme and asked if I knew anyone else. I wondered if you'd be interested?" Noor says. "You don't even have to be her official 'mentor' – just more of a friend if you want. I didn't mention it earlier because I wanted you two to meet first. See if there was any connection. And whatever you decide, you should still come to the art group."

I consider the idea. I wonder if I have been in Colorado long enough to be any help to Zainab; sometimes I still feel like I could use a "mentor" myself. But at least I have some understanding of where she has come from and maybe that will be of comfort to her. Maybe that is enough.

After art group, I meet Kate for her appointment. When I get to the maternity unit, she is already sat in the waiting room, repeatedly folding and unfolding the appointment letter in her hands. I give her a hug and sit down.

"They're running late," she says as I settle in to wait.

I can hear the gentle hum of chatter coming from the nurses' kitchen further down the corridor, the squeak of trolley wheels, the ring of the phone at reception. The air smells faintly of disinfectant and disposable rubber gloves.

The sounds and smells of hospitals are comforting to me. They remind me of being a child, sat in the waiting room of the hospital, waiting for my dad to finish work. One of the receptionists kept a colouring book for me in her desk. I would sit with it balanced on my knees, tongue poking out in concentration, the nurses sneaking me sweets from their pockets as they passed. That was while my dad was still able to work. Those were the best times.

Kate doesn't like hospitals. She puts the letter down and starts to pick at her nails. It's unusual to see her like this.

"Bad associations," she says when I ask if she's okay.

I'm glad she asked me to come. There are three other pregnant women in the waiting room and each one has a partner with them. One man in a suit sits engrossed in his phone while his wife flicks through a gossip magazine. Another younger couple hold hands and the man keeps leaning in to kiss her head and rub her belly. The third couple look like they are barely out of their teens. He has a short military haircut. She has a T-shirt that says *My heart is in the army*. It is a different world from the one I was in this morning. I feel like I am switching off one part of my identity and switching the army wife part back on.

"So how was this art-group thing anyway?" Kate asks me, trying to distract herself.

"It was good. Great, actually. I felt like I had a lot in common with them."

"Really? Like what?"

"Well, they come from other places. They have these sort of mixed identities, complicated stories – I feel like I can relate to them."

"I don't see what's complicated about it, Em. They're Iraqi or Arab or whatever. You're British. I'm American."

I don't say anything. I remind myself that she is anxious about the appointment and I am here to support her. Now is not the time to get into a debate.

"What's the art supposed to do anyway? Isn't it better to teach them how to speak English properly or something?"

"It's about expressing themselves," I tell her. "And creating a support network."

"Right…" she says.

I try to change the subject.

"Have you spoken to Dave recently?" I ask her.

"Yeah, yesterday. He got his days confused and called to ask how the appointment went."

"Did he sound okay?"

"Yeah. Busy. He said they were out having lunch with some important local guy today. Lamb grab, he called it."

"Oh, nice," I say.

"Dave hates them. He says everyone just sits on the floor and eats from the same plate."

"Our Iraqi team used to bring food in sometimes. I loved it. One time, one of the women I worked with brought in dolma, these vegetables stuffed with rice and meat. God, I could eat that now…"

Kate is studying my face.

"You really miss it, don't you." It is more of a statement than a question.

"Yeah, I do."

"You get that look. The same look Dave gets sometimes."

I think how alien it must be for Kate to see this longing in the people she loves, for a place that is far away and an experience she doesn't understand.

"What about Adam? Has he been in touch?" she asks.

"Not much," I say. I do not tell her the emails have been getting shorter. The Skype calls more difficult. Tense.

"Don't worry about it. It's good that he's got his head in the game," she says.

"Yeah. You're right. It was just easier when I was there too."

Kate leans back in her chair, her eyes wandering to the clock on the wall that now reads 2pm.

"What would be easier is if they were just home. I don't even know what our troops are doing in that damn country anymore."

"Withdrawals are complicated," I say. "They take time. A lot of Iraqis are scared about what will happen when the Americans leave."

"Let them figure it out amongst themselves. We've done enough already."

"But the Americans have caused problems out there too. And the British."

"We went there to liberate them and they're still killing our men."

"Kate, you know it isn't as simple as that."

She holds my gaze.

"Isn't it, Emma? Because all I know right now is my husband has spent years going to that godforsaken place. And for what?"

A nurse comes into the room.

"Katherine Jenkins?" she asks.

Kate grabs my hand and gives it a squeeze as she stands up.

"Wish me luck!" she says.

"Of course. Good luck!" I smile at her, and squeeze back, pushing down my rising frustration at her comments.

Kate disappears down the hallway and I am left sitting with the three couples, thinking about what she has said. Kate is my best friend here and yet major parts of our world view are fundamentally different. I am a stranger here too, on the edge, between one world and another. The truth is that I am a stranger everywhere now, even among my family back in England. In trying to know more of the world, I have inadvertently made myself alien in all of it. Accepted, embraced, but never fully belonging.

*

When Kate comes back into the waiting room she has a strange look on her face.

"Are you okay?" I ask her.

She nods quickly, her lips pressed tightly together.

"Are you sure?" I shoot a glance at the nurse standing behind her, but the nurse checks her clipboard and calls the name of the next patient.

Kate nods again, then opens her mouth and closes her mouth, reminding me of the giant carp that used to live in the lakes around the palace.

"I'm trying to hold it in. I should tell Dave first. But…"

"Wait," I start to say, "did you find out—"

"Girl!" she blurts out. "I'm having a baby girl!"

I jump up and hug her.

"Congratulations, Kate! Wow, congratulations!"

Kate hands me a picture of her scan.

"Look, can you see her? That's her head and those are her little legs."

It looks like the scan Rebecca sent me when she was pregnant with Sophie, but, with no explanation, Rebecca's scan had just looked like a black and white blur. Anna and I looked at the picture from my computer in Iraq, trying to work out what might be an arm or a foot, but we were clueless. I sent Rebecca an email saying it was wonderful and beautiful and then I never opened the picture again. But this scan is different. Kate points out the head, the legs, the heart and the black and white swirl become a baby girl.

I hug Kate close to me and feel her heart beating rapidly. No matter what our differences are, I need this woman in my life. We will get through this together.

27

"God, I can't imagine how weird it must be. All that time you spent visiting him and now he's back here. And you're just, well, in Colorado."

Anna sits in front of me with a glass of wine. She looks different to the last time I saw her. Her hair is shorter and a darker shade of brown. I can tell she is tired, by the way she intermittently rubs at the side of her eye. Her face pixelates briefly, then returns to full detail.

"Yeah, it's odd," I say. "Harder than I thought. You know how when you're there, most of the time everything is fine and there are just the occasional bad moments? Being on the outside is the opposite. Every minute he's not in touch I'm wondering whether something has happened."

"Stop, Em. You're making me feel bad about what I put my parents through."

"It's definitely given me a different perspective," I say. "Kind of makes me wonder how Adam dealt with it being the other way round for so long."

"He probably knew the roles would be reversed eventually," she says. "So what are you actually *doing* there? Hanging out with army wives? Hiking a mountain each morning?"

"No hiking mountains," I say. "I tried, but it didn't end too well. Actually, I'm going to mentor a new Iraqi family I met here. Help them settle in, that kind of thing."

Anna laughs.

"God, Em, you really can't let go, can you? An Iraqi refugee family in Colorado? You'll be telling me you're on a flight back here next."

Is this what Adam is scared of? Does he think I will leave him and go back to Iraq too?

"I just need some kind of purpose," I tell her. "I honestly feel guilty that I'm probably doing it more for me than for them. I miss it out there."

Anna gets it.

"I know, we miss you too."

"How is work going?" I ask.

"Busy," she says. "Same as ever. The backlog is bad; it has been for a while. We're just getting swamped with applications."

"And the staffing?" I ask. Staffing had always been a problem with that organisation. Everything was dependent on funding, so when the funding was low, people got laid off. Then a backlog would build up and at some point the funding would be renewed, then a whole new batch of staff had to be recruited and security cleared and trained.

"We're low, but that's nothing new," Anna replies. "I think the issue is the prospect of withdrawal. People just don't want to stick around to find out what happens next."

"I heard a similar sort of thing from Adam. They keep losing 'terps when their visas come through. Any word on whether they might agree on a military extension?"

"Rumours, but nothing official," Anna says.

I take a sip of my wine and her face freezes again, then returns. It's a bit early to be drinking here, but Skype dates with Anna are an exception. When I first moved to Colorado, we promised to have them once a month, but the routine quickly slipped.

"Anna, on the subject of 'terps, can you look up Adam's old 'terp on the system for me? To see if he's been caught up in the backlog?"

"Has he still not turned up?"

"Not yet. But his cousin Ameena moved over here while I

was still in Baghdad, so I wondered whether he had managed to get out too."

"Of course, I remember you helping her," Anna says. "Email me his full name. I'll take a look tomorrow."

"Thank you." I see her scribbling down a reminder on her hand. Anna wrote notes about everything, usually starting on her hand and spilling onto her arm when she ran out of space. In the summer once I saw her write a note on her thigh.

"So what are they going to do about the backlog. Are you recruiting?" I ask her.

"That depends, are you ready to come back to us?"

I know that Anna is joking, but her face becomes serious when I laugh but do not reply.

"Em… You're not actually considering it are you?"

"No… No. Colorado's great. I just... well, I miss it. The work. Being there. Hanging out with you!"

"You'll feel differently once Adam's home," she says.

"Probably. I just hope this mentoring gig will help a lot too."

"It was the right thing to do, Em… Leaving when you did. Not just because of what happened. Because of everything. It's not the same here anymore. Everyone is tired and cynical and just trying to work out what they'll do once the whole operation wraps up."

"I still feel bad about leaving."

"It was the right choice. You gave longer to this place than most people."

I nod, but it is a nod of acknowledgement rather than agreement. When I left Iraq it felt like a betrayal. Of Anna. Of everything. Even of myself, although I knew I couldn't do it any longer. I tried to get over what happened, but I couldn't.

Anna is the one person who knows about that evening. There were others there at the time, of course. People who were in the bar, the woman from the US Embassy who made the call, the Military Police. But all of those people exist only in the world of Baghdad. Anna is the only person who is in my real life too.

There was another day. A day that came after the petals and the dancing and the chill of the evening air. For me it is the day Iraq ends.

I was in the bar with Anna that evening. It had been a busy couple of weeks. We spent our days rushing through interviews, trying to catch up on paperwork, and wondering how much longer we could physically keep up that pace.

In the evening we sat sipping gin and tonics with zombie-like stares, but on one occasion we were interrupted by the appearance of a half-empty pint on our table. The owner of the beer, a brawny sunburnt man, grinned down at us both.

"Y'alright ladies? I hear this is the Brit table. Guess I'm in the right place then." He spoke in a thick slurring accent and made as if to sit down.

"It's more the quiet gin and tonic table," I said.

"Yeah. Emma and I need a bit of downtime," Anna added. "It's been a long week."

The man took a step back, although it was unclear whether it was intentional or to counter his swaying. He was smiling less now.

"Oh, *you're* Emma? You're the one who married a septic then, are you?" he asked, trying to focus on me. Septic tank. Yank. It was a term I'd only ever heard among private security contractors and British military.

"I married an American, yes." I felt my whole body tensing, my enunciation becoming more crisp. After such a rough week I was not in the mood to deal with this kind of shit. Whatever came out of his mouth next, I was ready to take him on.

The man looked like he was getting ready to say something else, when a more familiar face approached, Kieran. Kieran was another one of the British private security contractors. One of the good ones, we thought. He was ex-military himself

166

but had been teaching history in a secondary school some-where up north when one of his old army buddies had offered him a Baghdad gig that would let him pay off his mortgage in a couple of years.

"Hello ladies. All okay over here?" he asked, putting a firm hand on the other man's shoulder.

"We were just telling your buddy that we're having a quiet drink. Not really a big social night," said Anna.

"Of course," Kieran said, with a nod of understanding. "Sorry 'bout my mate here. He only arrived last week and he's been hitting the cat piss pretty hard."

He tightened his grip on the man's shoulder and steered him firmly away.

"New PSD, I take it," I said, turning to Anna. She raised an eyebrow.

"Yeah. Called Alec, I think. I heard he tried to take on one of the embassy Marines a few nights ago... I can't imagine he'll last long."

"Sounds delightful," I said.

Lisa, one of the political affairs officers from the US Embassy, joined us a short while later. We didn't spend much time with the embassy staff, but Lisa had a British husband and said that our accents reminded her of home when she was away.

"I just saw that new security guy stumble out the door. What a mess. I'm glad he's not supposed to be protecting me tomorrow," she said as she sat down.

"Yeah, he was over here being a pain," said Anna. "Kieran dragged him off."

"I heard one of the UN lot had some hassle with him last week. Watch out for him," Lisa said.

About an hour later, I decided to turn in for the night. Lisa and Anna were staying for one more drink, but I wanted to catch Adam on Skype before going to bed.

"Shall I walk back with you, Em?" Anna asked.

"No, then you'd have to come back on your own," I told her. "It makes no sense. Don't worry, I'm pretty sure that Alec guy will have passed out a while ago. I'll text you when I get to my room."

We were so careful about the buddy system usually, but not that evening. In truth, I wanted to enjoy a couple of moments on my own in the hot night air before returning to my windowless room.

I walked out of the bar and slowly through the compound, along footpaths bathed in the orange light of street lamps. I could hear music and muffled laughter from Baghdaddy's fading behind me, but other than that the compound was quiet.

I passed by the rows of CHUs. From a couple, the flickering light of a television screen slipped out between the blinds. Most were in darkness. There was the smell of smoke in the air and I thought I saw the glowing end of a butt brighten and then disappear further down the row as someone smoked a final cigarette on the CHU step.

Sometimes I found the number of people in the compound overwhelming, in the same way I used to feel overwhelmed looking at blocks of flats in London at night. So many lives stacked on top of each other. The IZ was full of people who had homes and families elsewhere, yet chose to be here in a strange bubble at the centre of someone else's war. Lots of lonely lives hemmed in by blast walls and barbed wire.

The night exhaled around me. I carried on.

I was about halfway to my room when it happened. I heard him first. The shift in the gravel at the edge of the path and the heavy breathing. Perhaps the smell of cigarette smoke had been him too. Was he out on his step, listening to the silence. Waiting?

He grabbed me before I had time to turn and shoved me up against a blast wall with the heavy arms of someone whose job was to be strong. His breath was stale on my face and his groin pushed into my leg.

A thick forearm pinned my head back against the concrete. But it wasn't who I thought.

"Kieran, what the fu—?"

"Sssshhhhhh," he said. I tried to scream but struggled to suck in air.

The other hand was already fumbling at my waistband, his fingers forcing their way between flesh and jeans. I had always known that this was a risk, but I didn't want to believe it was happening. Not now, like this. Not him. Not me.

"I saved you from that creep. Don't you owe me one?" he asked.

He pushed his fat warm tongue into my mouth and all I felt was rage. *Fight*, my brain shouted. *Fucking fight*.

I bit down, my teeth sinking into soft flesh.

He pushed me away and the back of my head hit the concrete of the blast wall, but I felt nothing.

"Argh!"

He bent forwards, hand over his mouth, then started to stand.

"You crazy fucking bitch, Emma. I'll—"

I never heard what he would do. My feet were already carrying me at a sprint back to the bar.

A warning message pops up in the middle of my laptop screen, obscuring Anna's face and telling me that my battery is low. I pick up the laptop and move from the sofa to the kitchen island, where I plug in the cable and perch on a stool.

"Okay, enough Iraq talk," says Anna. "On to more important stuff. Have you found me a cowboy yet?"

"Not yet," I smile. "There aren't too many of them coming into the art shop."

"What about at the bars?'

"If you go to the right one, I guess…" I say.

"Have you been out much since he left?" she asks.

"No, not really." The truth is I haven't been out to a bar on my own since what happened in Baghdad. It makes me feel on edge.

"God, Em, a normal social life is the main reason for not living in a conflict zone. Make the most of it!"

I hate to admit it, but she's right. We spent many evenings in Baghdad playing "If I were in London…" describing the bars we'd go to, the food we'd eat, the places we'd dance.

"There's a night out next week for the team wives," I tell her. "Some kind of morale-boosting thing. But I wasn't going to go."

"You should!" she tells me. "It'll be good for you. Worst-case scenario is it will be awful, and you'll have some great stories for me."

"Okay, I'll think about it."

"What's to think ab—"

Anna is interrupted by a familiar sound. My body tingles with recognition. My limbs want to push me off the stool and onto the ground. I am too close to the window and I need to move away from the threat of shattered glass. There is nowhere to hide under the kitchen island. I will have to crawl across the floor, get under the coffee table. Now comes the voice.

Incoming. Incoming. Incoming.

"Anna?"

Anna's face has been suspended momentarily in a look of surprise. Her face blurs back into movement and I can see that she is moving her mouth, but the sound is disjointed, chopping up her voice.

"Got to… Em… to go… I'll—"

I think I hear a low thud, but I cannot be sure. Anna's face disappears and my laptop falls quiet. Silence fills my house, but in my head the alarm continues to ring. I focus on trying to steady my breathing, on trying to calm the rush of adrenaline that is screaming through my limbs and telling me that I should be on the floor, hands over my head, taking cover too. A pop-up box on Skype asks me about the quality of my call. I try to close it, but my hands are shaking. I wait, but Anna does not log back on.

I walk a few steps across the kitchen and with each movement my legs feel like liquid or jelly or anything without bone, anything that will fail to carry the weight of a body. I slowly pour myself another glass of the wine and try to focus on the pale liquid as it fills my glass.

I check Skype again.

Anna is offline.

Anna is on the floor. Her hands are over the back of her head. The incoming alarm is loud, but the thuds are louder. The tremors move in shock waves through her body. She is alone. She closes her eyes and counts and breathes and tells herself she is fine. I am not there.

I take three large gulps of wine. I start searching Google and Twitter and Facebook for any news about attacks in Baghdad or attacks on the IZ, but there is nothing. Not that there would be anyway. I check Skype again.

Anna is offline.

Anna is under her bed. Dust is in her eyes and nostrils and mouth and lungs. Blood oozes from a cut on her arm. Her ears ring. I am not there.

I leave my laptop and sit on the sofa in the living room instead. I turn on the television, but there is a show with a car crash and a close-up of a woman with a gash on her face and blood running out of her ear. I turn it off. I get up and return to the kitchen.

Anna is offline.

Anna is under her bed, but there is no bed now because the ceiling collapsed and heavy rubble crashed down and now there is only darkness and no bed and no Anna and I was not there.

I wander from room to room in the house. It feels large and empty. I go and stand in the garden without a jacket and let the cold bite at my arms. My skin raises and my jaw judders and I hope that the cold will numb my thoughts or at least cause a pain that distracts me from my fears.

I do not know how long I am out there, but eventually I

return inside and the house is uncomfortably warm. I check my laptop.

Anna is offline.

But there is an email.

Subject: All fine

Hi Em. Sorry about that! Stupid incoming getting in the way of our catch-up. Did it remind you of the old days?! All fine here – apparently it's mostly VBC that's taking a hitting. Internet is patchy so I can't get back on Skype, but let's talk again soon. Anna xx

VBC. Adam.

Another email arrives.

Subject: Sorry

Shit, Emma, sorry. I sent that without thinking. I'm sure Adam's fine. You know what these things are like – more of annoyance than a risk! VBC is huge. It's probably nowhere near him. Xx

I want to email Adam. I've already emailed him today, so I need to think of an excuse. I can't tell him about the real reason or what happened with Anna. He will say I am panicking, that I should know better. It is late in Baghdad now. Perhaps he is in bed already.

Subject: Anna says hi

Hi love. I had a Skype date with Anna today. She said to say hi, so I thought I'd email you to say hi from Anna. She's going to check for Ali on the database. How was your evening?

Love, Emma

He responds straight away.

Subject: Re: Anna says hi
Hi babe. Good to hear you had a catch-up with Anna. Tell her I say hi back! Fingers crossed for news on Ali. I've had a quiet evening here. Watching a movie, then heading to bed. Another exciting day in the sandbox! Enjoy the rest of your day.
Love ya,
Adam

I wonder whether he has really been watching a film, or if he has been laying on the floor with his hands over the back of his head. He would not tell me if he had. There are moments of war that you keep to yourself in the hope of protecting those you love. These are not lies, but omissions. Of course, there is no protecting them really. Sometimes the imagination is worse than reality.

This is what we do. We try not to mix life out there with the real world. That way, when you come home, it can't follow you back. At least that's what we tell ourselves.

Adam does not know about the blast wall and the arm across my neck and the blood in my mouth. That's how I know he leaves things out when we talk. Because I do too.

28

Hi Em,

SO good to catch up last night! I miss talking to you. Stupid incoming for cutting us short!

I checked out Ali. He was on the system. He came in for an interview with us in July, but then there were some hold ups with his background checks on the military side – not sure what. Anyway, that got sorted and he was scheduled for the second interview in March, but he never turned up. Nothing after that. Sorry.

Let's talk again soon. AND GO ON THE NIGHT OUT. Remember my motto: Do it for the story.

Love

Anna xx

Hey babe,

Thank Anna for checking. It doesn't surprise me he was on the system. I don't have a good feeling about it, but I'll keep digging. Someone must know something.

Love ya,

Adam

29

Today I wake up in the middle of the bed. When he left, it seemed wide and empty. I woke each morning to the reminder of his absence, staring at a pillow no longer curved from the weight of his head.

At first I continued to sleep on my side, but my back felt cold without the warmth of a body to curl into. I learnt to fill the space that he left. Now I sleep on my front, my face in the hollow where our two pillows meet. My legs stretch out and I rest a hand where his face used to be.

My morning routine is gentle. I get up slowly, make coffee and take my mug into the back garden to enjoy the early sunlight. I water the flowers I planted before he left. The flower beds were just patches of bare soil then, but now there is growth. Sometimes I take a photo to show him. Sometimes I just sit and absorb the quiet. Sometimes I feel guilty that I can be happy when he is not here.

Tonight is the team wives' night out. Kate laughed when I said I was going, but encouraged me.

"Why not?" she said. "You should get the full wives' experience. Just drink before you get there and it will make the whole thing more enjoyable."

"Can't I convince you to come with me?"

"Without alcohol? No thanks! But I can't wait to hear how it goes."

We are going to Cowboys, the bar where I saw the Military Police the first time I came to Colorado. I am still not entirely sure I want to go, but I should. Anna is right. I should be making the most of life here. Olivia will be there and a couple of the other wives I have met. There is one called Sally who is also a yoga instructor. I've seen her around the commissary wearing lots of Lycra and brightly coloured hairbands that hold back her long dark hair. She reminds me of Jessica and Jessica makes me think of Sampath, but I don't want to think of that now. Not today. Today I just want to be normal.

At work I tell Penny that I am going out tonight. I keep announcing it to the world, as if telling lots of people will stop me backing out. As if they will hold me accountable.

"Good luck with that, sweetie," she says. "Watch out for all those handsy young soldiers."

"Penny! I'm a married woman," I laugh.

"You think that makes a difference to them?"

I know it doesn't, I want to tell her.

It is evening and I start to get ready. I put on the cheesy nineties RnB playlist that made Anna famous at UN compound parties and pour a glass of wine. When I get in the shower, the glass of wine comes with me. I do things like that now I live alone. After the shower, I pour another glass of wine, turn up the music and blow-dry my hair. Two glasses of wine in and going out doesn't seem like such a bad idea.

I stand in front of the open wardrobe, trying to work out what to wear. I've been living in jeans and T-shirts since he left.

The first dress I put on is Adam's favourite. It is a bright blue that makes my skin appear more tanned than it is. It skims my knee and has a slit that Adam likes because it shows off my legs. I turn in front of the mirror. I remember the first night I wore it and how we missed the restaurant reservation. I do not want to wear it when he is not here.

Instead I choose black jeans and heels and a dark green silk blouse. I run my fingertips over the material. The silk slides across my skin. For a moment, I feel lonely. I shake my head and return to the mirror, trying to get used to this unfamiliar version of myself.

When I first moved to Colorado, each day of getting dressed was a struggle. In Baghdad I had limited options. I never thought about what to wear, I just put something on. But Colorado was different. My Baghdad clothes were boiled and threadbare. My England clothes were too... British. Everything I put on made me feel more out of place. Eventually I went to the outdoor clothing store and now, at least from the outside, I look like everyone else. It is my words that give me away.

One more glass of wine and I am almost ready to go. I put on some lipstick but I have not worn it for so long that it looks clownish. I change my mind and rub it off again, leaving my lips red and raw. I check my handbag for money, ID, keys. I pick up my phone to add to my bag and there is an email from him.

Hey. Are you around for Skype?

I pause. It is 8pm in Colorado and zero five hundred hours in Baghdad. Early. He could be on his way out or on his way in. Or there could be something wrong. I reply.

Just heading downtown with the team wives. Can stay in if you need to talk though. All okay?

I think about putting down my bag and taking off my shoes. They're uncomfortable anyway. I could sit on the sofa and talk to Adam and it could almost be a normal Saturday evening. It's been more than a week since our last Skype conversation and I miss the sound of his voice.

The reply comes back quickly.

Team wives? Wow, that was unexpected. No worries, all fine here. I'll try to catch you tomorrow. Love ya.

I reply *Love you too*. I put my phone in my handbag and head out the door, leaving quickly before I change my mind.

*

When I get to the bar, I spot Sally quickly. She has a sparkly pink top and an alcohol-induced glow. She jumps up from her seat to hug me and tells me she's so glad that I made it. I'm clearly not the only one who started drinking early. I say hello to Olivia and some of the other wives who I have met before, who all have names like Liz-Beth and Mary-Ann.

Whatever conversation they were having dies when I arrive, so we sit around awkwardly for a couple of minutes until Sally announces it must be time for a round of shots.

One hour and another two shots later, we are all chatting and laughing. Despite the initial awkwardness, they are entertaining company and surprisingly open about their deployment struggles. The shots might have something to do with it.

Mary-Ann starts by announcing she's fed her kids pancakes for dinner four times this week. Liz-Beth says her Netflix addiction has become so bad that she woke up this morning spooning her laptop. Even Olivia seems more relaxed than usual.

Later in the evening I stand with Sally by the bar and she tells me again how happy she is that I came. I say I am happy too and I am surprised to find that I mean it, although my mind keeps drifting back to Adam's message. I check my phone to see if he has emailed again, but there is nothing.

While we wait to order more drinks, a couple of men approach us. They introduce themselves as Jared and Peter. They are both in town for some kind of training at the Air Force Academy. Jared is blond and stocky and does most of the talking. He has a cheekiness about him that I know Anna would like. Peter is quiet and tall, with dark hair and thoughtful eyes.

Sally tells Jared and Peter it's her birthday. I shoot her a questioning look and she shrugs with a smile. Jared buys us drinks and I feel a nervous twist in my stomach that this isn't quite right. Ten minutes later, Jared has finished his beer and is grabbing Sally's hand to drag her onto the dance floor. He gets more than he bargained for and I can't help but laugh as he tries to keep up with her moves, which involve lots of hair swishing and spins. A few of the other girls get up and join them. Jared winks at Peter from across the room.

Peter talks more now Jared is gone. He tells me that he is from California originally and that Jared is someone he met at the course this week. Nice guy but bullshits a lot, he says. He asks where I am from and when I say England he says he has always wanted to go to London. Peter tells me to call him Pete. We lean against the bar and laugh as we watch the dancing.

Peter tells me he got back from Iraq a couple of months ago. I become more interested. We talk about Iraq and exchange stories and laugh about how it was the worst and best of times all at once. Peter asks what brought me to Colorado and I tell him I moved here to be with my husband. My husband who I met in Iraq. He raises an eyebrow and says "deployment romance"? I nod.

"First time I've heard of one of those that's lasted," he says. I tell him Adam is deployed again at the moment. He doesn't say anything. I am not sure why I told him.

I finish my drink and now I feel ready to dance. I spot Olivia and Liz-Beth and Mary-Ann on the dance floor and I leave Peter to join them. Soon we are shouting song lyrics to each other under the flashing lights. We twirl around and hug and occasionally stumble as the floor pulsates with the beat of the music. I pull out my phone and we beam into the camera. I try to send the photo to Adam, thinking that he will be happy to see me with the other wives, but my thumbs are thick on the keypad and I don't know if it works. One song rolls into the next and I lose track of time.

At some point I go back to the bar and the room is moving more than it should be and I don't think I should drink anymore. I start to look for my jacket to leave, but then I feel a hand on the small of my back.

"You're not going yet, are you?" Peter asks.

I feel his fingers testing the smooth fabric of my blouse and I step away from his hand. The touch of someone who is not Adam clears the haze of alcohol from my mind.

"I thought we were having a good time," he says, leaning in towards me. I smell the alcohol on his breath and now I am back there with the forearm across my neck and the taste of blood in my mouth and the military policeman asking if I knew him, if I'd been drinking.

"I'm leaving," I say and push quickly away from him through the crowded bar. I head across the dance floor towards the exit, giving up on thoughts of finding my jacket. The other women aren't there now. I think I see Sally in the corner of the bar, but she is leant up against Jared. I could almost swear her lips are touching his, but it is dark and the lights are flashing and all I want to do is to get out.

I emerge into the cold night air with a gasp. I stand with my hands on my legs for a moment, trying to control my breathing. My thoughts. I straighten up to flag down a taxi and think that I am too drunk to be doing this on my own. I think about the buddy system in Iraq. I think about what happened the time I ignored it.

I shiver. The thin material of my top is no barrier against the cold and I hug my arms around myself, cursing the loss of my jacket. I consider going back inside to find it, but I don't want to risk bumping into Peter. I rub my arms and stamp my feet a bit, but it doesn't make much difference. This isn't me. These aren't my people. I don't belong here.

A couple of military policemen walk past. One glances towards me, then says something to his partner. Can they see I am out of place too? I wonder whether Noor remembers the US uniforms from before she left Iraq, and how she feels seeing them around Colorado Springs. I wonder if Ali managed to get out and if he's somewhere in America now too. I wonder if he goes out at the weekend and sees military police who don't know who he is, what he's done. Who he's saved. To them he is just another foreigner.

One of the policemen looks like he's about to come over, but a taxi pulls up and I clamber in. I tell him my address and when the taxi driver hears my accent he looks in the mirror.

"You don't sound like you're from around here," he says.

"No. I'm from England," I reply.

"Oh. You need to dress for the weather here. It gets real cold real quick."

I don't want to have a conversation, so I just nod and say, yes, he's right, and ask him if he got the address.

As soon as I get home, I take off my heels and pull on one of Adam's hoodies, which reaches halfway to my knees. I try to make tea in a mug that was in the sink, but I don't wash out the coffee dregs so the tea tastes strange. I start to cry and I tell myself that tea is a stupid thing to cry about. I drink a large glass of water instead.

I reach for my phone and send Adam an email. It is the kind of email I would never let myself send while sober. It is an email that doesn't help either of us.

I hate being in Colorado without you. I miss you. I wish you were home.

I sleep on the sofa, pulling my knees up into the hoodie. I do not want my empty bed tonight.

30

I woke up this morning with a dry mouth and a pounding head. I have drunk three cups of coffee and eaten a fried egg sandwich, but it hasn't helped. What I really want is bacon. Thick, English bacon, not the thin streaky kind that everyone eats in America. Perhaps if Adam were here we would go out for breakfast, to one of those places that serves stacks of pancakes and giant omelettes. But he's not here and it's almost midday and I'm still in my pyjamas. I called Penny and apologetically told her I couldn't come into the shop.

"Must have been a good night," she said, "I'm glad."

I feel nauseous. It's the kind of guilt and nausea mix that started plaguing my hangovers when I hit my mid-twenties. "The Fear", Anna and I would call it. The hangover guilt gathers like fog around the edges of my brain. I try to think back through the night. Sally and her friends. The shots. The two Air Force guys. The hand on my back. The panic. Sally leaning in, chin raised. Shit.

The worst part of it was the email I woke up to.

What? You hate being in Colorado? Are you okay? Did something happen?

I tried to ignore the pounding in my head so that I could reply.

Hey. I'm fine. Just a late night and a bit too much to drink – I got emotional. It was a fun time though. Sorry, I didn't mean to worry you.

The last thing I want is for Adam to be distracted worrying about me. The thought of that is worse than the hangover. Maybe that is where the guilt is coming from.

Back when I was at university, hangovers were almost fun. I'd often go out with people from my Arabic class, and the next day we would sit in lectures, resting against each other's shoulders as we tried to make sense of whatever Al Jazeera radio clip our teacher was playing.

In Baghdad, hangovers were less fun, mostly because of the low-quality alcohol and relentless heat. There was one particularly bad hangover the day after Anna and I went to a party on the UN compound. The 'bar' there was just another converted shipping container, same as the CHUs, that shook disturbingly when there was dancing.

The next day, we sat in the office, each clutching a large polystyrene cup of Coke and ice in our trembling hands. Anna periodically rested her head on the desk. I was on my third packet of salt and vinegar crisps.

"Never again," Anna said. I feebly shook my head to agree with the sentiment. That was when the incoming alarm sounded.

It had been a quiet couple of months, so the alarm was a surprise. It was the first and only time in my life that I have truly understood the figure of speech "a splitting headache". But I didn't just think my head was going to split open. More like explode, sending slivers of skull bursting in all directions. I briefly considered just staying in my seat and risking whatever fate came my way, but Nigel yelled, so we slid gingerly from our chairs onto the floor. The movement was too much for Anna and I heard her retching into the wastepaper basket next to me.

Even that Baghdad hangover was better than my hangover today. At least there I had Anna.

I lie on the sofa and stare mindlessly at the television. From my horizontal position, I scroll through Facebook. It looks like everyone in England is out enjoying a final enthusiastic burst of British summer. My sister Rebecca has just posted photos of Sophie, sat in a paddling pool in what must be the garden of their new house. Sophie is slathered in sun cream and wearing a bright pink swimsuit with frills. She is so much bigger than when I last saw her. I think about giving Rebecca a call, it's been a while since I spoke to her, but I realise I would only want to listen to her voice, because I am currently unable to form sentences myself.

I feel sick. My mouth is watery. I think maybe I should move to the bathroom just in case, but when I try to sit up my head pounds. Shit. Why did I let myself drink that much? Memories of the night come flashing back. The shots. Swirling to the music. The hand on my back. Shit. Why was I talking to him anyway? I was there with the team wives but just because some guy had been to Iraq I thought he was more interesting. I thought he was more like me. And Sally... shit. Sally and the man who wasn't her husband. I wonder if the other women saw. I wonder if there is a code among them, like there often is with the men.

Two more episodes of trashy television later, I get an email from Adam, asking if I'm around to Skype before he goes to bed. I drag myself to a sitting position and balance the laptop on my legs. Skype makes the familiar whoosh and pop sound that now accompanies every interaction with Adam and even finds its way into my dreams.

He calls. The emblem of a large pulsating telephone fills my screen. I smooth my hair down and hope I look less awful than I feel. I click accept and the circle of the loading signal swirls round for longer than normal. It is not a good sign.

Eventually Adam appears on screen, except he is not Adam. He is a blurred shape in the middle of the webcam window, which moves around to uncover and re-cover the light source behind it.

I hear him say hello, but the sound connection drops and his voice is lost before he finishes asking how I am. I answer anyway, but he realises the connection has gone down and asks "Can you hear me?" over the top of my answer. Then the connection is lost completely and his face is replaced by the infuriating circle that swirls unhurriedly as it tries to find him somewhere on the other side of the world.

The blurred shape is back. It talks to me.

Hey
Hey
Bad connection today.
Yeah. Weather?
Dust. How was—
Swirling circle.
Blurred shape.
My night out? Yeah, it was okay. But I—
Lost you. I said how was the night out?
It was good. I went with the team wives.
Yeah, I saw from the photo.
Photo?
Yeah, the – you sent.
Oh. Yeah, I forgot.
Did you—?
Pardon? I didn't—
Emma? Are you—
Swirling circle.
Connection lost.
Reconnect.
Can you hear me Adam?
Yeah, you're back. So you – fun?
Yeah, it was nice.

And the email?
Yeah, I… Sorry about that.
Do we – talk – about it?
No. No, I'm fine. It was just drunkenness.
I—
Connection lost.
Searching…
Searching…
Unable to reconnect

We switch to written chat.

Adam is typing…

Sorry babe. Video isn't happening today.

No worries.

Sure you're okay?

I'm sure. Just hungover. But how are you? Are you okay?
What did you want to talk about last night?

Nothing. It's fine.

Can we try to Skype again tomorrow?

I'll let you know. Busy couple of days ahead.

Okay. I love you Adam.

Love you too babe. Bye.

Adam is offline.

31

The day after the hangover, I told Noor I wanted to start the mentoring role as soon as possible. The night out had reminded me who I was, Colorado or otherwise, and more importantly – who I was not.

Noor told me that the objective of the first couple of visits to Zainab was just to build up a rapport with the family. It was up to them to choose how much or little of their lives they wanted to share. "It could be that they never really ask for any help," she said. "Sometimes just knowing they have someone there is enough.'

When I arrived at Zainab's house, I felt immediately at ease. At the door, she kissed my cheek, then took my jacket and dusted it lightly before hanging it up in a gesture that reminded me of my mother.

I am sat on her sofa now, balancing a tiny cup of coffee on my knees.

"How is the painting going?" I ask as she fusses with coasters on the coffee table.

"Well," smiles Zainab. "I've almost completed the painting you saw." Her English seems much more fluid now we're on our own, making me think it was nerves that caused her hesitation in the art group.

"Can I have a look?" I ask.

"Of course. I have a few I can show you."

"I paint too you know," says Zainab's daughter Farwa,

patting me on the leg from her position next to me on the sofa and making my cup wobble. Zainab has two children. Farwa, who has just turned fourteen, and Hassan, who is seventeen. Farwa looks a lot like Zainab. She has inherited the same almond eyes and the habit of pressing her lips together when she is thinking, which seems to be often. She is wearing a pink T-shirt, denim skirt and glittery Converse. She is chatty and bright and speaks almost flawless English. Her brother Hassan is different. He sits at the table in their living room and plays with his phone. He said hello when his mother told him to greet me, but hasn't said a word since.

"Oh, you do?" I say to Farwa.

"Yes. But not like my mum. I paint my pictures on normal-sized bits of paper. And I like to paint people, not just gardens."

Zainab returns with a pile of tiny canvases and I put down my coffee. Not one of the paintings is bigger than the one she brought to the art group. Some of them are backed onto light-coloured wood, but even those are almost weightless.

"Each person has their own style," Zainab says to Farwa. "Art is as different as people are. It would be a boring world if we were all the same."

"Your mother's right," I say to Farwa, taking the pictures from Zainab and beginning to look through them. Each tiny painting is the same garden, but from a different angle. One is a close-up of the bottle-green leaves of the fig tree. Another is a chair and a table, with a small bowl of olives. Another is a lizard, its body twisting in movement as it scurries up a wall.

"Are they all of your garden?"

"Yes. I don't have photos, so I paint it while I still have memories."

"Where did you live?" I ask her.

"Basra," she says.

"I have a friend from there," I say. At least I think I do, but there is still no news of Ali. Something is wrong. It shouldn't be this hard to find him.

Hassan's eyes flick up at my response. I catch his eye and he looks down again quickly, but I can tell it got his interest.

"You have a friend from Basra? Really? Oh my god, that's so cool," says Farwa. "How did you meet him? Or her? Is it someone in America?"

"Actually, I used to live in Iraq. In Baghdad," I tell her. I like the way she bubbles with questions and curiosity.

"What, seriously? Wow. But you're British right? Why were you there?"

"I was there for work," I explain. "I worked in immigration. Helping people to leave."

"People like us?"

"Well, I don't know the exact details of your family, but I did help Iraqis move to the US."

"We moved to Jordan first," Farwa says, "then here." That I knew. Noor broadly filled me in with the family's story before I came to meet Zainab. She said that Haider, Zainab's husband, was a businessman in Iraq. After the invasion, he won a contract providing logistical support to coalition troops. Noor said she didn't know exactly what that meant, but she understood that "big bucks" were involved. From what Noor had been told, for a few years the going was good, but then Haider began to receive threats, apparently linked to a soured relationship with an old business associate. The family applied to move to the US, but, of course, the visa process was slow, and when the threats kept coming, Haider decided it was safer to move his family to Jordan first, where they spent the next three years in limbo.

"Did you like Jordan?" I ask Farwa. She shrugs.

"I liked Iraq more. It's where my friends were."

I continue to look through the paintings Zainab handed me. There are so many of them. Fragments of the same garden, over and over and over again. A ginger cat. Weeds growing between paving slabs. The evening light. Endless attempts to capture a home that exists only in her memory.

"Have you painted all of these since arriving?" I ask her.

"No, I did some of them in Jordan."

"I love them, but I have to ask, why do you paint them so small?" I hold one flat on my hand and it fits my palm almost exactly.

"I have learnt only to create things that can be carried with me," she said. I imagine Zainab filling a suitcase, the taxi arriving in the middle of the night, the children being roused and piled into the waiting vehicle while still half-asleep.

"What about now you are here?" I ask. "Do you expect to move again?"

"I hope not," she says. "But if we do, I will be ready."

I think about my own home. The love atlas, the books on the shelf, my mother's painting. How easy would it be for me to pack up and leave? What would I take, if I could take almost nothing?

I hear the front door opening and closing. It must be Zainab's husband returning from his job as a UPS delivery driver.

"It's me. I'm going to shower and pray, then go out for coffee," he shouts in Arabic.

"We have a guest, my love," Zainab replies to him in English.

"Who?" he shouts back in Arabic, then appears at the living room door. When he sees me, he moves backwards slightly, shielding his brown uniform behind the door frame, then appears to think better of it and strides into the room with his hand outstretched.

"Hi, I am Haider. Nice to meet you," he says. "Welcome to our home."

"Hi, I'm Emma. Good to meet you too," I reply, standing up to take his hand.

"Emma is the lady from art group that I told you about," says Zainab.

"Right. The one who was in Iraq," Haider says, holding my gaze in a way that seems almost challenging. Defiant. I'd met plenty of men like this through my job in Baghdad.

Men who had been rich and powerful, and resented that they had to look to people like me for help.

"Indeed. Well, I don't want to keep you from your coffee. I'm sure we'll meet some other time," I say. Surprise and then suspicion flash quickly across his face.

"You understand Arabic?" he says to me.

"A little," I say. He does not need to know how much.

"Well, until next time, Emma," he says. "Enjoy your time in my home."

He ruffles Farwa's hair briefly and walks out.

I return to the sofa. I see Zainab looking at me, lips pushed together. I want to tell her that I am used to men like Haider, he is what I expected, but that doesn't seem appropriate.

"So now I've met the whole family," I say with a smile. Her face relaxes.

Farwa, who was silent the whole time her father was in the room, starts talking again.

"So why did you come to America, Emma?" she says.

"Mrs McLaughlin," Zainab corrects her.

"Emma is fine," I say. I want them to be comfortable with me. All of them. "Ah, that's a bit of a long story. I fell in love."

"Ooooh, tell us!" says Farwa excitedly.

Hassan, at the table, rolls his eyes.

"Mum, can I go upstairs to use the computer?" he says.

"Hassan, we have a guest. You're always on that thing," she scolds him.

"No, it's fine, really," I tell her.

Zainab looks at him crossly, but then she dips her head slightly and at the signal he pushes back from the table.

"Bye, Mrs McLaughlin," he says and then I hear him leaping up the stairs two at a time.

"Honestly, I don't know what he does on that computer so much of the time. He always wants to be shut away in front of a screen."

"He's a teenage boy," I shrug. "I think it's pretty normal."

"Em—, I mean Mrs McLaughlin. Can you tell me and Mama your story now?" says Farwa, squeezing my leg to move my focus away from her brother.

So I tell them. I tell them the story of Adam and Emma. Of Ameena and Ali. I tell them about Adam and how he wanted to help, and how I fell in love with an American soldier when it was the last thing I thought would happen to me out there. How I stayed there after he came back. How now I am here and he is back there. Farwa is enrapt throughout the story.

"What about Ameena and Ali? Where are they now?" she asks.

"Well…" I pause. "Ameena is in the States but Ali, I don't know…"

Zainab watches me intently. She notices something in my reference that Farwa doesn't. Farwa is too young.

"Have you been to see Ameena since you arrived?"

"Not yet," I say. In truth, it hadn't even occurred to me. The "USA" that I helped Iraqis get to feels like a different "USA" to the one I live in. The same way that the Iraq that leaves the lips of the military wives is different to the country where I lived and worked for three years.

"And Mr McLaughlin? When does he come back?"

"I don't know," I reply. "Not yet. But I'm sure he'll want to meet you all when he does."

"*Inshallah* he will arrive back safely," Zainab says, taking my hand and holding it tightly between hers. I look down at her hands. The slightly wrinkled skin, the polished nails, the gold wedding band. They are strong.

I blink back the tears that have unexpectedly filled my eyes.

32

Subject:
Hey. Not sure how to tell you this Em. I finally got news
on Ali. He was killed in February. He went to work with
a different unit and just didn't turn up one day. Someone
gave his mother compensation but no one wrote down
contact details so I don't know how to find her. Fucking
idiots.
Adam

Subject: Re:
Adam. Shit, no, that's awful. I'm so sorry. Are you okay?
Can you call me? Love you. Emma x

Subject: Re:
Sorry babe. I'd rather not talk right now. Don't worry
about me – I'm fine. I'll Skype you later in the week.
Adam

Subject: Re:
Okay. Stay safe. I love you.

Is that what he wanted to tell me?

I spend the afternoon moving listlessly around the house.
I wipe the work surfaces and the sink, but Ali's voice fills
my mind. I wonder whether he knew this was coming and

whether someone, anyone, could have done more. I try to breathe. To calm my thoughts. I vacuum the floor and try to drown out the voice in my head that says you should have known. You should have helped him. You should have stayed.

Has Adam known this since the night of Sally's party?

I want to call someone, to be comforted myself. But Ali is Iraqi. Kate won't understand. Penny will give me a hug and tell me to pray. Zainab will understand but she will understand too well and I am supposed to be helping her to settle in. Not dredging up old trauma. There is no one to call, so I must do something else.

I decide to try yoga. It has been a long time since I have moved my body through these routines. I first tried yoga at the suggestion of a therapist I spoke to after what happened to Sampath. I had a couple of counselling sessions with her. Talked over what had happened; how to deal with the moments of panic that would hit me unexpectedly in the gym or the chow hall afterwards. She taught me breathing exercises. Tapping techniques. Suggested yoga. We talked about Sampath, about the other stories I heard on a daily basis, but then she started to ask questions about my dad and that was too much for me so I didn't have the sessions any longer. Not until the other thing that happened anyway.

I retrieve my mat from the garage and roll it out in the back garden. I look around me, at the decking and the flower beds and the large safe-looking houses that look out onto wide tree-lined roads. Ali's death took place in a different world, a world where I once was and Adam is now. I don't know whether real life is here or over there.

I move through the positions and I start to sweat. My limbs are tight from sitting tensed in front of the emails. My chest is tight from what I have been told. I try to empty my mind, but it darts between Colorado and Baghdad. Jessica the aerobics instructor also led the yoga class on the IZ. I imagine her now in her neon Lycra and bright headband, guiding me through the routines. But then for a second Jessica flickers to Sally, and Sally is pressed up against the man under the flashing lights. I force my mind back to Jessica. I focus only on my body and my breathing. But now we are in Child's Pose with our bodies sinking into the ground and I see Ali beside me. He is on his knees too, his forehead on the floor, his body folded in prayer.

Jessica's voice continues to guide me through the breathing exercise.

Inhale slowly, she says. *Exhale.*

In breath number one, Ali gets home and his mother is at the door. She clasps his face between the palms of her gnarled hands. They called again, she says. They called and said they have a bullet for each of us. He takes her hands and kisses them, then presses them to his forehead. Do not worry Mama, he says. They just want to scare us. The lie is heavy as he tells it. They called him too.

Inhale.

Exhale.

In breath number two, Ali kisses his mother goodbye as he leaves for work. He locks the tall metal gate behind him and waves a greeting to his neighbour, who is washing dust away from the front of her house with a hose and broom. A vegetable truck crawls slowly past, laden with peppers and onions and the fat purple figs that are now in season. The seller honks his horn and shouts out his wares. Ali puts his key in the car door. He does not see the man emerge from around the corner, a dark metal object in his hand. His neighbour drops her broom and screams. His mother hears the shot as she rinses soapsuds from a dish at the sink. Dirty water runs down the gutter and mixes with Ali's blood.

Inhale.

Exhale.

In breath number three, he is on his way home. The traffic is bad and the journey is taking longer than usual. He cracks a sunflower seed between his teeth and extracts its fleshy centre with a deft flick of the tongue. His father's old prayer beads hang from the mirror and glint red in the sun. A Tamer Hosny song plays on the radio, the same one that I have as my ringtone. He winds down his window and lights a cigarette.

The traffic is caused by a temporary checkpoint up ahead. When he reaches it, they check his ID and pull him over to the side of the road. An officer leans into the vehicle to talk to him. Ali realises too late that the checkpoint is a fake. The policeman isn't real.

Inhale.

Exhale.

In breath number four, Ali is in a dark room. His hands are tied behind the back of the wooden chair he sits on. His head is bowed forwards and there is a trail of dried blood from his ear. The door opens and closes but Ali does not look up. He knows what comes next.

Inhale.

Exhale.

Inhale.

Exhale.

In this breath, the old woman with the gnarled hands is at the gate of the US base. She tries to talk to guards who do not understand her language. Their eyes are hidden behind dark sunglasses. She cries tears of frustration and they do not understand her, but she won't go away, so an interpreter is called. The interpreter knew Ali. He tries to comfort her with quick, low words and watches on uncomfortably as she is searched before being let onto the base.

They take her to a small room and give her a cold bottle of water. Droplets gather on the outside of the bottle. A senior looking soldier comes in and is unsure whether or not it is appropriate to shake her hand.

Dollar bills are counted across the desk. She takes them and her cheeks burn with anger and shame. She shoves the money into her bag and exits the base. She stands in a dusty road and the sun beats down and she wonders what happens now. She must find a way to get word to Ameena. Ameena must know.

Inhale.

Exhale.

And Adam?

Inhale.

Exhale.

Adam sits on his bed in a bare room. There is the distant sound of shooting from the PlayStation downstairs. Occasionally there is a whoop or a frustrated curse. He is alone. He picks up his phone. Puts it down. Picks it up again. He types.

Exhale.

Exhale.

Exhale.

Hey. Are you around for Skype?

I am in front of the mirror in a silk blouse. I am checking my make-up in the mirror. *Just heading downtown with the team wives.* My phone is in my bag and the door is shutting behind me.

Inhale.

With this breath, I open my eyes quickly. Stand up. Get off the mat. I do not know what I am doing here, practising yoga in my garden in Colorado while the birds are singing and Ali is dead. I feel helpless. Useless. This is not me.

33

The next few days are unsettling. Surreal. Everything is blurred around the edges, as if I am not inhabiting myself but watching my body go through the motions of living. I am detached from Ali's death by both time and space. I do not know how to inhabit this sadness. It fills my bones and my body aches and I am heavy with grief.

Eventually I send Kate a message to tell her what happened. I need to tell someone.

My father died when I was fifteen. So many people came to the funeral that some had to stand at the back of the church. My dad hadn't been inside a church since Rebecca's christening, but he knew it was what my mother wanted and funerals are for the living, not the dead.

I was an awkward, quiet teenager at the time. I stood glued to Rebecca's side as strangers came to offer their condolences. It was Rebecca who thanked them. Even though she was younger, she was always better at that kind of thing.

When the illness took hold of my father, everything changed. He cut back his hours at the hospital and eventually didn't go in at all. He moved into the spare room, lying propped up on pillows so that he could see the fields. His bones became visible and his hair thinned and his body was racked by a deep persistent cough.

I started to avoid the spare bedroom. I would get dressed

quickly in the morning and sneak out to school in the hope he would not wake. Sometimes he would hear me and call me in to say goodbye. I would try not to flinch as he pulled me in for a kiss and I felt the angle of his cheekbone against my fleshy cheek.

When he tried to be cheerful, I got angry with him.

"How can you smile when you are going to leave us?" I asked one morning.

When he was sad or desperate, I got angry too.

"You're supposed to be the strong one," I said. "You're not supposed to cry."

If you thought that being a doctor would prepare you for your own mortality, you are wrong. In the months before his death, I woke at night to the sound of him begging and bargaining with a God he had never believed in. I remember the strange feeling of being repulsed by his weakness and an intense shame that I could feel that way.

"Go in and see him," urged my mother continually. "He's still your dad."

While I went in less and less, Rebecca was the opposite. She had to be prised away from his side to eat meals and go to school. The closer she got, the further I withdrew. After the fear came silence. The nocturnal bargaining stopped. Rebecca told me he was at peace with his fate in the last few weeks. She would know better than I.

The day that he died, I did not see him at all. He called to me as I was at the top of the stairs, although it was barely a whisper by that point.

"Em. Emsie, come here."

"Can't, Dad, gotta go. Late for school," I yelled and rushed down the stairs and out of the door.

My mum turned up at my classroom just before lunchtime. I saw her pale face through the criss-crossed pattern in the small pane of our classroom door. She didn't need to tell me what had happened, she just hugged me tightly and guided us to the car. The funeral was a week later.

*

I never found out whether there was a funeral for Sampath in Sri Lanka. Perhaps there was some kind of service in his village, where people who hadn't seen him for four years wept as they wondered how they would afford to live without the money he sent home.

Jessica held a special aerobics class with a playlist of his favourite songs, but our hearts weren't really in it. The room felt more stifling than usual. One of the PSDs suggested we have a drink for him in Baghdaddy's, but that didn't seem right either. He never would have been able to go in there himself. Eventually someone in Green Beans put a framed photo of him on the counter, a grainy photo enlarged from his ID badge. It was a constant reminder of how little we knew him.

I may never know whether Ali had a funeral either. I don't even know whether there was a body to bury, whether anything was returned to his family to be bathed and enshrouded and laid in the ground facing Mecca. I wonder what Ameena did, on the other side of the ocean, when she found out. If she found out at all.

I think of all the women in the art group. Noor, Afsoon, Hope, Paz. I wonder who they have lost along the way and the different shades of grief they have traversed. It is built up, generation after generation. Layers of sediment and trauma are built into their foundations. The stories are passed down through families and as people move across borders and oceans they are ripped from their roots. A violent removal. They have all lived a thousand deaths.

Does Adam feel like we failed Ali too? If I had been in Iraq, at least I would have known about his application. Perhaps I could have pushed it through. If Adam had been there, perhaps the background checks and recommendations would have been quicker. But we weren't. We were both in Colorado.

"You can't save them all, Emma."

That was the advice that my boss Nigel gave me on the first day of my job in Baghdad.

"You can't save them all. All you can do is record their story in the most accurate, honest and detailed way possible, then pray to God that the system doesn't fail them."

Nigel's words resonated with me because I'd heard them before.

"You can't save them all, dear." My mother said those same words to my father one evening when I was a child. He was sat in his favourite chair with a tumbler of whisky in one hand while the other rubbed at his forehead. I was sat on the living room floor doing homework, but Mum told me to go upstairs for a while. I sat on the staircase, leaning against the banister and picking at the brownish carpet while I listened to find out what was wrong.

"You did your best, Bill," she said. "I'm sure of it. You can't carry them all with you." But he never did get over the patients he lost.

As I got older, I thought of my mum's comments and imagined my father walking around followed by the figures of all his patients who had died. Some held his hands. Others clung to the back of his shirt. The youngest was a girl who always sat on his shoulders, the girl he lost the day he drank whisky in the living room. When they diagnosed him, I wondered whether the ghosts had just become too heavy.

Until Iraq, I didn't fully understand how he felt, but now I do. I carry ghosts with me. Adam does too. Ali will forever walk beside us both.

There was a woman who I couldn't save not long before I left Iraq. I shouldn't have still been there at that point. It was after the bar incident and I wasn't dealing with anything well, but I was stubborn. I didn't want one person's actions to drive me out of the country.

Her name was Dina Al Wazzan. When I interviewed her, she was an intelligent, nervous young woman whose mannerisms reminded me of Ameena. She didn't have a son, but two young daughters. She came to the interview with both of her parents. The war had left her without a husband.

Dina worked as a journalist at one of the Iraqi television stations that was funded by the US. I recognised her face from the news channel we sometimes had on in the office.

I recorded her story as Nigel had instructed me to on that first day – accurately, honestly and with as much detail as possible. I interviewed her and her parents. I took down biometric data. I listened to her talk about the threats she had received. She recounted the ways they said they would kill her, each in a level of detail that made my stomach churn. She said it all without emotion, as if she were at work, on camera, reporting on the victims of the latest attack. It was only her mother who cried.

When I said goodbye to her that day, I went straight to my manager, by that time a man called Rick, and asked for permission to expedite the request. She was a single mother with a high-risk profession. He said no.

"We have lots of applications from single mothers at the moment, Emma, we can't just expedite them all. She still has both parents. She's not completely alone." I argued and argued, but Rick stood firm. On the scale of desperation, she was not desperate enough.

If Dina hadn't been a TV journalist, I might never have found out that she had been killed. She would have got through the background checks fine, perhaps, but then missed her follow-up interview. I might have checked the database and seen "did not attend" and wondered what happened, but I would never have known.

As it was, I did find out, just a few weeks later.

I was in the office at the time and happened to glance up at the television screen on the back wall just as her photo was shown. The first thing I saw was a professional portrait of her in a dark blue blazer and cream blouse. She was wearing thick eyeliner and a dark lipstick that made her face look much harder than the woman I had interviewed. There was a microphone in her hand.

"Turn up the volume!" I said, moving closer to the TV.

Hana and Mohammed looked up, surprised.

"What's happened? Is she dead?" I asked.

"Who? Dina al Wazzan?" Hana said.

I nodded without taking my eyes off the television screen, which was now a montage of her major reporting moments.

"Yeah, they found her body dumped last night. She's been missing for a week," Hana said. The montage was over and now replaced by a close-up photo of her body and clear gunshot wounds. I sometimes forgot that Iraqis were used to graphic footage of murders and attacks. The television stations didn't cater to the sensibilities of western audiences.

"Shit," I said, turning away from the TV, hand over my mouth. "Shit."

"Did you know her or something?" asked Mohammed.

"I interviewed her here," I said. "She knew they were going to kill her and she was trying to get out."

That night was one of the worst I had in Baghdad. I went straight to my room after work. I hadn't been to the bar much since the incident anyway.

I lay on my bed in silence and every time I closed my eyes I saw her. My thoughts were like the montage on the news, except now the montage was narrated by her steady modulated voice. She talked me again and again through what they had threatened to do to her. The images flickered and followed her narration in detail. Again and again, I saw all the ways they told her she would die.

I called Adam. Not on Skype but on his mobile. He was the other side of the world, organising equipment for team training that was coming up.

When he answered the phone, I cried at the sound of his voice.

"Emma, is that you? Emma – God, are you okay? Has something happened? What's wrong?"

"We lost her," I cried. "A woman came in and I interviewed her and it all took too long and now she's dead."

"Oh, Em, I'm so sorry," he said. "Babe, I'm sure you did everything you could. I know how you feel. I get it, I really do. Let me go upstairs and find a computer I can Skype you from. We'll talk it through. You'll be okay, Em, you really will. I love you."

I cried to Adam over Dina, but I never cried to my mother after my father died. Rebecca and my mother wrapped themselves in their grief. They let themselves break down, come undone. They stayed at home and clung to each other while I dreamed that their tears flooded the house and took us all under. I decided that I needed to be strong.

I was being strong when I studied hard at school, passed my exams, got a place at university. I was being strong when I went off to study a Bachelor's and a Master's, while Rebecca stayed at home. She trained at a local beauty salon, eventually set up her own business, stayed and supported my mum. I was being strong, but the thing about letting yourself break is that afterwards you can be pieced back together. My mother and Rebecca broke and began to heal. My fractures and cracks just crept deeper.

I thought I was being strong when I left altogether. When I came to Iraq.

It is different when I go home now. Each time, something more has changed. My mother decorated the kitchen and painted over the spot where Rebecca and I marked our heights in pencil as we grew. Rebecca's husband stores his tools where my father's fishing equipment used to be. My father's chair has been replaced with a trunk of toys for Sophie's visits.

"This isn't a doll's house, Emma," Rebecca argued. "You can't expect us to stay exactly where you left us, waiting just in case you ever choose us instead of them."

I knew it hurt my mother that I left.

"It's what your father would have wanted," she said. But

that was just it. I was more like my father than Rebecca, who took after our mother. So I knew that when I went back it was like a little bit of him had returned to her. I hated that responsibility and I hated that I was keeping him from her.

But now Rebecca and my mother are okay. As they have pieced themselves back together, they have found a way to fill the gaps left by my father, and now the gaps left by me too. I do not know how to find my place between them again.

My phone beeps, dragging me out of my thoughts. For a moment I have the strange hope that it is my family. I check my phone and try to ignore the mild disappointment I feel when I see it is Kate replying to my earlier message.

Oh, that sucks about the 'terp, Em. Sorry. Let me know if you need anything.

I wait for Adam to get in touch, but still there is nothing.

34

Subject: I miss you
Hey Em,
Sorry for not emailing for a couple of days – work stuff came up. It's been a pretty frustrating week. The usual bullshit. I'm sorry I haven't been very communicative. It's not that I don't want to talk, I just don't really have anything to say. Nothing positive anyway, not after what happened. I can't wait to be out of this place and back with you.
I miss you Emma,
Adam

Last night I dreamt that he was here. He smiled at me and I saw the slight angle of his left front tooth. He brushed a strand of hair from my face. I touched my fingertips to the tiny scar on his brow.

Last night I dreamt that he was here. I felt his skin against mine. The muscles of his back moved under the palms of my hands. His breath was warm on my neck.

Last night I dreamt that he was here and the nagging emptiness that has shared my bed for months was gone. The world folded and the oceans were crushed and mountains rose up from the plains and the land brought us closer together.

Sometimes it is harder to wake up alone after the promise of him, than when I remember in my dreams that he is not here.

35

I sit on the floor of the living room, in the same spot where we had the picnic before he left. Next to me is a large empty mason jar. I am surrounded by pieces. Fragments. Parts. Bits of stone and rock, tile, glass that has rounded at the edges. They are beiges and browns and reds and greens and the occasional sliver of blue.

Each piece holds a memory. I pick them up one at a time and turn them between my fingers. I twist them this way and that. I test the soft flesh of my thumb against their edges. I tease out their stories.

Here is the piece I picked up at the palace the day that Adam proposed. Here is the top of the Incline. Here is outside of the gym the day Sampath died.

I sit like this every evening now. I push the pieces around me into different shapes and formations, but always they seem to resist. I am not sure what I am hoping for, but when they are ready I will know.

This evening, tired and frustrated, I gather them between my palms and return them to the jar. I don't know if it is the pieces that are not ready or me.

36

I need to get out of my head. Since the news of Ali's death, things have got worse. I'm panicking more. It's like a trigger. It's set me off.

I Skyped with Adam a few days ago. He was ten minutes late to the call. At first I thought he could still be out working. Then I wondered if there was a sandstorm, the thick kind that gets in your eyes and ears and interferes with the internet. Or maybe there was a power cut and the generator hadn't come on. Or maybe he just didn't want to talk about the desert and the dust and eating the same meals every day.

But then I thought about other explanations too. In these other explanations, hot metal ripped through his body. An explosion tore him into a thousand pieces. Crimson blood soaked into the dry ground. A black hood made the night even darker.

When Adam finally came on Skype, he was fine. I acted like I was fine too.

"So how are things? What's up with you?" he asked.

"Not much," I replied. "What about you?"

"Same shit, different day," he said.

We do not talk about Ali, although his absence fills every conversation. We do not talk about Adam's homecoming, although I know the date must be getting closer.

I need to get out of my head, so I message Kate again.

Hey. Can I come and hang out?

The reply comes quickly.

Sure. Come on over!

When I get to Kate's house, she ushers me inside with a voice that is quieter than normal.

"We're just about to have story time," she says. "Dave doesn't get to read Noah's bedtime story because of the time difference, so sometimes we have one at Dave's bedtime instead."

I follow Kate to the living room, where I see Noah curled up on the sofa holding a teddy bear wearing a military uniform with a tag saying *Jenkins*. The laptop is open in front of him and I can make out the familiar blue window of Skype.

"Want to join us?" asks Kate.

"Are you sure? I don't want to interrupt. I can just wait in the kitchen or—"

"Don't be silly. Noah will love it," she says.

I look over to where he is waiting patiently. I don't think I've ever seen him sit still for this long.

"Hey, Noah, do you think Emma should join us for story time too?"

He nods, but doesn't take his eyes off the laptop.

I sit down on the sofa next to him and Kate sits the other side. It is the low deep kind of sofa that is made exactly for snuggling up with families.

Dave calls and Kate presses accept.

"Daddy!" Noah squeals, now sitting upright.

"Hey bud!" says Dave, his face appearing in front of us. "How're you? And let me see the bump – where's my kiddie number two?"

"Hi, sweetie," says Kate, as Noah kneels up next to her and puts both hands on the bulge of her stomach for his dad to see. "You've got a bit of an audience for story time today."

The video must have just loaded at his end.

"Oh, hi Emma! What's up?"

It is odd to be sat on Dave's sofa talking to him while he is in Iraq. I feel like I have been let in on an intimate routine.

"Hey Dave. I hope you don't mind me joining you."

"Are you kidding me?" he says. "It's great to see you! Hell, if I'd have known, I would have got Adam in here too and he could have helped me out with the voices!"

"My bad, I'll tell you in advance next time," says Kate.

I laugh. I don't know Dave well, but whenever I have spoken to him he has always put me completely at ease. There's something reassuring about him. It makes you want to confide in him, even though he's an enormous hulk of an SF guy. Really, he's a bit of a teddy bear himself.

Adam once told me that when Dave thinks one of his team needs to talk he opens a packet of Skittles and starts to sort them by colour. He has a theory that people concentrate on the colours and not the talking, so when he starts asking questions, people answer honestly without realising.

"I shit you not. It works," Adam said. "That's why Dave puts on so much weight during deployments. He probably gets through at least ten packets of Skittles a day."

"Okay, buddy, I've got a good book for you today," Dave says. He disappears off camera for a second and reappears wearing an eyepatch and holding a book called *The Homesick Pirate*. Noah squeals again. Pirates are his favourite. Kate looks over his head and mouths "Amazon" at me. I can't imagine what deployments must have been like before APO addresses and online shopping.

Dave starts reading the story. It is about a pirate who leaves his family behind to go on adventures. He meets mermaids and battles giant squid and finds hidden treasure, but each night he looks up at the stars and thinks about his family back home. Dave puts on an impressive performance as a pirate and occasionally adds in a few of his own "Arrrr, me hearty" and "Shiver me timbers" for good measure. I suspect he has been practising.

During the story, Noah moves from his position in the centre of the sofa and crawls onto my lap. He sits resting his head back against my chest, with the bear under one arm. I notice Dave miss a beat in the story as he and Kate exchange glances. Noah is a friendly child, but I've never seen him be particularly affectionate with anyone other than Kate.

At first I sit stiffly, scared that any movement will send him back to the middle of the sofa, but then I relax a bit and put an arm around him. His head droops to one side, leaning against my arm. Kate gives me a smile.

By the end of the book, when the pirate comes home to be reunited with his family, I am blinking rapidly. I'm pretty sure Kate is too. Dave takes off the eyepatch and gives us a wink.

I make the excuse of going to make coffee to give the three of them some time together.

"I really enjoyed that, Dave," I say as I get up.

"I can't believe Adam hasn't been reading you any bedtime stories," he jokes. "I'm going to have serious words with that man."

I laugh.

"Please do. I've been missing out!"

I go to the kitchen and from there hear the low murmur of Kate and Dave's voices, and the occasional giggle from Noah. Eventually Kate comes into the kitchen. Noah is lying on the sofa watching a DVD.

"The story makes him sleepy, even though it's not his bedtime. It gives me peace for an hour or so."

"That was really lovely, Kate," I say. "Thanks for letting me be there."

"It's no big deal," she laughs. "We do what we can with the distance. Some days Dave makes up his own stories. You should be here for one of those!"

I pour out coffee for me and fruit tea for Kate. I am as at home in her kitchen now as I am in my own.

"So how are you, anyway?" she asks. "I'm so sorry about the 'terp again, Emma, it must have been rough."

"It was," I say. "I think Adam's taken it badly."

"I told Dave to keep an eye on him. He said he didn't know anything about it but that Adam had seemed a bit quiet. What about you though? Didn't you know the guy too?"

"Yeah, not as well as Adam. Ali saved his life—"

"Shit."

"Yeah. I met his cousin too. I helped out with her visa application."

"Visa? Is she in the States now?"

"Yes, although I don't know where... We're not in touch," I say.

"Have you told Adam about your mentoring thing yet?" she asks.

"No," I say, hoping that I don't sound too defensive. "I haven't really had the chance, not with everything else that's going on."

"Sure," says Kate.

I've barely mentioned the mentoring to Kate. Since our conversation in the hospital, I've realised it's not something I can share with her. It's fine, I tell myself. We share different parts of ourselves with different people.

She stops and looks up at me.

"God, I can't wait for them to get back."

"Me neither," I say.

"I've always hated being away from him. You know, after the summer Dave and I got together, my parents had to physically force me to go back to college."

"But weren't you at high school together?" I ask.

"Yeah, but there were four years between us. I was friends with his sister and we were just kids when Dave left school and joined up. Then I came home the first summer of my physiotherapy degree and he was just back from the Q course. There were only two bars in town and we both wound up in the same one. He came over and said hi – didn't even realise who I was – and, well, that was it."

"Do you have any plans for when he gets back?" I ask.

"Not this time. He's usually pretty tired for the first week, so I think we'll just hang out at home so he can spend time with Noah before the chaos of this little girl's arrival." She runs a hand over her stomach. "But once he's out of the army… That part I have been planning. Summer hiking in Yosemite, a road trip through the Adirondacks in fall, maybe when the kiddos are grown up we'll finally make it to Europe. He always promised me that one day we'd eat pastries under the Eiffel Tower…" She drifts off for a second and I smile. "What about you? Did you find a homecoming outfit in the end?" she asks.

"Not yet," I say.

"Whatever it is, just make sure it's comfortable," she says. "They never get back when they say they will and there's nothing worse than hanging around for hours in a tiny skirt and too much mascara. I learnt that the hard way first time round."

I had been to Denver to check out the shops there. It wasn't even about the homecoming outfit really. It was just a way to try keep my mind off other things. Ali's death. Adam's silence. The latest unanswered job application.

I spent the day in Denver wandering around the shops and becoming increasingly frustrated. Nothing looked right. Nothing looked like me.

I dropped the last dress on the changing room floor and stood in front of the mirror, under the too-bright lights. I stared at my body and wondered what Adam would think when he saw it too. I looked at the tan line on my legs from a summer of sitting in the garden in shorts. I looked at the curve of my waist and the spot where he would rest a hand. Then I looked at the freckles on my torso that he used to join up with his finger while we lay in bed. I ran my fingertips over the soft flesh where my bra met my breast and tried to imagine how it would feel to have my skin under his. I let the back of my hand brush lightly down my belly, past my navel, skimming tiny hairs like the fuzz of a peach.

"I'm going to make some lunch for Noah. Do you want to join us?" Kate asks, opening the fridge.

"No thanks. I'd better go. I have the afternoon shift in the art shop."

"Are we still on for Thursday?" she asks. Thursday is

Thanksgiving. Despite the circumstances, I am looking forward to it. It was always a big deal in Baghdad. The chow hall would be decorated with paper streamers and the centrepiece would be a giant turkey-shaped cake.

"Definitely. I'm making mashed sweet potato, green bean casserole and some kind of English dessert, right?" I say. "Those seem hard to mess up."

"Exactly. And I will aim to provide an edible turkey," says Kate. She told me previously that Dave was famously talented at cooking the turkey, thanks to a technique his grandmother taught him, so it's usually his responsibility. "If it all goes wrong we'll order in a pizza and shove some turkey strips on top," Kate says.

"I'm sure it will be great," I say, picking up my bag and jacket that is hung over a kitchen stool. "Okay, enjoy lunch. And see you for our feast on Thursday. Give me a call if there's anything else you want me to bring."

37

Each night, I lie in bed and wonder if the final mission is today. It has become an obsession. It is the thing that stands between Adam and coming home. I know we are almost there.

Tonight in my imagination, Adam and Dave and the other men prepare for the mission in the team room. They stand around the table doing final checks on equipment. The old fridge that buzzes and flickers. They all know the plan. They have run through it countless times, played out all possibilities. They are ready.

There will be no Iraqi forces with them this time. It is just Adam and his team. On previous attempts the Iraqi Special Forces led the way and, technically speaking, this time should be the same. But time is running out and someone high up has decided to look the other way. As long as the mission is a success, the head will stay turned. If something goes wrong, who knows.

Adrenaline buzzes through them. No one wants to go home unsuccessful. It will hang over them whenever they think about this deployment, or all of their deployments, to Iraq.

"Okay," says Dave. "This is it. This is our last chance. I need your heads to be here and only here. It sucks that we'll miss Thanksgiving, but forget about that. I don't wanna have to tell your family you got shot by some Haji because you were pissed about missing the turkey."

"I'm not complaining," says Ramirez. "My wife's turkey is dry as shit and we have to have her whole goddamn family over each year."

A few guys laugh.

"There you go then. Count your blessings," says Dave.

At zero one hundred hours, the team load up into their vehicles. They each have their own routine, developed over countless missions and deployments. If you do a particular thing and everyone comes home safe, you damn well keep doing it. Ramirez wears his socks inside out. Lee cracks his knuckles one at a time, always left to right. Riley takes out a photo of his family and says a quick prayer, then stuffs it into his helmet. Adam won't tell me what he does himself, in case telling me changes anything.

The men enter the Humvees in the same order they always do. Dave slaps each of his team hard on the backplate of their body armour as they pass, then he climbs into the front seat. Adam says Dave has never been one to lead from the back.

The vehicles leave the compound and the men are out in Baghdad now. They head to the location they marked with a drawing pin on a map back on base. The lights on the vehicles remain off. They wear night-vision goggles that turn the black into shades of chemical green, like a video game. Heavy metal blasts through their headsets. The Humvee interior smells of sweat and cheap energy drinks.

Ramirez moves his head to the deep beat of the song, but Adam is motionless. He goes through the mission, the movements, the plan. I do not exist to him now. Nothing exists except the hours ahead.

The streets are empty, the city's inhabitants under curfew. The only movement the men see is dogs, scrounging for food among the trash at an hour when they are safe from being pelted with stones.

As they pass one building, Adam glimpses a young man, silhouetted against the flickering images of a television. He lowers a shisha pipe from his mouth and exhales slowly.

Smoke curls above his head, lit up by the changing colours from a television screen. Then he is gone.

They get closer. The houses are poorer now, the streets more potholed. Everything is soaked in darkness. The rolling blackouts hit this area at this time of night and no one in the neighbourhood has enough money for a generator. It is as they planned.

The men stop 200 metres from the target house. Some stay in the vehicles and some move towards the building on foot. Every piece of equipment is secured tightly to their bodies. The only sound they make is the light shuffle of boots on gravel, wet from the November rain. There is nowhere for the water to go so it collects in dips and depressions and transforms into a thick sticky mud that weighs the city down.

They get to the building and some of the men peel off, moving round to the back of the house. Dave crouches behind a wall at the front of the building, Adam squats behind him, followed by Lee. Everyone is in position.

Dave turns and motions the countdown.

Three.

Two.

One.

MOVE.

Dave's boot meets with the door, slamming it inwards. He stands to one side and Adam moves past him, runs up the stairs and clears one room, then the next. White lights and lasers sweep around in search of danger. More boots split off into different parts of the house.

There is a bedroom. A bed. A young woman screams and a man reaches for his gun, but it is too late. Ramirez pulls the man out of the bed, onto the floor. Adam puts a knee on his back, fastens the handcuffs.

In the room that Lee is in a child cries out. The man in handcuffs hears him and struggles. The child is comforted by an elderly woman, who holds his face close to hers. She wraps a blanket around them both, then rubs his back with arthritic

217

fingers. She looks at the solider guarding the entrance to the room. He wears a helmet and goggles and black fatigues like ISOF, but when he speaks to her the words are foreign. She cannot imagine a human inside the uniform.

Back in the first bedroom, an interpreter reads out a warrant for the man's arrest, written by a Baghdadi judge. The man has a dark moustache and greying chest hair that protrudes from under his vest. He has baggy underwear and bare feet and a face that is familiar to everyone on the team. They have searched for it for seven months. The man with the familiar face spits on the floor by Adam's boot, but Adam does not react. His job is done.

Now, Adam and his men are back in their vehicles. The prisoner is loaded up, ready to be handed over to the detention facility back at base. They return with their victory song booming through the sound system. Adam lets out a long breath and finally allows his mind to drift to the end of the deployment, to Colorado, to me.

Dave yells over the music on the headsets.

"Good work, guys, now let's get the fuck home. My wife will kill me if that baby arrives before I do."

Every night, I imagine a different version of the mission. Every night, it is a different collage of news stories and movies and things he has said after a drink. But the one thing that remains the same is that each night is a success; they all come home safely. So close to the end, I cannot let myself imagine it any other way.

38

While I am at the art shop I get a text from Zainab. *Hi Emma. Is there any chance you could come over this evening?*

I sense the tension in Zainab's house as soon as I arrive. She shows me into the living room and Farwa gives me a smile and a little wave from the sofa, but does not jump up to show me her homework or tell me about the new style she has learnt for braiding her hair. Zainab shifts around. I have not been to see them in the week since Ali's death and I wonder what has happened.

"Do you want to come through to the kitchen?" Zainab asks, changing her mind about the location.

"Sure," I say. Farwa watches us as we leave the room.

In the kitchen, Zainab fusses around, rearranging pots and wiping surfaces even though the room is spotless.

"Coffee?" she asks.

"Yes please," I say. "What's going on? Is everything okay?"

Five minutes later we are sat at her small kitchen table. I hold a small cup of cardamom coffee to my nose and breathe in deeply.

"I'm just so embarrassed," she says. "Neither of them has been suspended before. We had to go and sit in the principal's office while he asked questions about where Hassan could have picked up violent habits. And then Haider said it wasn't unusual for teenage boys to get into scrapes and the principal said that might be the case where we come from, but it was

219

an issue taken very seriously here. I was so embarrassed, Emma. I wanted the ground to eat me."

I try not to smile at the idioms that have begun to find their way into Zainab's sentences. The principal's comments annoy me. I am tempted to go and talk to him myself, but from Noor's description of him it might not be worth it.

"And Hassan won't tell you what happened?" I ask.

"Nothing. Just said the boy deserved it. I want to believe that it's not his fault; he's never been in fights before – at least not that I know of. But he's been acting out of character ever since we arrived in America. I don't know what he's capable of anymore."

"Try not to worry too much, Zainab. Haider's right – Hassan's a teenage boy. It happens."

"I just feel like I'm losing him. Like I can't get through."

"Is there anything I can do to help?"

"Can you try to talk to him, Emma?"

Fifteen minutes later I am sat on Hassan's bed, my back leaning against the wall. He didn't say much when I knocked on his bedroom door and asked if I could come in for a bit, just made a noise that I took to mean "okay". Since I've been in there he has mostly sat jabbing rapidly at his keyboard. I assume he must be talking to someone from the way he types a bit, pauses, types again, but I have no idea who. The thought concerns me. I read an article last week about the online radicalisation of young Muslim men and I can see how Hassan would be a prime target – a recent immigrant, struggling to settle in his new country, an impressionable age. Maybe that's why he's acting out.

As Hassan types, music plays from his computer. It is a mix of English and French and Arabic, but nothing I've heard before. The quality is grainy, but I think I can make out North African accents and a lot of lyrics about "the regime" and "the system".

"So you like rap then?" I say, making another attempt

at conversation. He nods. So far, all question have been answered with shrugs or one-word answers.

I examine my nails. I have been biting them more recently. I wonder if I should at least paint them again before Adam gets home.

"Do you like any American artists?" I ask.

"Not really," he says without turning around.

I shift on the bed. I need to go to the store to get the food for Thanksgiving. Zainab asked me if I wanted to join them and I felt guilty saying I already had plans.

I check my watch. I've been in here almost twenty minutes and it's becoming increasingly awkward. What did I think I was going to say to a teenage boy anyway? I could go back down and tell Zainab that I tried. That he's fine. That this is probably normal. Then a song comes on that I recognise.

"Hey, is this Narcy?" I ask.

Hassan turns round.

"Yeah. How do you know Narcy?"

"A friend played it to me once."

"Your friend has good taste," says Hassan and turns back to his computer.

"He does," I say with a smile. In my mind I am sat in Green Beans café again with Ali, the day he bought me the baklava. He is showing me a music video on his phone. We are getting sideways glances from other people in the café, but I don't care.

"He's from Basra, like me," Ali is saying. "Well, not him – his family. He lives in Canada. This one is my favourite. 'Phatwa'." I watch the video, which shows the rapper being searched at a US airport. "I hope it will not be like this for Ameena."

"She's strong Ali. She will be fine."

Ali's face flickers and now we are not in Green Beans but at the side of a road. He is kneeling, hands tied behind his back, gun pointing at his head. He lifts his head and looks at me.

"Emma?" he says.

"Emma?"

It is not Ali's voice but Hassan's. I wipe my forehead with my hand and realise I am sweating. Hassan has turned around in his seat.

"Yes?"

"What happened at school… It wasn't my fault, you know."

I try to refocus my brain.

"The fight?"

"Yeah. They were… They were saying stuff about Farwa."

"Like what?"

"Laughing and stuff. Farwa… She tries to be like the other girls, wearing lip gloss and learning the words to American songs. But she doesn't see how they make fun when her back is turned. I saw one of the guys put his jacket over his head, pretending like it was the hijab. It just made me flip."

Of course. He was protecting her.

"Oh, I'm sorry, Hassan. That's horrible of them." In my head I call them things far worse than horrible, but I am supposed to be the adult here, setting an example. In my head I would have hit them too. "Why didn't you tell the teachers that? Or your parents?" I ask.

"Why bother?" He shrugs. "The principal hates all the brown kids. He gives stupid sermons on being a good Christian and treating people equally, but he always punishes kids like me more."

My language is less controlled this time.

"That's fucked-up, Hassan. Is there another teacher you can talk to? What that boy did is wrong, but fighting him is not the answer."

"You just want me to stand by and watch them joke about my sister?"

"No, of course not. But getting into trouble will make things harder for you. You need a good school record, Hassan, especially to get into college."

"College?"

"Yeah."

"Who said anything about college?"

"Well, no one. But you're about the right age for applications, right?"

Again, that shrug.

"I dunno. Never thought about it," he says.

He starts typing again and I can tell that he considers the conversation finished. I stand to leave and as I do I catch a glimpse of his computer screen. It is not some kind of messenger as I had expected, but a long stream of words and letters and symbols on a white background. It looks like another language.

"Hassan?"

"Yes?"

"I don't want to pry, but what is that?"

"Nothing. Just my game." He types a bit more. A mix of square brackets and odd words that seem like instructions.

"What kind of game?"

He gives a frustrated sigh and I wonder if I have become that annoying older person asking obvious technology-related questions.

"This isn't the game itself. It's the code for it. I'm adding some bits."

"You're coding it yourself? Really? Can you explain it to me?"

He sighs again.

"Yeah. I guess. Sit here next to me."

"So he's been developing these whole multi-player games and then playing them online with his friends back in Jordan and Iraq," I say to Zainab.

"I had no idea," she says, her hands suspended halfway through washing up. "I didn't know that was even possible."

"It's incredible," I say. "Apparently, when you were in Jordan, he went to some kind of computer club, and then he taught himself the rest online."

"I remember the computer club!" says Zainab. "I had no

idea he was learning anything though. I thought they just hung out there and messed around."

"You know, he told me he hasn't thought about college, Zainab, but he seems to have a real talent. Perhaps it's something I could talk to him about more?"

"But higher education is so expensive here, Emma. I don't know how we'd ever afford it."

"Maybe he could get funding. I'm sure there are grants and scholarships he would be eligible for, especially with your story."

"You think so?"

"I do, but I need to research it. Are you okay with me talking to him about it more?"

"Of course," she says.

As I drive home, I have the same butterflies I used to get in Baghdad when I heard a case had been approved. I have found a way to help this family and I won't stop until Hassan is at college. Hassan is going to be okay and Adam is coming home and for a moment at least everything feels all right.

39

Today is Thanksgiving. I wake up early with a strange feeling, like I should be excited but I'm not. It is odd celebrating Thanksgiving without Adam. It reminds me of the feeling I used to have on Christmas morning as a teenager, after my dad died and the magic was no longer there. Today I feel nostalgic for a holiday that was never mine.

I turn on the television. On one channel there is a reporter live in New York, broadcasting amid the crowds gathering for the Macy's Thanksgiving Day parade. I turn over to a local channel where a firefighter from the Colorado Springs station warns people of the hazards of deep-frying their turkey.

I check on the jelly for the trifle that I left to set last night. I've used raspberry flavour instead of strawberry because I know it's Noah's favourite. The other dishes are prepped and waiting in the fridge.

I boil water in a pan and stir in two sachets of vanilla pudding mix. I haven't managed to find custard, but this pudding stuff seems similar enough. Someone who hasn't eaten trifle before won't know the difference anyway.

I messaged Kate last night to see if there were any last-minute bits she wanted me to pick up for her. I haven't heard back from her yet.

I gaze out the window while the mixture cools. It looks cold outside and there are low heavy clouds. It might even snow. Adam told me he would switch my car over to winterised tyres when he got home, but I'll need to do it myself before then.

I haven't heard from Adam today either. I expected a Thanksgiving email when I woke up, but there wasn't one. I wondered whether he had forgotten it was Thanksgiving altogether – the days do run into each other out there. But then I remembered the turkey cake in the chow hall and realised there was no escape from Thanksgiving in Baghdad. I decide to email him first.

Subject: Happy Thanksgiving!
Hey! Happy Thanksgiving from your Brit in 'Murica! I hope that you are celebrating with large amounts of tasty chow hall turkey. I might even attempt to cook you a proper Thanksgiving dinner when you get home. Kate is giving me tips.
Love you,
Emma

Then I send Kate another text message.
Hey. I'll be over at about twelve. Just finishing the trifle. Offer's still open to pick stuff up on my way.

The vanilla pudding is cool now. I scoop it carefully onto the combination of jelly and sponge cake. My phone rings. It must be Kate calling about some ingredient she's forgotten or to say we should have that turkey pizza after all. I wipe my hands on a dishcloth and pick up the phone without looking at the number.

"Hey. Happy Thanksgiving!" I say.

There is a strange white noise on the line and then I hear him.

"Emma, it's Adam."

"Oh, hey you! I thought it was Kate, but Happy Thanksgiving to you too! How are you?"

Adam speaks again. The line is bad and he sounds very far away. Muffled. As if he or the phone is underwater.

"Emma. Can you hear me?"

"Yes, I can hear you. Adam?"

"Em, listen. I haven't got long. Where are you? Has she called you?"

"I'm at home. Has who called? What's going on?"

"Shit."

"Adam?"

"You need to go to Kate, Emma. Go to Kate."

"Why? What's—"

"They just lifted the comms blackout. I couldn't call you earlier."

"Adam, what's happened?"

"Can you hear me, Emma? You need to go to Kate. It's Dave."

"No…"

"It's Dave, Emma. Dave is dead."

PART THREE
POST–DEPLOYMENT

40

Kate is leaving.

No one stays forever, I am learning that now. Some leave in ways that are more unexpected than others. But everyone leaves, eventually.

I sit in my car, around the corner from Kate's house. I can see the removal van parked out on the street, which must have been there since early morning. One of the removal men is leant against it, a phone raised to his ear. In his other hand is a cigarette. He flicks ash onto the road. I am envious of his cigarette. I have not smoked since Baghdad, but recently I have been thinking about it more.

I pull down the sun visor and examine my face in the mirror. It is blotchy and pale. I draw my fingers across the puffed-up flesh under my eyes.

Kate is out by the truck now too, talking to the removal man. Charlotte is balanced on her hip. I open the car door quickly, not wanting her to see that I have been sat here, gathering the courage to say goodbye. I pick up the bag of doughnuts that I bought on the way over, the way I used to when the men were gone. Or not gone, but away. Now gone means something different. I take a breath and leave the car, stepping out into the bracing air and the day of Kate's departure.

Kate walks across the lawn when she sees me. The grass is wet from the melting frost and I wonder if the damp will seep through her trousers, but she doesn't seem to notice. We meet in the centre of the lawn and I embrace her, feeling the cold of her cheek against mine. Charlotte gurgles between us, her woollen hat slipping to cover her eyes.

"You okay?" is all I manage to get out. She nods, lips pressed tightly together.

A figure appears in the doorway of the house. It is Kate's mother, June. She came down from Oregon the day we found out and has stayed here since. Her presence is reassuring. Strong. I can see where Kate gets it.

I wave to June. She calls for us to come indoors, saying she's just made a fresh pot of coffee. Kate draws away from our embrace.

"I definitely need more caffeine," she says. She looks tired, but who wouldn't, with a dead husband and newborn baby and house to pack up.

"Early start?" I ask.

"Early start and long night. Charlotte was up with colic, then when I came down to the kitchen this morning, Harvey had been sick and Noah had his hands in it."

She gives a tired laugh and I can't help but laugh too, even though it still feels strange to laugh when Dave is dead. For a brief moment our bodies remember happiness, but then the muscles of our faces relax out of their smile and Dave is still gone.

"That's a lot for first thing in the morning," I say to Kate. She nods.

We go inside the house. A couple of pieces of furniture are still there, but the photos, the toys, the piles of laundry, all the things that make it Kate's home have gone. Kate sees me looking around the house.

"Strange, isn't it?"

I nod. This place was a comfort to me while Adam was away, and again when he got back. There is something reassuring about the deep sadness of her house. There is no need to tiptoe around, as I do with Adam, navigating unspoken ghosts and feigning normality. In Kate's house we sit on the sofa, cuddled up with Charlotte and Noah and Harvey, eating food that June has prepared, trying to heal our wounds with love. I think it is better that way.

But now Kate is going back to Oregon. It's where her family and Dave's family all are. It is where the children will have grandparents, cousins, aunts and uncles. Somewhere Kate will have support. I told her I thought she was doing the right thing. Her mother couldn't be expected to stay in Colorado forever and Kate needed family around. I silenced the voice inside me that said, *no, don't go, not you too*. I have no claim to grief. My husband, a version of him, is still here.

I knew when Kate's family became my own that it wouldn't last forever.

June pours us each a large mug of coffee while I place the doughnuts on top of the paper bag. We sit at the kitchen table where I have sat with Kate a hundred times before, talking about our husbands' deployment or trying to talk about anything else.

"How are you, sweetie?" asks June.

"I'm okay thanks, Mrs Collier."

"And Adam?"

I take a sip of coffee, taking my time to answer.

"Quiet," I say. "Very quiet."

What I mean is he is silent. Some days the only sounds I hear from his mouth are those that escape his lips amid uneasy dreams. He is withdrawn. Sad. Angry. But all he says is he is fine.

"Don't worry, dear, that's normal. You know, my Bob barely said a word for years after he got back from Vietnam. He came back to himself eventually of course, but it wasn't fast. That's just the way it is with these army men."

Everyone keeps on telling me that this is "normal", but nothing about it feels normal to me. They say it is "understandable", given "what has happened". That is how people refer to Dave's death now.

233

"I'm sure you're right," I say. Kate is leaving and now is not the time to have this conversation.

June gives my shoulder a squeeze and says she is going to do some more packing in the living room. After she leaves the kitchen, Kate puts her mug down on the counter. She's doing that thing where she stares at me, evaluating. I know she is unconvinced by my response. After all the time we have spent together, Kate knows when I'm not telling her everything.

"How bad is it?" she asks.

"It's not good," I say.

"Has he spoken to anyone at work about it?"

"He says he doesn't need to."

I remember it being the same in Iraq. None of the men talked about things, not properly. No one wanted to be the weak link, the one to let the team down. Everyone just sucked things up and got on with it, at least until Dave and his Skittles came along.

"God," she says, shaking her head. "Dave would never have let him get away with that."

She's right. Dave forced the guys to talk, and there weren't many people like that. I had no idea how, or if, the other guys on the team were coping and I wasn't close enough to any of the other wives to ask. Kate had already warned me that the wives could be just as good at putting on a front as the men. They had learned from the pros that showing weakness was bad. They had their husbands to protect.

"I know," I say. "I've been trying to get him to talk to someone, but he won't."

"Until he asks for help himself, there's not much you can do," she says. "The support system is a nightmare to navigate. I hate to say this, Em, but there are so many messed-up guys that Adam won't be a priority."

I nod. I know. I've been on the websites, the message boards and forums. All full of the horror stories of the spouses of service members trying to get help. The help never seemed to come until it was too late. There was always something – a DUI, a battered wife, a scribbled note.

"How about you? How're you holding up?" she asks.

"I'm okay. Trying to keep up with the art shop, the mentoring, that kind of thing."

"You're still spending time with the Iraqis?" She puts her mug down.

"Yeah."

"You think that's a good idea?"

"Why wouldn't it be?"

"Because they killed my husband? Your husband's best friend?"

"Kate. These people I'm helping aren't the people that killed Dave. They're people that fled. Normal people like you and me that ended up in a shitty situation. I'm sure Adam gets that. I thought you would too."

"Look, Emma, you know I've always been supportive of your slightly weird liberal ways. You're European, you're different. I get it. But now? Think about who they are, who you're spending time with…"

"Kate, I'm sorry, but no. This family have lost people too. They aren't to blame for what happened."

What happened. There. Now I am saying it too. I don't want to have this conversation with Kate today. Not with everything else going on. She should be my priority.

"Let's not talk about this now, Kate. Are you all set? Is there anything I can do?" I ask her.

"I think we're sorted," she replies. She looks relieved too. We only have capacity for so much pain today and the threshold has almost been reached. "The new family moves in next week. I gave them your number, like you said. Hopefully they won't need anything, but it will be good for them to know someone in the area."

Kate's house is going to be rented by a military family transferring from North Carolina. I can't imagine different children playing in her garden or another military wife sat on the back porch where we had spent our mornings.

"You know I'm still here for you too, if you need anything," I say. She gives my arm a squeeze.

"Thanks, Em, I appreciate it. But just you worry about that husband of yours. I'm sure I'll be back," she says. I nod in agreement, even though neither of us knows whether she will come back or whether Adam and I will be here when or if she does.

We rinse our mugs and wrap them in bubble wrap, then spend the rest of the morning packing a few final things. Olivia stops by at lunchtime with a tray of sandwiches that we share with the removal men.

Things have been different with Olivia since she came to the hospital the day we got the news. Neither Kate or I had known that this was Olivia's second marriage. She lost her first husband – her high-school sweetheart and a nineteen-year-old marine – in the early days of the invasion. She said that it was something that she didn't tend to share, but it created a bond between her and Kate. It also made her previous insistence on the Family Readiness Group more understandable.

Olivia looks upset to see Kate leave and, from the absence of her usual make-up, I think she may have been crying. She didn't even get annoyed when Harvey jumped up at her and left a muddy paw print on her pastel blue skirt, she just ruffled his head and said he reminded her of a dog she had when she was growing up. I wonder what other memories the day is bringing for her.

"How's Mike doing?" I ask her.

She pauses momentarily.

"Oh, he's fine. It's great to have him back."

I wonder how he really is.

"And Adam?" she asks.

"Yes. Fine. Same."

Her new intimacy with Kate does not extend to me.

Before Olivia leaves she gives Kate a long hug and

mumbles something about being "army strong" and staying in touch.

Eventually, it is time for Kate to leave too. The removal van drives off first, then Kate and her family fill up the car. She and her mother are going to drive the long journey in shifts. The sky is heavy with clouds. The weather forecast says that more snow is coming.

"You should get going," I say. "How far are you driving today?"

"We're aiming for Salt Lake City, but I doubt if we'll get that far," she says. "My mum doesn't like being on the road in the dark. We can just find a motel along the way."

Five minutes later, Charlotte is asleep in her car seat. Noah is running a toy truck up and down the back of his grandmother's headrest. June is on the phone to her husband, letting him know they are about to set off. Kate stands by the open car door, ready to get in.

"Drive safely," I say and pull her into a tight embrace.

"I'm going to miss you, friend," she says into my ear.

"I'm going to miss you too," I say. "Let me know you get there okay. And... I'm sorry about everything, Kate."

She pulls back, wiping tears from her eyes, and I do the same.

"I will. And, Em, you've been great. You really have. Thank you. Say bye to Adam from me."

"I will. I'm sorry he wasn't here."

She gives me a final squeeze and then climbs in the driver's seat. In the boot, Harvey moves excitedly from side to side. His tail spills over onto the back seat and tickles Charlotte's sleeping face, causing her to stir. Noah presses his mouth up against the window and blows out his cheeks at me. Kate fastens her seatbelt and turns the ignition key. She takes one last long look at the house and then exhales slowly, her ribcage collapsing downwards. She holds onto the steering wheel, motionless, and for a second I wonder if she is going to change her mind or say something else, but then she pulls away. I am left standing on the pavement in front of her house, watching the red of her brake lights as she reaches the end of her road, takes a right turn and disappears out of sight.

I stand there a while longer, not wanting to go home. Eventually I turn and walk towards my car. Adam is back and I have never felt more alone.

41

At home, I sit on the sofa. Numb. I am still there when Adam gets back from work.

"Hey," he says.

"Hey."

He goes to the kitchen. Opens the fridge and closes it again. He pulls a plate out of the cupboard and a knife from the drawer. Still I sit. The bag of bread rustles. The knife is dropped into the sink. I do not need to turn my head to know what he is doing. The routine is familiar through its sounds. They fill the silence. He stands at the counter in the kitchen eating. And I sit.

When Adam got back from deployment, there was no great romantic reunion. He did not want me to meet him at the airport when he arrived or to pick him up from Fort Carson. He said that he was fine and there was no need to do the "homecoming thing". What he meant was that there was nothing to celebrate for a team coming home a man down.

After hours of waiting, tidying and re-tidying the house, changing out of my new dress and into jeans and a sweater, I heard the sound of a vehicle stopping in the street outside. I opened the door just as he was reaching it. There he was. Adam. Home.

I found my way into his arms without even saying hello. I buried my face into his chest and inhaled deeply. The smell of foreign laundry detergent mixed with aeroplane seats and a body stale from travel. But underneath it was the familiar scent of him.

"Hey," he said in my ear and I drew my head back. He smiled a sad, exhausted smile.

"Welcome home," I said and released the breath I had been holding for eight months.

"Thanks." He lowered his lips to mine and we kissed. Our mouths searched each other for familiarity. Then he lowered his face into the crease where my neck met my shoulder. I put my hand on the back of his head, holding him against me. I do not know how long we stood like that. When he eventually lifted his face, my shoulder felt damp, but he turned away quickly, saying he needed to get his bags from outside. I didn't see his eyes.

He came back carrying two large rucksacks and I shut the door behind him, against the cold and against Iraq. He was thinner than when he left and the skin of his face looked stretched over the new angles of his cheekbones. I reached up to touch his jawline, freshly shaven and pale where thick facial hair had previously protected his chin from the glare of the sun.

We stood for moment, just looking at each other.

"Do you want to sit down?" I asked, as if he were a guest. I sat next to him on the sofa, my leg against his, my hand on his knee. My fingers kept on contracting, squeezing, checking he was really there. He put his arm around me and held my body tightly against his. We kissed.

"How was the journey?" I asked.

"Fine. The first flight was late, but we made the connection."

"Did you manage to sleep?"

"A little."

"Was the flight full?"

"No. There was a spare seat next to me. It was fine."

We kissed again, searching, and maybe there was going to be more, but then we stopped. Amid the intense familiarity was something different. We needed to rediscover each other. To remember.

"Do you want something to eat?" I asked. "Drink?"

"Is there beer?"

"Of course."

I was pleased to have something to do. I went to the kitchen and he shifted around on the sofa, then got up to join me. I was stood in front of the fridge when he wrapped his arms around my waist. I leant back into his chest and pulled his arms more tightly around me and closed my eyes. The fridge beeped its disturbance, telling us the door had been open for too long.

I took a bottle of beer from the collection I'd been building up for weeks. Before he came home, I asked him what type of beer he wanted and he said he didn't care, so I'd bought one of everything I'd ever seen him drink.

He opened the drawer where the bottle opener used to be, but it wasn't there. He tried the drawer above and it was not there either. I opened the drawer at the side of the fridge and handed it to him.

"So you've been doing some rearranging, huh?" he asked.

"Yeah, sorry," I said.

He shrugged, momentarily a stranger in his own home. I ran through other things that might have changed location and made a mental note to move them back.

He returned to the sofa and I sat cross-legged, facing him, running a hand down his back. I knew not to smother him, but I needed to keep touching him, grounding myself to the man who had returned. He took a swig of beer and turned towards me, feeling my gaze. He reached out a hand to stroke my face and I felt the rough callouses of his palm against my cheek.

"What's up?" he said.

"How are you feeling?"

"I dunno. Tired, I guess. Like I don't want to think about anything for a while. What about you? What have you been up to today?"

I've been waiting, I wanted to say. *Waiting, waiting, waiting, as I have been every day for months.*

"Oh, you know, just sorting stuff out here. Running a few errands," I said. It sounded so trivial, so boring. I tried to see myself through his eyes. Who was this person I had become? We sat in silence as he finished his beer, then I got him another one.

"Steady," he said. "I haven't had a drink in a while. You trying to get me drunk?"

I laughed and traced my fingers down the muscles of his back again, my fingertips rediscovering the once familiar terrain.

"How's Kate?" he asked.

"Coping," I said. "I don't know how, but she is." Images flashed through my mind of the coffin as it was carried off the back of the plane, of me bottle-feeding Charlotte the day Kate couldn't look at her, of the small grainy photo of Dave in the newspaper that Kate threw in the bin only for her mother to retrieve.

"I need to drop by and see her," he said.

I nodded.

"She'd like that."

More silence.

The house felt transformed by his presence. It was no longer the place that I had inhabited alone for almost eight months. That place was already a blurry memory. The house felt full again, of him and me and us. But we filled it awkwardly, with a new sense of caution that I hadn't anticipated. Did he feel it too?

Adam put his bottle down onto the coffee table. He reached over and pulled me towards him. Onto him. I took his face between my hands and kissed him, gently, testing and teasing his lips. I had waited eight long months for this, but now it was happening it felt strange, like we were moving through a performance of what was supposed to happen.

Then Adam's kisses became deeper. His teeth grazed

my lips and I drew in my breath. He stood up, lifting me easily with him, and carried me up the stairs, surprising me with this increased strength. In the bedroom my hands fumbled awkwardly at the buckle of his belt. He moved my hands away and undid it himself, then pulled at my clothes, stripping them from me. I felt unexpectedly self-conscious at my nakedness.

"Hey, slow down," I said.

"Sorry," he breathed and continued.

We didn't make love, not in the way we had done before he left. The body that moved against mine felt different. Distant. The hands moved in a way I remembered, but the fingerprints of a stranger branded my body. I searched Adam's face but I couldn't find him there. He looked through me with empty eyes.

He came quickly and lay on top of me, his body heavy and hot. I wrapped my legs around him and pulled him close, overwhelmed. I wanted to keep him on top of me. Inside me. As if somehow, with our bodies intertwined, I could fix what had been broken.

Adam put a hand either side of my body and pushed himself up. His lips touched my forehead in a fleeting kiss and then he walked to the bathroom, shutting the door behind him. I lay naked, my body cold, and listened to the sound of the shower.

Later that night I struggled to sleep. I thought that when he got back I would sleep deeply, that I would finally be able to relax, but I was wrong.

At first we lay facing each other, our bodies intertwined. I draped my leg over his hip the way I used to. He put an arm around me and pulled me into his chest, his cheek resting against the top of my head. For a while I felt comfortable, secure. His breathing became deep and regular and I listened to his heartbeat and was thankful that he was home. But then his arm started to feel heavy and his hipbone dug into my leg and the air I breathed was hot from his lungs as it entered my own. His body became suffocating.

I tried to get space without disturbing him. I lifted his arm and slid carefully out from underneath. He stirred but did not wake. I moved as far across the bed as I could and sucked in the cold air, leaving only a foot stretched out to touch his leg. The smallest bit of skin-on-skin contact.

Sometime in the night he pulled me back towards him. I was faced away this time, with my back pressed against his chest and his breath on my neck. I felt my body weigh heavily on the arm that was beneath me. I shifted. Repositioned. Became frustrated with myself. Adam was home. Why was I not asleep, curled against him, as I had imagined I would be? This was what I had been waiting for.

When Adam first left, the bed felt huge. Each night it spoke to me of his absence as I reached out an arm to feel the cold space on the sheets where his body should have been.

But eventually it shrank. I learnt how to inhabit the space and enjoy the freshness of the sheets as I rolled from one side to another. Now he was back and I wondered how long it would take for the bed to expand once more.

In the kitchen, Adam finishes his sandwich.

"What have you been up to?" he asks. He has forgotten. Who is this version of my husband that forgot that Kate was leaving?

"Kate left."

"Fuck," he says. "Fuck. Why didn't you remind me?"

"I did, last night," I say. I look over at him and see the anguish in his face. "Don't worry, it's fine. I helped her."

I lower my head into my hands and rub at my eyes. I am exhausted. I feel like we are losing everyone. Ali. Dave. Now Kate.

Adam watches me from the kitchen. He comes over and sits on the couch next to me. He puts an arm around me and then draws me into his chest. I clutch his shirt between my hands. He is my anchor, this man. Whatever happens, he is what I need to cling on to. Somehow we will get through this together. He strokes my hair and my breathing slows. I am calmer.

"Thank you for helping her, babe," he says.

"We keep losing them, Adam. I don't want to lose you too."

42

When he came home, he brought back sand. Not fine white sand from the beach or colourful sand in a bottle with my name. Dirty sand. Dusty sand. Brown sand. It is the kind of sand I have seen before.

The sand got everywhere. It spilled out of his rucksack and started covering the floorboards. It filled every crevice and crack in the house. Then it filled the space between us grain by grain by grain. Now it is rising up around our ankles and knees and waists and we have to wade through it to try and reach each other.

"Is this why you left so much of yourself out there?" I ask. "To bring back all this sand?"

He shrugs and rubs a hand around the back of his neck. I think I see sand fall out of his earlobe too.

43

The day that Dave died I put down the phone and drove straight over to Kate's house. Kate was not there when I arrived. I banged on the door and the windows and shouted her name, but there was no reply. A neighbour emerged from the house next door. He had a beer in his hand and was wearing a plastic apron shiny with turkey grease. I had already forgotten it was Thanksgiving.

"An ambulance took her away early this morning," he said.

"An ambulance?"

"Yeah. A couple of soldiers turned up. Only saw them because my wife was up to brine the turkey. Next thing you know there's an ambulance at the door and they're taking her out in a wheelchair with an oxygen mask."

"And Noah?" I asked, trying to control the shake in my voice.

"The boy? He went in the car with the soldiers." He paused for a moment. "Is everything okay?"

He must know, I thought. After so many years of losing soldiers, the image of the black sedan and two death notifiers in their class-A uniforms had become etched in the nation's imagination. The vehicle had crawled through films and TV dramas and into the dreams of spouses, parents, friends and even children.

"I don't know," I said. He nodded, holding the beer can awkwardly at his side.

"We haven't lived here long. I don't really know her, otherwise…" He trailed off.

"I'd better go," I said.

"I hope she's okay. And, er, Happy Thanksgiving."

"Oh. You too."

I felt the man watching me as I turned around and got back into my car. From the corner of my eye, I noticed movement at the window of his house and saw other family members gathered there, watching. A young man stood with his arm around the shoulders of a woman who must have been his mother. She turned away when I caught her eye. It was not their tragedy.

I do not remember much about the drive to the hospital, except that I stopped the car twice to open the door and vomit. It was like moving through a sludgy dream. I prayed that there had been a mistake, that everything was okay and they were all going to come home. Like my father before he died, I bargained with a God I didn't know I believed in.

I think I ran into the hospital when I arrived. I might have shouted her name. A man and a woman in uniform found me, or I found them. One of them was holding Noah's hand. He was wearing an eyepatch and swinging a sword that Kate had bought him to match Dave's. I had bought him a toy parrot as a gift, which now lay forgotten on my sofa.

The first thing I did was bend down and hug Noah tightly. He said "Ouch, Emma" and looked at me with large confused eyes. It was the first time he'd said my name properly. I stood up and spoke to the people in uniform.

"I'm Emma McLaughlin, a friend of Kate," I said. "My husband is on Dave's, I mean, Master Sergeant Jenkins' team. I… I heard what happened."

I didn't say Adam called me. I didn't know whether he was supposed to call me yet.

"Oh, Mrs McLaughlin. Yes, someone was supposed to be contacting you. Mrs Jenkins asked for you."

I looked at my phone and saw missed calls from an unknown number, which must have been someone from the unit.

"I'm sure she'll be glad you're here. She's in the maternity unit at the moment. They've found her a private room... given the circumstances."

"The maternity unit?" I asked. "The baby... is the baby okay?"

"She's fine," she said. "Tiny, but fine."

I put out my hand to hold onto the back of a chair, steadying myself.

"She's... She's had her...?"

"Yes, ma'am. Mrs Jenkins went into labour after receiving the notification of death."

I imagined Kate opening the door, seeing the uniforms, standing aside and letting them into the living room. Sitting down. Watching their lips move but not hearing their words. Not needing to hear them. She'd been through it in her head a thousand times since Dave joined the army.

Adam said if you imagine a scenario enough times you would be prepared for it. I don't think it prepared Kate for this.

"I have been asked to inform you, Mrs Jenkins, that your husband has been reported dead in Baghdad, Iraq, at twenty-two hundred hours on November 24, 2011. On behalf of the Secretary of Defence, I extend to you and your family my deepest sympathy in your great loss."

The lips keep moving. They must be asking if there is someone they can contact for her. But she cannot focus. Something else is happening. The oxygen is leaving her body. A pain radiates out from her lower back. The baby is coming.

A nurse walked past us and the woman in uniform called her over.

"Nurse Rubio, this is a friend of Mrs Jenkins. Is she okay for visitors?"

"Of course, come this way," said the nurse.

As we walked through the corridors of the hospital, I noticed how quiet it was. Everyone was at home, eating turkey, celebrating with their families. The smell of chlorine and antiseptic filled my nose and no longer brought with it the comforting associations of my father – it smelt only of grief and fear. Now I understood what hospitals meant for other people.

The nurse was talking as we walked. She was a short woman with wide hips that rolled with each step. We walked slowly and I was grateful. I wasn't sure my limbs would have let me move any faster.

"You know normally we wouldn't have visitors this soon, especially as you're not next of kin, but it'll be good for her to see a familiar face, poor thing. It's not surprising she went into labour, given the news. A shock that big? That far along?" The nurse tutted and shook her head. "Poor thing," she said again.

When we got to Kate's room, we stopped outside and looked in through the rectangular window. I noticed the smear of a handprint on the glass and wondered who had stood in that spot before me, reaching their hand towards someone on the other side of the transparent barrier.

Kate was lying on her side, facing a Perspex box in which I could just about make out the outline of her tiny daughter. I was glad that she had her own space, away from the other new parents, fathers cooing and wiping sweat from their partners' foreheads. But in that room together, the two of them looked so alone.

"She can't hold the baby on her own while she's sedated, in case she falls asleep," the nurse explained.

"She's sedated?"

"Yes, she was in a bit of a panic when she came in, poor soul, not that you can blame her. The doctor gave her a dose to calm her down. That level of stress isn't good for the baby." The nurse flicked through a clipboard of notes as she spoke.

"But apart from the sedation, she's okay?" I asked.

"Physically, yes. The doctor said she's doing as well as can be expected. Emotionally, she seems like a strong woman, but the sedation will numb everything for now. It's too much for her to deal with all at once."

I saw the baby stir slightly, one miniature foot pushing into the air. Kate reached out to touch the edge of the box.

"Can I go in?" I asked. The nurse nodded. I wasn't sure that I was ready, but I knew I must.

The metal of the door handle felt cold under my hand as I pushed it down and I realised that my palms were sweating. As soon as the door opened, my ears filled with the steady bleeping of the machines attached to Kate and her baby, reminders of their continuing life.

Kate turned her head at the noise of the door opening, but it took a moment for her to tear her gaze away from her daughter.

"Kate," I said.

"Emma... You heard?"

I nodded, not trusting my ability to hold back the tears if I were to say anything else. I had to be the strong one now.

"I'm so glad you're here," she said.

I sat down on the bed beside her and held her hand tightly.

"Of course I'm here, Kate. I'm just... God, I'm so sorry." Over the following weeks I would hear these words of apology and condolence repeated to her until they were empty of meaning, but they were the only words I could find. Kate nodded, tears running down her cheeks. I felt a tight band constricting round my chest. I couldn't speak. I could barely breathe. It wasn't just grief. It was guilt. Guilt at the relief I was feeling, that it was her not me.

"Did you see her already?" Kate asked, turning towards the baby. "Did you come in while I was asleep? I think they've given me something. I just feel so tired."

"I haven't," I said, and moved around to the other side of the bed and looked into the case where a tiny but perfectly formed girl was lying, attached to wires and tubes. She had a mop of dark hair, darker even than Noah's, and a small square nose. Her eyes were closed, but one minuscule hand opened and closed as if reaching for something or someone through her dreams.

She looked so much like Dave that it took my breath away. I never thought that babies really looked like anyone. I thought it was something that people just said to placate proud but exhausted parents. But I could see Dave in every millimetre of her tiny features.

"Kate, she's perfect," I said. "She's just beautiful."

Kate smiled an exhausted smile. Her face was pale and clammy. Her own dark hair was stuck to the sides of her face with dried sweat.

"Do you think she looks like him? I look at her and just see his face, but I don't know whether that's just because... you know..."

"No, she does," I reassured her. "She really does."

"I can't believe he's gone, Emma. I can't believe it's really happened."

"I know, Kate. I know. Neither can I."

The small figure next to us stirred. We both watched her.

"Do you have a name yet?" I asked.

"Charlotte. It was Dave's grandmother's name – we decided on it as soon as we found out we were having a girl."

"It's a lovely name," I said.

"He always wanted a daughter."

"He'll be so proud, Kate," I said. "You must know that. He'll be so proud." I couldn't yet bring myself to talk in the conditional perfect, in the language of would have beens and could have beens and a world where Dave no longer existed.

She nodded, her eyes closing. I wondered whether I should leave her for a while to let her rest. But then her eyes opened quickly, as if some distant memory had pierced though the haze of exhaustion.

"Adam. What about Adam? Is he okay? Was he with him?"

"He called me. He's fine... He's..." I realised I didn't know. The phone call was short, fuzzy. I didn't know what had happened or whether he was injured or anything other than the fact that he was alive and Dave was dead. "He's fine," I said.

"Good," she said. "I'm so glad he's okay."

Again, that wave of relief and guilt swirled through me. Adam was okay. Dave, with his son and new baby daughter, was not.

"Emma?"

"Yes?"

"I need to close my eyes for a while. Will you watch her for me?"

"Yes, of course I will, Kate." I stroked her forehead. "I'm not going anywhere."

44

I am at the art shop again this morning. I decided to take on extra shifts. I need something to focus on, to get me out of the house. I need a reminder of the parts of me that are not just a wife struggling through her husband's return.

The art shop is my refuge now. I find the quiet predictability of it reassuring. When I am here, I can relax in a way I cannot at home. Adam's grief inhabits the house, appearing each day under a difference guise. Some days it sits quietly in the corner, a dark presence that sucks away light and joy. Other days it rages through the rooms, slamming us against the walls and leaving us gasping in the wake of its force. I do not know which is worse.

Some days I can't help but wish I had more than this job in a shop, but I'm not sure I would be capable of anything else at the moment. The job gives me stability. Helping Hassan with his college applications gives me purpose.

Penny is here again today. I have noticed that she is around more during my shifts at the moment. Noor comes in more often too. They are gentle around me and I know they can tell that something isn't right.

When Adam first got home, Penny teased when I came in late or tired. She and Noor joked that I was going through a second honeymoon period. They asked why I was hiding Adam away from them, keeping him all to myself. But now the jokes have stopped. Noor came to pick me up for the art group last week while my car was in the garage for a check-up. I asked her to text me when she arrived and said I would run out to the car. I hated myself for trying to keep her away from him. When I went out to meet her, I caught her glancing up at the figure that moved quickly away from the bedroom window.

Today Penny is organising stock and I am behind the counter when Noor arrives. She still comes in each Friday and sits in the corner of the shop with a coffee, talking about her latest project or her family or the trip that she one days plans to make back to Kurdistan.

"Hi Emma," she says today, with her usual warm smile.

"Hey, how's it going?" I say.

Penny emerges at the sound of Noor's voice. I have noticed the friendship between them take shape in recent months. They talk about their favourite artists, share recipes, and they even went to see a play together the other week. I would like to believe that the friendship is entirely based on their shared passions, but I can't help wonder how much of it is their shared concern for me. I wonder what is said between them when I am not here. They both know me, far more than most people in Colorado Springs, but they do not quite know me enough to really push. To challenge me when I say I am fine. Sometimes I wish they would probe more, but most days it is a relief. It would feel like a betrayal of Adam to discuss him with them. This is something I must deal with myself.

I go to make us coffee, and when I return, Penny and Noor are talking about the exhibit for the art group that Noor wants to plan. She has discussed the idea with me before. It is a way to showcase the group to the Colorado Springs community and demonstrate what refugees and immigrants can add to society. It is also a way to raise the profile of the artists themselves. Noor believes that some of the work produced, for example Afsoon's jewellery and Hope's clothing, could be sold in local shops. Noor had hoped to hold the exhibition in the school, but the principal has said no.

"He says that some parents won't think it's appropriate for the school grounds being used for such purposes," she says.

"Because we're foreign?" I ask.

"Because they are. Not you. You're white, so it doesn't count."

My identity as an outsider here is diluted by the colour of my skin.

"This is the same guy that gives Hassan a hard time. It was a nightmare trying to get a college reference out of him. Someone should really lodge a complaint."

"I completely agree," says Penny. Penny's world view has started to shift a little since her friendship with Noor. I have seen her drop her new friend's name proudly into conversations with old customers, as if daring them to comment, and watched her be offended by some news story or another on Noor's behalf.

"How are Hassan's college applications going?" Noor asks me.

"I think we're almost there," I say. "I'm seeing him this week to go over his personal statement one more time and then we're done. I never thought I'd ever learn so much about computer sciences or the US college system."

"Lucky you," Noor says with a laugh. "But really, that's so exciting. I saw Zainab at art group this week and she seemed super happy. I'm pleased for them."

"Me too. Sorry I couldn't be there again," I say.

"No worries. You know you're welcome whenever you can make it."

Penny, who has been deep in thought, speaks.

"Noor, your art exhibition... Why don't I ask my pastor if you can hold the exhibition at my church?"

"Really? Do you think that would be possible?"

Noor looks as surprised as I feel.

"Oh, I can convince him," says Penny. "I donated a whole

bunch of art supplies for the last charity auction he held. Far better than all the jars of jelly everyone else gave him. He owes me." She winks and I laugh.

"That would be wonderful," Noor says and then turns to me. "Do you think you'll have anything ready to put up, Emma?"

I feel my body tense at the question.

"To be honest, probably not," I say. "I just have a lot on at the moment. I'll definitely be there though."

It is not that I haven't tried. When Adam is out, I continue to sit on the floor in front of the love atlas and my mother's painting, pieces spread around me. I push them into different combinations and patterns. Last night I came close to something. The colours began to come together in a way that was familiar but I could not quite put my finger on. They prompted half-forgotten tastes and sounds and memories that remained just out of reach. Last night it was me who moved uneasily in my sleep, not just Adam.

45

The low sun has already settled behind the horizon as I drive home. There is frost on the pavement and heavy clouds threaten more snow, even though it is supposed to be spring. The Coloradan winter feels never-ending. I drive slowly and cautiously, other people on the road doing the same.

I am tired. I didn't sleep much again last night. Adam moves around while he sleeps. Makes indistinguishable noises. Once I think he cried.

Penny caught me dozing off sat at the chair behind the counter of the art shop after Noor left and told me to go home, but I didn't know how to tell her that home is the last place I want to be right now. The shop is free from the heaviness of habitation. At least outside there is space for me and my thoughts.

I open the door and Adam is sat, beer in his hand and volume on the television up high. I lean over the back of the sofa to kiss the side of his face in greeting. My lips scratch against stubble that I am surprised he can get away with at work. He reaches one arm back and pats the back of my head, his gaze not breaking away from the television.

"Hey," he says.

"Hey."

I pour myself a glass of wine in the kitchen and slump down next to him without removing my shoes.

"How was your day?" I ask.

"Shit," he says, expelling the word in a rush of sweet beery breath. I rub his leg.

"Wanna talk about it?"

"Nope." His eyes are still fixed on the screen. He is watching a football game between two minor league British teams. I don't know why he's watching it or how he found it. He's never expressed an interest in "soccer" before.

"How's your week?" he asks.

"It's fine. I saw Noor in the shop today, which was nice, and I'm helping Hassan finish his college applications this week."

"Of course. Hanging out with the Iraqis again," he says. "I don't know why I bother asking."

We don't talk about Iraq these days. "It was a shithole when we went in and it's a shithole now we're leaving," said Adam this week, when he changed the channel from a news report on the withdrawal. Without talking about Iraq it feels like our foundations have disappeared. Maybe Kate was right.

"What's that supposed to mean?" I say.

"You just can't quit," he says. "It's like an obsession to you – getting all involved in their business."

"It's not an obsession. I'm just helping them out."

"You're not in Iraq anymore, Emma. This is America. It's like we never even fucking agreed that you'd get your head out of that place for a while."

I won't take the bait this time. We've had this argument before and right now all I want to do is eat and sleep. I stand up and knock over two empty beer bottles that I hadn't noticed on the floor by the couch. I pick them up and take them to the kitchen.

"Want some dinner?" I ask.

"Not hungry," he says.

I open the fridge door, where there is only one bottle left of the two six-packs he bought yesterday. As I close the fridge, I notice the card from Adam's mum, stuck on with a magnet, reminding us of his dad's sixtieth birthday party. She's invited the whole family over for the weekend – the three sons, plus their wives and kids. We've already cancelled two trips to see them since Adam has got back and I know everyone else has sorted out their travel arrangements for the party.

"Have you booked tickets for your dad's sixtieth yet?" I ask.

"Not yet."

"The flight prices will get high soon. We don't want to end up having to drive it."

"I'll do it, Emma."

It's as if the more I ask, the more reluctant to book it he becomes.

I start clearing up the kitchen so that I have space to cook. There are a couple of empty bottles in the sink and a plate with a soggy piece of toast. On the counter is a knife, stuck to the work surface with peanut butter. I pick it up and drop it noisily into the sink.

"Babe, do you have to be so loud?" he says.

"I'm just cleaning up your stuff," I say, picking up a corner of the disintegrating toast and dropping it pointedly in the rubbish.

"Just leave it."

"I need space to make dinner."

"Get takeout," he says, his eyes now back on the television. "Or wait 'til the game's over."

"I don't want takeout. I just want to make some dinner so I can eat and go to bed."

He looks over again.

"Emma, will it really kill you to wait twenty fucking minutes?"

There are many things that kill us, but not this. I turn on the tap. I look over at Adam and notice that his fists are clenched in his lap. They were clenched when we argued last week too. Not high up in front of him but stomach-level, moving in small swift movements that punctuated his sentences.

"It won't kill me," I say over the tap, "but I want to cook

260

now." I squeeze green washing-up liquid onto a sponge and start to wash the plate. I sense Adam standing, but I do not look at him. There is a strange feeling in my stomach that I have felt before, but it is not a feeling that I associate with Adam. I feel the weight of his footsteps towards me, but I do not turn. The feeling gets stronger.

He does not say anything, but reaches into the sink and takes the plate out of my soapy hands.

"Adam. What the — ?"

He opens the back door and hurls the plate into the darkness. I hear a thump. It must have landed on the frost-covered lawn beyond the patio. I imagine it landing, cracked, but somehow intact. Rolling to a stop.

"Problem solved," Adam says.

He returns to the sofa, sits down, and I stand in silence. It is fear, the feeling in my stomach, even though I have avoided giving it a name. I feel the blood pumping through my body. I try not to tremble. It is fight or flight. Today I still have some battle left in me. Or at least I think I do.

I count in my head. Take a couple of deep breaths. Then I walk over to the television, turn it off, stand in front of it. He looks momentarily surprised, but his face quickly hardens.

"Are you kidding me?" I ask him.

"What?"

"All I want to do is make some dinner and you throw the plate into the fucking garden?"

"I asked you to stop and you didn't."

"You were an arsehole about it. I just wanted some food."

"You were crashing around. Was waiting really too much to ask?"

"Shit, Adam…" I am exhausted. Pain starts to hum around my temples. I can feel my eyes filling up, but I don't want to cry. Not now. Not in front of him. I put my face into my palms and massage the side of my head, trying to keep calm.

"Oh great. Yeah, that's right, have a little cry about it, Em. That will make things better."

He picks up the remote control for the television and turns it back on. He stares at the screen as if I am not standing there in front of it and a sudden anger flares up and burns brightly inside me. That is when I say it.

"You think Dave would want to see you like this? You think he'd be proud?"

They were not my words to say.

Pain and shock flash across his face. I want to take the words back, but it is already too late. I cannot stay there to witness the havoc I have wrought, so I storm to our bedroom. Slam the door. Hold my shaking hands in front of me and wonder what this deployment has changed in me too.

I sit on the bed for a while, practising the deep-breathing techniques that I learned while I was in Baghdad. Eventually I sleep.

I wake up the next morning lying on the bed fully dressed. Adam has not come to bed. I find him lying asleep on the sofa in the living room. His face looks even more gaunt than when he returned. I sit down next to him and he stirs, rubbing at his eyes as he opens them. This war has destroyed too much already. I won't let it destroy us too.

I stroke his head with my hand.

"Morning," I say.

"Morning, babe."

He moves back on the sofa and I lie down facing him. I am reminded of the nights we spent together in Baghdad, when we slept curled into each other in a single bed. My face is inches from his.

"Adam… I'm sorry for what I said last night. I shouldn't have said that… not about Dave."

He sighs.

"Yeah, well, I shouldn't have thrown the plate."

I put my hand on his side and he flinches at the contact, but I leave my hand there.

"Adam, I think you need to talk to someone."

He says nothing, just looks at me. I know he wants to look away, but our faces are so close that there is nowhere for his gaze to go.

"I just… It's not your fault Dave died and I think you're still punishing yourself for it. You did everything you could. Maybe talking to someone professional could help…"

It was Kate who had told me, not Adam. Kate had received the report, then asked and asked and asked until she understood the final moments of Dave's life. It was Kate who told me that Dave was shot in an ambush during an operation and that it was Adam who worked on him. It was Adam who tried to stem the blood that was pumping out of Dave's body. It was Adam who tried to stop the life from draining away.

I have asked Adam about it, but he won't say much. I do not know whether this is because he doesn't want to or that he simply can't. It's something I saw in some of the visa applicants who had been through trauma. Their mind decided it was better to forget.

Kate told me that one shot went through Dave's chest. The doctors said he never stood a chance, but still Adam tried. I have tried to reassure him many times that it is not his fault. He hears the words but he does not feel them.

'I'm the medic, Emma. The fucking medic,' he said to me when we finally talked about it. "It was my job to bring him home safely and I failed. Anything would be better than this. I would rather have not come home at all than come home without him."

"You don't mean that, Adam," I had said, my voice cracking. "You can't mean that." But I knew it was the most honest thing he had ever said.

"I can't get help, Em," he says to me now. "It's not that simple. They could stop me doing my job."

"Maybe a break isn't a bad thing."

"Without my work I have nothing."

I want to grab him. Shake him by the shoulders. Shout, *what about us? What about me? I left my job to come here.*

I have nothing else. Do not tell me your work is everything.
Instead I speak in a voice that sounds calmer than my own.

"Why would they stop you doing your job? I went to that briefing. There was all kinds of stuff about getting support."

"It doesn't always work out like that though."

He pushes his body up to a sitting position and I do the same. I face him on the couch.

"What do you mean?" I ask.

"Do you remember Scott?"

"Scott?"

"Yeah. He was in Iraq with me when we met."

"Oh, the short guy, kinda stocky?"

"Yeah, that's him. The team Bravo. Well, after the last deployment he had some marriage issues. He thought his wife had been fucking someone while he was away, although he never had any proof and she didn't admit to it."

My mind flickers to Sally in the bar, her body pressed up against a stranger. I never said anything to Adam and now I somehow feel that this makes me complicit.

"Scott went through a bit of a bad patch. Nothing major, but he realised he wasn't firing on all cylinders at work. He was getting pissed more than usual. So he did what they tell us to do. He asked for support. And do you want to know what happened?"

I have a feeling I probably don't.

"They transferred him off the team early. He still had a year left, but they sent him to some shit role in battalion ops. They said they just needed someone, but everyone knew what was going on. It was fucking bullshit."

"But... I don't get it. Why?"

"Because he didn't have his shit squared away."

"Are you sure that's why?" I ask.

"Positive. I'm just telling you how it is, Emma."

"But..."

I feel like I am fighting a losing battle here, but I have to persist. I have to try.

"But what?"

"Okay, so you can't ask for help, but there must be something you can do. Anything. Even just hanging out with the guys more. Maybe other people are struggling too."

"What do you expect us to do? Sit in a circle and talk about our feelings?"

"No. I just mean be around people who understand."

"I'm around them all fucking day."

"But to relax, outside of work…"

"Em, if you genuinely want to help me out here, the best thing you can do is get off my back. Yeah, I'm fucking miserable because one of my best friends died and I probably will be for a while. You just have to let me deal with it."

He stands up from the sofa.

"I need to get ready for work, babe."

And with that, the conversation is over.

46

"Okay, here it is, the last one… the biggie," I say to Hassan. "Are you ready?"

We sit in front of his computer on the University of Denver application website. He's applied to four other colleges in Colorado, but this is the one that he really wants. We've checked and double-checked his personal statement, uploaded transcripts (what he has of them) and references. Now it's time.

"Sure am," he says.

Hassan's finger flexes, *click*, on the submit button. He turns to me with a grin.

"Congratulations! College applications complete!"

I hold my hand up for a high five and Hassan shakes his head at my waiting palm.

"Too much?" I ask. He smiles and eventually lifts his hand to meet my own.

"Definitely," he says.

I am almost sad that the application process is over. It has been a race to get it completed, but one that has given me a sense of purpose. I don't know how I would have spent the countless evenings of Adam sitting silently in front of the television drinking beer, had I not been researching the details of computer science degrees across the state.

After the initial conversation with Zainab, things gained

momentum quickly. I contacted various institutions to ask about courses and funding availability. Unsurprisingly, more than one university was interested in having a bright young Iraqi among their student populace. A couple put Hassan in touch with current students so he could get a taste of what life at their university would be like. The University of Denver invited him for a private tour of the campus.

I'd noticed a change in Hassan since beginning the applications. Zainab said he seemed happier. He spent more time sat in the kitchen with his mother, talking about college options, instead of shut upstairs in his room. He even seemed more sociable with other kids from school.

Some evenings I would go round to Zainab's and join them, and we would compare research on what we'd found out about course details or entry requirements. We wrote what we knew on Post-its and stuck them to the kitchen wall, comparing institutions. When I was with them, I felt energised.

My favourite part of the process was helping Hassan write his personal statement. I felt like I was finally putting to use all the skills I had gathered in Iraq from interviewing visa applicants, coaxing out memories and details of significant life events. From that, I began to understand more of Hassan's story.

At first he was hesitant.

"I don't understand why you need to know about my childhood to write my personal statement," he said. "I don't want them to accept me just because I'm a refugee."

I knew how he felt. Mrs Edwards helped me write my personal statement in sixth form. Draft after draft after draft. She said I should include my father's death as part of my narrative and I was adamantly against it.

"It's not about trying to play the sympathy card," she told me. "It's about explaining who you are and what drives you. Your motivation to do good in the world comes from your father, Emma, it's obvious."

I explained this again and again to Hassan. I don't know

whether in the end I got through or whether he just gave up arguing.

"We just need to thread the pieces together," I told him. "They want to know how you became the computer-savvy Hassan that you are today, and how they can be the next step in that journey."

It took a long time for him to open up, but one day I took him out for a burger and finally the chipping away paid off.

"We used to go for burgers after computer class sometimes," he said. And then I asked more.

Hassan told me that when he was a child there was one computer in his school. It was locked in a classroom and he never got to use it himself. Every day he passed by that particular classroom he jumped up to look through the window, and he never once saw anyone use it. He was fascinated.

As he got older he got more access to computers, mainly through internet cafés where boys met to smoke, play games and occasionally talk to girls via messenger. When, in Amman, he heard about the computer club led by another Iraqi, he jumped at the chance. It ran from 3.30–5.30pm every Wednesday.

"I lived for that club," he said. "I spent every day just waiting for Wednesday to come around. As soon as the class was over on Wednesday evening, I just started counting down the days until the next one."

What Zainab had thought was just a bunch of boys hanging out in an internet café had actually been a course run by an Iraqi technology entrepreneur. He taught the boys and girls (only two girls, points out Hassan) basic coding and encouraged them to be creative.

"He told us to imagine what we would create if we could create anything, and then we worked backwards from that until we reached the very first possible step. The most simple thing we could do to work towards that goal."

After the course ended, Hassan and some of the other boys continued to teach themselves, via online forums and YouTube videos. Hassan was the only boy to master the more complex multi-player coding, so he started creating games they could all play together.

"It started as a bit of a joke," he said. "I met some other guys from Basra, so I made this game that simulated the streets of the city. We could meet up virtually in the coffee shops around the area we used to live. We could walk the same streets – past the school and the bakery and the market where we were sent to run errands for our mothers."

Through the game, Hassan had found a way of reclaiming his old life. He made an alternate version of the reality that he had lost.

"It got kinda popular," he said. "There are quite a few guys from Basra who use it now. Someone got in touch to ask if I'd make a Baghdad version, but I dunno… It's not my city. It wouldn't feel the same."

I was astounded at what Hassan had done.

Zainab appears in the doorway of Hassan's room.

"Is it done?" she asks.

"Yup," Hassan says with a grin. Zainab gives him a hug.

"I'm so proud of you, son. God willing, you will succeed. Whatever happens, I am so proud."

She turns to me.

"Emma, will you stay for dinner? I've made qouzi to celebrate."

I accept more quickly than perhaps I should have. I send Adam a message *Out for dinner. Will be back around 9pm.*

Haider is at work again, but Farwa joins us at the kitchen table. At first she struggled with all the limelight cast on Hassan over his college applications, but eventually she got on board and even started looking at courses that she would like to do herself. This has ranged from art history to astrophysics, so it is probably good she has four years to decide.

"Actually, I've decided to be a doctor," she announces this evening between spoonfuls of soft lamb and pistachio-sprinkled rice. Hassan snorts and she punches him in the arm. I am sure that whatever she finally puts her mind to, she will do it well.

I eat quickly. The food is delicious. I haven't had qouzi since I was in Baghdad and Hana brought the dish in on her birthday. She explained the preparation to me at the time, but it went on for so long that eventually I stopped listening. Zainab must have been preparing this all day.

"That was so tasty, Zainab," I say, as she starts to clear the plates away.

"I'm glad you liked it," she says. "I'll pack some up for you to take home."

Before I can protest she has gone into the kitchen and returns with a Tupperware container that is full to the brim.

"Give some to your husband, perhaps he will enjoy it too," she says.

When it is time to leave, I put the qouzi on the passenger seat beside me and the car fills with the smell of Iraqi celebrations. I feel protective over the family as their mentor, but I am quietly comforted by the maternal role that Zainab has taken on too. I enjoy when she fusses over me, makes me food, worries that my jacket it too thin. I feel cared for.

I look over at the qouzi, still hot in the Tupperware, and smile. But other thoughts start to cloud my mind. I think of Adam and remember the way that Iraq does not enter our home anymore. I think about Kate and remember our conversation in the maternity unit that day. *Lamb grabs, Dave calls them. He hates them.* Dave hates them. What do I think I am doing taking this food home?

I see a bin on the pavement and pull the car over quickly. A couple stroll past with their dog and I wait until they are out of sight, then get out of the car with the engine still running. I empty the contents of the container into the bin and turn my back as steam rises up into the cold night air.

47

The weekend of Adam's father's sixtieth birthday celebrations has arrived. I know technically he is my father-in-law, but I do not feel I know the family well enough to refer to him as that. I am almost surprised to be here, waiting for the door of the family home to open.

Up until the last minute, I wasn't sure whether we'd make it. I ended up booking the flights for us both, even though he insisted he'd do it. I worried that if I didn't, his mother might think that I was keeping him away.

Now, as we wait, Adam puts his arm around me, his fingers digging into my side. The gesture surprises me and I glance up at him questioningly, but his eyes are fixed on the doorway and the figure of his mother that has now appeared.

"Mom!" he says, his face breaking into a smile.

"Adam, oh my boy, it is so good to see you both!"

She takes a step towards us and wraps her arms around him.

"I'm so glad you're back," she says. All of her sons are back now. She has spent much of the past eight years with at least one son deployed, sometimes more. Now they are all home, for the time being at least.

She turns to me.

"Emma, honey." She hugs me too. This embrace is less easy. I know she finds it hard that her son married a woman she barely knows. Both of Adam's brothers married girls from their home state. The all-American type. The type that Adam's mum understands. The first time that we met was at the wedding and even then it was all such a rush that I didn't have the opportunity to spend any real time with her. Luckily, her and my mother bonded over a love of gardening and the stress of having children who work in dangerous places.

She ushers through the door and Adam keeps hold of my hand. In the living room, Adam's two nephews are sat in front of the television and jump up from the floor to greet him. His older brother, Chad, and his wife are on the couch. His other sister-in-law cradles a baby girl in the kitchen. His younger brother, Michael, and his dad are out in the back garden throwing around an American football but come in when they hear us, letting a rush of cold air into the room. This family is loud and boisterous and so different from my own.

"Son!" booms Adam's father, hitting him hard on the back.

"Happy birthday, Dad," says Adam. "How does it feel being another year older?"

"Feels same as ever, son. I'm still just as capable of whooping your ass at football," Adam's father says.

"We all can," says Michael. "Adam's big old brain weighs him down too much."

Michael gives Adam a playful punch in the bicep. Adam wraps an arm round his neck, pulling him in and ruffling his hair the way he must have done since they were kids.

"We'll see about that," says Adam.

"Boys, already?" says his mum. "Adam's only just arrived." But Chad has already pushed himself up from the sofa and Adam's dad is out the back door, Michael close behind. Adam puts his hand on my back.

"Won't be long, babe," he says, then kisses my cheek and disappears after them. Seeing him with his family makes me miss my own.

On the second day, I go to the store with his mother to pick up food for lunch. I am trying to be closer to her, the way she is with her other daughters-in-law. I want to talk about Adam.

"How does he seem to you?" I ask as we walk around the grocery store, me pushing the trolley as she fills it up. I know better than to interfere with her choices.

"Good," she says. "Same old Adam. Why?"

"I… He's different… at home. Not here. But at home, well, he's quiet."

She nods but says nothing.

"I'm worried," I say.

"Have you asked him about it?"

"Yes."

"And?"

"He says he's fine. That he can cope."

She drifts away and returns with two large packets of pasta, which she passes to me. I place them in the trolley.

"Well, there you go. If he says he's fine, then he's probably fine, honey."

She leans into the shopping cart and moves the bags of pasta to the other side, then rearranges the meat and the dairy.

"If you organise it now it makes it easier when we get to packing," she says.

As we walk down the aisles, she greets people. It is a small town and this makes shopping a slow affair.

"Oh, you must be Emma from England," one woman says, holding her hand between both of mine. That is what they all call me, "Emma from England". A constant reminder that I am not one of them.

The next aisle is quiet. I try again.

"What about Bob, or your other boys? Were they ever different after deployment? Or what about when Adam has been away before?"

She disappears without answering my question and returns with a packet of cereal. I try again.

"Mrs McLaughlin." We share a name now. "Were they? Different?"

She places the cereal methodically into the dried goods corner of the trolley and straightens up to face me.

273

"They've been to war, Emma. Of course it has an effect. But they are men. They find their own way of dealing with it."

"And if they don't?"

"Don't what?"

"Don't deal with it."

She raises her hands from her sides in frustration.

"They just do. It's not for us to interfere and tell them how. You're Adam's wife. Your job is to support him regardless."

This woman and her family are so different to my own. In my family it was my mother who encouraged us to talk about our feelings, to be vulnerable, even when we didn't want to be. Even when it seemed like a losing battle.

Adam's mother speaks again, her tone softer this time.

"Listen, honey, I can understand your concern. But honestly, you and Adam – you're still so new to each other. I've known him all thirty-one years of his life and, I can tell you now, that boy is fine."

"I hope you're right, Mrs McLaughlin."

"I've got three sons. I haven't been wrong yet."

When we get back to the house, Adam comes out to meet us at the car. He kisses me on the lips and takes the shopping bags that I have started unloading from the boot.

"Let me take those, babe," he says, carrying them back into the house.

"See, says his mother behind me. "He's fine." I desperately want her to be right.

We are only there for three days, but he is different at his parents' house. Better, on the surface at least. I wonder whether it is being with his family or being around other military men that helps. Perhaps it is neither and he is just better at acting these days.

He is more affectionate with me too. His leg rests against mine when we are sat at the dinner table. He pulls me onto his lap when there is no more couch space. I want to believe that my Adam is returning.

We go for a walk one evening and he holds my hand, our fingers interlacing the way they did in Garden of the Gods that day before he left. I let myself hope for a moment that maybe things could be different. As we walk, a piece of blue catches my eye. A bit of crockery that must have broken long ago and has been trodden into the path. I stoop to pick it up, my nails digging into the dirt to prise it from its place.

As we lie in bed that night, his body curls around me and his arm rests over my body. He kisses the skin behind my ear and whispers to me.

"Em, I'm going to figure this out. You're right, I'll try and hang out with the guys a bit more. It might do me good."

I say nothing, but turn my body to kiss him back and gasp silently as his skin finally starts to move against mine once more.

When we leave the next day, Adam's father holds him in a tight embrace and his mother keeps trying to give us plastic containers of food for the plane journey.

Adam steps back and puts an arm around me.

"Y'all need to visit us next time," he says to them. I smile and agree and insist that they must. I do not mention that I suggested to Adam that we invite them to us when he cancelled the last two visits, but he was against it.

Chad drops us off at the airport.

"Stay safe, guys," he says, passing us our bags from the boot of his truck.

"Always," Adam replies. "It was good to see you, bro."

We walk into the airport in silence. I want him to take my hand again, but his hands are in his pockets now.

"That was a good trip," I say as we wait for our boarding passes.

"It was fine," he says with a shrug.

48

At night he treads the streets of Baghdad. His night vision is not the plum colour of our sheets or the magnolia of our walls. It is grainy black and chemical green.

He never tells me where he has been, but I know. I transpose him onto images I have seen before. Last night, rubble-strewn streets with breeze-block buildings that have surrendered to the battle. The night before, an empty school, child-size chairs lying on their sides and paintings curled at the edges, licked by flames.

Tonight an infrared laser searches for a target. A pinpoint traces across the light green sky, then explodes into brilliant white.

While dogs dream, their paws paddle the air and rubbery black lips rise in muffled barks. Their owners watch on, nudge each other and smile. Sometimes Adam's limbs twitch too, but there is nothing endearing about a sleeping man who patrols the streets of a faraway country, in search of an enemy it is too late to find.

Sometimes half-formed words leave his mouth, guttural and aggressive. Get back, he barks. Get down. Get back. Get away. Sometimes they are of another language, learnt from interpreters and trainers, sounding heavy on his tongue. Sometimes they are not barks, but whimpers. Sometimes they form a name. I am an unwanted observer to his vulnerability. Always the sounds contain danger.

I do not wake him during these nocturnal operations. I do not want to walk into the stream of bullets flying from his gun or alert the enemy to his position with my intrusion. I do not want to disturb him as he shoves bandages into a gaping chest. Time is running out.

Mostly I worry that until his mission is complete he will never fully return to me. So I kiss him as he leaves for Iraq each night and pray that he will succeed so that he can finally come home.

Tonight I think he came close. It got down to hand-to-hand combat. Green on black and black on green. He grunted. Flesh pounded flesh. He grappled with a body, thrashing this way and that between dust and bed sheets. But then I entered his dream unbidden. The piercing sound of my cry rang out across Baghdad as his elbow plunged down through the night air to meet my face on the pillow next to his.

49

It has been a long time since I called her, but since we returned from Adam's house I have felt the pull of family. I want to hear her voice.

She answers on the third ring.

"Hello?"

"Hi Mum."

"Emma?"

"Yes, Mum. Hi. How are you?"

"I'm good, Emma. Is everything okay?"

I hear the concern in her voice. I am not the daughter that calls her just to chat.

"Yeah, it's fine. I'm just… I'm just calling to say hi."

"It's lovely to hear from you, darling. It's been a while."

"I know, Mum. I'm sorry. I just get caught up in things here, and then… you know… with the time zones and stuff…"

"It doesn't matter, you're calling now. How are you?"

"I'm… I'm fine."

"And Adam?"

"Yeah… He's okay too."

"Are you sure? You don't sound too certain."

"I am. It just takes a while, you know… Settling back in."

"I can imagine. You never seemed to settle when you visited us."

She's right.

"You must be so glad to have him back though, Em."

"I am. It's great... Really... really nice."

"Are you sure?"

"Mum. I..."

I want to talk to her. Want to tell her. I want to let her comfort me. But I can't.

"Mum, can we just talk about something else? How's the garden at the moment? Rebecca said you're painting again."

Even across the Atlantic she understands. She knows not to push too hard, too soon.

"Of course, darling, of course. Did she tell you about the new palette I bought?"

"No, Mum, but I'd love to hear more."

"Okay, Emma... But just remember, if you want to talk about anything else I'm always here."

50

Adam has gone out with the guys on his team tonight. Even though he promised he would while we were away, I didn't fully believe it. Not until he came home this week and said they were making plans for Friday night.

"I'm proud of you," I said and gave him a kiss on the cheek.

It was strange seeing him get ready this evening. I watched him put on his nicest pair of jeans and kissed his neck as he tightened his belt in the mirror.

"You look good," I told him. His reflection smiled at me.

I couldn't help but feel envious too. Even though I wanted him to go out with the guys and relax, I couldn't remember the last time the two of us had gone out together. I couldn't remember the last time we'd really had fun. But maybe this was the beginning, I told myself. Maybe things would get better and soon we'd go out together too.

After he left, I sat at the island in the kitchen and poured a glass of wine. I was there for a while, moving pieces of mosaic around the counter, but eventually I became frustrated and swept them back into the jar. Instead I ran a bath, put on some music, tried to relax. I had another glass of wine, put on fresh pyjamas and was in bed by 10pm.

Now, I wake up to the sound of my phone ringing. It is dark and the bed is empty and for a moment I think he is still out there and the panic rises in my throat. But Adam is in

Colorado now, not Iraq. The phone keeps ringing. It is not the Arabic pop song anymore; he asked me to change that after he got back. It is one of those irritating pre-set ringtones with a cycle of notes repeated over and over.

I grab the phone, checking the clock as I do so. It is 3am. No good calls ever come at this hour. I expect to see Adam's name, but instead *Zainab* flashes up on the phone. Shit. I answer.

"Zainab, what's wrong?"

"Emma…" I can hear the tears in her voice. "It's Hassan. I just got a call from the police. He's in some kind of trouble downtown."

"The police? Shit. Really?"

"They say he's been in a fight. Another one." Her voice shakes. "They aren't charging him with anything, but they want me to go and pick him up and Haider's working night shift so I don't have a car and I can't get hold of him."

"Don't worry. I'll go straight away," I tell her.

"Are you sure, Emma? I'm so sorry to ask."

"Of course I'm sure."

"I… I thought things were getting better with him, Emma. I don't understand."

"So did I. But it's okay, Zainab, we'll figure it out. Call the police officer back and give them my number. Tell them I'm on my way. I'll call you when I've got him."

"God bless you, Emma."

"I'll call you soon."

As Zainab was talking, I have been pulling on my jeans and socks. I don't bother changing my pyjama top but pull a hoodie on over it. I am angry with Hassan. Hurt. We worked so hard on his college applications and I can't believe he'd jeopardise all of that so soon.

I set off in the car. The streets are dead at this time of night. I do not turn on the radio. I just sit in silence and try to decide what I will say to Hassan when I get there. My phone rings again. It is an unknown number and I assume it must be the police officer.

"Hello?"

"Mrs McLaughlin?" says the voice on the other end.

"Yes. Is this about Hassan? I'm on my way. I'm about five minutes out."

There is a moment's silence.

"Er... No. It's Specialist Yates here, from the Military Police. I'm calling about your husband."

"Wait, you're what?" I push hard on my breaks and pull over to the side of the road.

"Yes. I'm in downtown Colorado Springs at present. I regret to inform you that your husband has been involved in an altercation. There are no charges against him, but given his current state of inebriation we recommend you pick him up."

"Where exactly are you?"

"We're at North Tejon with East Kiowa."

"I'm... I'm already on my way."

"Thank you, Mrs McLaughlin. We'll see you shortly." The voice disappears.

"SHIT!" I thump the steering wheel hard. "Shit, shit, shit." This can't be happening.

I call Noor, who answers the phone with a bleary voice.

"Noor, I'm so sorry to wake you. Can you get downtown? I need your help."

"So let me get this right, you're here for both this Iraqi kid and your SF husband?" the police officer asks me. The regular police officer and the MP are standing side by side. They exchange a confused look.

"That's correct," I say. I try to block from my mind the last time I talked to an MP. The blood in my mouth. My feet pounding the gravel. The look on Anna's face.

From what the policemen have told me so far, Hassan and his friends spent the evening smoking on benches because they were too young to get into bars. Adam and his teammates were drunkenly leaving Cowboys when they passed the group on the bench. Riley, the team Charlie, muttered something about "Haji motherfuckers" and the boys heard.

"What did you just call us?" one of the boys shouted, although it wasn't clear who. I remembered telling Hassan that he shouldn't tolerate racist comments and wondered if I had somehow played a part in this too.

The altercation didn't last long. Adam and his teammates turned around and there were a bunch of insults and a few shoves, but the police were on hand almost instantly. The presence of MPs in downtown on a Friday night suddenly made sense to me.

"Luckily we were just outside the next bar," the MP told me. "A bunch of SF dudes against those scrawny teenagers? I don't think it would have ended well."

Now, Hassan is sat with two other Middle Eastern-looking boys of the same age. I catch his eye and give him my best I'm-disappointed-and-your-mum's-going-to-kill-you face. Adam is sat on the pavement about five metres in the other direction, his head between his knees. He has avoided all eye contact so far.

Riley, who is still standing, hears what the police officer said to me.

"Hey. Hey. Wait. Did I hear that right? McLaughlin's old lady is here for the kid too?"

"Shut up!" the MP yells at him.

Adam puts his head deeper between his knees and runs both hands over the back of his head.

"No shit!" says another team guy, who I don't recognise. I watch Adam. These are his men. These are the people he has been trained to protect. To risk his life for. Who would he defend now?

"Yeah," Riley starts again. "She's the Haji-lover, don't you remember Adam telling us that—?"

"SHUT THE FUCK UP!" shouts Adam, raising his head.

283

"That's my fucking wife. I'll punch you in the throat if you say another fucking word."

His eyes lock onto mine. I hold his gaze for as long as I can bear.

Noor turns up about five minutes later, still fully in pyjamas. I try to remain calm as I explain to her what has happened. I see her glance over my shoulder at Adam, but she makes no comment. Instead, she calls Zainab to say that she is here with me and will bring Hassan home very soon. She passes the handset to Hassan and we watch as he says very little but just gives small nods and says "Yes Mom, yes Mom, yes Mom." After he finishes, I reach for the phone myself, but Noor grabs it and gives me a quick shake of the head.

"No, Emma. Just focus on Adam for now."

I look over to the pavement where he is still sat and I know she's right.

Hassan gets into her car.

"I'll call you tomorrow," Noor says. "Take care."

On the way back to the house, Adam and I sit in silence. His head rolls to the side each time I take a corner. I wonder how much he has drunk. I am angry and devastated and so many things that I say nothing. But then he speaks.

"Why do you always choose them, Emma?"

"What?" My eyes glance towards him and then back to the road.

"Why do you always choose them?"

"What do you mean, 'them'?"

"Iraqis."

"Adam, you're drunk. What the hell are you talking about?"

"You always choose Iraq. Iraqis."

"I just left the kid I'm helping so that I could bring you home. Is that choosing Iraqis?"

"What if that other one hadn't turned up, what would you have done then?" he asks.

"Other one? For fuck's sake, Adam. Noor. She's called Noor. You know that." But I do not answer the question because I do not know the answer and it's not something I want to think about more. "Is this just about tonight?" I ask, instead.

"Of course not."

"Then what, what else?"

"It's always, Em. I always feel like it's a competition. It's me or them. Me or Iraq. I fucking proposed to you, said I wanted to be with you for the rest of my life, and yet you still wanted to stay longer in that godforsaken place. Then you finally move here and we agreed you'd focus on settling in Colorado for a while, but first it's the Iraqi friend and this fucking refugee art shit and then next thing I know you've basically implanted yourself into an Iraqi family. I'm just waiting for the day you leave me to go back there."

My head is spinning.

"I'm not leaving you to go back there, Adam."

"You said you'd leave Iraq behind when you moved to Colorado and you didn't do that. Why should I believe you now?"

I sigh. Suddenly all the anger and frustration seeps from my body and is replaced by a tiredness that penetrates my bones.

"Even if I go back there to work, it doesn't mean I'm leaving you, Adam. You're my husband."

51

It is midday by the time Adam emerges. I spent the rest of the night lying awake, trying to convince myself his comments were just the alcohol talking. By 6am I was up, unable to bear the looping of the conversation in my head any longer. *You always choose them, Emma.* It wasn't so different from something my sister once said.

He comes downstairs and starts to make coffee without saying anything. I am sat at my laptop, looking at a pamphlet for that art exhibition that Noor sent me a few days ago for feedback.

"Morning," I say to him.

"Do we have any Advil?" he replies.

"Under the sink in the bathroom."

He heads back up the stairs and I hear the bathroom cupboard open and close. As he comes down, the pills rattle in their plastic container. He pours coffee. Takes a couple of noisy gulps. I told myself that I would wait until later in the day to talk about it all. But I can't.

"Adam, we need to talk."

"Now, Em? My head's ready to explode."

"Yes. Now."

"Fine. Talk."

"You need to get help, Adam. We can't go on like this. I barely even know who you are anymore."

"You're the one that wanted me to go out with my team, remember? You wanted this."

"But I didn't think it would be like… Adam, I didn't think you'd end up roughing up the refugee kid I'm mentoring."

"It wasn't 'roughing up', it was a couple of shoves. It's hardly a big deal."

"Hardly a big deal? Jesus Christ, Adam."

"Okay, so I won't go out with the guys after all. Is that what you want?"

"What I want is for you to talk to someone. This isn't you, Adam. Can't you see that? Can't you see how unhappy you are?"

"Yeah, I'm depressed as fuck. But I've told you, I'm not talking to a shrink."

"There must be someone. Anyone. The chaplain even."

"Why are you so desperate for me to talk to someone, Emma? You want me to talk about my feelings, what, like I bet you did when your dad died? You're such a fucking hypocrite. You barely even talk to your mom anymore and when you do it's just about gardening or the weather."

It is a low blow. It hurts because it is true. We all want to be known, but being known makes us vulnerable. Those who truly know us can see things that we have yet to recognise in ourselves. My brain won't even let me process his comments, so I continue, losing the fight to keep emotion from my voice.

"I want you to talk to someone because you're changing, Adam. You're… you're mean. That stuff with Hassan last night… Your comments about Noor… I'm starting to feel like I married a fucking racist."

"My best friend died, Emma. My best friend was shot in the chest by an Iraqi."

"And that's awful, but it was one guy, Adam. One Iraqi. What about Ali? Do you not even remember how we met, how you were trying to help him? How he risked his life to save yours?"

This doesn't make sense to me. It doesn't add up. How can the man I fell in love with be thinking this way? Which version of Adam is real?

"Don't you dare bring Ali into this," he says.

"Why, Adam? Because you know I'm right? That you're being insane. Yes, Dave was killed by an Iraqi, but that was one bad person. Did I start hating all the white guys in the world because one shitbag PSD tried to rape me?"

Silence.

"Someone tried to rape you?" he says quietly.

I say nothing.

"Someone tried to rape you and you never told me?" I thought I was protecting him by not telling him. Now I have used it against him at his most vulnerable.

He runs his hands over his head the way he did last night. I think I might vomit. The hand moves again. Over the head. Round the back of his neck. I can see him trying to process what I have said. Over the head. Round the neck. I'm not sure I've ever seen him look this sad before.

"Emma, I..." His hands are shaking. The trembling starts to extend to the rest of his body. What have I done, putting this on him? It was not something I wanted to throw out in an argument. "Emma..."

Over the head. Round the neck. Shaking. Then the hands stop and something in his face changes. Hardens. He looks at me and this other version of Adam returns.

"Well, Em, I guess that just proves that you suck at talking about important stuff too."

52

"Emma?"

"Noor. Hi."

"Hi. Are you okay? You sound… Have you been crying?"

"No, no. I'm just tired. I didn't sleep well after last night."

"Ah okay, good. I mean… Not good that you didn't sleep. But good that you're okay."

"Thanks so much for helping, Noor. Are they all okay? Zainab must have been distraught. I'll phone her later. I need to… I need to apologise."

"They're fine, Em. Hassan's been grounded for the rest of the month, but I explained things to her. Said it wasn't necessarily his fault, that…"

"Thanks."

"But Em, I need to talk to you. I don't think you should phone them. It's… Emma. There's no easy way to say this, but they've decided they don't want you as a mentor anymore."

"What?"

"They don't think it's appropriate, given Adam's involvement in what happened. And to be honest I agree with them, Em. You've got so much on your plate. You can't help everyone."

"They don't want me as their mentor? Zainab said that?"

"Well, no. Haider. But Zainab was there when he said it, and she agreed."

"But what… what am I supposed to do now?"

"What do you mean?"

"If I can't help them... If I'm not helping them... What am I supposed to do?"

"What?"

"What will I do, Noor?"

"Look after yourself, Em. Figure out things with Adam. I'm sorry... I... I had suspicions, but I didn't realise things were so bad."

"It's okay."

"You'll be okay, Emma. You're strong. You just took on too much."

I say nothing.

"I'm sorry to have to say this, Em, but promise me you won't call them, okay?"

Silence.

"Okay, I promise."

53

Now I am no longer mentoring, I return home straight after the art shop in the evening. I know Penny knows what's happened, but she says nothing. That's how bad things are.

When I get home today I expect to find Adam there. His truck is in the drive and his rucksack is on the floor by the sofa, but I cannot see him. I walk through the house calling his name and there is no reply.

Back in the living room I call his mobile and hear vibrations coming from the sofa. I push my hand between two cushions and scoop out the device. The anxiety that plagued me during his deployment creeps back, its tendrils wrapping around me. I have heard the stories of what some soldiers do after they return.

I walk around the house again. I am still wearing my shoes and the sound of their thud against the wooden floor echoes around our silent home.

"Adam?" I call. "Are you in?"

Nothing. *Breathe*, I tell myself. *Breathe*. But his words spin around my head. *It would have been better not to come home at all.*

I do not want to look in the garage, but I know I have to. Perhaps he is out there messing around with truck parts or digging out some equipment for work. Before his deployment he spent a lot of time in the garage, especially when he wanted to clear his mind, but since he got back he's only been out there to stash away his gear in a couple of large plastic boxes.

I open the back door and wrap my arms around myself, even though I am still wearing my coat. I walk briskly across the yard to the garage. The night air bites at my face and I shiver from the combination of nerves and cold. No light glows from the base of the garage door and I know the inside must be in darkness. My hand pauses for a moment over the handle and I consider going back inside. But I have to check. I push the handle resolutely downwards.

The metal is icy to the touch, so cold that it burns, and I pull my hand back quickly. I push the door open with a sleeve-covered arm and the hinges creak. Oiling the garage door was one of the things Adam wrote on his pre-deployment chore list but never got round to. I said I would do it myself, but I came out here so rarely during his deployment that it escaped my mind completely.

"Adam. Adam?" I say his name into the darkness once, twice, but there is nothing.

I might have shut the door and returned quickly to the warmth of the house, were it not for the smell. It is not strong, but out of place. I am accustomed to the smells of grease and old military equipment and stale workout gear that merge together in the still air of the garage. But there is something else in the mix this time. Alcohol.

I step back in shock when I turn on the light, even though it is not what I had feared the most. Adam is sat on the floor against the opposite wall of the garage. His feet are flat on the ground, his knees bent up towards his chest. His head tilts forwards and in a hand by his side is a half-empty bottle of whisky.

"Adam!" I gasp, rushing towards him. He raises his head and peers at me through bloodshot eyes.

"Please, Emma. I just want some quiet. Please just leave me alone."

"Adam, it's freezing out here and you're sat on the floor! Get up!"

"No, I'm fine."

"No, get up. Let's go inside."

I put my hand against his cheek and it is freezing. I have no idea how long he's been sat here, with the whisky providing a false blanket against the cold. I pull one of his arms over my shoulder and try to lift him, but he is too heavy. I stumble under his weight and he slumps back down.

"No, leave me, Em. Please, just go back inside."

"I'm not leaving you in the cold."

"It doesn't matter. I don't feel it. I don't feel anything."

"Adam."

"I don't. Nothing." He lowers his face into the palm of his hands. I pull his hands away and hold them between mine, trying to warm him.

"Come inside. Get warm. Let me make you a coffee."

"No…"

He drags his hands back to his face. A tremor runs through his body. I have seen him drunk since his return, but never like this. Never crying. I slide slowly down the wall next to him and put my arm around his shoulders, pull him towards me, try to absorb his cold body into mine. Another tremor racks through him.

"I'm sorry," he says.

"Sorry? Why? You don't need to be sorry…"

He takes gulping breaths.

"I failed all of you."

"Failed us? What do you mean?"

"You got attacked and I wasn't there. I should have told you to leave Iraq sooner. Or found that fucking guy and killed him…"

"No, Adam, no… That wasn't on you. I chose to be there, you know that. I looked after myself. It wasn't your call."

He tries to look at me but his eyes are out of focus.

"I'm supposed to protect you."

293

"Not when I'm there, Adam. That's not your responsibility."

I hate myself for having told him. Or for not telling him in the first place. I look at him now, shivering, coming apart, and wonder what part I have played in it. How much of this is down to me?

"I didn't protect you and I didn't protect Dave…"

"No, that wasn't—"

He cuts me off.

"You think Dave wasn't my fault either, Emma, but it was. You don't understand."

"I do understand. You did everything you could. The doctors said he didn't stand a chance. Kate doesn't blame you. No one does."

"No. Not that. The guys that killed him, they knew."

"They knew what?"

He rubs his face again, and then the back of his neck. He looks up.

"They knew we were coming. And when. They knew."

"But how is…? Why does that make it your fault?'

"It was Kareem."

"The 'terp?"

"Our 'terp. Our 'terp told them."

I remember our Skype conversations. *He's… He's fine… He's just not Ali.* I should have known then that something was up.

"But, Adam… it's still not your fault."

"Why won't you listen to me? It is!"

He is getting agitated as he speaks now.

"I knew something was wrong, Em. I could tell he wasn't right, but I didn't say anything. I always tell my guys, 'Trust your gut, trust your intuition,' and I was so messed-up about Ali that I didn't. I fucking didn't and now Dave is dead."

The weight of guilt has crushed this man. Shattered him into a million pieces. Perhaps this is why when he tries to piece himself together the edges don't quite line up. The shape isn't the same as before.

I kneel in front of him, grabbing his shoulder with one hand and his chin with the other. I hold his face hard and force him to look at me as I speak.

"I know this is hard, Adam, but…"

He throws my hand off him.

"You know this is hard? What the fuck do you know about it, Emma? Just because you knew some Sri Lankan dude who got vaporised in the IZ fun park, you think you know how this feels?"

I lean back on my hands as his words barrel into my chest, forcing the air out of me. I try to speak, but no words come. The wall between us is growing higher, wider, faster than I know what to do with.

Adam braces himself with an arm and stumbles to his feet. He storms unsteadily out of the garage and I hear the back door slam. I hold my breath and wait, praying that I won't hear the rumble of the truck engine. Nothing. I stand up and move cautiously towards the garage door, which trembles on its hinges. In the upstairs window I see the silhouette of Adam moving around our bedroom. Then the bathroom light goes on and steam from the shower starts to fog up the window.

I sit where I was on the floor, savouring the dull ache of the cold as it slowly creeps into my body. I understand why he sat here. I wait for the cold to reach my brain and silence the whirring thoughts. Of Sampath and Dave and Kate and Ali. And now into my thoughts, hand in hand with Ali, comes Ameena. Did we fail her too?

I thought having been in Iraq myself would make this easier. Now nothing feels further from the truth.

54

One morning when Adam and I were still in Iraq together, I drove to the PX on Camp Liberty.

Adam had asked me to run an errand for him. It was close to his leaving day and he wanted a gift for Ali – a kilo packet of Tootsie Rolls. Ali had a sweet tooth and loved the small cylinders of hard toffee. I was happy to go. Driving to the store felt like a brief moment of normality, even though there was really nothing normal about driving to buy sweets on a military base in Iraq.

I remember the drive in moments. Images paste together to form a collage of the journey in my mind, their order jumbled. Some flashes of the memory may be from a different drive, a different route, a different day.

I drove past one of Saddam's palaces that sat on a lake lit up by the deepening blue of the morning sky. I watched the giant fish as they broke the surface of the water, gulping at flies. I drove past the rows of CHUs where men who had worked the night shift now slept and then the rows of military vehicles that waited to roll out of the gates and into Baghdad.

Next I drove where water channels flanked the sides of the road, blocked from view by thick reed beds. There must have been a gentle breeze that day, because I remember how the reeds quivered.

There weren't any buildings in the area of the base where the reeds hugged the roadsides. No unmarked office buildings or warehouses. Not even a solitary "porta-potty". If you continued far enough you would eventually get to the water field, where packets of plastic water bottles were stacked baking under the sun. The harsh rays disintegrated the wrapping that held the bottles together and caused the warm plastic to seep into the water itself, giving it a strange artificial taste. Some people said that extra oestrogen was added to the water to control soldiers' testosterone levels. I don't know if I ever believed that – people said a lot of strange things about life on the base back then.

But I wasn't at the water field yet. I was still where the reeds lined the road. This is the part where the edges of the memory are sharp. Crisp.

I spotted the parked vehicle long before I passed it. The roads flanked by water channels were long and straight, so you could see far ahead through the shimmering haze of heat. A white truck was pulled up at the side of the road, the driver's door open, the sun glinting off the roof. It was strange. Wrong.

The speed limit was low on that part of the base and I drove past slowly. Next to the open door, the reeds were bent over where a human figure had pushed through them. Broken.

I did not stop. I was a lone unarmed female on a military base in Iraq. I was barely even supposed to be there. I couldn't just get out of the vehicle in the middle of nowhere, although some days I think that I should have done. I still do not know whether I wish I had.

I continued on to the PX, where I bought Tootsie Rolls for Ali and a large coffee from Cinnabon for myself. I could have driven back another route to RPC, but I did not.

The white truck was still there when I drove past, but it was not the only vehicle this time. A military police car was stopped behind the truck and an ambulance was parked in front. A policeman stood in the middle of the road and waved me by, motioning for me to keep a distance from the scene. The back of the ambulance was open and I tried to force my eyes away, but not before they had found the shape of a body under a sheet.

That night I dreamt of a man, partially submerged in the slow-moving shallows of a stream. The water trickled over pale flesh, undeterred by the obstacle in its path. It mixed with the blood that seeped from the body, absorbing the bright red fluid until it was no longer visible, and continued on between the reed stalks.

Where is Adam now? Does he stand at the edge of a water channel among the reeds, alert to the sound of an approaching vehicle, hoping despite everything? Or are his lips already closing around cool metal, my vehicle disappearing towards the water field, another person I have failed to save?

55

Anna's email arrives in early autumn, or "fall" as I have learned to call it now. The leaves have turned to blazing reds and oranges and there is a chill in the air. I am reminded of the walks I took with Kate and Noah this time last year, while the men were deployed. Kate would bend over her pregnant belly to stoop down and collect leaves for Noah's art projects. Sometimes we bought hot apple cider and wrapped our hands round the cups as we walked. We talked about life and love and what we would do when our husbands were home.

I went on a walk to the same forest a few days ago. I chose the steepest path and walked until my legs ached and my lungs burned from sucking in the cool air. I reached a viewing point and looked out across the changing foliage, but I could find only melancholy in the vibrant shades. Adam wouldn't come with me.

"What's the point?" he asked. I didn't have an answer.

I am sat reading the news in the kitchen when Adam comes in bleary-eyed. He sleeps in the spare room most nights now. He says it is better that way. It is easier for him to rest when he is not worried about disturbing me. But I struggle to sleep anyway. I thought that loneliness was a half-empty bed when he was deployed. Now I know that it is the sound of him breathing as he tries to sleep in a different bed under the same roof.

"Morning," I say. "There's coffee in the pot."

"Thanks," he says, rubbing at his eyes. He pours out a mug and retreats back upstairs, where I hear the sound of the shower being turned on. There used to be a time when he wouldn't start his day without giving me a kiss, but not anymore. Sometimes I let my hand linger for a moment when I pass him a plate or the keys to the truck, but he draws away quickly, as if he has accidentally brushed against a stranger's hand. We inhabit the space around each other awkwardly.

"Do you still love me?" I asked him last week.

"Of course I do."

"Then why won't you touch me?"

"I just… Who am I to touch you, Em? I don't deserve to. I can barely call myself a husband anymore."

It was then I realised he was punishing himself, not me.

Anna's email simply says: *Can we finally Skype, Emma? Please?*

Now I am sat in a café in front of my laptop, waiting for Anna to log on. I would have liked to Skype her from home with a glass of wine like we used to, but it's hard to talk freely inside the house these days.

Anna types a message. *Ready when you are!* I put on my headphones and press call. The sound of Skype dialling transports me back to Adam's deployment and the calls we used to have. For a moment I get the same flutter of excitement that used to accompany seeing his face. But it is Anna who appears.

"There you are, stranger!" she says. "God, I'm glad to see you. It's been far too long!"

"It's good to see you too!" I say. She is on R and R and is sat in the tiny kitchen of the London apartment she shares with a friend from her university days. Behind her I can see an open bottle of wine and a takeaway bag by the sink. It is an apartment I have visited myself, during a trip to the UK from Iraq. Anna invited me over and we attempted to cook together. We drank as we cooked and the food ended up burnt. We put it down to lack of practice because of so many chow hall meals, rather than alcohol consumption. We sat at the dinner table anyway, sharing a bowl of olives and talking about Iraq. Her head stayed in that place as much as mine.

"How long's it been since our last chat? Two months? Three?" I ask.

"It's been longer than that, Em! We've only spoken once since Adam got back."

"It can't have been that long."

"I'm telling you, Em, it is. But anyway, I have you now. So how are you?" she asks. The question I hate.

"I'm good," I say. "Really good. How about you?" If Anna notices the false cheer in my voice, she doesn't say anything. Perhaps I am getting too good at pretending. Anna is particularly observant of my moods, which I expect comes from living and working in such proximity. It is another reason I have avoided talking to her for so long.

"Great! I'm good too," she says.

We start to catch up. We talk about her dinner with her parents, where she's been on vacation recently, how everyone at the office is doing. Each time I think she may ask me a question, I ask her something else. But I can tell that she is holding back too. Eventually she says it.

"Actually, I have some quite big news, Em."

"Oh my god, are you pregnant? Engaged?" That seems to be everyone's big news at our age.

"Haha, no, Emma! Is that all you think is important these days?! I *am* seeing someone, but that's not the news. I'll tell you about him afterwards."

"So…?" I say, trying to work out what she might want to tell me.

"I've got a new job," she says.

"Oh, congratulations! Are you finally returning to the real world?"

Real world? Am I calling it that now too?

"Not yet," she says. "It's still with our lot, but in Afghanistan. They've asked me to head up the Kabul office."

I wasn't prepared for this. It is difficult to hear. I take a sip of tea and hope that the cup over my face gives me long enough to compose myself. I silently wish the internet would cut out, the way it does in Iraq.

"That's brilliant news, Anna," I say, hoping I sound sincere. It is brilliant. She deserves it. We both know that the organisation was lining me up to become a country lead before I left, but it is not her fault that I am not there and she was chosen.

"Thanks. I know it's a bit of a step up, but I'm ready for the challenge. And I think the change of scenery will do me good."

"Yeah, definitely. It's really exciting. So how long before you start?"

"Two months. I've got one more month in Baggers, then I'm taking a month out in between positions to sort things out and maybe sit by a pool somewhere."

"That sounds like a good plan."

"Yeah, I'm ready for a bit of a longer break."

That silence again. There never used to be silences between us.

"So, Em, there's something else."

"Oh?"

"Well, what are you doing at the moment?"

"What do you mean?"

"Workwise."

"Oh. Well, I'm still at the art shop."

"Do you enjoy it? I mean, is it enough for you?"

"Yeah. I do. It's… Well, it's not ideal, but it's fine for now."

"Okay…" I can tell there is more.

"What?" It comes out sounding more defensive than I intended.

"No, nothing. It's just that when I get to Kabul, I have to hire a deputy. I wondered if you would be interested."

"In being your deputy in Kabul?"

"Yeah. It's a good operation out there, Em. Great people and a decent amount of funding. I think we could really do something."

My mind is whirring. Kabul. Anna. The old version of me. It's all we ever wanted to do – something good. But do we end up helping at all, or just make things worse – for others and ourselves?

"I'm not sure the timing's right, Anna."

She pauses.

"Can I at least send you the job description? Just take a look. It would be the two of us again, Emma. It could be amazing."

It could be.

"Okay, send it over," I say.

An hour later she has sent me the job description and I have read it twenty or thirty times. The role and requirements look like they were written for me. Knowing Anna, they probably were. It feel it stir in me again, that desire for adventure. But maybe it is something else too. The desire to flee.

I finally reply.

Subject: Re: Skype!!

Thanks for sending that, Anna. It was so good to talk to you and, once again, CONGRATULATIONS! I'll have a read through the job description as soon as I get a chance and let you know what I think. One more thing, I have a favour to ask. While you're still in the Baghdad office, can you look someone up for me? Ameena Sabah. She's the cousin of Adam's 'terp who got killed and she relocated to the States while I was still out there. I just want some kind of contact details – a phone number or email address or anything. I'll understand if you can't, but honestly, Anna, I'll be eternally grateful.

Miss you,

Emma

She replies the next day with Ameena's email address and one line.

Are you sure you know what you're doing, Emma? Is everything really okay?

Even after this long, from so far away, she knows me.

56

The phone rings and rings and no one answers. As it rings, I sit and look at the painting opposite me. The summer day and the grass and the pond and the flowers. I focus on the colours, try to let them ground me. The phone keeps ringing and I am about to hang up, but then I hear a voice.

"Hello?"

"Hi Mum, it's me."

"Oh hello, darling. Sorry, I was out in the garden. I wasn't expecting you to call."

We have been in contact more recently and it has been a comfort. Nothing major, just occasional texts about the weather in England and how the conkers look like they will be late in falling this year. It has made me feel less alone. Last week she sent me a photo of a painting she is working on and I saw my mother as a happier version of herself.

"That's okay, Mum, I was just calling for a chat."

"Of course, dear. Rebecca and Sophie are popping in for a cup of tea soon. I'm sure your sister would love to talk to you."

"Yes. That would be nice."

My throat tightens. There is something that I need to say, but the words are stuck somewhere between my heart and my mouth. I force myself to breathe. There's something I have to do.

"Mum? I need to talk."

"Oh, Ems, thank goodness. Will you finally tell me what's going on?"

"I'm sorry," I say.

"You're sorry? For what, Emma?"

"I'm sorry for leaving after Dad died. For leaving you and Rebecca. I knew it hurt you, but I just… I thought I was being strong. But maybe I wasn't and I wanted to say I'm sorry."

"Gosh, you don't need to be sorry about that, my darling. Your father would have wanted you to go off on your adventures. You're so much like him, you see, so much more than Rebecca. That's why we always miss you desperately. Because you are a little piece of him that we have left."

I cover the mouthpiece of the phone as I cry.

"Emma, that can't be all. What's really going on over there?"

I take a breath and finally let the words come out.

"It's Adam. I feel like I'm losing him, slowly. I'm losing myself too, Mum. I just don't know what to do anymore. I don't even know who I am."

She talks and asks questions and for once I let her words soothe me. I let myself be comforted. This woman who survived the loss of her husband is a different version of the mother I remember. Calm. Reassuring. The empty hole left by my father is still there, but she has pieced herself together around it. She is stronger than I knew.

57

They call it hyper-vigilance. It is "enhanced sensory sensitivity". It is a heightened awareness of threats. It is being on edge often, always. It is a feeling that I know.

After Sampath's death, the scrape of a chair in the office was the tremor of a rocket making contact. Each song on the radio carried the wail of the incoming alarm.

When Adam was away, it was the obsessive refreshing of my emails. The panic if I went out without my phone. The way the word "Iraq" or "explosion" or "casualties" jumped out from any news report.

But now I am hyper-vigilant of him.

I tread lightly as I move around the house. I do not wash up when he is watching the television. I do not make plans for us or suggestions to socialise. I keep my phone on silent and go out to make calls.

I try to make myself smaller, lighter, quieter. But still the invisible eggshells crack and fracture under my feet.

It is an exercise in trigger avoidance. But I do not know which one of us is holding the gun.

58

I did not email Ameena straight away. I wrote messages, but I did not send them. The tone never sounded right. Too familiar or too formal or just too out of the blue.

Sometimes I considered telling Adam that I wanted to see her, but it was too much to talk about. To unpick. We could barely get through a chat about our day without arguing.

More than once, I deleted her email address. I told myself that contacting her was unethical. I was doing it for me, not her, and who was I to drag her into my turmoil after everything she had been through? But even after I deleted Anna's email from my inbox and Ameena's address from my contacts, it was still etched in my memory.

My desire to see her turned into an obsession. Eventually I pressed send. I needed to know whether everything we were going through was worth it.

Hi Ameena,
I don't know if you remember me, but my name is Emma. I interviewed you for your asylum application. I live in the US myself now. I just wanted to say hi and see how you're doing – don't worry, nothing work-related! I hope you and your family are well.
Best,
Emma

At first there was no reply. I wondered whether she had changed her email address. Then I wondered whether she just wanted to leave memories of Iraq behind her. Mostly I wondered whether she blamed me for what happened to Ali.

Almost two weeks later a response came. Polite but guarded. She said she was fine and living with her mother and son in Houston, Texas. She said it had been a hot summer, but they were used to that, and that there were lots of other Iraqis around.

Houston was a popular location for Iraqis relocating to the States and was already home to a sizeable immigrant community. As the first waves of interpreters and those associated with the US Forces claimed asylum, the state of Texas became a popular destination. Many Iraqis simply chose somewhere they had heard of from American soldiers and there were a large number of troops from Texas deployed in Iraq.

Later in the war it became a matter of connections. Everyone knew someone who knew someone else who had moved to Texas – a third cousin or in-law or distant relative. Gradually an Iraqi community developed and new arrivals were understandably attracted to a home away from home.

The emails between us continued. Talking to Ameena made me nostalgic for Baghdad – the Baghdad of drinking tea with Iraqi colleagues and watching the latest Nancy Ajram music video on YouTube and debating which stuffed vegetable in the pot of dolma was tastiest. I knew I had no right to miss the city in the way Ameena did. I had barely been outside the compound walls and I had no claim to the place, but sometimes I still felt an ache of longing for the city I never truly knew.

In my emails to Ameena I told her things I had never told anyone. I talked about how strange I found life in America and how much I missed my family. I tried to reach out to her, find common ground in our shared experiences. The irony of this is not lost on me.

After a few weeks of emailing, I asked if I could see her. I said that I would be visiting a friend in Houston, so perhaps I could stop by. *Yes*, she replied. *My mother will be happy for you to visit.*

I told Adam the same lie. If he heard the falsehood, he said nothing.

I am in a taxi now, on the ride from the airport to Ameena's apartment. It is my first time in Houston and it feels strange to be in a city after so long in Colorado Springs.

At the airport, I stood and watched people pass through the X-ray machine. I imagined they showed the real insides of those walking through them. What would Adam look like? Fragments. His insides are shattered, held together only by a sack of skin and sinew. As he walks, the fragments bump and knock against each other, gaining new chips and sharper edges. How do you begin to heal insides like that?

I can see the skyscrapers of downtown Houston in the distance now, but the address Ameena has given me is outside of the city centre. The taxi stops in a neighbourhood of identical apartment blocks which surround a gravel play area where two Arab-looking children play on the swings. Nearby, their mothers sit on a bench and talk. They watch me with interest as I get out of the taxi. One of them adjusts her hijab.

I find Ameena's apartment block and ring the buzzer. A voice comes over the telecom.

"Second floor."

The lock clicks open and I climb the stairs. The stairwell could do with a clean and a coat of paint. From behind closed doors, I can hear children, other families.

When I get to the second floor, Ameena is there waiting. With the passing of time, her face had become blurry in my memory, but now the lines of her features reappear in high definition before me. She has the same style and co-ordination I remember. She is wearing white trousers and a sapphire blue tunic, with a white scarf draped around her shoulders. Her eyeshadow is metallic blue. I am in jeans and a loose cotton shirt. Once again I feel underdressed in front of Ameena, but this time I do not have the excuse of living in the IZ.

Behind Ameena a child runs up the hallway and hugs the back of her legs, peering out at me warily with large dark eyes. For a moment I am not in Houston, but back in Colorado Springs with Noah appearing in the doorway behind Kate the first time I visited her house.

"Hi Emma," says Ameena. The "I" is drawn out and from just two words I can tell that her English has already taken on the faintest Texan drawl. "Welcome."

"Hi. It's good to see you, Ameena," I say. I am unsure exactly how to greet her, but she holds out a hand, which I shake. "Hi Yusuf," I say, crouching down. "You've grown up a lot." How old must he be now? Three? Four?

"You remember his name," she says and I register a flicker of surprise in her eyes before her face returns to its previous composure. "You must come in. My mother is waiting for you."

Ameena leads me down a narrow hallway. The walls are dotted with the family photographs she must have managed to bring with them. In one picture, Ameena is a child, standing in front of the Tigris with a taller boy I guess is her brother. In another, a much younger version of Ameena's mother smiles shyly next to a smartly dressed man who rests a hand on her shoulder.

I try hard not to react when I get to the photo of Ali. It can't have been taken long before he died because he looks exactly how I remember him, with his thin face and easy smile and thick dark hair. He is leaning against a wall, perhaps in one of the Baghdad palace complexes, a cigarette hanging down by his side. I want to stand and look at it for longer but Ameena keeps walking, so I follow her along the hallway, past a small kitchen and a bedroom to the living room.

It is a tiny apartment, especially by American standards.

There are no other obvious rooms, so the three of them must share a bedroom. Ameena would have received financial support for the family when they arrived, but it only lasts a few months. I have not asked how she supports them now.

We step into the living room and I am greeted by a strange fusion of Iraq and America. There is a La-Z-Boy chair which looks like it has barely been used and a low L-shaped sofa that is more what you might find in a Baghdad home. The material is a deep purple velour that I have only ever seen popular in Iraq. Next to the sofa is a coffee table and in the middle of the room is a large rug. I wonder whether they eat cross-legged on the rug or crowd around the tiny two-person table I glimpsed in the kitchen as I passed.

Ameena's mother is sat on the sofa when I enter the room and pushes herself up to greet me. She looks older and frailer than I remember, although perhaps it's just the oversized American furniture that appears to swallow her up.

"*Ahlan wa sahlan*," she says, greeting me with a smile. Her face creases and folds in a way that leaves her tiny dark eyes barely visible and she reveals teeth that are stained brown from many years of drinking sweet Arabic coffee. She must not have smiled at all the first time we met. She clasps one of my hands between both of hers and kisses my cheeks. Her lips suck loud noises out of the air and I am touched by the familiarity of the gesture.

"*Ahlan bikum*," I reply. "How are you?" I tried to practise my Arabic with Zainab, but it's been a month since I last saw her and now my tongue feels heavy and uncertain as it wraps around the words. I have asked Noor how the family are many times and she says "fine". I have asked Noor whether there has been news on Hassan's university applications and she says "nothing".

"I am very well, *alhamdulillah*," says Ameena's mother. "I am just sorry to receive you like this. We do not have a room here for our guests, not like back home."

I realise how strange this must be for her. Many Iraqis

have a special guest room where visitors are received, rather than having them traipse into the intimacy of family areas.

"Don't apologise, please," I say. "I understand that things here are different. I am still becoming accustomed to them myself."

The language I use is strained and overly formal as I scrape it from the recesses of my mind. Changing the conversation, I produce a box of chocolates for them that I bought hastily at Colorado Springs airport. I hand the box over with both hands. The packaging is squashed and battered after the journey, but Ameena's mother feigns delight with the skill of a seasoned hostess.

"Really, you are so kind," she says. "They look wonderful. I will tell Ameena we must eat them with our tea."

Ameena returns, as if on cue, with a tray of drinks. We do not drink the tea from delicate glasses but, rather, large mugs bearing the emblems of American sports teams, which she has filled up halfway. In a small dish next to the tea is a pile of American candy. She sees me looking at them and offers me one, but I decline. I cannot tell her that Tootsie Rolls make me think of Ali and the PX and the day I drove past the reed beds. What is Adam doing while I am here?

We sit and talk for a while about the family's new life in America. Ameena's mother seems particularly keen to reassure me that they have settled in well, wringing her hands together in the way I remember her doing during the interview in Baghdad. I gently remind her that I am visiting as a friend and not an official. She relaxes a bit, but not much. She must still worry that they could be sent back.

Ameena is more open. She says it was very difficult to start with, but at least now they have Iraqi friends and it is getting better.

"And what about work?" I ask. "Have you been able to use your nursing skills at all?"

"I work in Kmart," she says. She raises her chin slightly as she says this, as if daring me to judge her.

"Oh. Did you try and find work in a hospital? Perhaps I could—"

"Of course I did," she cuts me off. "I applied to six hospitals in the city and I got one interview. The woman who interviewed me had a son who was a soldier in Iraq. She said 'over her dead body' would I be allowed to get my hands on Americans here."

Ameena's face is defiant, but I can see she is hurt.

"What?" I say, horrified. "Did you tell her why you're here? Who you worked for?"

"Why bother? It makes no difference to that kind of person. Anyway, there are a lot of Iraqis in Kmart. It is easier."

From the little I know of Ameena's personality and everything I have heard of her life story, I know that working in Kmart is anything but "easy" for her. It must be soul-destroying. I wish I could somehow help her out, but I don't know anyone in hospitals in Houston. I am in no position to help her anymore. I am more of a stranger here than she is.

I try to keep the rest of the conversation light. We talk about the peculiarities of American culture, what Iraqi food they can cook with the ingredients available here, the kindergarten where Yusuf will start at the end of the summer. We do not talk about the obvious absence that hangs between us. Eventually I realise I have been there for two hours and am in danger of overstaying my welcome, although I am sure that neither Ameena nor her mother would ever indicate as much.

I make my excuses, saying that my friend will be expecting me. Ameena's mother, who has relaxed a bit by this point, tells me I must stay for dinner. I thank her but decline. She kisses my cheeks goodbye, then sinks back down into the giant sofa.

Ameena walks me to the door. It is she who brings up Ali.

"You heard about what happened to Ali, I take it?"

I am both relieved she has said his name and ashamed at my own cowardice.

"I did. I'm so sorry, Ameena. I wasn't sure how to mention it."

"He knew it was going to happen. He called me two days

before. He was trying to get out, y'know. He was going to come here, to be with us. We were finally going to… Well, it doesn't matter." She shakes her head.

"I'm so sorry."

"I asked him why he couldn't get the visa faster, like I did. I told him to email Adam, but he said that Adam had already done enough for our family."

"He should have contacted us," I say.

"Would it have made a difference?" she asks.

I struggle to answer.

"To be honest, probably not. There is always a backlog of applications. I was able to push through your application because you were a single mother with dependents. But Ali was a military-aged male. There are so many of those."

She holds my gaze and speaks in low English so that her mother cannot understand.

"Sometimes," she says, "sometimes I wonder whether we should have just stayed. At least we would have gone through it all together."

I lower my eyes to the ground. My thoughts race, jumble. I am holding Kate's hand as the coffin is carried off the plane. I am pressed up against the blast wall, with a hand scrabbling at the zip of my jeans in the hot night air. I am staring at Sampath's empty step in the gym. I am on the icy floor of the garage as sobs rack through Adam's body. I am the other side of the ocean from my family and their grief. Would it have been better to be together?

"Emma," Ameena says and I look up. "I don't know what brought you to us exactly, but I can see you are looking for something. I am sorry that you have not found it here."

I nod.

"I hope things get easier for you, Ameena," I say.

"They will, *inshallah*," she says. "And for you too. We have a lot to be grateful for."

She leans in and gives me the lightest kiss on either cheek and then the door is closing behind me and I am walking down the stairs. I emerge, blinking, into dry afternoon air and lean against the wall of her apartment building. My chest rises and falls. My ears are ringing.

On the floor I see a small white stone. I pick it up and squeeze it as tightly as I can, leaving angry white dents in my palm. The pain centres me. Helps me to breathe. With each contraction of my hand, I let her words circle through my body. *At least we would have gone through it all together.*

59

Today is my birthday.

Adam has gone to work already. I heard him get up this morning, stumble around to make coffee and then leave the house. It sounded like another restless night.

He hasn't mentioned my birthday, yet when I finally get out of bed I still enter the kitchen half-expectantly, hoping he might have left something. I am disappointed.

Last year he was deployed for my birthday. I woke up alone in bed just as I did today, but then the delivery man stopped by with a bouquet of pink and yellow camellias and a bottle of Prosecco. Adam didn't usually give those kinds of gifts, he says they lack imagination, but conflict zones tended to limit the scope of options for birthday presents. Tucked amid the flowers was a card with a message that the florist's assistant had carefully copied out from the email he had sent them. It was odd seeing Adam's words in looped feminine handwriting, with a heart dotting the "i" of birthday.

This time last year it was six weeks until he got home. This time last year, Adam was still Adam and Dave was still alive.

I make myself coffee and pull two envelopes that arrived last week out from the kitchen drawer. One is from my mum. She has made a card herself. It is a painting of cows in the field behind our garden and she has captured their large docile eyes perfectly, even in miniature. The second card is from my sister and her family. Inside it is a picture drawn by my niece

Sophie, of the three of us together with a birthday cake that looks like it might be on fire. *Soph says that 29 candles is too many for a cake*, Rebecca has written on the back. I laugh out loud and surprise myself with the noise.

I slide the drawing under a magnet on the fridge door. A photo of Adam and I falls off as I do so, but I place it on the counter rather than putting it back up. Upstairs, I stand the two cards on my bedside table where my phone is charging. I check to see if Adam has called or sent a message but there is nothing.

I have taken the day off from the art shop for my birthday, but now I am unsure what to do with myself. I check my watch. It is around midday in England. I told my mother I would call her early evening their time.

I have breakfast and then spend some time browsing mosaicking websites, still on the search for inspiration. I have stopped going to the art group and I miss the companionship and creativity of the other women. Noor said I should continue coming, but I couldn't bear the thought of making Zainab uncomfortable. She needs that space more than I do.

Later in the morning I decide to walk to the local supermarket. I usually drive, like the rest of America, but the walk will kill some time and maybe some fresh air will make me feel better. I consider buying things to make a birthday dinner for Adam and I later, but he is unpredictable these days. Last night I made dinner for us and he said he wasn't hungry, then sat and ate crisps on the sofa while I threw away half of what I'd prepared.

I decide to buy myself a birthday lunch instead. As a child, I used to ask for jam sandwiches and custard cream biscuits for lunch every birthday. I don't know when or how the routine started, but I know my sister does it too. That is what I want today, a taste of home. It feels like the closest I can get to my family right now.

In the store, I roam the shelves. I knew that I wouldn't find real custard cream biscuits, but I thought I would find some kind of American equivalent. I end up buying Oreos, which I'm not even sure that I like, plus a loaf of bread and strawberry jam or "jelly" as the label calls it.

At the cash register, the middle-aged lady surprises me by asking if I'm okay. I force a smile and say I'm fine, just a bit tired. I return home and sit on the porch with my birthday lunch for one.

I bite into a sandwich and my phone rings with an unknown number. I let it go to voicemail, then listen to the message. It is Anna. She sings "Happy Birthday" down a crackly line, then reminds me it's not long until she goes to Kabul and asks if I have made a decision on the job yet. I haven't. Every time I try to think about it, the thoughts come in waves and swirl around each other and I feel like I am being pulled under by the current. I delete the voicemail and tell myself I will email her later.

My phone makes another noise and it is a text message from Kate:

Happy birthday Emma. I hope you have a wonderful day. Noah and Charlotte send their love. Say hi to Adam from us too!

We last spoke about two months ago. Kate said that she was doing okay and was beginning to take on some physio clients while her mum looked after the kids. She said Noah's clinginess got worse for a while, but he was much better now and making new friends at school. Charlotte was taking her first steps and smiles at everyone and everything. She still looks just like Dave.

When Kate asked how I was doing, I said fine. In the background, I heard her mother shout that dinner was ready.

"I have to go, Em, but call me if you ever need to talk," she said. I did need to talk, but I never called.

I check my watch again. It is 5pm in the UK. I dial my mother's number and she answers after a single ring. She has been waiting.

"Happy birthday, baby girl!" she says down the phone.

"Mum, I'm twenty-nine!" I say.

"I know, darling, but you're my first. You'll always be baby girl to me. How's your day been so far?"

I tell her about my trip to the store ("Shop, Emma, we call it a shop!"), my failed quest for custard creams and my lunch of jam sandwiches.

"Gosh, I didn't know you still did that! I would have posted over the biscuits if I'd known. I still can't believe your father managed to convince you it was a special birthday custom," she laughs.

"Wait, Dad started it?" I ask.

"Yes, don't you remember? It was the year you turned five and I had the flu. It was awful. I was stuck in bed for about a week, so your dad was in charge of looking after you. He was having a busy week at the hospital too, so on your birthday when he came home from work and was too tired to cook he managed to convince you that jam sandwiches and custard creams were a special birthday feast for children once they turned five. Rebecca was so excited when she turned five too! I remember how she cried on her fourth birthday when you told her she couldn't have jam sandwiches because they were only for big girls."

My mother is laughing and I am laughing too, even as the tears roll down my face. I can feel tiny fragments of memory shifting around inside me, finding each other and fusing together. I remember the smell of the hot lemon and honey he took my mother, the rustle of the biscuit packet as he opened it, the way he had spread the jam with a spoon not a knife.

"It's so good to talk about him, Mum."

"I know, darling. It must be hard with no one there to remember him with."

We talk for nearly an hour. I tell her about Ali and my visit to Ameena and finally about Anna's offer.

"Are you going to take it?" she asks me.

"I don't know, Mum. I don't think I can, not with Adam the way he is. I don't even know if I want to go to Afghanistan, I just know that I want something. I want to feel like me again. It's like my life has ground to a halt."

"I'm sure you'll make the right decision. But remember, darling, there are people all over the world who you can help. It doesn't always have to be in a war zone."

I am sat on the sofa when Adam gets home from work. He says hello as he passes, goes to the bedroom and changes into his gym kit, then says "Catch you later" as he leaves again through the front door. I say nothing. Sometimes it helps him to work out. Sometimes it makes him less angry. I drag myself off the sofa, pour a glass of wine, then return to my previous position.

By the time Adam gets back from the gym it's 9pm I ask if he's eaten and he says he picked something up on the way back. He opens a beer, then goes off to shower. I flick through TV channels and try to decide whether I can be bothered to make myself something to eat.

"Shit!" The shout comes from the bedroom. I flinch and wine spills down my hand. Heavy footsteps come down the stairs. "Why didn't you remind me it was your birthday?" he asks.

"It's not a big deal," I say.

"It *is* a big fucking deal. It's your birthday." He presses his palm into his forehead. "How did I forget? I'm such a fucking idiot. Okay, get your stuff, we're going out."

I sit motionless on the couch as he disappears up the stairs again, then reappears moments later in a clean T-shirt, pulling closed the belt on his jeans.

"Are you ready to go?" he asks me.

"Go where? Adam, it's late already. Let's just stay in. I don't need to go out."

"Em – it's your birthday. We're going out, end of story."

Although I am glad he has remembered, this is not what I want. What I want for my birthday is for us to sit on his sleeping bag and balance the laptop on his footlocker and watch a movie the way we used to. I want to order takeout and eat it straight from the container and then when I get tired I want to lie with my head in his lap and for him to stroke my hair as I fall asleep and miss the end of the film. But he says we are going out and so I find myself getting into the truck beside him and trying to convince myself that this is a nice idea.

"Where do you want to go?" he says as he reverses out of the driveway.

"Um, I'm not sure, I mean this is a bit sudden—"

"One of the bars downtown. Or we could grab some food – have you eaten? Hey, how about the Mexican place? We haven't been there for a while. Yeah, let's do that! I could eat again."

He gets like this sometimes. Frantic almost. Like the energy saved up during his lows all comes bursting out at once.

We haven't been to the Mexican restaurant since before he was deployed. That's more than a year and a half ago now. I'm not sure I want to go, but maybe we will find an old version of us tucked in the corner table or between the pages of the familiar menu.

Adam has turned up the volume on the radio and is singing. The highs make me just as uncomfortable as the lows.

"Come on, babe, it's your birthday, join in!" he says. It sounds forced. Strained. I shake my head and try to give him a smile.

I can tell as we pull up outside the restaurant that it is shut already. The inside is dark and the colourful papel picado that hangs from the ceiling is barely visible.

"Shit," says Adam, slamming his hand against the steering wheel. "Why are they closed?"

"It's late," I say, "and it's a Tuesday night. They probably didn't have any customers. It's fine, Adam, let's just go home. We can have a drink there."

"No, wait, I see someone!" he says and starts getting out of the truck. "You see that guy mopping? I'll ask him to open."

"No, they're closed. Adam! What are you—?"

Before I can finish my question, Adam is out of the truck and banging on the glass door of the restaurant. I get out quickly to follow him.

"Hey. Hey! You!"

I see the man who is cleaning the floor look up, surprised. The tables are empty. They have been cleared of cutlery and the selections of hot sauce bottles. The last customer must have left some time ago.

"I'm sorry, sir, we're closed," says the man, opening the door just wide enough to talk through. "We're just finishing cleaning up and then—"

"No, look, sorry, but I need you to open again. Just for a little while. It's my wife's birthday, you see, and we want to come in."

"I'm sorry, sir. Perhaps you would like to reserve a table for tomorrow? We open at five."

Adam is gripping the door frame and his foot is wedged in the door to push it open further. The man who works at the restaurant is a small guy, maybe in his late forties. I am grateful not to recognise him from when we used to come here. He looks intimidated by Adam.

"You're not listening to me," says Adam. "It's her birthday today. Just open your fucking restaurant. We're paying customers."

The man takes a step back from the door and it swings open. He shoots a glance behind him to the entrance of the kitchen, where other staff have gathered to see what's going on. One of them takes a phone from his pocket, ready. I catch his eye. It's the waiter who used to serve us. I look away quickly.

I can feel Adam getting increasingly agitated and all I want is to be out of this situation. Away from these staring people. I do not trust what could happen next.

"Adam, please, let's just go home," I say, taking hold of his arm. "I'm not hungry anymore. Let's just go back, I'm tired."

"No, Emma!" He throws my arm off with a force that

323

causes me to stumble back and for a moment I think I might fall.

I hear one of the women from the kitchen gasp and my cheeks burn.

"Oh, babe, sorry, I…"

He reaches out to me but I say nothing. I turn and walk quickly towards the truck. I climb in and slam the door. Adam follows me and sits in the driver's seat apologising. Then he starts to drive and shakes his head and says he's sorry and he doesn't know what is up with him these days. He says that he loves me. He says, "You do know that I love you, right, Em?"

We pass by a twenty-four-hour Walmart and he pulls into the car park. I do not follow him when he gets out of the truck. All I want to do is go home. I just sit and stare and try not to cry. I know that tears provoke him. I don't know what I'm doing here. I do not know how to continue.

Adam reappears and gets back into the driver's seat with a plastic Walmart bag. He opens it up and pulls out a packet of custard cream biscuits, the US version of the kind I had been looking for and for a moment I realise he remembered, but it is not enough. He opens the pack and holds it out towards me.

"Happy birthday, babe," he says. "I'm sorry about this evening. I'll make it up to you, I promise."

"Thanks, but I'm good," I whisper.

"What?"

"I'm good. I don't want one."

He hits the side of the truck and I jump.

"It's your birthday, Emma, and I bought those fucking birthday biscuits you like. Stop being so goddamn miserable and eat one."

He holds them out again and this time I take one. I bite into it. My mouth is dry and crumbs stick to the back of my throat as I try to swallow. I am no longer sure that this man feels like home.

60

The roof caves in first. The ceiling that I thought was beams and bricks and mortar starts to crumble. A few grains of sand start to trickle down, then more. We were already wading. Haphazard pyramids of sand form and then collapse under their own weight. And now the sand pours down all around us and I can see no door in this collapsing structure we used to call home, so I stay. I cover my eyes as the sand burns like pinpricks into my cheeks, fills my hair, my ears, my nostrils. I open my mouth to take a breath and now the grains are on my lips, between my teeth, under my tongue.

Eventually the cascades stop. I try to free my arms, to push myself upwards through the sand. A sound fills my ears, the howling of the wind. I look up in my roofless home into a chemical orange sky. The gale screeches and whips overhead and takes bites out of the newly exposed brickwork, eating away at the walls. I am paralysed. All I can do is stare.

I thought we were stronger.

61

I stand outside the exhibition, nervous about going in. Penny persuaded me to come. Since she convinced her pastor to host the event a few months ago, she has thrown herself into its organisation, advertising it in the shop and distributing flyers to customers. Noor said Penny has even stopped by the art group a few times to get to know the women. I have noticed her in the shop wearing one of Hope's blouses. One of Afsoon's rings.

Noor also said it would be nice to see me there, although she understands my hesitancy. She says that the women would like to see me, but I don't know if that includes Zainab. I got a Facebook message from Afsoon a few weeks ago, asking where I was. I told her that I was just really busy at the moment.

I hear a voice behind me.

"Emma, is that you?"

It is Marie-Luz. I am pleased to see that she continued at the group.

"Hey, how are you? It's good to see you!" I say. "How's it all going in there? Are you exhibiting your worry doll collections?"

"Ah, not the worry dolls," she says. "I started a new project. A cookbook! I've written and illustrated old family recipes."

"That's a great idea," I tell her.

"*Thank you*. One of my little girls dropped a doll in the stew I was cooking. What a weird way to get an idea right?"

"Haha, it's perfect. I think a lot of great ideas come from the most unexpected places."

"I made it into the book's title actually. *Worry Doll Soup*."

"I love it."

She smiles.

"Okay, I've got to get back in there. You're coming in, no? Everyone will love to see you."

"Sure, I'll just be a minute," I say.

She nods and disappears into the church building. I take a breath and follow after.

Inside, the hall is full. I spot several regular customers from the art shop, as well as the owners of a few local businesses I have come to know through Penny. There are many other people too. Members of the congregation perhaps, members of the local community.

Several paintings are displayed on easels, while other women have tables to show off their work. As well as the women I recognise, there are others who must have joined recently or been members before I was there. I see Hope standing proudly next to two racks of colourful clothing and give her a wave. Afsoon sits in front of a table that displays her jewellery, much of it hung delicately on some spiralling branches she has brought in. Laura has hung up large swathes of textiles she has embroidered: cushion covers, bed throws, table runners. Penny moves between the crowd, greeting people, gesturing towards this woman or that. She looks like she's in her element.

I see Noor coming in my direction.

"Hey, it looks amazing in here," I say. She gives me an excited hug.

"Oh, Em, it's going so well! We're getting a lot of interest. Three gift shops in Manitou Springs have already said they'll stock Afsoon's jewellery!"

"Noor, that's brilliant. I'm so proud of you."

"Thanks, Emma," she says with a smile. "You should have a walk around. Have you seen Zainab yet?"

"No," I say. "Is she on a table?"

"Oh no," says Noor with a smile I can't quite figure out. "You'll find her in no time. Go and look around. She told me she was hoping to see you."

I walk through the exhibit, saying hello to people I recognise, stopping to chat and catch up with the women in the group. People know my name here and that is a comfort. I stop feeling nervous and let myself enjoy the greetings, the easy conversations. None of them know what things are like at home, to them I am still just Emma. As I look at their projects, I am full of pride and admiration. These women with complicated stories and complex identities are finding their way through life. They are exploring who they are and what their identity means to them. They continue to try where I am failing.

I do not notice a stand for Zainab as I wander through, although my eyes search for her. But then, near the back of the hall, there she is. The table of coaster-sized paintings is there as I had expected, but what really catches my eye is the large canvas that Zainab stands next to. It must be a metre tall and almost a metre wide and on it I see her garden. All the tiny details of her previous paintings have come together. The plastic furniture, the teacup, the bowl of olives, the tree that is heavy with fruit, the ginger cat that winds itself around the table legs. With a painting this size, she has put down roots.

"Zainab," I say and I walk towards her. "This is… It's beautiful."

"Emma. It's good to see you. Thank you." Her smile is still shy, but there is something else there now. A beautiful, quiet kind of confidence.

When I decided to come to the exhibit, I told myself that

I would give Zainab her space. The exhibit wasn't the place to talk about what had happened. But self-restraint fails me and the words tumble out before I realise what is happening.

"Zainab, I'm so sorry about everything. About what happened with Adam. He's not normally like that, I promise you. He's just different since he got back. But he never would have really hurt Hassan, I promise you. At least I don't think... But anyway, I understand Haider's decision and I'm sorry, Zainab. I miss you and I'm sorry."

At first she says nothing, but I think I catch the smallest exhalation of a sigh. I wonder if I should leave now, but then she takes a step towards me and puts a hand on my shoulder.

"Do not be sorry, Emma. These men... Adam, Haider, Hassan. They are not so very different. Don't you see? The war follows us everywhere. Your husband brought it back here with him. So did mine. We're fighting the same battles."

"I wanted to help you, not make things worse," I say.

"You did help, Emma. You did."

Zainab reaches into her handbag. She pulls out an envelope and puts it in my hands. I see the University of Denver logo stamp on the front.

"Is this...?" I look up at her and she nods. I turn the envelope over in my hands. It is crumpled at the edges and I can see that it has already been opened and closed hundreds of times. I carefully pull out the letter and unfold it. *Dear Hassan, We are pleased to inform you...* My eyes barely make it past the first few words before Zainab is speaking.

"A full scholarship! Can you believe it? Hassan, going to university in America! It's really happening!" I look at her face and am reminded of Ameena and her hopes for Yusuf's future. These are the moments we live for, that make the rest of the suffering worth it.

"Oh my god, Zainab, congratulations! This is huge! When did you find out?"

"Two days ago. I wanted to call you and then Noor said you were coming, so I thought I'd tell you in person."

"Is Hassan happy?"

"He's ecstatic. So happy. We're so grateful, Emma."

"No, you don't need to be. Really, this is all Hassan. He is a talented boy."

"But we wouldn't have known where to begin without you. Here, I got you something. Just a little thank you…"

"Oh, Zainab, you didn't need to get me anything." The truth is that I still feel guilty. What happened with Adam could have jeopardised everything. I do not deserve their thanks.

But Zainab is fishing around in her handbag again. She pulls out a dark blue mesh bag the size of my hand that shimmers in the light. It is tied shut with a ribbon, but as she places it in my hand I feel the contents move against each other. I untie the ribbon and tip the bag carefully into my open palm. A selection of small pieces spill out. Ceramic, stone, glass – all in brilliant blues and greens and turquoises. They are perfect.

"I thought they might help," she whispers.

And for a moment I am speechless. I am known.

62

When Adam has gone to bed, I sit at the kitchen island and once again pour the pieces from the jar. I pick up each one, examine it, remember its story. There is stone from outside the gym in Baghdad, and another one from the step the day Sampath died. There is the piece from the top of the palace on the day Adam proposed. There is our wedding in Garden of the Gods, our last walk before he left, my trip to Texas. I hold each piece and close my eyes and will myself to remember. And then, when I am done, I carefully open Zainab's bag.

I pour all of the new pieces in one place at first, but then I being to shift them around and the jewel-like colours mix and merge with the reds and pinks and beiges and browns that are already there. There are blues and greens already too, softer shades, but these new additions seem to draw out their colour and make them glow.

Soon the new pieces are mixed with the old and I continue to move them. My hands are opened wide, my palms moving flat across the surface of the pieces, testing them this way and then that. Then I start to feel it.

I leave a few fragments in their position and move others around them. I smell something sweet in the air, hear the buzz of an insect, feel a light breeze against my skin. I move them again. I push the blues furthest from me this time and move the light greens closer. In the middle, I place the darker and more vibrant greens, threading through them with pinks and reds. I feel an ice lolly melt and drip down my arm. I see my mother in the doctor's jacket streaked with colour. I feel a large hand reach down and ruffle my head.

I look across at the living room wall and there it is, my childhood. The garden, the flowers, the tiny pond. My mother's painting. And now, in front of me, with fragments from all the periods and places of my life, it starts to take shape again. A silent call. An invitation. All the pieces of me.

63

It is Thanksgiving, again. I stand in the kitchen peeling sweet potatoes, half an eye on the floats of the Macy's parade that flash from the television screen in the living room. It is hard to believe that a year has passed already, yet it also feels like an eternity. I barely recognise the couple we were back then. Although I struggle to recognise the couple we are now.

I asked Adam if he wanted to do something to mark today. Perhaps lay some flowers on Dave's favourite hiking trail or visit the plaque in his memory at the top of the Incline. Even go to Old Chicago where he and Dave used to go for pizza and football on Thursday nights. He said no.

The sweet potatoes peeled, I begin to chop them into chunks and put them into a pan of water on the stove. I'll boil them now so they are ready to be mashed later and mixed with butter and cinnamon, in the tradition of the country I have come to call home. Neither of us even wants a Thanksgiving meal really, but I doggedly persist in trying to create new memories so that our love does not exist only on a compound in Iraq.

Yesterday I sent Kate a card to let her know I was thinking of her. Last week I saw a video she posted on Facebook of Charlotte taking wobbly steps across the living room towards Noah, who was waiting with open arms. He looked so much more grown-up than when they left, taller and without the rounded cheeks of his toddler years. Then Kate turned the camera on herself and smiled into the lens. She looked different too, her hair cut into a short dark bob.

Everyone is moving on except us. We're stuck in a purgatory, somewhere between Iraq and real life. The readjustment period may take time, they said, but they meant months not years. He could be sent away again soon, before we have even recovered from the last time. Maybe there is no more recovering left to do. This is just who we are now. Changed.

Adam left the house early today. *Will be back around 1pm*, says the note he left. I am grateful he left a note at all.

I rub salt into the skin of the turkey and wait for the oven to heat up. As I move around the kitchen, I think of last year. Preparing the trifle to take to Kate's. My phone vibrating on the counter by the sink. Adam's voice from far away.

I sit on the sofa to watch the rest of the parade. I get up again, mash the sweet potato. Return to the sofa. One o'clock passes. Then two. The turkey is ready. A pecan pie waits in the fridge. I call his mobile, but there is no answer. I wait. I drink a glass of wine. Three o'clock passes and I call again and leave a voice message.

"Hey, it's me. Just checking you're okay. If you need more time alone that's fine, just… Well, just let me know."

I try to control the anxiety in my voice, but the words come out with an unnatural high pitch. Things have been bad lately. Worse.

I stand in the kitchen and pour another glass of wine. I look at my watch again. Half past four. I put my hands on the work surface, close my eyes, draw in a breath and try to calm the anxiety that claws at my stomach.

The images begin to flicker, unbidden, the same way they did when he was deployed. But these days the scenarios that chase one after the other through my mind are not Adam in uniform, or a lone bullet in a dusty street, or an explosion that lights up the Baghdad night. They are Adam, at home, where he is supposed to be safe.

I open my eyes, but the scenes have already started. They

are harder to stop at the moment, harder to control. In the first sequence, Adam is in the mountains, far out in the forest where we would go for Sunday drives before he went away. The trees around him are aflame with the last crimson leaves of the season. He stands on a rocky outcrop, taking in the view. Silent. But now I see he has something in his hand. He closes his eyes against the cold taste of metal. A shot rings out, reverberating against the hillsides. Birds erupt squawking into the November air.

I shake my head, trying to clear it. Take a cold sip of wine. It doesn't work.

In the next version, Adam is drunk. He has been out driving the back roads, swigging beer from a six-pack. Rock music blasts from the stereo and his windows are rolled down, despite the gnawing cold of the air. The road is narrow, with steep sharp corners, which he navigates with one hand on the steering wheel. The tyres spit out sharp gravel as he turns. Then something jumps out in front of him. An animal. A deer? It smashes through the windscreen and now there is another corner coming up, but it is too late and he can't see and now his truck leaves the track, tumbling down through thick tree trunks until one finally brings the vehicle to a halt.

The third version is interrupted when I hear a key in the door. I wipe a relieved hand across the cold sweat that has gathered on my forehead.

Adam comes in, pushing the door open hard so that it hits the wall and adds to the dark mark where it has made contact several times before.

"Hey," he says. "Smells like cooking."

"Yeah, Thanksgiving dinner. I thought you were going to be home at one."

I am not sure whether I can smell alcohol from him or whether I just imagine the scent that has become so familiar when he enters the house. He tries to take off a boot but loses balance and falls sideways, his shoulder slamming against the wall.

"You okay?" I ask.

"Yeah. Fine," he replies. I notice his eyes are red and sunken, more than the usual combination of sleepless nights and beer leaves them. His face is blotchy and pale.

He is sitting on the floor now, pulling off his boots like a child.

"Want something to eat?" I ask.

"Sure."

I heat up vegetables and put them on a plate with slices of dry turkey and ham. He sits on the sofa and I hand him the food.

"You not having any?" he asks.

"No, I ate something earlier," I lie.

He turns over the television channel to what remains of the Thanksgiving football fixtures, then increases the volume. He barely blinks as forks of food find their way to his mouth. There is a strange vacancy to his stare.

Before Adam left, I used to love watching American football with him. It wasn't the sport itself, but the enjoyment he took in explaining the game to someone new. Before a big game we would often go to Rudy's for dinner, the BBQ joint he'd told me about in Baghdad, and over stacks of moist brisket he would explain to me which team was predicted to win, what it would mean for the league tables, which players I should look out for. It was the excited conversation of lovers discovering each other's passions. It was a keenness to know the other, and be known ourselves.

It's not like that anymore.

In the kitchen, I wash up the dishes from cooking. It doesn't need to be done straight away, but I don't want to sit next to him while he's like this.

Adam puts his plate to one side and stands up. I tense, wondering whether the noise of the cutlery scraping the bottom of the sink was too loud, but he goes to the fridge to get a beer. I say nothing, but as he closes the fridge door he sees me look.

"What?"

336

"Nothing, but... Are you sure you want another beer?"

"Yes."

"Okay."

I continue to wash the dishes, but then I can't help myself. I speak again.

"Have you called Kate?"

I see the small muscle at the side of his jaw twinge.

"No. Why?"

"Just... Because of what day it is."

He puts the beer down on the sideboard so hard I think the bottle might crack. He raises his hand and rubs his fingers against his brow, leaving pale pressure marks when he takes his hand away.

"Did you ever think that maybe Kate wants the world to leave her the fuck alone today? That maybe she doesn't need the reminder?"

"Okay, I'm sorry," I say, taking a step back. "It's just..."

He looks up. There is a hardness to his eyes. A stranger stares out at me.

"What, Emma? It's just what?"

"It's just that I think Dave would like it if you still checked in on them once in a while."

There. I've done it again. Adam takes a step forwards and pushes me hard. I smell the alcohol on his breath as the back of my head hits the wall, sending a photo frame with a picture of us on the Incline smashing to the ground. I taste blood in my mouth from where my teeth are knocked shut over my tongue. For a moment I am not at home in my kitchen with my husband. I am in Iraq, being pushed against that blast wall, a forearm across my neck, another man's face too close to mine.

Then I am in Colorado again and it is Adam's face shouting at me. I watch his mouth move and hear his words, but I feel like my brain is shrouded in cotton wool. My ears are swimming in the water of the Tigris. This is happening to someone else. This is not Adam. It is not me.

337

"Don't fucking talk to me about Dave. You have no idea. No fucking idea!" the man who is Adam yells. His eyebrows are low. His face is contorted. Spit flies out of his mouth and lands by the woman's foot.

"Adam!" she shouts. "Stop!" His fist is raised.

In this movie of us, time slows down. His fist is already moving when our eyes lock. There is a flicker of recognition and for the smallest fraction of a second we both remember who we are. Who we used to be before everything broke. His eyebrows lift and his mouth begins to form a silent "o".

Then time speeds up again and his fist slams into the wall by the side of my head. I think I scream. He pulls his hand away and his knuckles have split from the force.

"Fuck," he shouts. "Fuck!"

My legs give way and I slide slowly down the wall until I am sat among the shattered glass of the photo frame on the kitchen floor. I try to take a breath but my throat has tightened, so it is more like a gasp as I suck in air. Exhaling is just as difficult and the gasps turn into sobs.

Then Adam too is sinking and now he is sat, legs out in front of him, back leaning against the kitchen cupboard. The blood from his knuckles seeps into the dark fabric of his jeans. His hands are shaking. He looks from his fist to me, his eyes wide with shock and confusion. He is no longer the cold angry stranger, but Adam. Scared. Vulnerable.

We stare at each other. My throat loosens and I swallow and try to take slow, deep breaths. A weight descends so heavily upon me that it is as if I am being pushed into the ground. It is the knowledge that we are broken beyond repair.

I struggle to clear the white noise, my ears ringing from the explosion of us. Adam shakes his head, his eyes still wide.

"How did we get this bad?" he asks, looking again and again between his trembling hands and my face. "How did *I* get this bad?"

I try to move. Each motion is an effort. My heavy limbs are weak and useless and I think I might be sick. Eventually

I manage to crawl amid the broken glass and across the kitchen floor.

Adam's whole body is trembling now. His head leans back against the kitchen cupboard. His skin is clammy and pale. Tears run down his cheeks. When I reach him, I lie down. I curl up on the floor with my head in his lap. I take his bloodied hand and hold the palm against my face.

"I don't know," I tell him. "But we can't do this anymore."

64

He does not cry when I tell him I am leaving. He knew it was coming, we both did. I wanted to save him, but I couldn't. He needs to figure out a way to save himself.

He does not cry when I tell him I am leaving, but part of me wishes that he would. I wish that there was a part of us still strong enough to fight for this. To break the pattern. To be normal. But that is not how war works.

Perhaps the end was written from the beginning, but we were blinded by the romance of the battle. Conflict will always call to people like us. Even as we watch our comrades and loved ones get chewed up, spat out, destroyed. Even though we know it will destroy us too, eventually. Even though it already has. But this time I want it to be different.

He is sat on the sofa when I tell him. I sit beside him as he slowly flexes the fingers of his bandaged hand. It is late afternoon and the sun is low in the sky. The first snow of winter settles lightly on the ground.

"Kabul?" he asks. I told him about Anna's offer eventually, in the days after what happened in the kitchen. Everything came out then.

"No, nowhere like that. Not now. Not yet," I say.

"Then where?"

"England."

"England? To do what?"

"I've got a job with a refugee support organisation, working on their youth programme. They have a lot of young Iraqis on the scheme."

"Of course, got to get that Iraq kick somehow," he says. I am too tired to argue, so I don't reply. He speaks again. "I'm sorry, Em. I didn't mean it like that. It's still one of the things I love most about you, the way you always want to help people. I'm… I'm sorry I wouldn't let you help me."

"Me too," I whisper.

He opens and closes his hand, working the tendons.

"Where… Where will you stay?"

"With my mum to begin with. After that, I don't know."

He nods.

"I think it will be good for me," I say. "There's stuff I want to work through with her. And Rebecca. Get to know them again… Give them a chance to know me."

"It sounds like it will be good for you," he says.

"I hope so."

He rubs a hand round the back of his neck.

"Em, there's something else… I'm sorry that you didn't feel you could tell me about what happened in Baghdad."

"About the guy who attacked me?"

He nods again.

"That wasn't your fault, Adam. It was me. I thought I was protecting you by not saying anything."

"I know the feeling," he says.

"It didn't work out great for either of us, did it?"

"Not really," he replies.

We sit in silence a little longer and then I stand up, folding and unfolding a small piece of paper in my hand.

"Adam, I got this number… In case you change your mind about speaking to someone."

I do not expect him to reach out and take it, but he does. He examines the piece of paper. The phone number. The doctor's name.

"I'll miss you, Em," he says.

"I'll miss you too. Try to look after yourself, Adam."

"I'll try."

I am at the airport now. My old rucksack is over my shoulder and my passport in my hand. I stand at the gate, waiting to board, and my nostrils fill with the familiar smells of disinfectant and cheap airport carpet. My phone beeps and for a moment I let myself hope that it is him, but it is my mother.

Darling, I hope you got to the airport okay. Let us know your flight is on time. Rebecca will be there to bring you home xx

I switch off my phone and hand my boarding pass to the flight attendant stood waiting by the scanner. I look at my watch. I called Adam's brothers before I left because I knew he wouldn't. Michael arrives tomorrow. Chad should be getting to the house about an hour from now.

I walk down the connecting bridge, surrounded by the hum of other travellers. Just before I step onto the plane, I close my eyes, open my lungs for one long breath and hear my father's voice.

Yes, there it is, you can keep going now.

ACKNOWLEDGEMENTS

The story of this novel began long before any of its words were written, in Barnett's of Wadhurst bookshop, where I walked in aged thirteen and asked for a job. Since that day the influence of bookshop owner Richard Hardy-Smith has shaped who I am as a writer and a person. The bookshop was, and still is, a home for me. I cannot describe my happiness at finally having my own novel on the shelves that I organised for the next six years. Richard, thank you for your love and patience.

The first words of *Pieces of Me* were born at the Under the Volcano writing workshop in the town of Tepoztlán, Mexico. I have been visiting this magical town since I was eighteen and it has always found a way to draw me back when I have needed it most. I would like to thank UTV founder Magda Bogin for her unwavering support and wisdom in helping me to develop the manuscript and Owen Sheers, whose words during that retreat made me decide it was a book worth writing. Thank you also to Rebecca Levi and Kavita Bedford for sharing quesadillas and writing dreams, and to Alejandra Quiroz Vargas, my Mexican sister. Ale, your love and generosity know no limits and I hope we will still be having pozole parties together when we are old.

Many people's feedback helped shape the novel as it grew, but I would like to give particular thanks to fellow writers Jon Stapley and Jill Germanacos. Jon, our writing and pub sessions were legendary. Jill, thank you for talking me out of pressing delete.

From awkward teenage poetry to debut novel, Jennie Worthley has believed in me through every part of this writing journey and helped me through more crises than I care to remember. Amy Cormack, Sarah Karmali and Megan Richmond have been here for a lifetime of helping me to celebrate the successes and push through the lows. Elba Rodriguez was the best workout and wine partner I could have asked for. Ivon Pezer always kept me smiling. Thank you all.

I have tried as far as possible to be accurate in my portrayal of life in both Iraq and the USA and many people have helped with that. Any inaccuracies in the book are entirely my own. I would like to thank everyone I met during my time in Iraq, the USA and beyond; a whole mix of nationalities, military and civilian, people who left and people who stayed behind. You have all helped make this novel what it is. Special thanks for help on this manuscript go to Emily Gucwa Duff, Robert Yick, Arianna Dini, Theo Bell and Kate Davies. Kate, thank you for your friendship and guidance both in Baghdad and in life.

I have worked on this novel in many corners of the world. Iraq, Tunisia, Mexico, the US, the UK, Germany, Spain and even on a small sailboat crossing the Atlantic (that's a story for another time). Throughout my travels I have met so many people who have inspired and encouraged me. To name you all would take another book, but I hold you in my heart. Thank you.

This dream would not have become a reality without my wonderful agent Ella Diamond Kahn, who immediately shared my vision for the novel. Her unwavering support and optimism have been a reassurance throughout this process and I am grateful to have such a passionate champion of my writing. Thank you also to the London Book Fair's Write Stuff competition for bringing us together.

Thank you to my editor Lauren Parsons for her expertise and all of her excitement for the novel. I will be forever grateful to Lauren and all of the Legend Press team for helping me to launch this story into the world. I am so happy to be on this journey with you.

To my family, I put you through a lot, I know, but you deal with it all with love and humour and I am so thankful for that. Dad, you always get the worst bits, thank you for helping me through them. Mum, thank you for encouraging me to dream big. Charlie and Alice, I love you both and I'm sorry, I never did figure out that word count.

To James, the life of love and adventure that we are building together means everything to me. You have taught me about courage and perseverance and I am eternally grateful to have you by my side. Tomorrow we will do beautiful things.

COME VISIT US AT

WWW.LEGENDPRESS.CO.UK

FOLLOW US

@LEGEND_PRESS